Jacqueline Dumas's first novel, *Madeleine and the Angel* (Fifth House, 1989), earned rave reviews, was a finalist for the W.H. Smith/Books in Canada Best First Novel Award, and won the Writers Guild of Alberta Fiction Award for 1989. When she's not in Edmonton, where she lives and writes full time, Jacqueline loves to travel. She has hitchhiked across Canada and the U.S., and has spent time in Central and South America, the Caribbean, and Europe, including a year in Paris and a year in Granada.

The Last Sigh

Jacqueline Dumas

FIFTH
HOUSE
PUBLISHERS

Cover illustration and design by John Luckhurst/GDL

Printed and bound in Canada
93 94 95 96 97 / 5 4 3 2 1

The publisher gratefully acknowledges the assistance of The Canada Council, Communications Canada, and the Saskatchewan Arts Board.

Historical names and places in this novel are used fictitiously, and the protagonists are the product of the author's imagination. Any resemblance they may bear to real persons is coincidental.

CANADIAN CATALOGUING IN PUBLICATION DATA

Dumas, Jacqueline

The last sigh
ISBN 1-895618-21-5

I. Title.

PS8557.U3954L38 1993 C813'.54 C93-098089-1
PR9199.3.D85L38 1993

Fifth House Publishers
620 Duchess Street
Saskatoon, SK
S7K 0R1

In memory of Giuseppe Vannelli
(1947–1973)

To Mike and to Louise

Acknowledgements

The poem, "El silencio," is from *Federico García Lorca: Obras Completas, Tomo 1,* Aguilar s a de ediciones, Madrid 1980. Other snatches of poems are from the same book and from *W.B. Yeats: The Poems,* ed. Richard J. Finneran, Macmillan, London 1984.

Thank you for financial assistance from the Alberta Foundation for the Literary Arts, The Canada Council, and the Wayman foundation.

Gracias mil al simpático y generoso pueblo del Albayzín.

Special thank you and abrazos to Martha Gould, friend and editor por excelente.

Dale limosna mujer,
que no hay en la vida nada
como la pena de ser
ciego en Granada.

Francisco A. de Icaza

(Give the beggar alms, woman, for there is no one so wretched as he who is blind in Granada.)

Coeur qui soupir n'a pas ce qu'il désire.

French saying

Outset

EVA BONILLA BELIEVED IN BOOKS AND IN THE wisdom of others. To prepare for her trip to Granada, she had read everything she could find about the south of Spain. Now she was on her way: a Canadian flying to Europe for answers.

It was true, reading often raised more questions than it answered, but Eva did not like to be surprised by life, and she hoped that in paying close attention to the thoughts and habits of others she might discover not only clues to their behaviour, but signs to guide her own. Perhaps, this time, she would not be caught off guard.

In the adjacent seat, her six-year-old daughter Resa had stopped fidgeting. Eva checked her watch—eighteen hours since leaving Edmonton, twenty minutes before the scheduled landing in Málaga. Why did children do that anyway? Hours of are-we-there-yets and superhuman struggles to keep themselves awake and cranky, only to fall asleep just before arrival.

In Amsterdam she and Resa had boarded what was supposed to be a nonstop flight to Málaga, but it made an unannounced landing in Madrid, at which point all passengers were told to disembark—for customs clearance, Eva had figured out. Most of them had charged to the terminal while she had dragged behind with an uncooperative Resa. Then the two of them had stood, resigned Canadians, while the elbowers jostled their way to the front of the control lineup and rushed off with validated passports. After a while Eva had noticed that the front of the line was increasing in density and not getting any shorter, expanding like the opening bellows of an accordion as people ¡Adios!ed their way in from the sides. By the time she had started a bit of elbowing and adiosing of her own, it was too late and she could only watch helplessly, Resa's hand clutched in her own, as their plane taxied off down the runway. After more confusion, and help at last from a sympathetic Italian woman who did some multilingual shouting on their behalf, they had been ushered into a standby lineup from which Eva had been too anxious to stray. Finally, exhausted and hungry, they had boarded a later flight to Málaga. All this to avoid the Madrid airport in the first place.

Damn, thought Eva, we might as well have booked the flight straight through to Granada.

"Try to stay awake just a little while longer, sweetheart," she said. "We're almost there."

"My head hurts," Resa whined.

Eva eased back Resa's seat and felt her forehead. No temperature, not yet at least.

Resa closed her eyes and rubbed them.

Eva sighed and eased down her own seat back. She unzipped her bag and reached in, feeling first for the velvet pouch. The pouch was still there, at the bottom of the bag.

She took out her book and opened it. She usually had one with her, this a small hardcover on bullfighting written by an Englishman who had lived in Spain for thirty years and was trying his best to be fair.

The Andalusian bull is not so much a product of nature, she read, as it is a freak of selective genetics, and thus it owes its life to the very fact that it is to be killed. It is bred to viciousness, its role as propitiatory victim a privileged one.

Eva reread the paragraph but could not decide why it bothered her. She continued.

Early on in its life the bull is studied in the field, goaded by men on horseback in order to determine what fierceness and prowess it might exhibit in the ring. Never is the bull in the field allowed to face a human on foot, for fear that it might learn something of man's habits and thus become too dangerous for the individual who must one day confront it in the ring. It is essential that on the fateful day of its death, everything that the bull is to experience be experienced for the first time.

And the last, I suppose, Eva thought.

The day of public deflowering arrives: the stands are filled, the cuadrilla marches in, the gate is opened, and the bull trots out from its dark pen into the bewildering glare of potential glory. Confused, it paws the clean smooth sand and charges madly about from barrier to barrier, churning up dust as it searches for a way out, for from the very first moment of release into apparent freedom, it has been set on escape. But the fate of the bull has already been determined, its killer chosen, by lot.

Before the killer can attend to his business, however, the bull must be properly prepared—weakened by pikes, provoked by banderillas—all in all, taught how to attack. Only then will the matador take full charge.

The good matador can halt, moderate, and command the bull, twist it to his will. He senses how far he can go, how much to taunt and tease it, when and how to slap it in the face with his mantle. He challenges the bull directly, and knows exactly when to flee, but only a little, not overdoing it, backing off just enough to give the bull confidence. He seduces it with slow voluptuous sweeps, leads it on with loving lengthened passes of the red muleta, keeping his own movements to a minimum, allowing the bull to show the way to its own death. When the time comes, he braces himself, and at precisely the right moment steps forward with his estoque, the slender sword which he has been hiding behind his little cape.

Eva turned the page.

The bull is admired to the extent that it can hold up to the torture. After, parts of its body—the ears, the tail—are sliced off and saved, like trophies from a slain opponent in war are bagged by the victor.

Or like relics, she thought, the fingers and toes of dead saints.

The dead bull minus its cut-off bits is dragged from the ring by a team of garlanded mules to an eager team of butchers. Its meat will be eaten, and its heart. The heart of a brave bull is especially desired.

Eva thought of the Iroquois swallowing the heart of Jean de Brébeuf.

She learned that more than one bullfighter had received his education in a slaughterhouse, and that, like the slaughterhouse, the corrida was strictly regulated by the government. The pikes which were made for the unique purpose of piercing the thick skin of the bull were carefully inspected and sealed. The bulls themselves were inspected. Outraged purists campaigned against small bulls and shaved horns, some even protesting the modern practice of protecting the horse with padding. With all of these contemptible indecencies, the purists complained, the bull had become nothing more than a desiccated wineskin. How was such a bull to taste death in its perfection?

Will I ever grasp all of this? Eva wondered. Do I want to? But she read on.

A minority of theorists, wrote the Englishman, emphasized the sporting aspect of the corrida: the snaring of the prey in accordance with a solemn code of ethics.

Eva thought of other regulated death industries: public executions; the rules of war of the Geneva conventions. Why was it so important–not to stop the killing altogether–but to have stringent rules of how to kill? As if the harder the bull pushed against the steel blade, the more legitimate was the killing of it.

The Englishman himself seemed to value the corrida as a work of art, stressing the fact that most newspapers in Spain placed the coverage of the fiesta de toros in the entertainment section. The corrida, he said, was the enactment of a tragedy, the fiesta de toros the legitimate heir of the Roman circus, with the trickery and subterfuge of art having been introduced to bring about the death of the bull.

Was the cheering crowd, then, made up not of vulgar clods, but of irrepressible aesthetes out to enjoy a play? Would a like group of people in North America be glued in front of the TV appreciating *Othello* on PBS?

The seat belt and no smoking signs pinged on. The airplane hit a pocket of turbulence and fell like an out-of-control elevator, then levelled off again.

Resa sniffled and settled against her mother's arm. Please don't get sick now, Eva implored silently. She shut her book and closed her eyes.

Oh, if only she had someone to discuss things with once in a while, another adult, so that the weight of living would not be so completely on her shoulders. As it was, she was always having to make decisions for the two of them, and she didn't think she was very good at making decisions.

If only Tony were still alive.

Since his death, she felt as if her real life were on hold much of the time, a state of suspension in which she waited for things to happen, her behaviour a series of knee-jerk responses to actions initiated by others.

But maybe she was fooling herself. Maybe she had always been like this, even during her years with Tony.

It was six years now since his death and the birth of Resa, and barely three months since the death of Teresa Benabo—Tony's mother and Resa's grandmother and namesake.

Mrs. Benabo had died just before Christmas, her final month in the hospital having been an especially difficult one for Eva, who had no car. Despite one of the coldest winters on record, she had taken the bus to the hospital every second day to fluff the pillows of an old woman who had generally disapproved of her. But had she had a choice?

Eva sometimes questioned that she had ever been as close to Tony as she liked to believe. In those moments she would look at Resa and recite to herself that yes indeed, she had had a lover, she had lived with him and she had had his baby, a baby with his dark hair and eyes. And not having married him doesn't imply that I lack the widow's right to grieve, she assured herself.

But Tony had died and been buried in Granada—drowned in the river, Mrs. Benabo had told her. This far-off death and burial attested to by his mother exaggerated Eva's fear that he had never really belonged to her. How did one mourn from such a distance?

The signs pinged out and Eva reopened her eyes. Resa was sucking her thumb.

No, thought Eva, I must not allow the few years Tony and I had together to be reduced to a fantasy.

She reopened her book.

To understand Spain, wrote the Englishman, one must understand the corrida as an indelible mark on the Spanish soul. He quoted Kazantzakis: the idea of bullfighting went back to early man, to the moment when the wild beast showed up at the mouth of the cave and man assumed that it was a god offering himself to be killed and eaten. The Englishman discussed how the ancient Iberians had sacrificed bulls to honour their gods, and how Hercules had gone to Iberia and killed Geryon and his oxen.

In this scenario, the fiesta de toros was not so much spectacle as sacrifice, a pagan rite that had been transformed into a modern auto-da-fé in which the bull's death was expiatory rather than tragic, and the crowds assembled to witness a holy feast of killing.

Eva read about the two schools, the two philosophies of killing. The first was the Ronda school, which held that the end, the goal of the corrida, was the final thrust of the sword, and all else preparatory. The second school was the Seville one, which preached that each act of the fight was an end in itself, and the final stroke merely the ending. But no matter which school the torero adheres to, insisted the Englishman, the bull that faces him in the ring owes its life and its death to him, for if there were no bullfights, this particular bull never would have existed.

The sort of logic that gives parents the right to kill their children, thought Eva.

There seemed to be more words for the different types of bulls and the moves of the matador than there were words for snow in the Arctic. The matador performed revoleras, afarolados, arrucinas, galleos, chicuelinas, mariposas, manoletinas, verónicas (the moisture and blood softly wiped from the face of the bull), and naturales–as if there could be anything natural in preparing one's victim for the kill.

Like the two schools, there were also two acceptable methods of killing. One was called "matar a volapié," in which the matador flew off his feet and used the impetus of his own body to drive the sword into the neck of the stationary bull. The other, more classic way of killing, and the one admired by the Englishman, was "matar recibiendo," in which the matador stood deathly still to await the final charge of the bull. The matador was not to move his feet until it reached him, at which point he aimed and sunk the sword into the sweet spot. The bull, wrote the Englishman, is said to desire the plunging sword, and rushes forward to receive it.

The signs above her pinged on for the last time and the descending plane was submerged in clouds. Eva slipped the book back into her purse and closed her eyes once again.

Resa opened hers and wriggled half out of her seat belt to look out the window. Being inside the clouds was disappointing–they weren't fluffy and white, it didn't look at all like you could bounce around and play on them. And you couldn't see a thing. It was a bit scary, like that time she got lost in the fog at that lake with all the weeds. It was like being in the middle of nothing.

Then the airplane sank through the cloud cover into a thinly veiled sky and the lights of Málaga were revealed, the reflecting sea beckoning in the distance.

A few minutes later the wheels of the Aviaco 727 rumbled down, the hydraulics whined, the nose lifted up, and the plane bumped to the ground. Thrust reversers braked and tires gripped the tarmac.

The whole aircraft shuddered and rattled. One of the doors of the overhead compartments flew open, but nothing fell out. Several of the mostly German and English passengers applauded.

Eva relaxed her grip on the armrests and opened her eyes.

With that directness of gaze peculiar to animals and small children, Resa, now up on her knees, was studying the energetic man who had been sitting across the aisle from her mother. He was medium in height and compact of build, dressed in bright blue slacks and an open-necked shirt, the kind that is worn on the outside of the pants, like a jacket. His hair was dark and neatly combed, curling up at the collar. He had eyebrows that flew out in all directions, and, incongruous with the dark hair on his head, a mass of red beard, which he kept stroking. His fingers were elegant and expressive, the nails of the right hand long, thick, and clean.

During the descent, he and a group of fellow Spaniards had not stopped talking, their voices rising to compete with the screaming engines. And now, contrary to the crackling instructions from the loudspeaker, the man was standing in the aisle, jabbering, gesticulating, prompting the others into laughter, so that when the plane jerked to a stop he lurched sideways into Eva's lap. He scrambled up, smiled foolishly, apologized, reprimanding his brutish clumsy self and the even more clumsy landing—the pilot must be Catalán, ¡eso! a Catalán flying an airplane that has been patched together from the scraps of the ancient Romans—and the rough runway—the government is probably waiting for the Moors to come back and fix it ¡Ojalá! and then ¡Hola, hija! noticing Resa, leaning across Eva to pinch the what-a-delightful-child-you-are's cheek, grinning and dipping his hand into his pocket to fill her palms with the caramelos that had been passed out earlier by the crew. ¡Qué guapa! You remind me of my own little girl—it's two months you know since I've seen her, two months! ¡Imagínate!

Resa looked the man back straight in the eye.

He laughed and turned to Eva—"She's no timid foreigner, that little girl of yours."

He told her he was on his way home after eight weeks in Disneymundo, at the Epcot Center. That's Manolo, interjected someone, Manolo who makes the best guitars in all of Andalucía, the Junta chose him to represent us, so he could display his guitars in America. I was only supposed to be there for three weeks, said Manolo, but I stayed seven. I took four guitars with me, each in a different stage of completion so the Americans could see how they are constructed, but the guitars were barely out of the packing case before everyone was clamouring to buy them, so I sold all four on the first day, no, not the first day, the first morning, all four guitars in one morning, can you imagine such a thing? Everyone agreed that this was indeed an amazing thing. Of course, then I had to stay longer than I had planned, in order to complete all the guitars, and then, just as I was tying the last string on the last of the guitars, the woman who bought it asked me to stay and play for her little girl's birthday party, so what could I do? Everyone muttered and nodded, What can you do, that's life for you.

"Entonces, here I am, an errant guitar maker on my way home, soon to embrace my own sweet daughter and my own loving mother. And you, señora—this *is* your daughter ¿verdad?—you are in Spain for a holiday? For the Semana Santa perhaps?"

"Well, I don't know . . . we will be here for Holy Week I suppose, but we've come for other reasons, too."

"Ah, for other seasons too. Muy bien, well said."

Most of the passengers were now standing pressed together in the aisle, and with the engines shut off the air in the compartment was dry and stale. Eva realized that he had misheard her, but she decided to let the misapprehension pass. By way of response, she stretched her lips into a smile. Her cheeks felt like a cracking mud mask.

Finally the exit door was opened and the line of people began to lumber out. ¡Adios! señora, hija, ¡adios! called Manolo. Eva waved feebly, and told Resa to stay put until everyone else had deplaned.

"Are we there yet?" asked Resa.

"Not quite. We still have to get to Granada." After we find our suitcases, thought Eva, realizing that there would probably be more complications because of the missed flight.

"I'm hungry," said Resa.

Eva tightened her lips and opened her purse, taking out a small box of raisins—the last—and handing it to Resa. "Here, chew each one ten times."

Inside the Málaga terminal, Eva discovered that the last flight to Granada had left half an hour earlier. But there were buses, la señora could take a taxi to the bus station if she did not wish to wait until morning.

On top of everything, the automatic luggage feeder was broken down. The passengers were told that the suitcases would be delivered by hand. But what about *my* luggage, said Eva to a man in uniform, it was on a different plane, the one we were supposed to be on. No hay problema, señora, don't worry, your bags are on the way, they are being carried out as we speak. How could she make the man understand that her luggage was undoubtedly sitting in another room?

Oh, what did it matter anyway. The suitcases were going to appear any minute now, and the other passengers were going to bully their way into all the cabs before she even had a chance. And if she did manage to get a taxi to the bus station, she would still have to figure out which bus to catch and how to buy the tickets, and if they actually boarded the bus, there was still the drive to Granada, and it would be late when they got in and she would have to find the Hotel de los Tilos, and somewhere in there she had to get Resa something to eat. Oh, if only it were tomorrow already.

Eva tried to calm down, to shut out the indignant German voices and the fretful English ones which were deploring Spanish inefficiency. All big airports are the same, she said to herself, none of them are efficient or pleasant places to be. No sense panicking over events you can't control. She took a deep breath and put on a reassuring smile for Resa.

Resa, of course, was not fooled by her mother's outward composure, but sensing an anxiety greater than her own fatigue, an anxiety that alarmed her, she slipped her own cool hand into her mother's clammy one just as two workers wheeled out the first carts of luggage.

Somehow, miraculously, all of their bags were on the second cart. Eva took Resa outside to the taxi line, stopping first to buy a copy of *El País*.

†

Later, on the road to Granada, cushioned from the vibrations of the bus by her mother's folded jacket and comforted by the TV burbling above the windshield, Resa would breathe in the smell of the jacket and fall into a deep sleep.

Earth and Sky

EVA FINALLY RELAXED AND SQUINTED OUT the window, but outside was black and the most she could see was her own reflection in the glass.

†

Had the bus been travelling in the relentless blaze of the afternoon sun, she might have seen white villages clinging like goats to the sides of mountains, and, in open doorways, shadows moving sideways behind those billowing curtains which in the south allow the air to enter while keeping out the heat. Had it been early morning, she might have made out once-fertile fields now so neglected as to have become rock meadows, and, grazing near the rocks, enchanted black steeds mounted by ghostly warriors who, still as death, guard the mouths of blocked-up caves. Or she might have caught a glimpse of the earth-bound spirits of not-quite-domesticated Jews and Gypsies eking out their livings under cover of the dim haze.

As for those who had bartered and sliced their way across the land before the Islamic invaders to trample their own share of men, women, and children, few traces remained. Almost nothing of the ancient Iberians, Phoenicians, Celts, Greeks, Carthaginians, Romans, Suevians, Alans, Vandals, and Visigoths. The axed fragments of these cultures are entombed in the museums of the world, where one may view limestone goddesses seated on lion-footed thrones, and curious man-headed bulls with tails forever poised to whisk away nonexistent flies. And in the cool Spanish grottoes of naked Astarte and Adonis, clothed Mary and Jesus now receive homage.

†

Eva picked up her newspaper, but the same interior lights that were bright enough to prevent her from seeing outside were too dim to read by. She stuffed the newspaper into the seat pouch, settled back into her seat, and tried to pick out what she could from the general din of Spanish surrounding her.

"Why read the words of strangers when you can talk with your neighbour," said a familiar voice from across the aisle.

She turned her head in curiosity. The energetic man from the plane, the guitar maker–Manolo–was grinning at her through his red beard. She had been too preoccupied with Resa to notice him.

"Once again fortune has seen fit to place us side by side. Do you not think we should listen to her? After all, when that fateful day arrives and death knocks on the door to escort us from this world, we shall be judged not by what we have read, but by what we have done or not done."

She was pleased that he had recognized her. She smiled back much more warmly than she would have to a like stranger on a like bus in Canada.

†

It has been said that most history is the story of the victors, or, in the words of Francisco de Carbajal, the Demon of the Andes, as quoted by Ricardo Palma, nineteenth-century librarian of Lima: Nobody who becomes king is ever called traitor.

The rapists, the hackers and the slashers, the thieves–they are the authors of history, ruthless soldiers and men of fortune who purloin reputations as sensitive civilizers. History is rewritten to accommodate the most recent criminals–the rebel son who has murdered his father, the brother his brother–and their methods of war–different ways to kill large numbers of people efficiently–are studied meticulously, so that stories of skirmishes, sieges, abatis, scalings, raids, bombing runs, all acquire the status and mystique of religion. Most history is the story of death.

But the unwritten story of the survivors, the story of life, continues subversively in kitchens and bedrooms, passed on in the language that really counts–the profane one of food, of touching, of smiles and gestures, of song and of dance, of poetry, of love. Flowers push apart stones to seek the sun; trickling brooks do reach the river.

†

The bus slowed and Eva could see streetlights.

"Loja," said Manolo, thrusting out his chin and raking his beard with his long fingers.

The bus wound its way through the town, up a small street, and stopped. A woman near the front got off.

"I thought this bus went straight to Granada," said Eva.

"It does, and usually it doesn't pass through Loja at all, but the driver couldn't very well leave someone on the side of the road at this time of night."

No one else seemed to have been surprised by the detour. I must have missed something, thought Eva.

The bus backed up, turned around laboriously, and began to wind its way back the way it had come.

"Are we following a river?" asked Eva.

"The Darro."

"Almost right, my friend," said a raspy voice from directly behind Manolo. "This is indeed one of the two rivers which flow through Granada. But it is the Genil which comes to Loja, not the Darro."

Manolo shrugged. "Whatever."

Eva turned to look at the source of the raspy voice—a well-groomed man with banker good looks: thin nose, thick white hair. He was dressed casually but expensively.

"Señora," said Manolo, "let me present Don Angel—Señor Don Miguel Angel Sanlúcar—a very good friend of mine from Granada."

Eva extended her hand back across the aisle.

"How do you do, my name is Eva."

"Encantado, Señora Eva." He squeezed her hand and suavely inclined his head. "I could not help but overhear your comments, señora, and I was very interested in your observation about the road. In this case you are right, the road does follow the river, but you might like to know that in these towns and villages, it is not always the rivers and canyons that cause the roads to wind. Here it is common for people's homes to determine the path of the streets. And often, a road is only as wide or as narrow as the distance between two particular houses permits it to be."

"In Miami the roads were wide and straight," said Manolo, "and along them the houses were strung out, as if the neighbours didn't want to talk to each other. And the houses so huge, with many doors of escape, as if the members of the family didn't want to talk to each other either."

"In America everything is built for the convenience of the car," said Angel.

"Don Angel knows a lot about America," said Manolo. "He goes there often. And like me, he has just returned."

"From Miami?" asked Eva.

"No no, not from Miami, from a history conference in New York. Normally I do not take the bus, but my plane was late coming in and I missed the last flight to Granada."

"Yes I know, the same thing happened to us." When she said "us" she glanced at Resa.

"Tell me, señora, is that beautiful child your daughter?"

"Yes, my daughter, Teresa."

Resa responded in her sleep, sighing and extending one leg across her mother's lap.

"Don Angel, you may be named for the angels," said Manolo, "but that little girl is a *true* angel."

"Absolutely angelic. She does not look at all American."

"That's because she's not," said Eva.

"I knew it," said Manolo. "From the moment I saw her on the airplane, I thought to myself, that child is Andaluza."

"That's not what I meant," said Eva. "I mean she's Canadian, not American."

"Canadian. She looks even less like a Canadian," said Angel.

What's that supposed to mean? wondered Eva.

"Don Angel has been to Canada too," said Manolo—impressed by the fact, thought Eva.

"Where in Canada?" she asked.

"Toronto," said Angel, proudly.

As if that's Canada, thought Eva. "What did you think of it?" she asked.

"It was very interesting . . . everyone lives well there, each family in its own large brick house."

"Well, not quite everyone, I don't think," said Eva, slightly irritated but not sure why. Perhaps she was just overtired.

"You speak Spanish very well, señora," said Angel.

"My father spoke it—he was Mexican—and I studied it at university."

"Ahh, I see."

"We have large houses here too," said Manolo, "but not many Spaniards can afford to live in them. Most of our houses are small and pushed together. In Miami I went inside an American house—the first man to buy one of my guitars invited me to meet his family. I saw a bedroom big enough to sleep the entire family—parents, children, grandparents, the dog—but it was just *his* bedroom, for him *alone.* And his wife had one exactly like it, with an attached bathroom, and each of his three sons had his own room. And the beds, you should have seen the beds: so big a couple could sleep together and not hear each other snore." Had she been to Miami?

No.

"Of course," said Angel, "nowadays our houses are larger than they were, for instance, in the days of the Muslims." Did la señora know that when the Christians took over Granada in 1492, the houses were so tiny that each soldier claimed two, three, even six houses for his family?

No, she hadn't known.

"The streets themselves were so narrow that the tops of the houses reached across and touched one another. King Fernando ordered that the main streets be widened and the houses razed, so that a hospital and cathedral could be built."

"Both in honour of the Virgin Mary," said Manolo, "but at Jewish and Moorish expense. It was not by chance that the houses destroyed were in the judería."

"Of course not, hijo. But such were the times."

"Have the times changed that much, Don Angel? It seems to me that the powerful are always building monuments to themselves on the backs of the powerless."

Angel shrugged his head sideways and addressed Eva again.

"Actually, señora, my friend Manolo and I are in agreement—wide streets and narrow thought are one of the classic routes to power. Take your cities now, they were built by optimists who had not yet learned to distrust their governments, so from the beginning your neighbourhoods were uniform, systematic arrangements of buildings separated by avenues wide enough to accommodate tanks. In North America you are still shocked by the excesses of your politicians; you believe casting a vote on election day will make a difference."

"I don't know, I think we're getting more cynical than that," she said.

"If you want to experience the difference, try taking a walk through one of our older neighbourhoods. It might strike you as a disorderly, ill-kept madhouse, but it is because we in Andalucía have come to expect nothing good from our politicians. We prefer the streets and alleyways of our towns and villages to be mazes without signs–nothing which might aid the intruder. In one place the same road might be wide enough to allow the passage of a truck and, a few metres down, two burros could not pass side by side. Sometimes a road will taper into a footpath, or abruptly drop off into steep steps, or it might die out at the front door of your Aunt Josefa."

Suddenly the bus sped up and again Eva could see only reflections in the glass.

"Señora," said Angel, "do you know? We are now following in the footsteps of los reyes católicos–Fernando and his wife Isabel. They passed through these very same villages through which we ourselves are about to pass–almost five hundred years ago, and more than seven hundred years after the first Muslims had crossed the Straits of Gibraltar to defeat Don Rodrigo, king of the Visigoths. Throughout those seven hundred years, the Christians jabbed away until only one pocket of infidels remained–the Islamic Kingdom of Granada. At the time, of course, the worst enemies of Christendom were locusts, hail, and the plague, but ¡no importa! the politics of the day required infidels."

"And do you know why the Moors in Granada resisted longer than the rest?" asked Manolo.

Eva wasn't sure if she did know. She was listening attentively, but it was a strain, and speaking even more so. Her last comment had been ignored–maybe "cínico" wasn't the same as "cynical."

"No, why?" she said, giving Manolo the most encouraging smile she could muster.

"Because they believed they were defending the gates of heaven," he answered. "They were convinced it hung suspended directly above them. So pure were the waters of Granada, so serene was her sky, that they knew they must be living in God's shadow."

"Allah's shadow," corrected Angel.

Manolo leaned across the aisle and said pointedly to Eva, "When Fernando saw Granada for the first time, in the distance, he said to his wife: For you, I will pick out the seeds of that pomegranate one by one."

Eva couldn't tell whether or not he was being facetious.

She did know that the Reconquest of Granada had begun with the forged papal bull that allowed Ferdinand, the teenage heir of Aragon, to marry Isabella, his counterpart in Castile. In an undercover manoeuvre designed to guarantee him the crown, Ferdinand disguised himself as a mule tender in a merchant caravan, travelling over mountains and across plains to meet his future bride.

"Queen Isabella must have been an amazing woman," said Eva, making a renewed effort. "I read that she gave birth to each of her five children in a different place."

"Where her soldiers went, the queen went," said Angel. "She followed them, moving her court from city to city and camp to camp, pursuing her enemies as they retreated. Moorish infidels! Devils in paradise! she would shout. Her knights had the red cross of the Holy Crusades stamped on their tunics and on their white pennants.

"Alhama fell first, to the Marqués de Cádiz–"

"–Don Angel's ancestor ¿verdad?" said Manolo.

"My direct ancestor," said Angel, puffing out his chest. "The Marqués led the battle against Alhama, the most important of the battles to precede the fall of Granada. After Alhama, the others fell easily–Lucena, Loja–"

"Loja which we just left, señora," said Manolo.

"–then Baza, Purchena and its valley, the sierras of Filabres and Bacar, Almería, Guadix," continued Angel. "The queen gathered them in, one after the other, clutching them to her bosom like rosary beads. But you know, señora, they only whetted her appetite, for it was Granada she wanted, Granada she lusted after with her whole body and soul. And when finally it was in sight–Granada, object of her desires–she had the town of Santa Fe built, for succour. Santa Fe–a hive in the vega to shelter the queen bee while she waited for her honeyed prize."

"That was in 1492?" Eva said.

"The preceding year. But in 1492 occurred three events from which we Spanish have never recovered."

Angel paused.

"First," he said sticking up his thumb, "the defeat and expulsion of the Muslims. Second," he uncurled his index finger, "the Inquisition. And third, the discovery of America." He shook three fingers at her for emphasis. "Three events of monumental importance."

"You're forgetting number four," said Manolo, "the expulsion of the Jews."

"That belongs with the Muslims," said Angel.

Eva was tired. It wasn't only the language–it was the oral onslaught of information.

"How far are we from Granada?" she asked. I sound like Resa, she thought.

"Not far," said Manolo, "we're almost there. Too bad it's so dark. For your first time, it would be much more romantic if you were to enter Granada in the early morning, with the first rays of the sun, so that you could lose yourself in that moment when night meets day, and the light seems to be hesitating between the moon and the sun and the white houses of the Albayzín are robed in ruby and lapis lazuli . . . but I do not think you are a romantic."

How would you know any such thing? she thought.

She could sense him examining her profile and turned her head to look at him. His eyes were smiling. Why? Had she missed something?

"Did you know, señora, that the Moors believed the moon to belong to them, and the sun to the Christians?" he said.

No.

"Of course, the siege of Granada was not at all romantic," said Angel. "The sad reality is, that while the queen and her soldiers waited outside the walls of the city for the Christian god to deliver it to them, inside, the Islamic king and more than 25,000 of his soldiers waited for *their* god to rescue them . . . Meanwhile, in the midst of all this waiting and praying, an ordinary Christian, an unknown explorer who would one day become much more famous than the queen herself, was arriving in Santa Fe to talk to Her Majesty about his plans to sail a new route . . . "

"An ordinary Christian, or a marrano?" said Manolo.

"You mean Christopher Columbus?" said Eva. She had never read anything about his being a Spanish Jew. "I thought he was Italian, or Catalan or something."

"Cristóbal Colón? ¡Catalán!" said Angel. "Señora, ¡perdone usted! but that canard is part of Cataluña's worldwide campaign to exaggerate its own importance. Those Cataláns would claim Jesus Christ as one of their own if they thought they could get away with it."

"But Colón *could* have been marrano," said Manolo.

"It's true that he was very secretive about his past, and that there are conflicting stories about his origins, but the most credible version is still the most common one—that he was from Genoa."

"He could have been Jewish and also from Genoa," insisted Manolo. "Otherwise, why would he have loaded his ship and ordered his men to board the night *before* he was to set sail, which was also the night *before* the edict expelling the Jews was to take effect? Does that sound like mere coincidence?"

Angel waved his hand dismissively and once again addressed Eva. "In any case," he said, "we in the south would far prefer Colón to be an Italian Jew than Catalán. You see, Colón is still a source of pride to us, although it is entirely possible, of course, that in a few years no one will want to claim him as one of theirs."

"King Fernando had Jewish blood too," said Manolo, "and Franco was a Jew, descended from a family of conversos."

"Which explains everything and nothing," said Angel. "But to get back to our story, Colón came to Santa Fe explicitly to see Queen Isabel. He had been chasing after her for six years, begging for her support. Each time she sent him away more brusquely than the time before. He was beginning to get on her nerves. Then one day out of the clear blue sky she said, Mister Colón, stay, I want to talk to you."

"But alone," said Manolo.

"Yes, alone."

"It's like the Secret of Fátima," said Manolo. "Why did the queen change her mind? What was said?"

Angel laughed. His teeth were yellowed and slightly crooked. "But unlike Colón's meeting with Isabel, the words of Our Lady were written down; a document exists . . . "

"Colón was with King Fernando when Granada surrendered," said Manolo. "Isn't that right, Don Angel?"

"Indeed he was, hijo."

"Centuries after a Moorish king had dreamed that the poplars of Granada would one day fall to the ground."

"The surrender occurred during the night of the New Year of 1492. The troops entered the palace of the Alhambra and claimed it for all of Christianity. In the morning, Colón watched with his own eyes as the pennant of Saint James was raised on the Torre de la Vela. His ears were deafened by the shouts of the army–¡Santiago! ¡Castilla!–and he fell upon his knees beside the king and queen and all their soldiers, weeping with them as the choir of the Royal Chapel sang the Te Deum."

"And Colón was also present when Boabdil el Chico, the last Moorish king, delivered his sword to King Fernando," said Manolo.

"Boabdil's real name was Abu Abdallah," said Angel, "but we can use his popular name."

Eva's mind had started to drift, but the mention of Boabdil's sword stopped it.

Angel said to her, "I think my friend is basing his assumptions on a painting that is in the Capilla Real."

"No I'm not."

"What painting?" she asked.

"One of the Rendition of Granada," said Angel, "in which Boabdil, sword in hand, meekly approaches Fernando."

"I think I've seen a photograph of that sword." She tried to sound casual.

"There is indeed a sword displayed in the Army Museum, a sword said to be the sword of Boabdil. But my research—which includes a letter from Boabdil to one of his cousins—indicates that the sword in the museum actually belonged to one of Boabdil's subordinates."

It seemed to her that Angel had hesitated before answering. And was she imagining it, or had Manolo just glanced slyly her way? But Angel continued talking and the impressions vanished as quickly as they had come.

"In the end," Angel said, "everything—Boabdil's kingdom, his earthly paradise—all of it, fell prey to the jealousies and schemings of the harem."

Here we go again, Eva thought to herself. War, bloodshed, defeat—they're always the fault of women.

"You look doubtful, señora," said Manolo.

"Oh I don't know, it's just that I remember reading something about all those party leaders—"

"—the Reyes de Taifas," said Angel.

"Yes, well didn't they have something to do with the Muslim downfall? I mean, weren't they fighting amongst themselves when they could have been banding together against the Christians?"

"And?"

"Well, I was just wondering, that's all. It seems to me that, oh, I don't know . . . "

"What? That a wife can't be ruthless? That a mother can't be blinded by ambition on behalf of her son? Or that Boabdil's mother could have been such a woman?"

"Of course there are such women. It's just that I was wondering if Boabdil's weakness didn't have as much to do with male intrigues at court as with female ones."

"You mean 'Cherchez l'homme' rather than 'Cherchez la femme.'"

"I don't know enough about it, really."

Disconcerted at having had an opinion flushed out, she was saved from further divulgence by a small commotion near the front of the bus.

Stop! a man was calling. ¡Oye! Stop the bus!

"It's Chico," said Manolo. "*Rafael* el Chico, that is, not Boabdil."

The man, Chico, staggered backwards until he was in the aisle between Eva and Manolo. He mumbled something and Manolo shouted ¡Hombre! and something else to the driver that Eva didn't understand. People turned around and chuckled, and she thought some of them were asking the driver to stop. A woman said something about an overflowing gas tank, and the driver braked abruptly and pulled over as the passengers pitched forward. Manolo grabbed Chico's arm to stop him from falling. The driver opened the front door and pointed outside, saying something about a gas pump, but Eva saw nothing. Manolo and the man who had shouted "stop" helped Chico up the aisle and down the steps into the dark outside—all to general amusement.

"What's going on?" asked Eva.

"It's nothing," said Angel. "Chico won a lotería, that's all."

A lotto?

After a few minutes, a grinning Chico lurched back up the steps, followed by the two men. They were greeted by cheerful noises, and the driver closed the door and pulled back out onto the road.

"How often does that happen?" said Manolo, gliding back into his seat. "Winning twice, never mind once. Think of it, Chico won two bottles of aguardiente, that's why he was drowning. But now he can enter the city as contentedly as poor Chico the Moor was morose in leaving it."

"En efecto," said Angel. "Before he left the Alhambra for good, our poor Boabdil had his ancestors exhumed. Then he gathered about him the rest of his entourage—his women, his unarmed soldiers—and it was this group of humiliated Abencerrajes, with little to guard but a few cases of dug-up bones, that escorted the last Islamic king out of Granada and into the mountains of the Alpujarra."

"The saddest and angriest of those women was his mother, Morayma," said Manolo. "When Boabdil stopped to look one last time at his lost kingdom, she said to him: Lloras como una mujer lo que no has sabido defender como un hombre."

Eva translated in her head: Like a woman, you bewail that which you did not know how to fight for as a man.

"That spot is the last place from which Granada is visible," said Angel. "To this day, it is known as el Suspiro del Moro."

The Sigh of the Moor.

"What happened to Boabdil in the end?"

"When his wife died in the summer of the following year, he sold all his properties in the Alpujarra to Christians and retreated across the water to Fez, where he lived until his death."

"And when he died his body was put in a swift flowing river so that it would be swept out to sea," said Manolo.

"And Morayma?"

"Who knows?" said Angel, shrugging his shoulders as if to say, Who cares?

"And while all this was going on, Columbus was preparing to sail?"

"Oh yes, Colón had received everything he wanted."

"You mean the backing for his expedition . . . "

"That too, of course, but I meant the gratification of his frivolous demands, the sops to his vanity—the right to bear those grandiose titles: Viceroy; Governor of All That He Should Discover; Grand Admiral of the Ocean Sea . . . "

"The right to wear gold spurs," said Manolo. "Sin embargo, it is curious, that the day Colón set sail was also the day it became illegal for Jews to remain on Spanish soil—despite the fact that many of them had helped in the siege and capture of Granada."

"The times, hijo, the times . . . But you're right, it is ironic . . . Colón, going forth into a world he had not yet imagined, and at the same instant in the same harbour, hundreds of thousands of people staring into the past, waiting for the sea to part."

Manolo said something quickly in Spanish, which ended with "niña, cariña."

"We learned the names of the ships in school," said Eva, hoping she was guessing right about the subject matter. "The Niña, the Pinta, the Santa María . . . it always sounded to me like the chorus of a song."

Manolo said something else—about a song of whores, Eva thought.

Angel laughed. "And the Santa María was in reality Loose María, because of what she had been before Colón renamed her.

The sailors always called her by her original name—Maríagalante."

"So, el señor Colón and his ships with names of whores set out to bring us glory on behalf of God and his saintly queen," said Manolo.

"And like whores, they brought misfortune," said Angel. "We sent horses, and what did we get in return? Lung cancer and syphilis."

"I thought it was the other way around," said Eva. "I mean, that's what I've read, anyway, that syphilis travelled from Europe to America."

"Everyone knows that the first recorded case was the result of the union of an Inca with an alpaca," said Manolo.

Oh no, she thought, another of those stories, like the one about AIDS originating in a sex act between an African and a monkey. And it was not as if the civilized maladies, those acknowledged to be from Europe, had not been lethal to America. Eva thought of the smallpox epidemics, of the legacy of lopped-off heads and poisoned stomachs, of gouged-out eyes, of nameless men in dark cloaks prepared to slit the throats of children.

"Poor Colón," said Angel. "When everything was over, he had nothing. Spain had nothing."

"Nothing but rather a lot of gold," she blurted out.

The two men laughed.

"Unfortunately, most of the gold ended up outside of Spain, to pay war debts," said Angel. "The Crown was broke, which is why we had the Inquisition. After the Expulsions, there were not enough people left to pay taxes."

"And no one left to do the work," said Manolo. "Those Christians were lazy, more interested in making fortunes in far-off lands than in tending the home garden. When they took over, indolence swelled into a national disease. The crops in the countryside were not watered, and in the city, the houses fell to ruin."

Eva thought she had read the same idea, but phrased more generously (was it by Richard Ford?), that for the Spaniard, pleasure is the absence of exertion, existence in itself being happiness enough.

"It's true, the Christians were not very interested in growing trees and flowers," said Angel. "But you have to understand, the long wars had taught them little more than how to fight and how to consume."

"In the time of the Moors, our country was much more beautiful than it is now," said Manolo. "Mientras más Moros más ganancia."

The more Moors, the more profit.

"An old saying," said Angel, "and like many popular sayings, it does contain a grain of truth. The expelled were the productive ones: the farm workers, the carpenters, masons, weavers, dyers, shoemakers, blacksmiths, merchants, tailors, tanners, the artisans, the potters . . . "

" . . . the poets," said Manolo.

"Sadly enough, the poets too."

"And when the poets were expelled, civilization itself was expelled."

"In a way, the Reconquest was our first civil war, the beginning of the end of happiness for everyone: Jews, Muslims, Christians alike. At first the Christians seemed to gain a lot, but everything got out of hand very quickly. And the newly baptized were never truly converted, not in their hearts. They spoke Arabic in secret and addressed each other by their Muslim names, and because their baths were forbidden, they washed in the dark. They bided their time, certain that those who had been forced to leave would return with their Turkish and Syrian brothers in one huge avenging army. The exiles themselves believed they would be back. Many buried their gold and silver in the gardens or walls of their houses, to be recovered later."

"In the mountains surrounding Granada are treasure caves guarded by enchanted soldiers," said Manolo. "Every hundredth year on Good Friday, or maybe it's when Good Friday falls on a full moon, I can't remember, those soldiers are visible."

"Good Friday is barely a week away. Perhaps this is one of those years, what do you think, Manolo?"

Eva looked at Angel and he winked.

"Perhaps," said Manolo. "I will ask my mother, she will know. Incidentally, señora, if by any chance that is a Ring of Solomon on your right hand, then on the appropriate day you have only to switch it to the forefinger of your left hand and all those enchanted soldiers will reveal themselves to you."

She was surprised. She had forgotten about the ring.

"Superstition," said Angel. "Don't pay too much attention to our friend, señora. Manolo is the privileged descendant of one of those conversos we were just talking about. As a baby, he sucked in streams of cabalistic notions at his mother's breast. My background is quite different, as you may have gathered. I, despite my interest and fascination with all ethnic groups, am by rights a cristiano viejo—an old Christian. As I already mentioned, I am the direct descendant of the Marqués de Cádiz who led the key assault on Alhama."

But Eva was more interested in Manolo. "Tell me about your family," she said, turning to him.

"My lineage is not quite as pure as that of Don Angel."

Again, she couldn't tell how much irony, if any, he was speaking with.

"Hijo, you know as well as I that the whole notion of limpieza has been exaggerated," said Angel. "The facts are that despite the rhetoric, here in the south it was not long after the first wave of expulsions that both Jews and Muslims were quietly encouraged to stay, and by 1550, there was no great racial difference between the Islamic and Old Christian populations–the differences were social, not biological. The only thing of note was the father's lineage and religion. Your mother might be black or morisca, as well as both your grandmothers, but you could still join the Christian elite. Even the doors of the religious orders and colleges were opened. The enforcement of limpieza was just too impractical."

"You're descended from conversos?" Eva said to Manolo.

"Yes, on my mother's side. If not for the combined facts of the Jewish expulsions and Colón's first voyage, I would not have been born."

"That sounds intriguing."

"You have heard of Fray Juán Pérez?"

"You mean the monk who sent the secret message to Isabel, after which she supposedly changed her mind about the expeditions?"

"The same. Well, on the eve of Colón's departure, Fray Juán went to the docks to give his blessing to the expedition. Just as he was disembarking from the flagship, a young Jewish woman ran up and threw herself at his feet. She cried out that everyone in her family was dead, that she was terrified of the ocean, and that if she were forced onto a boat she too would surely die. The young woman was beautiful. Fray Juán took pity on her and brought her back to the abbey, as his housekeeper."

"And?"

Manolo spread his arms.

" . . . I am the latter-day result of the kindness of the monk."

He paused–for effect, Eva thought.

"So you see, while it is true that I am descended from conversos, I am also descended from the most virtuous of Christians."

Eva didn't know what response was expected, so she raised her eyebrows and smiled as noncommittally as she could.

Manolo continued. "Colón was so grateful to Fray Juán for

everything he had done, he left him his most valued possession."

"You mean his son Diego," said Angel.

"Don't tease me, Don Angel. We both know that children are not possessions. What I mean, of course, is Colón's most valued *material* possession."

Eva waited patiently while Manolo again paused dramatically.

"His most valued material possession was the sword of Boabdil."

Once more, Eva had the impression that Manolo was trying to gauge her reaction.

"Here we go again," said Angel. "This is not the first time we have had this discussion, but for the benefit of la señora, do tell us, hijo, what in god's name Colón was doing with the sword of Boabdil."

"The queen had given it to him."

"Really? Queen Isabel had given the sword to Colón?"

"When she declared him Admiral. It is a fact."

"A fact of history so obscure that I, a historian, have heard it from one source only: my good friend Manolo. Tell me, hijo, where is this sword of yours today?"

"Who knows?" shrugged Manolo.

"I thought it was in that museum," said Eva.

"I for one know that it is not," said Manolo.

She looked at him inquiringly.

"Everyone knows that museums are full of fakes. The scientists keep the authentic objects for themselves. They take what is valuable and leave behind worthless trinkets for the people."

"Whatever one chooses to believe about archaeologists, and scholars in general, in truth they have saved and cared for many important works of art which the so-called people would have blithely left to rot," said Angel.

Oh no, thought Eva. There goes the conversation again, down another Spanish alley. The bus hit a bump and Resa's knee bent sharply into her mother's stomach.

"No importa," said Manolo. "What comes from the pueblo belongs to the pueblo—the people are free to do what they wish with their heritage."

"And who exactly are 'the people'?"

"Take the last pueblo we passed through. If the fathers of those villagers made some sculptures, the sculptures belong to the villagers and to their children, not to some stranger or museum on the other side of the mountains."

"And if your villagers decide to smash the sculptures?"

"That is their business. The sculptures are theirs to preserve or to destroy. No one has the right to come in and take what does not belong to him. It would be the same if my mother possessed, let's say a key, a key that had been passed down from that same young woman who threw herself at the feet of Fray Juán. Imagine if I was to find the door into which that key fit, and that the door was attached to a house that had been seized by a Christian soldier in 1492. Is not my claim on the house more than that of the descendants of the thief who stole it from my family?"

"The question is irrelevant. Such a house would have been torn down centuries ago."

"Perhaps, but the key to that house would be our claim to our past."

Angel stretched and took another tack. "The truth is, it would have been unusual for Jews to be so optimistic as to keep their house keys . . . "

This is unreal, thought Eva, all this talk of Boabdil and his sword, of exiles and their house keys. It was as if her inner concerns were in balloons above her head for all to read and comment on.

"For the expelled Muslims," continued Angel, "it was a different matter, of course. So certain were they of God's favour that most took their house keys with them to Barbary."

She glanced up at the luggage rack.

The overnight bag was still there, safely above.

"Is there something you need?" asked Manolo. "Can I get something down for you?"

Eva hesitated. She knew there was nothing to worry about. But ever since leaving Edmonton the bag had been in her hand, at her side, or under her feet, and although now, with the bus in motion, the bag was in no danger of being lost or stolen, she felt a twinge of insecurity at being separated from its contents.

Manolo was already standing, reaching up.

"Which one is it? This one? The black one?"

"Yes, thank you."

She moved Resa's legs and he set the bag gently in her lap. She unzipped the middle compartment and felt for the velvet pouch.

Of course it was still there, tucked in the corner.

She felt a sudden need to have the pouch with her, on her person with her passport and money and snapshot of Tony and other irreplaceable items. She fished the pouch out of the bag and stuffed it in her pocket, and immediately felt calmer. In the next moment she realized just how tired she was. The stresses of travelling, Resa's demands, and now the ceaseless talk had drained her. She needed to retreat into herself.

"Excuse me," she said to the two men across the aisle. "I think I'd like to try and close my eyes a bit."

"Muy bién, señora," said Manolo, "I'll let you know when we reach Granada. Sleep with the angels."

Or had he said "angel," referring to Resa? The conversation was slipping away again, but Eva was too exhausted to care.

†

When Tony had died, it wasn't Eva the government had called, but his mother, Teresa Benabo. Mrs. Benabo had summoned Eva to her apartment and told her: I've bought us each a ticket to Spain.

Spain? Eva had thought he was in Italy.

At the Edmonton airport Eva had been refused permission to board–too pregnant. Then I will go on my own, Mrs. Benabo had said. After all, I am his mother.

And so it was Tony's mother who had gone to Granada, his mother who had identified the body and arranged the burial so far from home. Eva had returned by herself in a taxi to the apartment she had shared with him.

For the longest time she had stood in the open doorway and stared at the shelves jammed with books, his mixed with hers. In the hall closet, his Gortex jacket hung empty on the hanger and his Nikes with the partially supinated heels stood slightly pigeon-toed, as he had in life. She understood that he had died, but it felt more that he had vanished into thin air.

Unable to bring herself to move the shoes, to touch the books, she sank down to the floor, and noticed one of his running T-shirts scrunched up in a ball at the back of the closet. She grabbed it and pushed her nose into it, staying that way until morning. When the sun came up she crawled to the couch, still holding the T-shirt, and fell asleep listening for the swoosh of water on the shower curtain. She didn't bathe for five days, and slept with the shirt on her pillow.

On the sixth day, in the same hour that Mrs. Benabo was burying her son, Eva gave birth to his daughter.

It wasn't the birth, but the commonplace of having to name the baby that shocked Eva out of a general collapse of will. A nurse rolled the baby into the hospital room. She needs a name, the nurse said. I don't have one, Eva said. The nurse placed the baby in Eva's arms and left the room, and Eva looked at the little crying face and thought: For you, the present is eternal; you have not yet learned hope.

That night Tony came to her in her sleep, and Eva said to him all the things she had not been able to say to his hearing ears. Holding on to herself, hugging her own shoulders, she cursed, cried out the unvoiced expiations and explanations, the trivial elucidations of misconstructions, the words of love, begging to hold him one last time, desperate to have him back just one more night. She was awakened by the cries of the baby being wheeled in for her night feeding.

The baby sucked fervidly at her breast, and Eva gazed back into the intense, undiluted little eyes. The baby mewed. So this is it, she thought, this is what all the fuss is about. And she thought she understood what had been Mrs. Benabo's previous resistance to her.

Teresa, she said when the nurse returned in the morning, her name is Teresa, after her grandmother.

When Mrs. Benabo came back from Granada she took one look at the baby and saw the eyes of her son staring back at her. That little bundle of baby is my only connection to anything that matters, she said. She told Eva to move in with her. I will take care of little Teresa while you go to work–please, she said, humour an old lady.

Eva wavered, but by the end of the month she had packed some of her things into a Budget rent-a-van and taken them to Mrs. Benabo's. The Salvation Army hauled off the rest.

Mrs. Benabo doted on her granddaughter–it was she who gave Teresa her nickname. Little Resa smells just like her father did . . . and those feet, just look–his used to turn in exactly like that. Eva, for the first months at least, emitted that ambiguous scent of the newly widowed, and her long black hair seemed thicker and blacker than before, her hesitant smile wiser and more melancholy, so that Mrs. Benabo warmed to her and eventually came to think of her as family.

As for Eva, the five years with Tony's mother provided her with more warmth than she had received during her entire growing-up years. Her own mother had been an unhappy, self-absorbed woman who had withdrawn into herself after the death of her husband, and Eva had learned as a child to expect little and make do with the small pleasures that can intimate happiness–the smell of rain, its sound on the roof, the approving smile of a teacher at school.

In her early twenties, Eva's Canadian mother had gone to Mexico City for a holiday. She had met Juán Bonilla, the most exquisite man she had ever seen, and fallen instantly in love with him. They had been married, and Juán had eagerly flown back to Edmonton with his new wife, bringing with him dreams of an expansive future. Then one day he had realized that he was working hard and going nowhere. He had slacked off, lost his job, and given in to lethargy and claustrophobia. How are such feelings possible, he had wondered, in this country of limitless vistas? He had decided it wasn't his fault: his spirit was snowbound–by the climate, but especially by the Canadian temperament. He stopped going out and passed long evenings muttering at the TV, cursing his wife for his misery. He would declare that he was returning to Mexico, that no warm-blooded man could be expected to hole up like a squirrel in such airless, closed-up rooms for months on end: it was unnatural. You'll see, one of these days I'll go back home, he would say. Fine, let's go, his wife said one day. No, he said, when I go, I go alone. Why did you marry me? she asked. Because you told me life was better here.

She had thought he loved her.

She turned to drink.

Eva was six when her father died–of what, she never knew, but she always imagined that he had fallen asleep in a snowdrift.

She learned to open cereal boxes and cans of soup, to scramble eggs and boil macaroni, and got in the habit of coming straight home from school, alone, unwilling to introduce other children to her increasingly unpredictable mother. In the evenings she stayed in her room. Sometimes merely keeping out of her mother's way used up the time. It was understood that she was not to ask about her dead father, of whom she remembered less and less.

At age fourteen she went through a religious phase, spending hours rearranging her collection of medals and holy cards, hoping that one day she too could be a saint. The saints were perfect. They smiled. They dispensed boundless love.

One of her treasures was an Our Lady of Guadalupe dashboard magnet with a dark complexion, like her father's, and her favourite holy picture was of a swooning Saint Teresa of Avila falling back with parted lips and offering up a crucifix, a book, and a pierced heart.

One day Eva lost her Lady magnet and the religious phase was over. She turned to reading, and discovered that although she acquired facts and concepts easily enough, she had difficulty applying the knowledge to her own life. She became the person whose silences lead others to believe that she sees the world exactly as they do and is therefore entrusted with their secrets, a chameleon taking on the colours of other people's expressed thoughts and emotions.

She finished high school and went straight to university, not out of ambition but because she had been awarded a scholarship. Rudderless yet imbued with an unspecified yearning for things Latin, she drifted into Romance Languages and became reacquainted with her childhood Spanish. She continued to live at home, although she and her mother rarely spoke.

When Eva was in her final year of university, her mother died, at age forty-five, of cirrhosis of the liver. After the funeral, Eva stayed in bed for a week, not out of mourning so much as a failing of the spirit, a shut-down of all systems following extended use: she had grieved her mother's absence long ago.

On the seventh morning she jumped out of bed with the knowledge that she was going to move into an apartment and sell her parents' house.

A few months later, while she was at the bank investing the money from the house sale, a mutual acquaintance introduced her to Tony Benabo.

Eva reads Italian, the friend said. Great, said Tony. He was an associate professor in metallurgy, an expert in ancient bronzes. He had a letter from the Department of Antiquities in Naples. He thought he had the gist of it, but would she mind having a quick look at it, just to make sure? She liked his eyes. Sure, love to, now was fine, why didn't he come over to her place? Her new apartment was right around the corner. He told her that he had spent the previous summer extracting and examining slag samples from a Lucanian site in the south of Italy. The presence of the slag indicated a furnace might be buried in a neighbouring farmer's field, and the letter granted him permission to dig in the field.

That was the beginning. He left the letter at her place and returned later that night to retrieve it. She found his vitality irresistible; he found her placidity mysterious. He stayed for three nights and two days, and a month later, moved in.

She had not known she was lonely. She had always assumed that she didn't require the intimacy sought by other people, didn't need the heat. But Tony's enthusiasm for every little thing he did—his enthusiasm for her—made the world around seem painfully fresh and alive. Before long he became all that mattered to her—no, not that—it was that now, everything mattered. She was no longer content to coast along through her courses, slapping assignments together, writing routine papers, surviving exams, not thinking any further ahead than the next class. Now she wanted to do things: see the world, meet people. She wanted babies.

It was only since Tony's death that she had begun to doubt him: to wonder why, two weeks before his death, he had abruptly left the dig in Italy to fly to Granada, when that very morning the archaeological team had located the furnace. Since the prospect of excavating the furnace was the reason he had returned to the site for the fourth year running, what could have been so important as to impel him to leave at that precise moment, and without telling her?

She turned to his books, but was disappointed to find no connection between the dry technical texts and the burning lover who had cancelled classes to spend those first three nights with her. It was his letters, along with five packets of snapshots, that came to redefine the large part of the few years she had spent with him.

Often when she woke in the night, she reread the letters—one from an earlier trip to Granada, a trip she had known about—and the later ones from Italy. The photographs and letters verified to her that she had been loved, and that the love had been flawless.

The letter from Granada said: More than anything I want to bring you here. We'll rent a carmen with a garden and a fountain and we'll go from room to room making love all through the night and all through the day. In one of the letters from the Italian dig, he had written: I've just come back from Naples. I miss your voice. I wish I could talk to you, but there's no phone here. The director took me to Pompeii, and then to Herculaneum where the new city is gradually being disembowelled to reveal the old. Do you remember me telling you about Avebury, how sheep graze in fields of standing stones? (She didn't.) Herculaneum is to Pompeii what Avebury is to Stonehenge—the persistence of life in the face of death. In modern Herculaneum, people shout, cars honk, and trains whistle above the ancient smothered city with its deserted cardines paved with lava. By contrast, in the ruins of Pompeii I felt like a tourist in a graveyard. He had included a snapshot of himself at the top of the crater of Mount Vesuvius. A strong wind whipped his hair and clothes. In another photograph, he squinted into the sun while behind in the distance the Bay of Naples was a milky haze absorbing the barely visible mountains.

Near the end of his second summer at the dig, she had met him in Italy. The trip was not planned.

He had phoned her from a village near the site. Please come, he said, I'll send the ticket and instructions. I still have a few things to do, but you can help with some of it, and after, if there's time, we'll head north.

She still had the list of instructions: get an International Driver's Licence; get tetanus shots; bring a hat, sunglasses, hiking boots, gloves; don't bother with a purse–it's better to carry your money and passport close to the body. From Frankfurt take the overnight train to Rome; in Rome, stay near the station at the Hotel Villafranca; take the espresso to Reggio Calabria on August 16; get off at Sapri–I'll meet you there.

He met her in a borrowed Fiat and took her down the coastal road and up the winding one to the village with the telephone. She had a picture of him standing beside the red Fiat.

Each morning, at dawn, he climbed five kilometres up the mountain to the site. The first two mornings she had trudged up with him, only to discover that despite what he had said, there was little to do for someone with no experience. She was useless at sorting his samples, and in any case she found the digging itself to be all too domestic. The site was divided into rectangular parcels, each assigned to a different couple who seemed to spend the day weeding and sweeping out the little plot. Gardening and housekeeping, thought Eva, like playing house under a hot sun. She opted to spend equally mindless mornings on the beach twenty minutes away, and afternoons in the village walking from one end to the other, stopping to read or take pictures, or to just stare over the wall, awaiting the end of Tony's day.

During the first week she had gone through five rolls of film. The photos called to mind the village and the resonance of male voices–in the bars, the men playing scopa, slapping down cards with gusto and great roars–and the women at the wash house, their rough hands pummelling and scrubbing in the icy water. In the evenings, after the chores were done, the young women walked up and down the main street in twos and threes, and the young men poked each other in the ribs and draped their arms across each other's shoulders, swaying like male chorus lines before the audience of girls.

At the wash house on the hill the women were curious about her. They examined her closely, like a suspected jailbreaker. Was she the foreigner Roberto had married and brought back to the village? No. Then she must be the American niece of Alessandro the butcher. The German cousin of Francesco's wife. They eyed her suspiciously. What was she doing here in the village then? She was on the excavation? Then why was she at the wash house at this time of day? Oh, her *man* was on the dig, she was doing his laundry! They lent her pails to soak the clothes in, a brush to scrub them with, soap to replace her own inadequate brand. They teased her and gave animated gestured explanations on how to use the system of the three tiers of water: prewash in the bottom basin; soap and scrub in the middle; rinse in the top, where the water is the cleanest.

The final week, she and Tony had taken the train north while the rest of the country seemed to be heading south to the forests and the mountains and the sea. A photograph taken from the balcony of their room in Naples confirmed the city in her mind as grimy, rundown, overcrowded with people and cars. She had two snapshots of Tony with the pigeons in the Piazza del Duomo, reminding her that Milan at the end of August had been silent and empty, desert clean, as if from Naples they had travelled halfway around the world and not just a few hundred kilometres. They had spent one night in Naples, and two or three in Milan. Or was it four? They had bought a nineteenth-century engraving of opening night at La Scala.

The longer she examined the photographs, the less they served to prompt her memory and the more to assert themselves as the sole embodiment of the trip, as if her memory was adjusting itself to exclude events that had occurred outside the moments captured by the camera, so that these unchanging snippets could become the certified record of that summer, just as the photograph of a great-great-grandfather dressed for the only time in his life in a borrowed suit can become for his descendants the single and false representation of the man, obliterating all else.

Thus Frankfurt was the cold city represented in the tight-lipped face of a grim young man staring into the camera from the window of a black sedan. The train ride to Rome was reduced to postcards of the Swiss Alps. Of Rome itself, she remembered the Colosseum, and the Vatican, where she had taken a picture on the steps of St. Peter's of a group of priests bustling off like self-important businessmen, leather briefcases in hand.

She knew she had wandered with Tony through the ruins of Paestum because in two of the pictures he was leaning against a pillar in front of the Greek temple. But she could barely recall the rest of the day, the afternoon they had spent at the beach, bobbing and drifting in those huge, amazing waves that never quite broke.

Had it all been so simple? Had she and Tony really taken life so for granted? The photos were the evidence that she had been in Europe that particular summer, but where was the evidence that she had been changed by the trip? The photos and letters proved that Tony had existed, but they intensified the feeling that he had vanished into thin air.

This feeling took on a surreal quality when Mrs. Benabo gave Eva the velvet pouch, the one she had just slipped into her pocket.

Two weeks before she died, Mrs. Benabo asked Eva to fetch it from the back of a dresser drawer at home.

Eva did so and brought it to the hospital.

Open it, Mrs. Benabo said.

An old map and an old key.

For Resa, from her father.

From Tony?

Family lore had it that in the fifteenth century a lone Benabo ancestor had been driven out of the Kingdom of Granada. The ancestor, Alfonso Abenabó, had been the last surviving son of an Abencerraje official and his wife, both of whom had been favourites of King Boabdil and had benefited greatly as a result. They had been killed in one of the palace intrigues that preceded the fall of Granada to the Christians. Alfonso had remained loyal to King Boabdil, following the king first into the Alpujarra and years later to Fez. Like the other exiles, Alfonso had been forbidden to take anything of value with him, but, also like the others, he had expected to return one day, so he had buried his valuables in the garden and kept his house key.

"The very key you are holding in your hand," said Mrs. Benabo.

Eva was astonished. Tony had told her none of this.

The key felt substantial in her hand. It was about four inches long, of wrought iron, with a circular shaft and the sharp seasoned smell of aged metal. The years had smoothed and rounded its edges.

The map was a black-and-white plan of a house and garden, with the point of a tiny red sword marking a spot in the garden. It could have been the plan of a house and garden anywhere in the world.

The original map disappeared long ago, said Mrs. Benabo. This is a redrawing.

For almost five hundred years the key and a copy of the map had been passed down in the Benabo family, son to son, along with an account of what had transpired up to that point—"like an oral log," said Mrs. Benabo. During that time, successive Benabo men had returned to Granada to try and locate the site of the house.

"As far as I know, I was the first woman to be let in on the secret. You are the second, and Resa will be the only one to actually possess the key. It is supposed to open what is probably a nonexistent front door of what may have been the Benabo house, in the old district of Granada known as the Albayzín. The red sword marks the spot where Alfonso Abenabó buried his strongbox the night before he left with Boabdil for the mountains. As you can see, the map is useless unless you know exactly where the original house was."

Eva was dismayed that Tony had never mentioned his Spanish ancestors, let alone told her their story.

"My husband was middle-aged before he became interested in doing anything about the treasure," said Mrs. Benabo. "The last few years, I hardly saw him. He worked at two jobs, day and night. At the time I thought he was saving to buy us a house, but it was really so he could retire to Spain. He never made it, poor man. He died too soon, like his son after him. And now, there are no Benabo men left, only a little girl."

Eva had told Tony everything about herself—humiliating details about her mother, her father, her own misguided blunders—and he had chosen to keep all this from her.

"When my husband took ill, Tony was still very young—much too young to lose his father, and too young for his father to properly explain things to him. So I was entrusted with the secret. When I finally did tell the story to Tony, his initial response was sober and silent. Then, over the next few weeks, he pressed for more details. Was I sure there wasn't anything else? A map of the ancient Albayzín that might show the location of the house? A list of names? Of objects? Some seemingly trivial fact I might have forgotten? He became obsessed with the idea of going to Granada. Perhaps it was his way of dealing with his father's death, poor boy."

Still, the fact remained: Tony had not trusted Eva with what was most important to him.

"Men seem to adore their secret societies with their bonding rituals—they can be so sheeplike about such things," said Mrs. Benabo. "But if the whole affair seems a bit too much like tablets in the desert and Arks of the Covenant, it has often been the promise of the key that has kept the Benabo family going. In keeping quiet until he could pass on the key to the next in line, Tony was following tradition."

There was more.

Buried in the Abenabó garden was not only a chest filled with the usual gold and jewels, but something of amazing and unaccountable worth—the sword of King Boabdil himself.

For despite the fact that Muslims were not allowed to keep weapons, King Ferdinand had taken pity on Boabdil and allowed him to keep his sword, with the proviso that he not use it against any Christian, and later, when Boabdil decided to leave Spain for good, he had given the sword to the young Alfonso Abenabó, whose father had died fighting for the king.

"When King Boabdil left the Alpujarra for Fez," said Mrs. Benabo, "he was very depressed. He said to Alfonso: No longer am I worthy to carry a sword.

"Years later, Alfonso joined forces with a group of men who stormed into Granada, assuming that those still capable of bearing arms would rise up with them. But even the sight of Alfonso brandishing the sword of their exiled king was not enough.

"That night an old Moor took his añafil to the top of a tower and sang out into the silence of the night: Muy tarde viniste, Zaide; Trajiste pocos, y venís tarde. Too little too late. The old Moor sang the lament in Arabic, but my husband used to sing it in Spanish.

"Alfonso heard the song of the old Moor and decided that it was time to accept defeat. The uprising had failed. He made it back to his former house and hid the sword alongside the strongbox. Soon after, he was arrested and deported along with most of the rest of the moriscos of the Albayzín."

Does any of this have anything to do with me? wondered Eva.

Then she asked the question she had been afraid to ask.

"That summer, the summer he died, had Tony planned to go to Granada?" He had told her he would be spending the whole summer in Italy.

Mrs. Benabo had pushed herself up on her elbows. "I'm sure he had no such plans. Otherwise he would not have left the key and map here, with me. He would have wanted them on his person."

Again Eva wondered: why hadn't he left his most treasured objects with her?

"It's impossible to believe that he would have gone to Granada just then unless it had something to do with this business," said Mrs. Benabo. "He had been twice before, but you already knew that."

But not why.

"What do you suppose he did there?" Eva asked. How did one look for a treasure?

"I imagine he conducted himself as the family has always done, which is to say, as discreetly as possible. You see, they have never known what would be the legality of their situation should this treasure actually turn up, and anyway, legalities can change to suit the latest group of officials. The Benabos assumed that should one of them find the treasure and it become known, the state or some local politician would find a way to confiscate it. My husband told me to stress that whatever Tony's choice of action, it be done *calla'ito,* on the quiet. I'm sure Tony would have taken this directive as seriously as he did the rest. And anyway, he was very superstitious."

He was?

"If you ask me, this whole business was very directly involved with his death."

What was Mrs. Benabo saying? She had already said that he had drowned in the Darro River.

"My son was found floating in the river with a bruised and broken arm, a broken jaw, and a bump the size of a melon on the back of the head. The police said he probably slipped, injured his arm trying to break the fall, hit his jaw, rolled over, hit his head, and fell into the river. Now I ask you, does that make any sense?"

Eva was feeling dizzy.

"The fact is, my son would never have allowed himself to drown like that in the middle of the night, and in such a puny river as that. It wasn't like him."

Why had Mrs. Benabo mentioned none of this before? Eva wasn't sure she could cope with this hollowing out of her most solid touchstone.

"My dear," said Mrs. Benabo, falling back on her pillows, "there is so much about life you have yet to learn."

Eva had felt pale, filled with unearned emotion, and she had thought of Plato's reflections in the cave.

"I have something that might make you feel better," said Mrs. Benabo. She pulled a ring off her finger and pressed it into Eva's hand.

"This ring also has a long history. It has been in *my* family for many many years. My mother gave it to me, and it's for you now, and of course I would like Resa to have it one day, too."

Eva was tremendously moved.

It looked big for a woman's ring, but it fit the middle finger of her left hand. Two golden triangles were interlaced to form a star enclosed by a silver circle.

"The ring is very special. It's supposed to bring luck, but luck is not something I require any more."

"I can always use a little," said Eva.

"If you ever go to Granada, you will need more than a little."

"You think I should go?"

"That's not what I said."

"Can you tell me more about the ring?"

"You mean about my own background."

"Yes." Eva knew only that Mrs. Benabo had come from central Europe before the Second World War.

"I suppose you're right to want to know. After all, my story is part of Resa's story too."

"Yes."

"My roots also go back to Granada, but farther back than my husband's. My people were there before any of them–before the Nazarites, the Modharitas, the Idristas, the Berbers.

"The ring belonged to one of my foremothers, Ruth Shulam Delcampo, a poet who was among the first group of Jewish exiles.

"Expelled families had only a day or two to prepare–the time to say good-bye, to pack a few things, no more than what they could carry on their backs. Selling anything was almost impossible because the neighbours knew that the leftovers would be free. But worst of all were the betrayals. The lists of those to be deported were compiled with the help of loved ones–friends falling all over themselves to be greedy spies, children turning in their mothers and fathers to receive as reward the property of their slain or captive parents.

"Exiles were forbidden to keep jewellery, but Ruth somehow kept her ring. Many exiles did not make it to the ships, countless dying on the road of grief, of weariness, of hunger, or they were robbed and butchered by the very guards assigned to protect them, but she made it to the coast. The ships were overcrowded, rat-infested, and once out of port, at the mercy of pirates. But she, Ruth Shulam Delcampo, managed to reach the shores of Barbary."

"Why didn't more people stay and let themselves be baptized?" asked Eva.

"To spend their remaining days being watched like criminals? Trembling with the terror of being discovered in clean clothes on a Saturday? In dread of being invited out to dinner? Those who stayed had to keep their doors open on the Sabbath, so that any passerby could check that they were not following forbidden rites, and they had to eat pork conspicuously, because in the trials, abstention alone was proof of guilt. Their neighbours would invite them over for meals and announce—this animal was killed in an accident, or, it was bitten by another animal before it died. Any converso who refused to eat the unbled meat could be arrested.

"But in the end, I suppose you're right: it didn't much matter who stayed and who left, because everywhere we've gone, our people have had to struggle. Ruth Shulam's descendants eventually found their way to Europe, but Europe certainly didn't want them back. And I came here with my husband, but I'm not sure Canada really wanted me either."

After Mrs. Benabo's death, Eva sometimes wished that someone, a fairy godmother, would appear to give her step-by-step instructions in how to cope, as if grief might be stayed by the right prescription, as if the right prescription might eliminate pain in the same way that Tony's photographs and letters had led her to disregard so much of her unrecorded past with him.

No fairy godmother, and Eva found herself checking books out of the library, all of them about Spain.

One book told her that Spain was a blend of East and West, of Don Quijote and Sancho Panza, of Ignacio de Loyola and Teresa de Avila, so she read Cervantes and the writings of the two saints, finding comfort in the preferred saint of her fervent youth. She read about the Civil War, about the aspirations of Catalonia and the Basque region, approaching Andalusia cautiously from the north. Finally one day she carried home a stack of books by Europeans who had travelled south: Ford, Brenan, Hugo, and a couple of Italians. The next week she brought home *The Complete Works* of Federico García Lorca, which led her to a book of Arabic poems from Islamic Granada.

Most of the poems were extravagant praises of Granada, litanies that struck a familiar chord. Instead of Virgin Most Chaste, Tower of Ivory, Queen of all the Saints, she read City of Silk and Gold, City of Perpetual Snows, Damascus of the West. Granada the Unsurpassed: to breathe in her air was to sample the perfume of heaven; to drink of her waters was to sip from the fountain of paradise; to lie in her shade was to luxuriate in the delectable coolness of God's shadow. The sons of Granada were braver than lions and more generous than cocks; they cried pearls not tears, and they smiled with ruby lips to uncover gums like pomegranate flowers, and teeth to rival the Pleiades.

The Arab poems led her, inevitably, to a collection of Jewish poets of Muslim Spain. But she was disappointed: Ruth Shulam Delcampo was not mentioned. Most of the poems, translations from Hebrew, were on biblical themes. None of them were by women.

One spring morning, three months after the death of Mrs. Benabo and the morning after having finished reading *The Last Abencerraje* by Chateaubriand, Eva woke up, pressed her nose into Tony's T-shirt, and realized that the scent had faded away. She got out of bed with the absurd knowledge that she and Resa were going to Granada.

That day Eva quit her job. She gave away her dishes; she sold her books and records. She carefully folded the unwashed T-shirt and buried it under a tree.

You know so little about life, Mrs. Benabo had said.

†

The bus was slowing again. Eva opened her eyes and rolled her head from side to side until her neck cracked.

Resa was still asleep. She did look like Tony—his curly black hair, his almond-shaped face. But not his white skin. Resa's was dark. Like mine, thought Eva.

"Feeling better?" asked Manolo.

"Much."

"We are passing through Santa Fe. Will you be getting off?"

She smiled at him. "I thought you already decided I'm not a romantic."

He smiled back. "Romantic or not, you will soon be in Granada."

"Señora, I noticed that you spent no time in Málaga," said Angel. "Most tourists spend a few days there before continuing on to Sevilla or Granada."

"Should we have?"

"No no," said Manolo. "Málaga is fine, but you can see what's of interest in a single morning—there's the Alcazaba, and the bullring, and the house where Picasso lived as a boy . . . you can always visit Málaga on your way back."

"When will that be, señora?" asked Angel. "When are you planning to return?"

"I don't know."

"Why plan to leave before you have arrived, right señora?" said Manolo. "And it can take forever to visit Granada. The Alhambra alone can take a lifetime . . . "

"I can't wait to see the Alhambra. I've read so much about it."

"I'll take you through if you like; I know it very well. I give private tours. Whenever there is an important dignitary, I am the one who is called. Last year I was guide to los reyes, Juán Carlos and Sofía. They had planned on spending one hour in total, but the entire afternoon went by before we even made it to the Generalife . . . Don Angel, are you finished your work yet?"

"I still have a little more to do . . . And by the way, señora, I too would be happy to give you a tour. I'm working on some restorations in the Alhambra, and living there at the same time–for the convenience."

"Like Washington Irving," said Eva.

"Yes, but he wasn't the first, you know, and I'm sure I won't be the last–just the latest in a long line of Christian usurpers, Fernando and Isabel, of course, having been the first. And what about you, señora? Do you have a place to stay in Granada?"

She knew where she wanted to stay, but she had not reserved because she had lacked confidence in her telephone Spanish.

"We're probably staying at the Hotel de los Tilos."

"An excellent choice. Inexpensive, clean, and in la Plaza de Bibarrambla–very central."

But no matter how overpriced and inconveniently located, Eva would have chosen it. Los Tilos was the hotel from which she had received Tony's only letter from Granada.

The hotel is on a plaza surrounded with bars and shops, he had written. In ancient times the plaza was the site of jousting matches, and in medieval times of autos-da-fé.

†

Eva's first view of the city was unanticipated.

It wasn't that she had been expecting the unearthly Granada of the poets or the fanciful one of the travel writers, but neither had she expected so much traffic and carbon monoxide.

Where were the narrow streets of the arcane Orient, the stark white houses of Tony's postcards? She saw only drab buildings with the false bas-reliefs and cupids of western Europe.

She chided herself on her naiveté. After all, Granada was now part of post-Franco Spain, and the government was even planning to enter the Common Market. What had she expected? The golden walls of King Haxix?

†

At the bus depot, Manolo hailed a taxi for her. He knelt and pinched Resa's cheek, then lifted her into the back seat. He shook Eva's hand good-bye.

"Welcome to Granada," he said. "Whenever you want your guided tour of the Alhambra, come and see me in my guitar shop. It's in the Albayzín, on Elvira, at the bottom of the hill and not far from your hotel. I also live in the Albayzín, but our house is up top, near la Plaza del Cristo. Everyone knows me. Just ask for Manolo. Manolo Carmona, a su servicio, señora." He bowed and shut the door of the taxi.

Carmona. Manolo Carmona, the guitar maker. Of course. Why hadn't she made the connection sooner?

†

A week after she had given Eva the key and the ring, and a week before her death, Mrs. Benabo had said, out of the blue, "There's a guitar maker in Granada named Manolo Carmona. He lives with his mother and his young daughter. They were very good to me while I was there, especially his mother. They knew Tony quite well."

Mrs. Benabo had closed her eyes.

"Manolo makes beautiful guitars. He also fancies himself as somewhat of a curandero. His success rate with beautiful young women is apparently quite high, but if I were to need a real cure, I would visit his mother, who is renowned throughout Granada for her healing hands."

†

Was it possible? For Eva to come thousands of miles, and have her first contact in all of Spain be with this same Manolo Carmona? The man who had been with them on the plane, on the bus, and just now, guiding her and Resa into a taxi? And what about the uncanny discussion on the bus about Boabdil and his sword? About buried treasures and house keys?

†

Eva entered the hotel, her ring hand fingering the pouch with the map and the wrought iron key that Mrs. Benabo had so carefully wrapped in white tissue, like a gift.

Dreams

IN SLEEP THE DEAD WANDER IN AND OUT OF OUR dreams as they please.

Helpless, asleep, Eva was enveloped in her dead lover's Mediterranean savour, as if Aphrodite herself had preserved and sprinkled his fragrance onto the pillow, infusing the dark with comfort and soothing Eva into flighty dreams.

Tony floated above, then came to her like a sultry breeze. Together they lay near a river in a meadow thick like snow with butterflies and sank with the sun, blood-red and rolling below the horizon and over the edge of the earth. Fish skimmed the water like skipping stones, flashed back sprays of light.

But there was no meadow; there were no fish: there was nothing in the water save a tomb-black space. The heavens were the cold grey ice of an overcast day. The sky pressed closely, too heavy, too intimate.

He twisted out of her arms and dove into the water. He swam. Exuberant, he stroked straight into the tomb-black space.

She tried to avert her eyes. ¡Socorro! he called, crying out not to her but to his dead mother. And then the river sucked him in.

†

Eva sat bolt upright in the bed of her room in Los Tilos Hotel.

†

Oh love, what were you doing here? What am I doing here?

The night before, the taxi from the bus station had crossed the

River Darro. At the point of crossing, the river was hidden, covered over, at its most secret.

"Is this your first time in Granada?" the driver had asked.

Ah, then he had something to show her. He spun the steering wheel and squealed the tires around the next corner. The street curved and narrowed dramatically.

"Look," he said, taking his foot off the gas pedal.

The sight almost took her breath away–high above, the square towers and walls of the fortress of the Alhambra shone red out of the blackness, and above it the white summer palace of the Generalife floated like a silver castle. At the same moment a sleepy Resa looked up and saw the palace of Aladdin in the Arabian Nights.

"The word 'Generalife' comes from the Arabic for 'house of artifice,'" said the driver. "In the days of the Moors, the waters of the fountains sparkled like crystal, and the plants and flowers resembled gold and emeralds."

Lush orchards formed by the embrace of Allah, Eva had read. She imagined Muslim kings with their viziers and soldiers, their harems and poets, all beguiling the evening in the gardens and woods behind the walls.

"For us Granadinos, the Alhambra is our moon; by day it is our sun."

Then the taxi rounded another bend and the moment of magic was behind them.

†

Granada: Christian by day; Moorish by night.

†

Resa opened her eyes. The room itself was still dark, but her mother was in the corner, reading under a lamp. Light was also coming in through the doors off the balcony.

"Good morning, Resa love," smiled her mother, looking up.

Resa crawled out of bed and went to the French doors. The plaza was empty. Last night it had been full of people.

"It's very early yet," said her mother. "Your body clock is still on Edmonton time, but most people here are still asleep."

When they had arrived at the hotel last night, the man at the desk had spread his arms and raised his shoulders and talked in a loud voice to her mother.

There are no rooms, her mother had said. The man says this is a busy time of year, that Holy Week begins in a few days. We'll have to try elsewhere. Her mother had looked so tired and sad that Resa had felt like crying. Then she had noticed the man squinting down at her over the desk, and suddenly his expression had changed until it was like the one on her fuzzy puppy with the droopy ears that she liked to snuggle at night.

The man had scooted out from behind the desk and started gabbling, saying smiling things in Spanish that she couldn't understand but that made her smile too. He had bent down and lifted her up, saying ¡Qué princesa! and, in English, What a child, what a beautiful bride you will make one day! He had pressed her cheek to his prickly one and kissed her on the forehead and set her back down. Then he had said to her mother, Listen, I just remembered, there is a room you can have, it is over the plaza. The little girl will be able to see the processions–each year they pass right by here.

Resa didn't know what processions were, but she was pretty sure they could fly. She had just been dreaming about brightly coloured birds that had come to take her for a ride. Maybe those birds were processions, and they flew by every year on their way home. Or maybe they were more like those flying dinosaurs she had seen pictures of, with talons big enough to snatch up small children. If they were like dragons, she hoped they wouldn't be the sort that breathed out fire when they got mad. But whatever they were, it sounded like processions travelled in groups, and you should stay close to your mommy, just in case.

"Mommy, can we go on the balcony?"

"I think it'll be a bit nippy out there," said her mother.

"Please?"

"Oh, all right, but first let's get a sweater on over that nightie of yours."

She helped Resa into the sweater and woolly slippers, and took two chairs out to the balcony.

But Resa wanted to be closer than that. She waited until her mommy was sitting and climbed into her lap. "Are the processions coming yet?" she asked.

"Not until next week."

Still, you never knew, they might be early this year.

She cuddled against her mother and the two of them watched the plaza wake up.

The stores weren't open yet, but in front of the still-darkened windows street vendors began to unfold collapsible candy and cigarette stands. The first patrons were greeted by a blind lottery vendor singing out his lucky numbers, the tickets hanging from his neck like garlic bunches. Pigeons settled around the fountain to plump their feathers, and were shooed off by old men waving their arms to appropriate their places. Two teenage boys with guitars came and sat beside the old men. The boys slumped facing each other, knees touching, and exchanged rolling runs–a conversation between guitars. On a nearby stone bench another old man sat with his back to the sun and seemed pleased with himself and the unkempt children who had come from who-knows-where to dart and dash about.

The sky lightened, and people in housecoats appeared on other balconies to stretch and lean over the railings. Waiters in black pants, some in pale yellow shirts, others in white, materialized to unlock doors and carry out batches of tables and chairs, unfolding and arranging them in clusters in front of their respective restaurants. Natty men sat down to drink coffee and read their newspapers. A family appeared, and more vendors, weaving through the tables to sell this and that– Kleenex! 3 packages! 100 pesetas! Mendicants with professional slouches begged outright, one plump baby propped on a woman's hip extending his hand to the complacent coffee-drinkers.

The Plaza de Bibarrambla was now bright and filled with activity. Resa was getting restless; she wanted to be part of the life below. She examined the sky, but there was nothing moving, only a few wispy clouds high above.

Eva nuzzled her nose in her daughter's hair and squeezed her.

Resa took another peek at the sky, just in case, then wriggled out of her mother's grasp.

"Well," said Eva, standing up, "I guess it's time for breakfast. We'll unpack later."

They dressed, and Eva removed the key from the pouch and slipped it into the pocket of her jeans–why, she didn't know. She placed the pouch with the map under a pile of T-shirts in one of the suitcases.

By the time they sat down, Resa knew what she wanted–those thick, golden fingers of dough which most people seemed to be eating. The family at the next table was sharing them, breaking pieces off and dipping them into hot chocolate. When the waiter came, Resa pointed–Churros y chocolate, he told her.

Eva ordered a coffee.

The waiter returned with their order and watched Resa expectantly. "¿Qué? ¿Te gusta, niña?"

"It's yummy, like doughnuts and chocolate pudding."

He laughed, delighted. "¡Qué lista!" he said to Eva over his shoulder.

Eva smiled and took a guidebook from her bag and opened it.

"Leche, señora, leche."

She looked up. The woman with the baby was making another pass between the tables. The baby rolled his velvet-painting eyes and whimpered, holding a chubby hand out to her, palm up. Eva wasn't sure how one dealt with beggars, so she handed him a churro. No no, the woman shook her head, no señora, ¡Leche! the baby needs milk, leche. The well-coached infant wrinkled his brow and whimpered again.

Eva fished a few pesetas from her bag and handed them to the woman, who backed away mumbling a mechanical blessing.

Resa was kneeling on her chair, gobbling up the rest of the churros. Eva took a sip of coffee and went back to her guidebook.

She read that the Plaza de Bibarrambla had once been surrounded by lime-washed buildings with tiers and tiers of windows. It had also housed the huge silk market known as the Alcaicería, a miniature city with two hundred stores and ten gates to keep out men on horseback. At night the market was patrolled by dogs.

She turned the page to a picture of Columbus kneeling before the queen—the monument to the capitulations in the Plaza Isabel la Católica—the taxi driver had pointed it out yesterday.

Eva read that west of Granada was the vega, and to the east, the high mountains of the Sierra Nevada. Granada itself was dominated by three steep hills. From the Plaza Isabel la Católica she would be able to see the first of them: Mount Alhambra, whose gardens were still filled with roses, citrons, pomegranates, aloes, prickly pears, orange trees, peach trees, quince, and the emerald green shrubbery of kings. Opposite, to its north, was the rival hill of the Albayzín, once surrounded by three leagues of walls with twelve gates and one thousand and thirty towers. Today, the summit and slopes of the Albayzín hill were a crowded labyrinth of houses bordering narrow streets and small squares. The third and adjoining hill, Sacromonte, was burrowed with mostly abandoned caves. Slicing through the city were two rivers: the Darro and the Genil, which eventually joined up far outside the city.

"I'm done," said Resa, sucking her fingers.

Eva closed the book. "Good," she said, "where should we go first? The Alhambra or the Albayzín? The palace or the guitar shop?"

"I want to see the palace."

"The Alhambra it is, but let's check out the Alcaicería on the way."

†

The wonder of that day would stay with Resa for the rest of her life—a multitude of legs that ambled and sauntered; arms and hands that gestured and beckoned and pointed; voices that laughed, sang, shouted, called out to one another—harsh, unapologetic, uncanadian voices that sailed from terraces, bounced off walls, and leapt over streets with no trace of timidity; and the eyes—alert, interested eyes that looked directly into her own, seeing her and acknowledging her. The traffic was aggressive and undisciplined—along one wide modern avenue cars and motorbikes brayed nonstop—but then later, in the Albayzín, three donkeys munched quietly in a narrow cobblestone street.

†

For the moment, she and her mother made their way to the far side of the plaza to the Alcaicería, which Eva found to be a single disappointing alley of souvenir stalls. A few merchants were putting out their wares, but none was open. A Gypsy woman offered her a flower. Eva smiled and shook her head no, but the woman insisted, pushing the flower at her—"¿Por qué? ¿Por qué?"

"Resa, let's go over to the church," said Eva, beginning to cross the cathedral square.

The woman pursued them, her raucous ¿por qué?s scraping at Eva's ears.

"Let's go in the church for a few minutes," said Eva, trying to pretend the woman wasn't there. "It's getting hot."

She and Resa entered the church, and sure enough, the woman did not follow.

Outside had been unmediated light; inside was dim and dank.

"It's kind of scary," said Resa.

"But nice and cool. And now that we're here, why not have a little look-see?"

They walked around the outer aisle, peering into the gold-laden chapels of the various saints and mothers of God. Nuestra Señora de las Angustias, the patron of Granada, and the other Virgins glowed from the depths of their dark enclosures, their carved faces painted in tears, their squat medieval bodies dressed in fancy velvet and lace.

"They're wearing real clothes, just like dolls," said Resa.

Here and there an old woman bent her head in prayer before a sputtering votive candle, but the overwhelming impression was of extravagant power and immense weight.

In the Royal Chapel, Fernando and Isabel lay in state, protected by elaborate iron railings, florentine angels and the fathers of the church. Off to one side lay the smaller and outranked figures of Juana la Loca and Felipe el Hermoso. The marble effigies of the Catholic Monarchs dominated the entire chapel, eclipsing the immense altarpieces and gilding that covered the walls.

Resa scrambled up the spiral wooden steps of a pulpit to get a better view of the sepulchres, then scrambled down just as quickly. Her mother took her hand and led her down the stone steps to visit the tombs themselves.

If the Royal Chapel was Catholicism at its most lavish, the crypt was the quintessence of self-denial. A simple iron crucifix hung on the stone wall behind the plain lead coffins—four adult and one child-sized—that housed the bones of Fernando and Isabel (side by side, even in death) and Felipe, Juana, and the infante Miguel. The air that Eva had declared a cool relief now seemed musty and closed, as if holding the aroma of the settled dust of centuries.

"The smell of intestines. The guts of Spain."

The clipped male voice startled Eva. She hadn't noticed anyone come down behind them.

She turned and looked up: sunglasses, despite the gloom. A bony face, thin moustache, short blond policeman's hair, unswarthy complexion—decidedly unmediterranean-looking. The man was tall, not much older than her, perhaps in his mid-thirties. He stood stiff and erect, hands behind his back, directly facing the coffins.

"Above, the public face of Spain. Extravagant emotion. Bravado. ¡Soy yo!"

The accent was flat American.

"Down here: reality. Unadorned. The sobering truth of mortality. Acceptance of the inevitable. ¡No se puede!"

He delivered the words staccato, like sprays of fire from a machine gun.

"Spaniards are pagans at heart. Pagans don't serve God. They adore him. So Spanish churches are like African fetish huts. With their stores of bones and bits of body. A femur here. A pelvis there.

A tooth. They dug up Teresa of Avila five times after she was buried."

At the mention of her namesake, Resa pressed her face in her mother's stomach.

"Five times, at least. To get a different piece. The left hand. A finger from the right hand. An arm. A foot. A few ribs. A chunk of bone. Strips of flesh torn off and distributed. The heart. The head. Most of her neck is gone. So is one eye and part of the jaw."

As casually as she could manage, Eva took Resa by the shoulders to nudge her up the steps, but Resa needed no encouragement. She rushed ahead, checking first to make sure it was her mother who was behind her. The man followed and continued his commentary.

"Interesting head. Colour of dates. Sits on a satin pillow, what's left of it. A red pillow with silver embroidery."

They were back in the main chapel.

"Actually, Teresa hated the Andalusians."

Saints aren't supposed to hate, thought Eva.

"Detested them. But used them to try to enter heaven. As a child she ran away. South. So the Moors would behead her. So she could go straight to heaven as a martyr."

After the crypt, the chapel seemed almost giddily frivolous–the busy ironwork, the stained glass windows too high up to read, the hundreds of statues stuffed into niches, the huge paintings hanging from the walls.

"This chapel is more than reliquary. It's a giant vault. Full of jewels. Books. Paintings."

"It was Isabel who paid to have it built, wasn't it?" said Eva.

"With our gold."

Our gold? She examined his blond hair, his face around the dark glasses. Perhaps he meant "our" as in "New World," she thought.

"Isabel left behind a fortune to honour herself. All this–propaganda paid for by its victims. Queen Isabel. Ha!"

The laugh was like a gunshot, and it startled her.

"Isabel. Daughter of a deranged princess. Mother of a deranged queen."

Resa started walking away, taking long, obvious steps. When her mother didn't follow, she ran back and began to tug on her arm.

"Resa, please," said Eva, not wishing to be rude–and one of the paintings had caught her eye.

In the foreground stood a man with white gloves holding a sceptre. Behind him was a crowned queen on a magnificent white horse, and behind her, another rider, dressed in sumptuous red, being approached by a dark man on a black horse. The Alhambra and the Albayzín were visible in the distance. The dark man appeared to be offering his sword to the man in red, but the focal point of the picture was the queen.

"*The Rendition of Granada,*" said the stranger.

This must be the painting Angel mentioned on the bus, thought Eva. She contemplated the grand scene in the picture and the imposing tombs of the Catholic Monarchs. "It's ironic to think that they should be remembered almost as adjuncts of Columbus," she said.

"Even more ironic–the real hero is totally forgotten."

"Who's that?"

"Martín Alonso Pinzón."

"The captain of one of the ships?"

"He was more than that. Columbus owed everything to him. History has never acknowledged the debt."

"What did Alonso Pinzón do?"

"Columbus met him at the monastery of La Rábida. Alonso had a map with him. Obtained from the cosmographer of Pope Innocent."

"Didn't Columbus already have his own map?"

"An outdated one. A useless one sent by Toscanelli to the King of Portugal. It was the map from Innocent that made the difference. One look at it and Fray Pérez wrote the queen. She summoned him. Now, time after time, she had turned down Columbus's project. Yet when Fray Pérez showed her Alonso's map, she changed her mind. On the spot."

"How do you know this?"

"I know."

"So you're saying Columbus wasn't the great visionary he's made out to be?"

"He was an ungrateful pig. Alonso Pinzón was the true hero. The man of action. He provided the ships. Columbus had planned to man them with jailbirds. But Alonso rounded up real sailors from his home town. Made the expedition possible on a practical level."

"A sort of Spanish Gabriel Dumont to Columbus's Louis Riel."

"What?"

"Nothing." How silly of her. How could she expect anyone from outside Canada to have heard of Gabriel Dumont or Louis Riel.

Resa said, "I'm cold, Mommy. Let's go."

"In a minute, sweetheart."

"God is style. Style is power. Look at the king and queen. Flat on their backs, but lying in style. Style. That's what counts here."

Is he as sure of himself as he seems? she wondered. He emanated an unsettling quality that intimidated and fascinated her, an insolent assurance that was holding her fast. But why was he wearing sunglasses indoors?

"The local myth says the Christian God smothered the light of Allah. Zapped the joyous boulboul. Pure crap, I say. Churches are monuments to the power of death. This church is the reality of Spain. Austerity in the crypt. Gaudiness up here. The extremes."

Resa was tugging again on her mother. "Come on, Mommy, you promised we'd go to the palace."

"Going to the Alhambra? I'll take you up there."

Eva could feel his breath on the top of her head.

"Mommy-y-y . . . "

"It's very kind of you to offer . . . "

"I'll give you the grand tour."

Resa pulled on her mother's hand and dropped to the floor. "Owwie! You scratched me with your ring!" she wailed.

Embarrassed, Eva stooped down to look at Resa's hand, but Resa would have none of it. "You hurt me, Mommy! Ow ow ow!"

Eva straightened up again. "She's very tired," she said apologetically. "Thanks so much, but maybe some other time."

For the first time he turned to face her, but still did not remove the dark glasses. He spread his arms in mock abdication and bowed slightly.

"Until next time then. Granada is small. We're sure to meet again. But first, a warning."

He gave her a close-lipped smile. His lips were smooth.

"Watch yourself. In a few weeks everybody will know everything about you."

He spun on his heel and walked off in the direction of the sanctuary, disappearing almost as quickly as he had appeared.

Eva's skin was tingling. Too long without, she thought to herself.

Resa sniffled and let her mother pick her up and kiss her slightly pink finger better.

They left the shadows of the cool church and emerged into a hot crowded street. The bright sunlight momentarily stung their eyes.

"Let's see now, where are we?" said Eva, conspicuously examining the map.

"I don't like that man," said Resa.

"Here we are, not far from the Plaza Nueva." Close to Manolo Carmona's shop, thought Eva. Maybe later. "Let's go, sweetheart. That way."

Across from the plaza was the bottom of the Cuesta de Gomérez, which led to the top of the Alhambra hill.

"Okay, this way to the palace."

The River Darro was also indicated on the map, but here in the new part of the city, it was cemented over.

And for the second time since their arrival they crossed it without hearing so much as a trickle.

Who would guess there's a river under our feet? thought Eva.

†

The sun beat down on Resa's hot dry head as she and her mother climbed the Cuesta de Gomérez. The slope was lined with little shops, the windows crammed with odds and ends–wooden boxes, ornaments, jars and pots, keys.

"Are we almost there?" Resa kept asking. "Where's the palace? If we're getting closer, why can't we see it?"

The road was steep and narrow, but just past the huge Gate of the Granadas her mother chose another route, and they were in a wide avenue with flowers, shrubbery, and tall cypresses that filtered out the sun. They came to a shaded bench and sat down, and Resa looked at the sky through the treetops. No processions yet, but a bird sang.

After a while they got up and before they knew it the walls of the Alhambra were before them: one minute nothing, and suddenly here it was, all of it.

They entered the grounds through the Gate of Justice.

†

King Haxix had finished the Alhambra one hundred years after the first stone was laid–that much Eva remembered, and that throughout its eight centuries, it had gone from being centre of politics to barrack for soldiers, to prison for pimps, to home for beggars and bandits, and finally to its present incarnation as tourist mecca.

She and Resa wandered under the stalactite ceilings and horseshoe arches, through rectangles of light and dark and bright patches that shifted with the moving sun. They marvelled at the carved birds, monsters, and fruits–grapes, apricots, figs, oranges, peaches, olives, and pomegranates of wood and plaster–and at the tapestries woven in these same animal and fruit motifs. The walls dripped with chiselled, unreadable poems. Windows became picture frames enclosing the outdoors–green trees and flowering shrubs and the countryside beyond. And in each room was the sound of water, the music of fountains.

Eva had anticipated ostentation, but the whole exuded an air of grace and freshness. Like a secret kiss on the cheek, she thought as she looked out a mirador. Perhaps Boabdil's mother and his wife had stood here together, in this very spot, surveying their future with helpless resignation. Eva thought she heard a rustle of silk, and her captivation was complete.

For her part, Resa ran fingers over the stuccoed poems, hid amongst the columns, and watched the goldfish swim in the pond of the Patio de Arrayanes. She looked out miradores that were like her own dark eyes, and she tried to follow the windings and twinings of the traceries on the walls, but each time she became lost in the lacy arabesques, until after a while the walls seemed themselves to move, and to awaken new and confusing feelings–a familiar strangeness that was like the awakening of the passions of youth, when longings are still dreams.

She discovered a small domed room off the Court of Lions in which some people were standing with their ears pressed against the wall and others seemed to be kissing it. Then she noticed that each person was alternating between the ear pressing and the kissing, and that the lips of the kissers were moving as if they were talking, not kissing. Her mother entered the room and took her to the curved wall–Stand here, she said, while I go to the opposite side of the room. When I get there, put your ear to the wall. Resa did so and heard her mother as clearly as if she were talking into her ear, but her mother was still on the other side of the room. Careful, her mother's voice said, the walls have ears. The wall murmured and groaned. Resa cried into it, Can you hear me Mommy? and her mother on the other side of the room laughed silently and whispered yes.

Eva led her daughter outside into the gardens of the Alhambra and into the wooded heights of the Generalife. Inside the Generalife, water trickled down the middle of a staircase handrail.

"Did you know," said Eva, "that once upon a time, a long long time ago, a sad little princess lived here? No one ever saw her smile. Months of sunshine didn't cheer her up. Not even her father the king, who loved her more than anything, could get her to smile. Then one day it started to rain, and the king happened to look out the window.

He saw his princess slipping and sliding in a small patch of mud, laughing her head off. The next day he ordered that the whole yard be turned into mud, and from that day on, whenever it wasn't raining, the gardeners had to water the yard."

Eva and Resa meandered back to the Alhambra, and then, standing atop the Alcazaba, they looked across at the hills of the Sacromonte and the Albayzín, the one a moon village of caves, the other a white hill of houses with roofs the baked ochre of twenty generations of sun. Below the Albayzín sat the cathedral, like a thick and lumpy tumour.

Resa often had flying dreams in which she soared like a bird, her arms extended into wings. Or sometimes she was stretched out on her stomach peering over the edge of a flying carpet, and her shadow, perfect as a Chinese paper cutting, sluiced over the hills and valleys below. She would swoop down and see animals in the forest and lonely princesses in faraway castles.

As she examined the white mountain of houses, she knew that inside the square courtyards would be stone seats and flower pots, fountains and fruit trees. She had no vocabulary to express what she felt, so she said simply, "Mommy, I like it here."

"So do I," replied her mother.

But where to start looking in such a maze? And from up here, all the houses looked the same.

"Let's go back to the hotel," she said. "I think we've done enough for one day." Tomorrow, the guitar shop.

On the way down, Resa was sure she saw the man from the church getting into a car in the parking lot.

"Mommy, I think that man is bad," she said.

Eva didn't hear. She was looking down at the gorge where the Darro had surfaced to dribble past the church of San Pedro in a scanty greenish-brown stream.

Tony had told her stories of rafting in whitewater rapids, and once he had taken her canoeing on the North Saskatchewan River. They had tipped into the rumbling fast-flowing water and he had readily pulled them out of it.

Mrs. Benabo was right.

How was it possible for him to have drowned in such a river, a river which was almost not there?

Hot and Cold

THE NEXT MORNING AFTER WHAT WAS TO become a habitual breakfast of churros and hot chocolate, Eva and Resa made their way to Manolo Carmona's guitar shop on Elvira. The shop had no sign, but as Manolo had promised, everyone knew where it was.

A man who was sitting braced in the doorway stood up, bowed, and stepped aside onto the sidewalk. Eva peered through the windows and tried the door, but it was locked. No hours were posted.

"Do you know when the shop opens?" she asked in Spanish.

The man, who looked Asian, gestured to show incomprehension. She repeated the question in English but received the same non-answer.

"Well then, Resa love, I guess it's plan B. Let's try and find Manolo's house." She consulted her guidebook. "He said it was close to the Plaza del Cristo . . . and judging from this map, that should be an easy walk from here . . . up the next street."

She nodded to the man, who bowed deeply.

Within minutes, she and Resa were in a world of divers odours and streets devoid of cars. They came to a corner with a choice of five directions, and paused. Eva opened her map.

She heard shouts, ¡Arré! ¡Arré! and looked up to see a train of mules descending one of the streets, hooves clacking like castanets on the cobblestones. The driver was showering the mules with abuse and praise, goading the lead male, hitting him with a stick—¡macho-

macho-macho-o! ¡firmé, firmé-e-e!—and cajoling the unenthusiastic females—¡viejas! ¡reviejas! get a move on, slapping them on the rear and swearing like a pimp keeping his girls in line.

The donkeys passed, and Eva chose to go up the way they had come down. But soon the road forked in two, and the one she chose forked again, and when that one ended at an iron gate she realized she was lost. There were no street signs, and the map in the book was almost useless. Distances were not to scale, bends were not indicated, and sometimes two streets that appeared on the map to run side by side were in fact one above the other. Streets and alleyways twisted and rose and fell and turned back in on themselves, sometimes dropping into vertical steps taking Eva and Resa back to where they had started. Deadends were unmarked surprises.

In the middle of one otherwise deserted lane a mother stood in the sun, rattail comb in hand, carefully inspecting the head of a squirming boy. Sigue, sigue, she said, pointing in the direction from which they had just come. Once they came upon an old man sitting in a stairway, his eyes half-closed and arms folded across his chest. When Eva apologetically asked if they were going in the right direction, he answered Directo, directo, señora, waving his arm upwards like a baton, indicating that they must keep climbing. Farther up they met a bored-looking woman in slippers and a terry cloth housecoat sitting on a wooden chair in a doorway, the kitchen discernible behind, the street in front her living room. Bare legged, knees apart, she was cleaning a chicken. From inside the house came rutting sounds—two female voices and a male one—not nearly muffled by a tinny ghetto blaster. The woman on the chair tossed some entrails into the gutter running down the centre of the street, and a couple of emaciated cats, one without a tail, the other missing an ear, approached cautiously, pounced on the leftovers, and escaped through the iron bars of a window in a derelict building down the lane. No, señora, la Plaza del Cristo is not far, said the woman, Sube, sube directo, no está lejos, you will see.

Yesterday, from the heights of the Alhambra, the Albayzín had been lush green patches framed in white: mingled city and grove. But now, from street level, the exteriors of the buildings gave no hint of what might be inside, as if they had been designed specifically to hide. The high blank walls gave off smells of urine. Eva saw no restaurants, no bars, no evidence of commerce. I'm hungry, I'm thirsty, Resa kept saying, I want to go home.

They climbed one chalky street after another, sweat pouring down their faces and soaking their backs. Raw snippets of song tumbled from an open window, but the singer was nowhere to be seen.

How could I have been so stupid, thought Eva. I'm nothing but a typical tourist setting off in the heat when any nitwit with half a brain in her head would have known to stay in the shade with her feet up and a cool drink in her hand. How dumb can you get? And poor Resa, what kind of mother am I? Selfish, I'm irresponsible, foolish, blind.

Finally she decided to give up, to head back to civilization and refreshments–assuming she *could* find her way back down. We can always come back tomorrow, she thought, we'll take a taxi up one of the main streets.

Resa too had had enough. No way was she taking another step. She was ready to scream, she would lie down in the middle of the street and kick her legs if she had to.

And then, at the moment of their defeat, Eva and Resa caught a whiff of jasmine, and their hot cheeks were caressed with the softest coolest breeze either of them had ever felt.

"We've reached the top!" cried Eva.

Below was the cathedral, hulking over the new part of the city, and in the distance, the vega.

"Mommy, look!"

In the other direction, at the end of a street, a plaza filled with people–drinking, eating, gesticulating.

So that's where everyone was.

They entered the plaza and observed the noisy scene from under a scrawny tree. Green metal tables and chairs spilled from the sidewalk, between parked cars and into the street itself, so that vehicles and pedestrians passed within inches of the seated patrons. A church with a square white steeple marked the far side of the plaza, and a crucified Christ the near one. The stone base of the Christ had a particularly battered look to it, as if it had been torn down and reassembled at one time. Some of the tables were set around the crucifix, the diners gathered as at a mock Last Supper. Eva could not see one empty chair, and it didn't look as if anyone was prepared to get up.

"Welcome to la Mesón de los Milagros," said an astonishing voice. The voice had the huskiness of a lifetime smoker, and suggested nights of skidding to the edge. "Join me–I would be delighted to introduce a fellow Canadian to the pleasures of this bar."

Another Canadian! Eva wondered that she had not noticed her immediately. The woman was sitting alone, a drink in her right hand and a cigarette in the left. Her thick-jointed fingers gripped the glass as if in fear of having it taken away; the thumb and forefinger of the other hand formed an O around the cigarette, like holding a teacup. Her nails were bitten short but painted hot red, and her hair was blond and youthful-looking. Next to the healthy hair the deeply wrinkled face was shocking, and as with many old women, the heavy powder and bright lipstick only served to dramatize her advanced age. Overall, the impression was one of jadedness, with a certain vulnerability in the shoulders.

She looked familiar.

"Come on, don't be shy," the woman insisted. "Moncho will bring more chairs. You can be sure he's already noticed you."

As she spoke, a man in jeans and blue leather shoes approached with a full tray balanced on one arm and three metal chairs slung under the other.

"I brought an extra one, señora, in case you need it," he said. He whipped open the chairs, at the same time maintaining the tray poised high in the air.

"Thank you, Moncho."

"This is very kind of you," said Eva to the woman. "We've just this minute walked up from Elvira–it seems like we've been trudging around in circles for hours."

Moncho smiled at Resa and lightly pinched her cheek. "Señorita, I will be right back to take your order."

He left, working his way through the tables.

"Moncho's a cantaor–a flamenco singer," said the woman. "His wife Pepa used to dance–actually, she still does once in a while, but only on feast days, and only if she's not in the kitchen. She's the niece or something or other of la Faraona or la Macarrona or la Papatuna, I don't remember. Her stage name is la Luz del Sol. Unfortunately the beam of sunlight has widened and she's more like the Criada del Cristo, cook and scullery maid of the Plaza del Cristo."

"You don't mean it! This is actually the Plaza del Cristo?"

"Mmm."

"It's unbelievable. This is where we were headed when we got lost."

"Well, this bar *is* called the House of Miracles."

"Mommy," interjected Resa. "I'm thirsty, and I want something to eat."

"Yes, sweetheart. We'll order something as soon as the man comes back."

Eva examined the menu board. "What do you suggest?" she asked the woman. "I don't know any of those dishes."

"Have the boquerones–fresh-fried anchovies. And maybe a tomato salad. That should fill you both up."

Moncho came back and took the order. "And to drink?"

"Is it safe to drink the water?" Eva asked in a low voice.

"You're lucky he can't understand you. Water's sacred here. People talk about it in the same reverent tones that the French use for wine."

"Agua, por favor."

"¿Con gas o sin gas?"

"Ask for tap water," said the woman.

"Del grifo."

Moncho nodded approvingly and went off.

"As a matter of fact, these people sing about *water,* women and song. Each well in the mountains has its aficionados. One person will write a song to the waters of his village, and another will sing, 'Ayy ayyy . . . Drinka-aoooo the watera-a-aooo of my-y vil-lagea-a-aoooo . . . '"

Eva laughed. "What about here?"

"In the Albayzín? You have two wells to choose from: the one at San Nicolás and the one up at San Miguel alto."

"You sound like you've spent some time here, and from your accent–maybe a few years in Britain?"

The woman raised an eyebrow and took a swig from her glass.

"But how did you know we were Canadian, before we spoke, I mean?"

"Isn't that why you wear that? So people will notice?"

The woman waved her cigarette at the maple leaf pinned to Eva's lapel. Eva had bought the pin at the Edmonton airport in the unquestioned belief that the outside world loves Canadians, and that it is thus of great importance when travelling to demonstrate that one is not a dreadful American.

"You probably think that leaf will protect you from all sorts of disagreeable things, such as being disliked. You think that once they realize you're just a decent Canadian, thieves will not rob you, vendors will not cheat you, and strangers will rush up to shake your well-meaning hand." The woman drained her glass. "I mean, you don't see Frenchmen with miniature fleur-de-lys cufflinks or Englishmen with union-jack tie clips. They know who they are. It's only Canadians who run around the world wearing silly little flags and pins. All it serves is to attract other Canadians. And what if a Spaniard did notice your pin? He would probably think you were a crusader, or that you work for the Red Cross, or, even worse, that you work for the government. Half the people in Granada don't even know where Canada is."

Eva laughed uncomfortably. "Well, you can say my pin is silly if you like, but it did attract *you.*"

"Exactly, another Canadian."

"Thank goodness, we were about to drop dead of exhaustion."

While they were talking, Moncho brought the water. The woman quickly lifted her glass and motioned to him for a refill, but he was already rushing off to another table.

"I hate Canada," she muttered, banging the empty glass on the table.

"What do you mean?"

"Just that, I hate it."

"Why?"

"What do you mean, why? Are you sure you want to hear? I have a whole rant."

"Yes."

"Right, you asked for it.

"I hate Canada because it is filled with muted immigrants whose colour was strained out in the second generation. It all began with the first colonists, that batch of French illiterates whose children blossomed into ideological dinosaurs who steal every issue and turn it into a nationalistic one. And after the French rabble, the rest of Europe shipped off its undesirables: it was the signal that anyone was welcome. The disgraced, the fanatics, they came in droves—narrow-minded evangelical sects bent on self-preservation, whose self-righteousness regenerated into mean, spiteful children who cling to hatreds with origins in far-off villages whose names they can't even pronounce. And they're still coming, each new group hating the others, but not overtly, oh no—they snip out of the sides of their mouths at each other until they get their citizenship papers. And what about the ones who get stuck in Canada by default? Canada was just supposed to be a stopping-off place for them, a stepping stone to the glorious U S of A. Instead we've become a consolation prize for those the Americans don't want. We're a population of rejects, of fearful inward-looking people who have taught our children to distrust expressed emotion or thought. A country that conceals all of its nastiness inside idyllic haystacks."

Eva looked at Resa, nervous that her daughter should hear such talk, but Resa's attention was directed to a group of children across the plaza who were kicking a ball in a circle. What did this woman really mean? That good citizenship could be equated with class, that the decent people had stayed where they were and the other sort had gone to Canada? Maybe those first immigrants had gone about it all wrong, maybe they had been blind to the beauty and sanity that surrounded them. But wasn't the history of the world the story of migrations? Eva thought of her father, of his desire for a better life. It's not like that, she wanted to say to the woman. These days, it seems only those with money need apply, legally obtained or otherwise.

But, "You're not serious," she said.

"You think Canada deserves to be taken seriously? A country that thinks Wayne and Shuster are funny? Worse–thinks Stephen Leacock is funny?"

"We've had Cheech and Chong since then. And Rich Little."

"Who?"

"Never mind. Do you mean that Canada shouldn't be taken seriously because our comedians aren't funny?"

"Exactly. In Canada, what's intended to be funny is not, and what's intended to be serious is absurd. I mean, think about it. You live in a country in which the politics of its writers is determined by the size of the latest government grant to their union. A nation that requires one to lick the back side of a foreign queen in order to post a letter. One in which *being nice* is considered a virtue rather than a lack of moral courage. The whole idea of being nice is so disgustingly Canadian, it could drive one to drink . . . Where is that Moncho, anyway?"

"You remind me of Voltaire. Wasn't he the one who described Canada as nothing more than so many acres of snow?"

"I don't see why he wouldn't say the same thing today. I mean, each successive boatload or planeload of immigrants seems to end up blunted in some way–immobilized. Maybe it's the snowdrifts."

Eva thought again of her father.

"How long since you've been back?" she said.

"I left years ago, and made the mistake of returning–just the once, mind you, but it was a close call—I almost didn't escape. Blandness is surprisingly contagious. Before you know it you've become more passive than an old-fashioned bride, and you start to believe, along with everyone else, that somehow such behaviour is laudable. You think that other people are doing things *to* you. You don't say: we've sold out; you say: the Americans have bought us up, and after we were so nice to them and everything. Every once in a while we jump up and down a bit, but not too high, and we complain, but not too loudly, that being nice isn't enough to make everything fall into our laps. Then we snivel: It's not fair. I have my own identity, we whine, and copy the antics of our neighbour to the south, but covertly, in such a way as to reap the overflow benefits without taking any of the chances."

"You don't think we suffer from a national inferiority complex?"

"Rubbish!" spat the old woman. "Try a national smug complex. How many times have you heard: I'm proud to be Canadian? As if one can be proud of an accident of fate. We're so disgustingly smug about our niceness, and it's not as if our country suffers from an overabundance of intelligence, either. We've always looked without for our roots, right from when the first drunken European stumbled out of his ship . . . which reminds me . . . Where is that Moncho, anyway?" She banged the glass down again. "Moncho! Moncho!"

He appeared at her elbow and set a fresh drink in front of her. She took a long swallow and her anger vanished.

"By the way, how do you do?" she smiled pleasantly, letting go of her glass long enough to shake Eva's hand. "How rude of me not to introduce myself. I'm Isabella Flowers, a pinless wayward Canadian."

Isabella Flowers. No wonder she looked familiar. In Canada she was a living legend. Last year Eva had noticed a copy of the first edition of *Bleeding* priced at $600 in a secondhand bookstore.

"Pleased to meet you," replied Eva, instinctively treating the mood swing as she had her mother's humours—by ignoring it. "I'm Eva Bonilla, and this is my daughter Resa. And actually, I do know who you are. I've read *Bleeding*—I've even read it twice."

"How refreshing to meet someone who greets me with, 'I read your book,' rather than, 'I saw your picture in *Maclean's* magazine.'"

Eva didn't say that it was an article in *Maclean's* that had compelled her to rush out and buy the infamous novel.

The publication of *Bleeding* in the thirties had soaked Isabella Flowers in instant notoriety and won her Canada's top literary award.

It was said that the book had been written in one hot blinding flash, after which she had chosen a life of debauchery and had abandoned writing altogether.

As a teenager, Eva had read, Isabella Flowers had run off with a Hungarian Gypsy poet almost twice her age called Zendi the Magnificent. The two had hitched rides on steamers and ended up in the south of Spain, and it was while living in the caves of Sacromonte that she had written *Bleeding*, a story of obsessive passion that had caused frissons of scandal back home. The novel had been reprinted umpteen times and been translated into umpteen languages. It had been performed as a play on Broadway, in London's West End, and been made into a Swedish sex film. Her work (the one novel) and life (squandered genius) had also been examined in countless academic papers and newspaper articles. Some years ago—Eva couldn't remember just when—Zendi had reportedly died of an embolism in the arms of an Idaho cowhand.

"Yesterday I was reading Milan Kundera," said Isabella. "He said: 'Before we are forgotten, we will be turned into kitsch.'" She contemplated her half-empty glass. "In Canada I was turned into kitsch years ago."

"And here?"

"They don't know or care who I am. They call me la Católica—not to my face, of course."

"Why la Católica?"

"Queen Isabel was notorious for her extreme virtue . . . take it from there . . . " Isabella laughed, more a bark than a laugh. She seemed pleased with herself. "If you're around here long enough you're sure to acquire a nickname too. And oddly enough, there's a tendency to become one's nickname, or its opposite."

"You mean someone might look at my maple leaf and call me the Crusader, and next thing I'll be off to North Africa with the Ladies of the Sash?"

"More likely you'll get something mundane, like: La Canadiense."

"I thought you said no one here knows what one is."

"And it's not important either. Whatever your nationality, you will be granted the same courtesy that is extended to the stranger who shows up at the tent in the desert. What does matter is whether you're buena gente or mala gente. But be careful—once you're pegged, that's it. You're good or bad, one or the other, until everyone-who's-ever-known-you-and-their-descendants has died. So choose your friends with caution."

"Does talking to you count?"

Isabella smiled coyly and took another long drink.

"Imagine actually meeting you, Isabella Flowers, and here of all places. I really did love your book." Eva didn't want to say that she had been confused after the first reading, and that the second hadn't helped much.

"Call me Bella."

"Bella. Do you live here now?"

Bella's head suddenly plopped to one side and she lowered her voice melodramatically. "I might live here, I might die here," she slurred. She raised the cigarette to take a drag, but it was one long ash. The ash dropped to the table, and she brushed it to the ground. "So . . . " She lit another cigarette and snapped her head to attention. "What brings *you* here? Granada gets millions of tourists, but not many bother to come up here, not to this bar, at least."

"No wonder, it's not exactly easy."

"You walked up on your own?"

"Yes."

Bella leaned across the table conspiratorially. "Weren't you afraid of being robbed or something? Of having your daughter kidnapped by Gypsies?"

"It never even occurred to me. Is there a danger?" Eva glanced at Rosa, whose attention was still fixed on the group of children across the square.

Bella dropped her head to one side and barked.

"Oh," said Eva. "You were pulling my leg."

"You looked so earnest. But would you like some sincere advice?"

Eva guessed so.

"Dear girl, you look confused . . . Here's my advice: trust everyone and no one."

"I'm not sure I understand."

"Would you like an aphorism instead? All right: 'In Granada, everything is theatrical, even the sunset.' I don't remember who wrote that—probably some Englishman . . . Or would you prefer a cigarette?" She pushed the pack towards Eva.

"No thanks, I don't smoke."

"No, of course, you wouldn't."

Eva let the comment pass. "It's probably not what you meant," she said, "but the first time I saw the Alhambra, it did occur to me that it made the night look like a backdrop."

"Some days I could swear I'm just an apparition at the end of some wizard's wand," said Bella, "or an actor in a mystery play. And you know, when you're out in the street, you might as well be on stage, you're observed that closely. And you had better play your role properly, oh yes. On the other hand, you're also a member of the audience, and some evenings you may choose to stay on your balcony and watch the action from your private loge."

Bella tipped her glass back and stuck out her tongue to catch the last drop. "So, are you here for Holy Week or something?"

"Well, yes . . . no . . . "

Bella set down her newly empty glass but didn't let go of it. She stared at Eva and waited. Her pale blue eyes seemed to be looking into the very bottom of Eva's soul. They were the liquid sort of eyes that can darken with emotion or be as pale and removed as the sky of a cold English winter.

" . . . oh, I don't know any more," said Eva, "it's all so complicated . . . unfinished business, I guess." She looked over again at Resa, who was now standing, watching the other children.

"You see, my husband . . . Tony . . . he died here . . . "

Bella continued to scrutinize her.

" . . . six years ago, but I wasn't able to come then, they wouldn't let me on the plane . . . I was pregnant, you see, with Resa . . . His mother came instead . . . "

"Teresa Benabo."

"You knew her?"

"I knew your husband better."

"You knew Tony? Actually, he wasn't my husband, not really, we weren't married, but we had been living together for almost five years . . . and I've never even seen his grave."

"I can show you."

"Mommy, look at all those little fishes!" said Resa, jumping back up on her chair.

Moncho set the basket of bread and the dishes of boquerones and salad on the table. He handed Eva and Resa each a fork.

"Another drink, Moncho," said Bella.

"Whatever you wish, señora," and he scooted off again.

"Mommy, where's the plates?"

Eva wasn't paying attention; she was still trying to digest what Bella had said.

"Mommy, the plates!"

"Share from the middle, like in a Chinese restaurant," said Bella. "You can eat the fish with your fingers."

Resa started eating, but Eva was thinking: the famous Isabella Flowers had known Tony, well enough to offer to show his grave. And he had never so much as mentioned her name.

"Look!" said Resa. "There's the nice man from the bus!"

The man from the bus? Indeed, Manolo Carmona was walking towards them from the direction of the church, waving, greeting people as he advanced. The red beard was unmistakable.

"¡Orí!" he called.

Eva had forgotten all about him, that finding him was the reason she had dragged Resa up here in the first place.

"¡Buenos días! to all of you. I see you compatriots have met."

"Buenos días, Manolo," said Bella. "Won't you join us?"

"¡Qué aproveche! But what a pleasure it is to see you both again. And how is my little Teresita today, my Risita?" He pinched her cheeks. "And how do you like our food?"

"I love these little fishes."

He laughed. "And you, Señora Eva, how do you like the little fishes? I see you have already managed to find the best bar in the Albayzín."

"Manolo-o-o ¡Pri-mo-o!" called Moncho.

"¡Mon-cho o!" Manolo called back. "That's my cousin."

The two men grabbed shoulders and slapped each other on the back and shook hands.

"Primo, la señora Eva and her beautiful daughter are my new friends," said Manolo.

"Ah, your friends, in that case, the next round of drinks is on the house."

"What will you have?" said Manolo.

"Nothing for me, thanks," said Eva. "I've had enough today."

"You have to have something," said Manolo.

"I'll bring the cognac," said Moncho, rushing off.

"Please sit down, Manolo," said Bella.

"Thank you." He smiled at Resa and touched her hair as he seated himself in the extra chair. "So, how are you enjoying Granada?" he said to Eva.

"Very much, thank you."

"Have you decided to stay awhile?"

"Oh yes, I think so."

"Qué bien."

Manolo was delighted, he hoped they would stay for a long time, he would find them an apartment, immediately if they liked, one that rented by the week. He knew of an available place, completely furnished with everything they would need: sheets, blankets, towels, dishes, everything–they could move in next week, earlier if they wanted. But first, he told Resa, she and her mamá must come to his house and meet his mamá and daughter. He had told them all about them, and his mamá had insisted that he bring them home.

"One look at you and she will adore you, Sonrisita mía with the gypsy hair." He mussed Resa's curls. "You come tonight, because you know what? Today is my little Puri's birthday–she is ten years old."

"A birthday party!" said Resa.

He turned to Eva. "Señora, you must know what joy it would give my mother to meet this wonderful little girl, she has such gracia."

"Well, it sounds lovely . . . "

"Mommy, let's go ! Let's go!"

"Yes, I insist . . . And you too, Señora Isabel, you must come."

"Thank you," said Bella, "but I don't think I'll be able to make it."

"That's too bad. Ah, here comes your other compatriot, la señora de mucha campanilla." He stood up. "I must go. You are at Los Tilos?"

"Yes," said Eva.

"I'll come to your hotel later and get you."

"That's very nice. What time?"

"Luego, esta tarde."

"What time later?"

"Later, this afternoon."

Four? six? seven?

He shrugged. Later.

Eva gave up. "Okay, see you later then."

"¡Hasta luego!"

"¡Hasta luego!"

"¡Qué le vaya bien! ¡Adios!"

"¡Adios!"

Bella joined in with her own good-byes.

What a lengthy ritual, thought Eva.

"¡Hasta pronto!" And he was gone.

"Sharp eyes, he saw her way before I did," said Bella.

"Who?" said Eva.

"The marching muppet."

A woman in a large green hat and matching dress was striding purposefully across the plaza. She was big-boned and tall, well over six-foot, and charging directly towards their table, the head leading, the rest of the body following at an incline—a person who will brook no nonsense. Even in Canada she would have stood out; here in Granada, where the men are economical of build and movement and the women's heads are uncovered, she seemed to insist on more than her share of space.

Despite the heat, her dress was buttoned up to the throat.

She does look like an overgrown muppet, thought Eva, but an angry one. Her outfit reminded Eva of a co-worker who had once gone lunch-hour shopping and come back with four identical pairs of pants in all the available colours—red, pink, brown, and navy—and matching sweaters, shoes, plastic earrings.

"Oh, *there* you are, Bella! I've been looking *everywhere* for you!"

Moncho arrived with the cognac.

"Where's my cousin?"

"He had to leave," said Bella.

Moncho set a coke and the bottle of cognac and three glasses on the table. "Help yourselves," he said. "Please enjoy."

The woman in green assumed the extra chair and looked imperiously about her, as if challenging he-who-would-dare to question her right to be here, at this very moment, in this lofty Plaza del Cristo, in front of the Mesón de los Milagros, in this very chair in which she herself had chosen to sit.

She pursed her lips at Bella's cigarette and glared at the hand clutching the empty glass.

"Well Bella," she sniffed, "aren't you going to say hello?"

Here and There

ALTHOUGH RUTH KOSTYK HAD BEEN SEARCHing for Bella, the actual sight of her was almost more than she could bear. Who did Bella think she was anyway, boozing it up so early in the day, chain-smoking as if there were no tomorrow. The gall. But you had to hand it to her, she always did seem to manage to find a drinking buddy. This one looked like one of those skinny feminist groupies, what with that long straight hair and those big hooped earrings.

A bit *too* casual, if you ask me–probably wears those jeans and sandals all year round. Now be civil, Ruth said to herself, introduce yourself.

She stuck out her hand and smiled firmly. "How do you do? I'm Ruth Kostyk, I'm a writer."

"Pleased to meet you. I'm Eva Bonilla, and this is my daughter, Resa."

Bella reached for the cognac and squeaked out the cork. "Cognac, anyone?"

"Now Bella, you know I can't sit and drink in the sun."

Ruth could feel her forehead stretching. Relax now, don't let her get to you.

"*You'll* have some," said Bella, pouring a few fingers into Eva's glass.

"Oh no, not for me," she said.

"It would be rude not to have a little," said Bella. "Moncho would be insulted."

"Oh. Well okay, just that bit you've already given me, then."

Talk about being rude. How did Bella get away with it anyway? If she wanted to drink, that was one thing, but arm twisting other people into doing it too, that was too much. Go ahead, Ruth told herself, say what you think.

"It must be nice," she said, "but I can't drink like that in the middle of the day. I get migraines you know. Red wine is particularly bad, of course, and cheese, especially blue cheese, and for some reason I've always had trouble with Chinese food, I suppose it's the MSG, and then the traffic doesn't help—do you suppose there's a shortage of mufflers in Spain? Honestly, haven't you noticed how noisy these people are, don't you just wonder if they ever go to bed? I've already had to change hotels once. I was staying at this place on Constitución, but it was one ongoing racket—I had tried the Parador but it was booked solid—now I've managed to get a room at the Washington Irving, although I have to say that's not much better, you still get those bells ringing at four o'clock every morning, honestly, every night, ring ring ring, for those soldiers who were murdered who knows how many hundreds of years ago in the Alhambra, that's what I was told, anyway. Back home in Toronto I have double glass on all my windows—I require absolute quiet you know, I can't tolerate noise of any kind."

"So you're also Canadian?" said Eva.

"Yes, I don't suppose she's told you anything about it, but I'm here to do a piece on Bella. I'm on paid assignment from the *Toronto Comet,* although I would have preferred the *Galaxy*. I don't usually do this sort of thing, you know, I'm mostly a fiction writer, but *some* of us have to earn our living after all, and I suppose it does make a certain amount of sense that they would ask me, both Bella and I being from the same town and all, although we never actually knew each other until later, of course."

Her head was beginning to pulse, just above the right eye. Hang on, keep control, she said to herself. "And you, where are you from?" she asked Eva.

"Edmonton."

The West. "How interesting, I've lived in Toronto for years now, wouldn't live anywhere else, unless it were another large city of course, Paris or London maybe. Are you on holiday? I suppose you are. Must be nice, I've always envied tourists, how you can flit here and there looking at this and that without a care in the world. A writer of course is *always* working, after all you *never* know what you might be able to use for a story—I was talking to Peggy Atwood about this just last month—I don't imagine we writers are ever *really* tourists I said, travellers maybe but not tourists . . . "

"A foreigner is a foreigner is a foreigner," muttered Bella.

I suppose she thinks I didn't hear that, thought Ruth.

"Did you walk up, by any chance?" asked Eva.

"I took a taxi." Ruth's right eye was starting to throb. "Oh dear, I hope I didn't forget my sunglasses," she said, digging around in her purse, " . . . ah, here they are. I don't like to sit too long in this bright sunlight, you know, it can trigger an attack, but as I do have to speak to Bella, I have to take that chance."

"Mommy, can we go now?" said Resa.

"Soon," said Eva. She opened her bag and took out a pad of paper and a pen and handed them to her daughter. "Draw for just a little while and then we'll go back to the hotel and get ready for the party."

"Promise?"

"Promise."

I suppose people will think you're being impolite looking at them through these dark glasses, said Ruth to herself, but that's their problem. "I'm photophobic," she said, "but Bella knows that, speaking of which, *Bel-la,* I've been chasing after you for two days now and *honestly,* I'm sure I've never met anyone so hard to track down, and today I left the hotel so quickly I didn't have my full ration of coffee. I could really use a café doble about now, and I don't know about you but I know how *I* like my coffee, and that's a decent cup of it, not those miserly thimblefuls they serve here, I mean really, even those so-called café dobles are so tiny—that's the second thing I learned to say, 'café doble,' the first was plain old 'café'—but honestly, how *do* you get service around here anyway? I mean, these Spaniards, they're charming enough and all that, but what's charm if it can't give you a cup of coffee when you need it? Anyway Bella, now that I've found you, when do you suppose we can start the interview? How about this afternoon?"

Bella looked as if she had had the wind knocked out of her. Her head was lolling to one side and her eyes appeared to be unfocused.

There she goes again, pretending to be drunker than she really is, thought Ruth.

Bella looked towards the inside of the bar and appeared to revive. "Excuse me," she said, jerking to her feet, "I have to go."

And she was gone, winding her way through the tables and disappearing into the bar.

"Honestly," said Ruth to Eva, "I don't know who works harder for their pennies than us writers. Do you know, I've been trying to do this interview for almost a week now. It's not as if the *Comet* will cover my expenses indefinitely, even if I *am* doing a feature on the renowned Isabella Flowers, even if they *do* understand that I have to spend a certain amount of time getting a feel for the place, absorbing the right atmosphere and so on, but I'll tell you, if she keeps it up, I'll be tempted to chuck it altogether, after all, money's not everything. It's so childish the way she avoids me, and when I *do* find her she's either incoherent or recovering from the effects of the night before, I mean *honestly,* I don't like to say anything against the poor old dear, but I've put aside my latest novel for this job, and that's more frustrating than you can imagine. Anyway, what about you, are you a student or what?"

"Pardon me?"

"Are you a student?"

Eva looked blank.

"A student? A friend of Bella's?"

"Oh, no, I just met her. But she seems very nice. Very engaging, I mean."

"Engaging," repeated Ruth. "That's not the first word that would have popped into *my* head." This girl looks rather naive, said Ruth to herself, I think you should set her straight, before she gets overly impressed by Bella. "I do have my own theory about her, you know. Listen, seeing as you just met her, I think you need to know a few things about Bella, just so you're aware–she can have a devastating effect on people, you know, I've seen it happen. You may have noticed that she has a certain presence, a way of sitting perfectly still that can make people feel totally inadequate–it brings out their desperation. I met someone a couple of years ago, a reformed alcoholic, who said that she had taken her first drink in thirteen years just from sitting for too long at the same table with Bella." Ruth lowered her voice. "And she gets followed around by young homosexuals, you know–they trail after her like she's Judy Garland or something . . . Tell me, have you read Bella's book? I'll bet you haven't, because everybody in the world seems to have bought it, but tell me honestly now, how many people do you know who have read it from one end to the other?"

Eva looked confused, then said, "Actually, yes, I've read it."

"And that's another thing, and this isn't me talking, it's the opinion of most of the writers I know—all this fuss over Bella is a bit silly, and not just because she hasn't written anything for years, although it's true, she hasn't you know, not one word for the last fifty-three years, and that's a very long time to not write and still be considered a writer, don't you think? And lots of writers don't even think *Bleeding* was all that good in the first place, I mean, one of my best friends, a very fine novelist I might add, but I can't tell you his name, that would be betraying a confidence, he said, and these are *his* words not mine, that *Bleeding* is a conventional display of self-absorption that bears no more interest than a teenage girl's diary, and he's not the only one, another very good friend of mine said that once Bella finished that little book she had said everything about herself there was to say, and the reason she never wrote another thing is because she *had* nothing else to say, and she had nothing to say because she has absolutely no imagination for other people, mind you, *I* admire Bella a great deal, I'm just telling you what some of our most respected writers say. They say she's not a real writer, she's an *ex*-writer, just like when you quit teaching you're an ex-teacher—you get a watch and you take up hobbies. Think about it . . . Now what was I going to say? Oh yes, my theory. Now if you ask me, the reason Bella gets all this attention has nothing to do with how good or bad her book is—it's because she *used* to be *beau*tiful. Of course I love the dear old thing and all, she *is* from my home town and everything, but have you ever noticed how it's only the *attractive* women writers who get the attention?"

Eva was gazing towards the bar, a vacant smile on her face.

"Have you?"

"I'm sorry, have I what?"

"Noticed how it's only good-looking writers who get the attention."

"No, I haven't."

"You haven't noticed! You can say it's just luck, but how come beautiful people get all the luck? They are cultivated by the *right* people, they get reviews beside big photographs of themselves looking all hot and steamy, and before you know it they've become popular and their books are selling like hotcakes. Then they get on the talk shows and say all kinds of outrageous things and get fawned over by the host, and more books sell, and it doesn't really matter what they write or how they write, all the media cares about is voyeuristic sensationalism—sex with a dog, lesbianism, whatever. Honestly, I don't care who reads or doesn't read my books, but the public should be aware of how certain writers get all the attention. I mean you've seen some of them, how they sit there giving the most intimate details of their sex lives, for free, too—I mean it's positively embarrassing. You know the routine—the guest demurs, the host coaxes, and finally the guest relents and tells this perfect stranger and this absolutely anonymous audience all about how her father screwed her, and then some woman in the audience gasps, everyone bursts into thunderous applause and there's a break for commercials. At least Bella's never stooped to that level, I have to give her that much."

"Do you think she's coming back?"

"Probably. There's still some cognac left."

"I'm finished, Mommy," said Resa. "Can we go now?"

"In a minute, love . . . You and Bella are both from the same town, but I gather you didn't know each other when you were growing up."

"Are you kidding? She's *much* older than me—she had run off with that phoney poet *long* before I was born. You must have heard the story."

"You mean about Zendi the Magnificent?"

"Zendi the Fake is more like it. He was no Hungarian Gypsy, he was Jean-Paul Cardinal from the Soo, and Bella was no teenager, she was twenty-three. He got her pregnant and was so afraid of what her father might do that he talked her into running off with him and getting an abortion, but first her mother slipped her some money and she and Zendi flitted around the continent until the money ran out, at which point her mother managed to sneak her some more money. And despite everything, during all those years her family had the nerve to look down their noses at our family. My parents may have been shopkeepers, let me tell you, but at least they were honest and hardworking."

"Your parents had a store?"

"They owned the general store in town, but the Flowers, they had to be better than everybody else, only the shops in Toronto and New York were good enough for them. Do you know, in all the years, that family never bought one single thing in my parents' store, not one. And nobody else in town liked them you know, nobody liked the Flowers, until Bella wrote that book and became famous, then suddenly everyone was their friend. You have to hand it to those Flowers, my mother used to say, they sure know how to get all the attention. First they had their Holocaust and now their daughter writes a scandalous book."

"The Holocaust?"

You have to explain everything to this one, thought Ruth. "Well, and this is my mother talking, not me now, how come, she used to say, how come there's so much fuss about the Holocaust and you never hear anything about the millions of people killed in the Great Terror–it's Holocaust this and Holocaust that, and Flowers this and Flowers that. My poor mother, if she could see Bella now, I know exactly what she would say. Well that's life for you, she'd say, that Flowers girl sat down and scribbled for a few weeks, and look at her, fifty-three years later, still collecting fame and fortune from that one slim volume of self-indulgence."

"But didn't *Bleeding* win a Governor General's?"

Ruth could feel her face reddening. Keep calm now, keep calm, she told herself. "That wasn't a *real* G.G.," she said, "Bella got it at a time when the awards were still being given out by that bunch of amateur writers, what are they called now? The Canadian Authors Association."

Ruth's notion of writing awards was akin to Olympic medals in the world of figure skating–a skater worked hard and progressed slowly through the ranks until it was her turn to get the prize, whether or not the pertinent skate was good.

†

Ruth Kostyk's own literary reputation, such as it was, rested on the art of the short story–more specifically, on her competent and realistic depictions of small-town Ontario. Yet, despite six collections, critical attention had been sparse–mostly from small literary magazines–and virtually nonexistent from outside her own country, although ten years ago she had received a query from a Finnish publisher about her third collection of stories, *Summer Sauna*. She had sent two copies of the book by return mail, but had never heard back. Subsequently, she had come to two conclusions: that Prairie writers were coming into vogue, and that only novelists had a chance of gaining wide readership. So she had moved to Moose Jaw and written a novel.

The novel had been panned by the most influential reviewer in Toronto (hence the country) under the headline, *High and Dry*. He had said that although the huge swells of prose were pleasurable enough, the lack of climax had left him feeling perplexed and disappointed. Perhaps Ms. Kostyk should stick to short fiction, he had advised. She seemed to lack the all-encompassing vision, the panache and the will to resolution, the deceptive simplicity and poetic vision of, to take an example from her own home town, the great novelist Isabella Flowers.

Unable to break into the popular fiction market, Ruth had moved back to Toronto and tried the academic one. Her next project had been a ninety-page book entitled *Turbulent Tides: Ficti/one/thical Form and the For(e)aging of the Fem/i/nine into the Fem/I/nist,* in which she had rescued Emma Bovary from the confines of the "rigid male mind" of Gustave Flaubert and set her down on an Atlantic ice floe headed south, using the free-floating Emma to expound a theory of language as imitation of the movements of the sea, a metaphor for the undulations of the humin/wominly soul. (Unfortunately for Ruth, the tide of academic interest had already turned to "Nordicity.")

Her theory was no more absurd than others which had generated salary increments for their proponents, but she had never taught at a university (thereby suffering from a lack of legitimizing connections) or even taken so much as a creative writing course (thereby lacking a mentor to sponsor her ideas).

Turbulent Tides had been reviewed by a Red Deer College professor who had chastised her for ignoring the great body of criticism that existed in Canada, and for writing as if her ideas were unique ones which had sprung forth like Athena from the head of Zeus. But a collection of her stories had turned up on CanLit courses at two Maritime universities, and a master's student at the University of Alberta had decided to adapt her thesis of ocean/female imagery to the prairie/masculine fiction of W.O. Mitchell, and had sent her a questionnaire to fill out.

Despite the setbacks, Ruth had remained optimistic, retaining movie and translation rights for all her books.

†

"What do you suppose happened to Bella?" asked Eva.

"That's easy, she probably saw some man in the bar, I mean I don't like to say anything, but it's kind of pathetic, a woman her age, I mean she does like her men, especially the young Gypsy ones, and once she gets a few drinks in her, well there's no telling what she'll do. I worry about her, the poor old thing—all that carousing around can't be good for the heart. Now wait, I know what you're thinking, you're wondering why am I doing this, why would I go to all this trouble for one lousy interview, well it's not what you think, it's called *writing for a living*. I need money to support myself, and I don't care if you do think I'm prostituting myself, but I'm not lucky like Bella, I don't have an independent source of income, and I can't always afford to work on what I want to. If I were a less honest person I would be sorely tempted to fudge this whole interview and get on with my own interests. Did I tell you I'm working on a novel? It's my second one and I've had to postpone it to do this article for the *Comet*. I thought I'd be able to earn a few bucks without too much trouble, but this job's turning out to be more hassle than I bargained for."

"Mommy, can we go now?" said Resa.

"In a bit, sweetheart."

Resa kicked the table leg. "You promised."

"Just another few minutes." To Ruth she said, "What's your new novel about?"

"Oh, I never discuss what I'm working on."

"Sorry."

"Do you want to know why? I'll tell you why, because all writers are thieves, and if you're not careful they'll steal your best lines—but you're not a writer, of course, so I guess there's no harm in talking to you about it, at least not in a general way. I've decided to write about the wave of Ukrainian immigrants who came to Canada before the War."

"I admire writers. It must be hard coming up with new plots all the time."

Not exactly profound, but there was something sincere and appealing about this young woman.

"Hmmph, plots are the easy part. I'll tell you, drop me anywhere in the world and an hour later I'll have ideas coming out my ears. As a matter of fact, just yesterday I was reading in the *Herald Tribune* about a bunch of rare books that were discovered missing from the library of the University of Granada. What's extraordinary is that these books were never catalogued, so nobody knows how many books have disappeared because nobody knows how many there were in the first place. Imagine—there were no proper records of anything—not the medieval manuscripts, the medical treatises, the Arabic poetry—none of it. So how did they find out about the theft, you ask? By chance. Three months ago a professor went to fetch a particular manuscript off the shelf, and it wasn't there. At first everyone assumed the book had been misplaced, but once they started looking, they realized that dozens and dozens of other books were missing, too. Hardly any of the books were catalogued, but you can bet they're doing it now."

"Mom-m-my," said Resa. She stood up and knocked her chair over.

Eva picked it up and whispered something in her ear.

Children can be so irritating, thought Ruth. "Now I recognize a good story plot when I see one," she said, "and this one's so good I might postpone my novel a little longer–not that I'm interested in writing formula mysteries or anything like that, but at the very least I should be able to get a short nonfiction piece out of it, you know, earn a few extra bucks without compromising my principles. What do you think?"

Eva was smiling first at Ruth, then at Resa, back to Ruth, patting Resa's hand, making just-one-more-minute appeals to her.

Why doesn't she just ignore the child? wondered Ruth. How else are children supposed to learn respect?

"Good idea, don't you think?" she said.

"Sounds like a great idea. Excuse me, but we're going to have to get going. Resa needs her nap."

"No I don't."

"I think we should both lie down a bit."

"But I'm not tired, Mommy."

"Well," said Ruth, "I was just leaving anyway, so don't stay on my account. But we must get together again–you'll have to tell me all about yourself. I seem to have done all the talking today. Next time, you can talk. What did you say your name was again?"

"Eva."

"Eva, and this dear child. What's her name?"

"Resa."

If you're going to leave, get up and do it now, said Ruth to herself. She felt another unwelcome twinge in her temple. Take control now, don't let it take you over.

"I'm going to call a taxi now," she said out loud. "Would you like a ride down?"

"That's kind of you, but thanks anyway."

"Suit yourself. See you next time."

And she walked briskly away.

†

Just the other day, she had had one of those dawn attacks that seemed to strike with particular severity. As usual before going to bed, she had tried to make the room black and silent, but it hadn't been enough.

The attack had begun with a disoriented awakening out of an atrocious and incoherent dream. She had lain still, shivering and sweating, cold and hot at the same time. The throbbing in the right temple had intensified and she had pushed her head hard into the pillow, but the ache had spread to her neck and down into her shoulders, and her skull had felt as if a wedge were being driven into it, tearing her brain in two. She had pulled the covers up over her head, shutting out the light that was seeping in through the spaces in the warped shutters. But she could do nothing about the drip-drip of the bathroom tap and the horrid little motorbikes outside that attacked her nerve ends like angry wasps, and, worst of all, a sick sweet smell of jasmine.

Old and Young

EVA OPENED HER EYES. HAD THERE BEEN A noise?

Resa's head was in her mother's lap, the book they had been reading on the floor.

Eva's neck hurt from being on the pillow—a hard lumpy tube stretched like a sausage across the top of the bed. She cracked her shoulders back and looked at her watch: 7:00 P.M., already. Did this still count as afternoon? She should have known to eat earlier. Now they would have to wait until at least 9:30. She remembered something she had read: Spanish timetables are not meant to indicate the hour at which an event is to begin, but the hour before which it will not begin.

Still, I must have got it wrong, she thought. Either the party is another day, or I misunderstood completely and there is no party.

†

What a day. First, the Plaza del Cristo materializing out of nowhere, then meeting Isabella Flowers and Ruth Kostyk, and running into Manolo after having temporarily forgotten about him, then Bella vanishing before she could be questioned about Tony.

Ruth reminded Eva of something, someone—a small dinner party in the past, a politician seated next to her. In person the politician had seemed much as he had on television, perhaps too much so, saying the same things, in exactly the same words. On television, he had sounded as if the public were his intimate, but at the dinner table, his words served not to establish any sort of intimacy, or even mutual acknowledgement. It was as if he were delivering a lecture or a rehearsed speech, and she existed only as his audience. When she spoke, he seemed to be using the time to plan what he was going to say next. From a distance he can establish an intimate feeling in a crowd, she had thought, but up close the effect is the opposite. Nothing I might say will change or affect him in even the smallest way.

That's what it is, thought Eva–when Ruth said next time *you* get to talk, it was as if she believes that conversation is a series of alternating monologues in which pleasure is to be derived only in speaking. Ruth has delivered her monologue and she will tolerate my right to deliver one too.

And that business about the Holocaust–Ruth had spoken as if there were a scale of horrors, an atrocity competition with a possible winner.

But it had not occurred to Eva to voice these thoughts. Instead she had watched silently as the authoritative green hat had swooped away in the taxi. Eva had gone into the bar to pay for lunch, but Moncho had said, No, it's okay, the señora's friend, la Católica, had taken care of everything.

The walk back down to the hotel had been as quick and easy as the walk up had been tortuous. Here and there in the narrow and solitary streets something bright had flashed against the dead white of a building, only to disappear behind another.

†

There was a knock, five solid raps.

Eva wriggled out from under Resa and went to the door.

Three pairs of large dark eyes looked up and unabashedly examined her. One child, a boy, was dressed as a harlequin; the second, a girl, was a princess in a foil tiara and what might have been an old communion dress; Puri the birthday girl was in a splendid purple flamenco dress sprinkled with white polka dots and trimmed with overlapping tiers of flounces. Behind the children stood Manolo.

"Good, we were wondering if you had perhaps gone downstairs for a drink," he said.

"I'm sorry. Have you been here long?"

"No no, I only knocked a few times."

"We were dozing."

"A late siesta."

"Jet lag."

The princess was the first to notice Resa. "¡Hola!" she said confidently, stepping around Eva to the bed. Resa sat up, looking disoriented.

"¿Cómo te llamas?" demanded the princess.

Resa stared back at her.

"Se llama Teresa," answered Eva. "No habla español."

"¿Qué?"

"She can't speak Spanish."

"Is there something wrong with her tongue?" asked the harlequin.

"No."

"Then why can't she speak?"

"She does speak," replied Eva, "but she speaks English, not Spanish."

"What?"

"She hasn't had time to learn it yet."

The children did not seem to understand.

"You children will have to teach Risita to speak," said Manolo.

Eva went to the bed and kissed her daughter on the top of the head. "Come on sweetheart, let's get those party shoes on."

When they were ready to go, Manolo knelt down to Resa's height and said to her in English, "We'll find you a costume to wear as soon as we get to my house."

Off they tramped, Puri leading: into the elevator, through the hotel lobby and into the Plaza de Bibarrambla, past the cathedral, across the Gran Vía de Colón and around a corner to a butter yellow Seat with the right front seat missing. The polka dot ruffles of Puri's dress bounced on the stones and the white communion dress dragged in the dust. The harlequin hopped from foot to foot.

Manolo slid behind the wheel of the ancient Seat and the five passengers squeezed into the back seat.

The trip took five or ten minutes, but by the time they arrived up at the small plaza where the Carmonas lived, it was dark. The excited children took Resa's hand and pulled her towards a doorway.

"She'll be all right . . . Look," said Manolo, touching Eva's arm.

Across from them was the Alhambra, lit up as on the first night but somehow larger and more magnificent. The Generalife shimmered like a mirage in the desert.

Eva sighed.

"It is marvellous, isn't it?" said Manolo. "Each season, each year, each day and night of the year, it is different."

"Is it possible to visit at night?"

"Until you've gone inside at night, you haven't seen it."

"If I had known it was open late we could have gone yesterday."

"Don't even think of it—a woman alone with a child, it's much too dangerous—too many vipers in the bushes. When you decide to go, say the word and I will take you . . . For now, let's go in the house."

Inside, thirty or forty people of all ages and both sexes were wandering to and from the house and patio. Resa was propelled into a room by a clump of women and girls—Don't worry, señora, we'll fix her up.

Out on the patio, flamenco music crackled from a small ghetto blaster turned up full volume. Eva was poured a cup of sherry from a large vat. After a while, Resa emerged from the house, completely transformed into a miniature woman in a bright blue flamenco dress. Her eyes were outlined in kohl-black, her lips painted a brutal red, and her curls pulled back in a shiny black bun. Two tiny red carnations were fixed over her left ear.

She came running up to solicit her mother's admiration—"You look wonderful, sweetheart"—and was gleefully yanked away by Puri and her friends.

The girls and women danced sevillanas and rumbas. To Eva, the women with their plump arms and unshaved armpits were dancing versions of Beryl Cook's lusty cleaning women. Now and then a man condescended to lead his wife in a pasodoble.

Others arrived in good time, including the Asian-looking man from the guitar shop, an old old woman in a black dress and black shawl, and what appeared to be a family of seven or eight brothers. A wiry man of about sixty came and stood next to Eva. After a time he stretched out his hand and offered her some sunflower seeds, which she declined. He looked familiar.

"Soy Rafael, son of Tonete the blacksmith."

That's who he was—Rafael el Chico, the drunk whose full bladder had brought the bus to a halt on the highway.

"My wife Encarna's over there. Before we were married she was an artista, in the style of her mother before her and la Faraona before her."

Eva looked over at the dancing group of women and girls.

"No no, not there." He turned and spat a spray of husks into the corner. "My wife does not do the sevillana. It is an ugly dance, not for artistas. Over there, over by the lamp, that's her leaning against the wall."

A middle-aged woman with smudges of black around her eyes and a cigarette dangling from between her lips was singing: "Fumando, esperando, a mi amor . . . " Three other women were laughing and clapping, encouraging her.

"Ah, and there's la Abuela. ¡Abuelita! ¡Abuelita!" shouted Rafael. "Here she comes, la Abuela."

The old old woman was hobbling towards them on her cane, her thin mouth one more wrinkle among many.

"Let's all sit down," said Rafael, indicating some empty chairs to the women.

"Hijo," said the old woman, grumbling into her seat, "eh, what can you do? My dog's half-lame and now he's gone blind. How's he supposed to keep the thieves away?"

"As long as the thieves don't know he's blind, they'll stay away. As long as he can bark, that's what's important."

She grunted. "I don't know, a blind dog and a blind-drunk man, what good are they? And you? How is la Encarnita?"

"Very well. She's over there with her cousins." Rafael sat down between the two women and adjusted his genitals. "Don José didn't come?"

"He didn't come and he didn't want me to come. But as soon as he started to snore I crept out. The devil will keep him company till morning."

She sniffed and shook her head.

"But what can you do? That's life. Who is that beside you?"

"A friend of mine."

"You must be Don Molina's new wife."

Eva remembered the Italian village and the women at the wash house. She smiled and shook her head no.

"I saw you sitting today with la Católica, at the feet of el Cristo. My first husband used to sit there in that very place, day after day. He was a drunk too, another borracho, and no sooner did I bury him than this one comes along, another exactly the same. Except that Moncho doesn't have a tragaperras machine, so this one spends his time in Paco's bar not Moncho's, but just like the other one he'll drink every duro I have, and the rest he'll shove straight into that machine. All the little fruits spin round and round, the machine buzzes and dingles, but it never spits any money into his palm. If la Luz wasn't kind enough to fix me a tortilla now and then, I might never eat. But what can you do? On top of everything, my legs are bothering me again."

She rubbed her leg and pointed to her shoes. The backs were bashed down so her heels stuck out.

"I do that to ease the discomfort. I must speak to María Mercedes about it, she'll be able to help me."

"Who is María Mercedes?" asked Eva.

"You must be a stranger. Are you the one the bank manager brought back from Madrid?"

"María Mercedes Heredia Carmona, otherwise known as María Mercedes de Ana," replied Rafael.

"Mercedes de Ana, whose hospitality you are presently enjoying, señora," said the old woman, jabbing two fingers at Eva.

"You mean Manolo's mother?"

"Mother of Manolo, and granddaughter of Ana la Sabia, the wisest woman who has ever lived in our midst."

"They say she was born on the stroke of midnight," said Rafael, "on a Good Friday."

"Who?" asked Eva. "Mercedes de Ana?"

"No no no no no," said the old woman, impatiently flapping her hand. "Ana la Sabia, of course. She could open hearts, mouths, throats. She could stop tongues."

"If only she were alive today to stop some tongues," winked Rafael at Eva.

"Careful, hijo, that your cavern of a mouth doesn't get filled with flying camel dung. I will tell you about la Sabia. My mother told me la Sabia could spot rotten fish before it started to smell, and that before she could so much as crawl. My mother also said that before she was even born, while still in her pregnant mother's womb, la Sabia cried out, so loudly that she was heard not only by her mother, but by my own mother herself, who was still a girl then and was standing with her aunt in front of the fountain of Avellano."

"That's where I'm from, Avellano. The water from its fountain used to be the best water in all the province," said Rafael.

"It was common knowledge that the head and life lines on la Sabia's left palm were joined as one, joined as one, I say. Everyone went to her–women, men, young, old–everyone."

"Not any more, Avellano doesn't have the best water any more, not since the Fascists polluted it. Now it is Alfácar that has the best water. Alfácar, that's where my brother lives."

"We don't have anyone like that now. Oh, Mercedes is fine if you want to make someone fall in love with you, or if you need a net to throw over your husband's wandering affections."

"Mercedes helped el Curro find his missing ring," said Rafael.

"But her grandmother la Sabia would have been able to tell him the name of the thief. When I was a small girl, my mother told me the following story. One day little Ana went to the market with her mother, as always. Her mother was chatting with Carmen la Canastera when Ana, seen by others but unnoticed by her mother, very deliberately crossed the street to a stall of oranges in front of which stood a stranger, a man who was telling everyone he was a muleteer from Sevilla. Ana, who had barely learned to talk, looked him dead in the eye and said, in a measured voice: Ladrón. Just that: Ladrón. All conversations stopped dead. The stranger frowned and he called out, But whose child is this, insulting an honest man in such a bold fashion? Let her father step forth and discipline her. No one moved. Little Ana continued to stare fiercely at the stranger, and soon he began to back away. Ladrón, she said again. Each time he took a step backward, she took one forward, not taking her eyes from his. Finally the man could bear it no more. He reached in his pocket and pulled out one bracelet and three gold rings and dropped them on the ground. None of the jewellery had yet been missed by its owners. Such, señora, was the power of Ana la Sabia."

"Still," said Rafael, "Mercedes is wise in her way. She can sense if you're ill or in good health, and you go to her for your ailments. Lorca himself used to go to her."

"You mean García Lorca, the poet?"

"They were friends, very close friends," said Rafael.

Eva was impressed.

"Lorca went to her for advice, but he didn't take it when it counted. She warned him the Fascists were coming to get him, but he didn't believe her. I'm a poet, he said, and no one kills poets. Of course, as soon as they got their grub-infested hands on him, they murdered him."

"Pah! You men and your politics," said the old woman, spitting over her left shoulder. "So, señora, tell me, if you're not Don Molina's wife, and you're not the bank manager's wife, you must be the wife of the new doctor. He married a foreigner."

"No," said Eva, "I'm no one's wife. I've just arrived, from Canada."

"Ah, yes, Panamá. That's across the ocean, isn't it? Panamá. It must be very beautiful. You young people, it's not like it used to be. Nowadays you do exactly as you please: leave your families, dart off here and there looking for this and that and finding who knows what. Where does it lead, all that activity? We don't know our own neighbours any more. No one cares about anyone else, not like in the old days. In those days, if a man beat his wife, the other men would chase him out of town, and the wife and children would be looked after. Now . . . pah! The man can beat his wife to death with a stick and be sent to jail, and there's no one who will care for the children. Not that we didn't travel in our day. When I was a little girl my father took me to Sevilla. King Alfonso went by in a carriage and looked straight at me, but he wasn't king yet, he was still a small boy."

"Sevilla's not as far as Panamá," said Rafael.

"I'm not from Panama, I'm from Canada, like Bella–Isabella Flowers . . . like la Católica."

"Now if there's a creature more godless than that drunken husband of mine, it's la Católica, eh Chico?" The old woman crossed herself. "Eh, you've seen how she wobbles off after any old gitano who still has the strength to untie his belt."

The woman rubbed her leg again and struggled up out of her seat. Rafael stood up to help her.

"I must go see Mercedes about my leg," she said. She spit over her right shoulder. "But you wait and see, hijo, one night some jealous gitana will slit the throat of that Católica. Every sin carries its own punishment. Hasta luego, hijo . . . señora."

"So, Panamá," said Rafael, reseating himself. "I like travelling, too. Last month we went to Córdoba, my wife and I. My brother and his family live there. Have you been to Córdoba? Muy bonito, Córdoba, but next to Granada?" He shook his head in seeming disappointment. "It's true, Córdoba has the Mesquita, which is impressive in its way, but so sombre, a dark forest of pillars keeping out the sun. I prefer our Alhambra, with the light and the open views of the vega and the sierra. The city of Córdoba is beautiful, of course, but flat as my wife's tortas, and the only way to get a view is to climb to the top of the minaret. I didn't want to climb all those steps, but my wife did, all 267 of them. And she said it was a waste of time, because when you get to the top there's really nothing to see."

Calgary versus Edmonton all over again, thought Eva.

Rafael reached across and grabbed an apple from a bowl and

offered it to her. When she shook her head no thank you, he pulled a knife from his pocket, flicked it open, and began to peel the apple. The parings dropped to the floor.

"Córdoba is not clean like our Granada either, and not nearly as healthy. We went to sit in a park to eat our lunch, and you should have seen, señora, all the garbage, and all those pigeons hopping around our feet, and the water, you can't drink the water there, it's very very bad, so bad my brother bought us a bottle to bring with us to the park. Can you believe it? Having to buy water? And it wasn't just the water we had to buy. Señora, you can't imagine! Do you know that in the bars of Córdoba you have to pay for the tapas. ¡Cojones! 600 pesetas for drinks and a few fingers of fried fish! ¡Imagínate! And one afternoon my brother took us to see an old bridge. It was an admirable enough bridge, but I'm sure it wasn't as old as our own old bridge here in Granada, the one that used to cross the Darro. Then he took us to la Placeta de los Capuchinos. Now that, I have to say, that was better, with pretty designs in the sidewalk, but even so, the workmanship was not as good as that of our own plazas, the stones not as well placed, not inserted with as much care. Mejor puestos en Granada. All the same, it was interesting to see. And there was one thing truly worth seeing, and that was the monument of Manolete! Ah yes! Manolete, now that was a man! That was a matador! My wife's uncle was a picador in his service, you know."

Three men—a young one and two older ones—entered the patio talking and spitting sunflower seed husks.

"There's my grandson, Juanito," said Rafael. "What a boy! He works as a scratch in la Discoteca el Cadí."

He must be the young one, thought Eva. "Who are the other two?" she asked.

"The one with the white mane is my cousin, Don Elías. Don Elías has taught all my children, starting with the oldest—Pepita, Juanito's mother."

"And the other one?"

"The bald one with the face like paper is Juán Pepe the panadero."

He appeared to Eva to be inebriated.

"Pepe's wife must be sick again," said Rafael. "She's not with him."

"¡Abuelito!" called the young man Juanito.

"Excuse me, señora—I must go speak with my grandson."

The bald baker with the paper skin lowered himself with great concentration into the vacated chair.

"Hola. Soy Juán Pepe."

Eva shook his hand. "Pleased to meet you. I'm Eva."

"Eva Perón or Eva Paradisiaca. You are Eva, I will be your Adán. Adam and Eve. What do you say?"

Eva could think of nothing to say, so she said nothing.

"I can tell you a story. When Fernando III died, he went straight to heaven, because he was a saint, of course. Santiago took him by the hand and introduced him to the Virgin Mary, who said, Now Fernando, because you and your people are favourites of mine, you have only to tell me what you want most for your country, and your desire will be granted. Fernando thought for a moment and replied, Oil, garlic, and corn. Granted, said Our Lady. He thought again and said, Sunny skies, brave men, and pretty women. Granted, said the Virgin. Well, he thought, My people could surely use fierce bulls and good cigars. Of course, she said, no problem. Is there anything else you would like your people to have? One more thing, he said. Good government. No, no, said the Virgin, that is not possible. Were I to grant you such a thing, not one angel would remain a single day longer in heaven. So, you see, señora, that's why, except for our politicians, who are sent to us by the devil in hell, we enjoy the same pleasures as the angels in heaven. Granada is like the Garden of Eden, and you and I could be like Adam and Eve . . . Tell me, señora, do you like Granada?"

"It's one of the most beautiful places I've ever seen."

"I suppose you have been to Barcelona."

"No."

"Well don't bother. Once we went there to visit my wife's sister and her husband. And you know how they entertained us? They drove us to see the factories! ¡Fíjate! Here, when they come to see us, we throw a party, we invite the neighbours, we have a good time. But they? They showed us where he makes his money. Can you imagine such a lack of manners? And that's my wife's sister, too. But if you're going to marry a Catalán, what can you expect? ¡Mal educados! We're never going there again, I told my wife. Your sister can come here if she wants to see you, but even if we're in the area, we're going to keep driving, right through to France. France, now I like France. I used to work there, you know. Are you from France, Madame? I like French women."

Rafael walked by. "La señora is not from France, she's from Panamá," he called.

"Ah, Panamá. Then you must come out with me and have a copita. There's a place around the corner."

Eva noticed he had no teeth, his mouth a tear in an onionskin face.

"No. Thank you, I'm enjoying the party, and anyway I can't leave, my daughter's here too."

"It would be fine to leave your daughter here with Manolo and his mother. Mercedes is a curandera, you know. Do they speak French in Panamá? I like French. Je suis un chien andalou, un chien amoureux, un Andalou amoureux. Do you speak French?"

"No I don't, and I'm not from Panama; I'm from Canada, but not the French part, the English part."

"When I worked in France, many years ago now . . . Comment ça va? Je vous trouve jolie . . . See? I still know some French . . . well, we were out one night, my wife and I, with our new friends, another couple from the car company, and we had a little wine to drink, we were having such a good time, singing and dancing—my wife wasn't dancing, just the other woman and me, and her husband was playing records and singing along, well we were dancing and she kissed me, the other woman did, right in front of her husband and in front of my wife. Her husband stopped singing and I waited to see what he would do, but he said, Embrasse-le encore, Rose, that's what he said, Do it again Rose. That was her name, Rose, and he said to me, Pepe, we're good friends, and friends help each other out. I know about your wife's problem. You see, señora, my wife is mala, muy mala. It's her kidneys, poor woman. Ever since she was a young girl, she's had bad kidneys, and it hurts her to make love, so she never wants to. Well, my wife was looking at us and Rose kissed me again and I was embarrassed, but then my wife said to me, It's okay, Pepito, go with the other woman. Because my wife can't do it, you see, it hurts her too much. So I went with the other woman, but just for a few hours, not the whole night, and my wife understood—she understands, señora, if I go with other women. It's been four years now—you can imagine how hard such a thing is on a man. Do you have a husband? No? Then you can come with me. There's no reason why not. You have no husband to worry about and I have a wife who won't mind, not at all. As long as it's with an outsider, she understands. So come, mon Eve du jardin d'Eden, come have a copita with me."

"I'm sorry, I really can't," said Eva.

His lips stretched in a toothless grin, exposing his upper gum.

"You understand, it's been four years, Evita, four years, don't you see, and my wife doesn't mind, she really doesn't. Es lógico."

"No, really."

"Well, okay, I guess Manolo did meet you first. Do you have an ailment for him to cure? You're very pretty. He tried to cure my wife, you know, but that was different, she's much older than you. She drank ass's milk for thirteen days and milk of almonds for seven, and he gave her a herbal infusion each evening, followed by a massage. It helped a little–he's very good at massaging. Oh, but times are changing. For example, if you hurt your leg you don't have to go to Manolo any more–there's a spray you can buy that will take away the feeling in the muscles. Zap! and you won't feel another thing. Now his mother, she's the one with true gracia. If you need help with an ailment of the heart or mind, you're best to go to Mercedes, and, just in case, to pray to la Virgen del Pilar. Still, some women prefer the hands of Manolo, especially the younger ones."

Eva was trying to decide how to get up and leave without being too obviously rude when Manolo appeared.

He poked Juán Pepe in the shoulder. "¡Primo! ¿Ehhh? What's up? Pestering la señora? Hijo, this is Tonio's widow."

So you do know who I am, thought Eva.

"Come on, get up from that chair and find someone else to charm. Come on. Up you go."

He crooked his arm and Juán Pepe used it to pull himself up.

"I'm sorry señora," said Juán Pepe, "I didn't know, please excuse me. Tonio was muy buena gente."

Juán Pepe made his way to the vat of sherry. Manolo nonchalantly hitched his crotch and sat down.

Three or four lamps lit the dancing group of women and children, Resa among them, and the smaller group of men and boys who were sipping sherry and beer, talking to one another and watching the women dance. Manolo held out his hand and offered Eva some sunflower seeds.

"Señora?"

"No, gracias. And please, call me Eva." She thought, if that ridiculous Juán Pepe can call me Eva, surely you can.

Manolo spat some husks onto the floor.

"I know that you make guitars," said Eva. "Do you also play?"

He splayed his fingers and wiggled them to indicate so-so.

"I play mainly to try out the guitars, to check the sound, and if

Puri wants to dance and she needs someone to accompany her. But a real guitarist must play eight, ten hours a day. I don't have the time, señora."

"Eva."

"Muy bien, Eva."

"Puri seems to be a very good dancer."

"She takes lessons from la Luz, my cousin's wife, who dances in the style of Carmen Amaya. La Luz was never as famous, of course, but when she went to America, she had her picture in a big New York magazine, and she went on a tour of Japan."

"Flamenco's popular in Japan?"

"Very popular. It was a Japanese guitarist who played for la Luz when she danced in Tokyo. Many Japanese come here every year to learn how to play or how to make guitars. Their work is very good—technically that is. They are supreme copyists."

"Is that man from Japan?" She nodded towards the man who was sitting quietly by himself, watching the dancers. "He was sitting in front of your shop this morning."

"That's Yukio, my assistant. When he was a small boy in Japan, his parents took him to see la Luz dance, and he decided right then and there that when he grew up, he would come to Spain. This summer he came here and discovered my shop. I am teaching him to construct a guitar."

"Does he pay you?"

"Pay me? Of course not. Why would he pay me? All he does is watch, and ask questions."

"But don't you mind teaching him for nothing? Aren't you afraid he'll compete with you?"

"Afraid, you mean, that he will mass-produce guitars for half the price I can make them? Sabes, tomorrow morning, if I go to my shop, he will be sitting in the doorway, waiting for me. If I don't go to work until the afternoon, he will wait. If I decide not to go until three days from now, he will still be there, waiting for me, the master. Can you imagine a Spaniard being so eager to work and learn? There is not one young person here in the Albayzín who has ever come to ask me what I know."

He lowered his voice.

"And anyway, I haven't told him about the apple."

"The apple?"

Manolo spit out some more sunflower husks and smiled, slyly.

"The apple in the case. It's a trade secret . . . Anyway, knowing how to craft a fine guitar is not only a skill to be learned–it is a colour of the soul."

"I would love to visit your shop."

"Come around next week some time."

"When is a good time?"

"Anytime."

"Morning or afternoon?"

"Either one, doesn't matter."

"Monday?"

"Whenever."

"Maybe we'll go Monday morning then."

Eva took another sip of sherry. She had been trying to figure out when would be the best time to ask Manolo what she really wanted to know. The sherry helped her decide that now was probably as good a time as any.

"How well did you know my husband, Tony?" There, she had said it.

"I knew him well."

How well? she wondered.

"His mother, too. A wonderful woman, so open, so warm. How is she?"

"She died, you know, last Christmas."

"I'm sorry to hear it, but not surprised. My mother had a feeling about it. She also had a feeling that you were coming to Granada, so I was on the lookout for you. I guessed who you were–not on the plane, but later on the bus–it was not so much you as your daughter. Risita has her father's, and her grandmother's, eyes."

"Where is your mother? Is she here?"

"She had to deliver an infusion to her aunt who has arthritis, but she should be back soon. She is anxious to meet you . . . ¡Mira! Look at Risita! ¡Qué guapa es! A real little gitana that one! Punta y talón, punta y talón ¡ale! ¡ale!"

Resa was springing up and down with Puri and two other girls, imitating them as best she could, stomping down her heels, lifting her arms over her head, one after the other, hand to the mouth and waist and up again.

"Pick the apple, put it in the basket, then you eat it," laughed Manolo, clapping his hands. "¡Ay-ay-ay que la Mariquilla, ay-ay-ay que la quiero ver!"

"How did you meet Tony?"

"When he saved my Puri's life."

This was too much. Again, Eva experienced the unsettling sensation that she had actually known very little about the man with whom she had decided to spend the rest of her life.

"I remember the scene as if it were yesterday," continued Manolo. "Puri was younger than Risita is now. She had gone with me to Moncho's plaza. I sat down to have a copita and Puri ran off to play with her little friends. The children were playing with a ball, and it bounced out into the street. Puri chased after it, so quick no one had time to think. At that same moment, a moto ridden by Pepito—the son of my cousin Juán Pepe who was just talking to you—came around the corner, heading straight for Puri, who was bending and reaching for the ball. Your husband Tonio happened to be walking in the opposite direction, towards the approaching moto. He leapt in front of Pepito, who as usual was going much much too fast—you know how it is with young men. Tonio grabbed Puri and jumped out of the way with her in his arms. The moto caught the back of his leg, ripping the pants but causing no other harm. Pepito lost control and crashed into the base of the statue of Christ. His cheek was torn and his nose broken, and his arm, but nothing permanent. A good lesson."

"And Puri was all right?"

"Yes, just frightened."

Tony had never told her any of this.

"Until the moment that he stepped in front of that speeding motorcycle, none of us had ever set eyes on him, but after that . . . " Manolo pressed his hand to his heart . . . "Tonio could have made the claims on me of a brother."

"You became close."

"I told you, close as brothers. As for my mother, he was like a son to her. We loved him very much—I, my mother, Puri—all of us. He was part of our family."

"Did he talk about himself?"

"Oh yes. Very soon after the accident with the moto, he told us the story of his family, about his Abencerraje ancestor, Alfonso Abenabó. Naturally I took him to the Alhambra and showed him the blood stains of the thirteen Abencerrajes who had been lured into the Hall of the Ambassadors to have their heads sliced off. But Tonio said that that had happened before Alfonso's time."

"What else did Tony tell you?"

"About his mother, and how she was descended from Delcampos. That was when we knew for certain that it was fate which had brought us together. You see, my mother has Delcampos on her mother's side of the family. They have been in Granada for hundreds and hundreds of years, since long before the Moors came . . . "

"He obviously told you a lot about his past." And little of his present.

"He wanted to find out more about his roots, but he was more interested in the Abenabó side than in the Delcampos. So I introduced him to Miguel Angel Sanlúcar."

"You mean the historian who was on the bus with us?"

"The same."

It seemed that Tony had known everyone. Eva wondered why, that summer, he had chosen to show her the north of Italy—desolate Milan in August, where neither of them had felt at home. Why not bring her here, which was obviously of special importance to him?

"I thought the Delcampos were expelled from Granada," said Eva.

"Not *all* the Delcampos were expelled. And I'm a Carmona too, of course, on my father's side. The Carmonas were left alone by the Inquisition because they were Gypsy. Gypsies were infidels, but they had no gold or silver to confiscate. You see, only those with money were expelled. The rest were forced to convert. You must understand, greed is the real soul of Spain. Greed, and jealousy of all who do well in life."

"I doubt that Canada is any different," said Eva.

"But in pictures, your country always looks so clean, filled with snow and forests without end. When I think of Canada I see an open and generous vista."

Dotted with isolated pockets of selfish, inward-looking people, according to Isabella Flowers. Maybe the soul of Canada was not so much avarice, as small-mindedness.

"Speak of the devil, here's Don Angel now." Manolo leapt to his feet. "Don Angel! You already know my good friend from Canada, la señora Eva."

"Of course. How are you, señora?"

"Very well, thank you."

"Don Angel, la señora Eva has—"

"—Eva, please." After all, Manolo said "Tonio," not "*Señor* Tonio."

"Eva has been asking me about our history, about the Inquisition, and the Delcampos. She is Tonio Benabo's widow, you see."

"Señora, I'm amazed, he said nothing about a wife."

"We weren't actually married, but—"

"—but he was your husband," said Manolo. "Marriage. Pah! What couple needs a piece of paper from a corrupt government or church to know that they belong together? The institution of marriage is just another method of extorting money from the people."

"All that time on the bus together, and I didn't know who you were," said Angel. "I'm doubly pleased to know you, Señora Eva. And allow me to tell you how sorry I was about your husband's death. He was truly a wonderful man. It must be hard for you, to be left alone with a small child."

Manolo excused himself to get drinks.

It seemed that every time she got close, the opportunity slipped away. Well, Angel knew Tony too, she thought. Maybe Angel will tell me something.

He sat down and said, "El señor Tonio and I had many stimulating conversations. He was very interested in our history, particularly in the period of the Expulsions and the Inquisition. He had a very curious mind."

"What did he want to know?"

"Everything, even the way the baptisms were handled. I have never believed that the conversions were a bad idea in themselves, but the implementation was a farce—water splashed at people huddled in groups, mothers shielding their children, everyone trying to hide behind someone else. All these stories have been passed down through the generations. Even today, Manolo can proudly describe to you how the Carmonas hunkered down behind a group of tall Moors, so that no water actually touched them. And because these so-called converts were given no formal instruction, they remained heretics at heart, going through the motions like puppets whose arms and legs swing when the strings are pulled."

"I guess most people would have done whatever they could to avoid incrimination."

"Absolutely anything, for when you were arrested you disappeared from human view as if the earth itself had opened up to swallow you. Your trial might last two years, four years, no one knew; you could be dead or alive. If your family was lucky, they saw you reappear at some public auto-da-fé, to be condemned to prison or ten years in the galleys, or let off with two hundred lashes and a heavy fine. Sometimes an inscription of your name and offence was hung around your neck and you were paraded through the streets on an ass. At the very least, you were sent home wearing a san benito."

"What was that?"

"Usually a yellow tunic with a red band—an indelible mark of disgrace which had to be worn at all times in public. In fact, the san benito was the origin of the outfits you will see on the penitentes tomorrow in the processions."

"Who got sent to the stake?"

"Those who were named negativos, and as you know, negativos were burned by the thousands." Angel shook his white head slowly. "A sad chapter in our history. Even God was unhappy at the excesses of his Church. During those years the poorest harvests ever were recorded, and a pestilence attacked the clergy. In one village not far from here, twelve out of the thirteen priests died, and the thirteenth lost his mind. And if that was not enough, locusts descended from the sky in clouds so huge the sun was blocked for days, and devoured everything in their path. And it was not just here that catastrophe struck. In Aragón in the north, one hundred years earlier, the Carmelites had preserved the tears of a weeping image of the Holy Sepulchre. When the Muslims were expelled, this holy fluid suddenly evaporated."

Resa came giggling up to her mother, to touch base. Eva hugged her, Angel fussed over her, and she ran off squealing with the pack.

"You can imagine bringing children into such a world," said Angel, "and trying to care for the ones you already had. Childbirth became a public affair. To ensure that your baby would not be circumcised or given Muslim names, a Christian midwife had to be present. And death itself was no longer private. If your father died, you were closely watched to ensure that you did not wrap his corpse in clean linen before lowering it into the ground. Cleanliness, of course, was the most unchristian of sins."

"It was a sin to be clean?"

"Clean blood, dirty skin: personal filth was next to godliness. Only Jews and Muslims washed. The very mention of a bath was heretical. If you were working in the fields and it began to rain, and you stood too long allowing the water to wash over your face, you could be tortured and sent to jail for five years. When the devout Saint Eufaxia entered a convent of one hundred and thirty nuns, not one of whom had ever washed her feet, Gil de Avila called them flowers, a sweet garden perfumed by the good smell of sanctity . . . Do you know the colour, 'isabelino'?"

"No."

"The daughter of Philip II, whose name was Isabel, made a solemn vow not to change her dress until a particular siege was won. No doubt she thought the siege would be over quickly, but it lasted more than three years. She kept her vow however, and the royal garment acquired a distinctive colour all its own, a sort of yellow shade that came to be called isabelino. But history has a way of catching up with such nonsense. You have seen the fountain in Plaza Isabel la Católica?"

"Yes."

"It is the most typical and the most ironic monument in all of Granada. Imagine, the Catholic queen who outlawed bathing, being drenched by a flow of water night and day, week after week, year after year . . . Have you been to the north?"

"Not yet."

"When you go, in some of the bars you may notice signs that say: No singing or dancing. What they mean is: No flamenco. Why no flamenco? Because flamenco is really the zambra. You see, señora, despite what I've been telling you, Andalucía has remained the sum of what it was before the arrival of the Christians. For on Sundays, the conversos went to Mass, but only to escape the fines, and on Fridays and Saturdays they furiously swept their floors and left their doors open for all to see. But whenever the opportunity arose, they worked on Christian feast days, harder and with more pleasure than on other days. They continued to bathe surreptitiously, even on the coldest days in January. They brought their babies to the church to be baptized, then rushed home to wash off the chrism. Boys were secretly circumcised after the Christian midwife left. Brides and bridegrooms went to the altar camouflaged in Castilian clothing, but upon returning home, they changed into Moorish ones and sang the zambra. In short, old Granada went underground.

"And let me tell you, Señora Eva, old Granada is still here to enjoy. Lose yourself in our labyrinthine streets. Enter the chamber of the Ambassadors in the Alhambra, close your eyes, and listen for the whispers. But be wary of what you hear. I may be a Sanlúcar, a proud cristiano viejo, but I'm telling you, all we Granadinos have had duplicity bred into us."

"Is that a warning?" she smiled.

He did not return the smile. "Serious advice. You must be careful of the friends you choose."

"How do I tell who's who?"

"With your eyes." Angel put a well-manicured finger below his left eye and pulled down at the skin. His raspy voice deepened. "And of course, watch the man who smiles too easily—he is probably scheming to sell you a cat for a hare."

You've been smiling rather a lot at me, she thought. "Are you suggesting I should be careful of you?" she said.

"It depends. In which way do you mean?"

Manolo returned with three drinks and sat down. Eva took a large sip of hers. She was starting to feel giddy. "How about Manolo, should I be careful of him?"

"Careful?" Manolo opened his brown eyes wide and stroked his beard, which looked dark and lush in this light. "Why be careful of me?"

He really did have expressive hands, such beautiful fingers. Eva took another sip. "Don Angel was just giving me survival tips, telling me stories . . . "

"Stories, or myths?"

"Is there a difference? I once heard Tony say: To the archaeologist, myth is prehistory."

"Well said, Señora Eva," said Angel. "But there are usually several versions of a single event. How do we know which to believe? Take the naming of our city. We are told that the Phoenicians knew it as Karnata; therefore Karnata is the origin of the name, Granada. No, we are told by another person, in the eighth century, Granada was a thriving town known as Garnatha Alyehud, or City of the Jews. And still a third will say, no no, King Aben Habuz had an equestrian statue of himself erected at what is now San Cristóbal, and he named it Garbnaath, or Naath of the West in honour of his wife, and gradually that name was corrupted to Granada."

"I read somewhere that it was founded by a daughter of Hercules, and that Granada was the name of her cave . . . "

"There, see what I mean? My personal favourite claims that it is a corruption of Garnata, or Cava de Nata, the daughter of Count Julian the Traitor. Nata de la Cava was said to have given herself to Don Rodrigo."

"My mother says Granada was named after that cave in Alfácar," said Manolo. "Its mouth is blocked up now, of course, but in Moorish times it was a holy place where curanderos helped people who were suffering from the effects of the evil eye."

"I know that story. It was reported by several writers during the reign of King Haxix–"

"–the alchemist who had walls of gold built around the Albayzín."

"I see you're well-informed, Señora Eva. Yes, the reign of King Haxix was a time of great wealth, a time when the city was reputed to have some seventy thousand houses."

"Is it true that under the Moors, most people could read and write, even women?"

"Up to a point, but this golden age of Muslim feminism is largely a myth. Families traced agnate lineages which sought vengeance and wealth, and glorified warlike deeds of the past. Marriage laws made it permissible for non-Muslim women to marry Muslim men, but Muslim women were rarely allowed to marry non-Muslim men."

"But weren't many of the women educated? Weren't some of them even poets?"

"Yes, but if you think women were truly free, you've been reading too much romantic propaganda."

"But I'm sure I've read that the Catholics were much more intolerant than the Muslims." Eva was surprised at her persistence. It really must be this sherry, she thought.

"It's true, they always imposed Christian names on their conquered people–your continent is a case in point. But that was because Catholicism sought to incorporate everyone, regardless of race. Here in Granada, it was important to erase Arabic names precisely because so much importance had been attached to purity of race, to tracing male lineage back to Mahoma the Prophet."

"And then came the Christians, and all the mosques were converted into churches."

"What do you expect? The Christians won the battle. Would you require them to retreat behind the brownish grey walls of their medieval convents? And anyway, the Muslims had torn down temples and synagogues to build their mosques. They crossed the water, and before you could say 'Bib el Bonut,' there was a mosque on every corner. Same foundations, same stones."

"Still, I've read that under Muslim rule there were many Jews with responsible positions."

"Oh yes, but they were barred from the highest offices. Jews could only climb so high–the caliphs used them like the popes did: as tax collectors and translators. And bigotry was everywhere. Why just last night I was reading a poem, a frenetic diatribe against a Jewish official called Yusuf Ibn Ezra, written in 1066 by one Ishaq Aben Abu."

"1066, the Battle of Hastings."

"Very good, Señora Eva. Also the year that Halley's Comet flew from the sky to terrify much of Europe."

And four hundred years before the parents of Alfonso Abenabó had been killed. Aben Abu–that sounded very much like Abenabó without the accent.

"Time should not be divided into such arbitrary dates," said Manolo.

"Ah, but without exact dates there is no history, only anecdote."

"The people are swallowed up by such dates."

"About the poem . . . " said Eva.

"Yes, as I said, it was written against Yusuf Ibn Ezra, who had risen high in the court and lived in the Alhambra palace. Sources say he had amassed an immense personal fortune–through occult ways, it was believed. He aroused much jealousy and many failed conspiracies. When Ishaq wrote his poem, it became the catalyst for the murder of Yusuf and hundreds of innocent Jews in the surrounding area."

"Perhaps the appearance of the comet had something to do with the massacres," said Manolo.

"Who knows? Now, of course, Ishaq is remembered only for the effect of that poem: the work itself is of no literary merit."

"And Yusuf's fortune?" asked Eva.

"Yusuf's body was displayed, his house plundered, his library destroyed, but most of his fortune was never found."

"So Granada's treasure stories do not all have to do with enchanted Moors," said Eva.

"Indeed not. Spain was accustomed to plunder. I imagine many people had the habit of hiding what they valued. You see, Señora Eva, in the end, avarice rules all men."

There was that idea again. She raised her glass to take another sip, but the glass was empty.

"Remember Jonah in the Bible? Before being swallowed by the whale, he was on a ship bound for Tartessus in the south of Spain. Tartessus, you may remember, was the city that existed during the reign of Solomon, an unwarlike city given over to the arts, but filled with gold and silver."

Like some of the civilizations encountered by the Spanish explorers, thought Eva. In his last letter to her, Tony had written that one day he wanted to take her on a cruise, to follow the trail of Hercules. The golden apples of the Hesperides grew in Spain, he said.

"The Carthaginians demolished Tartessus. That is what happens to cultured, peaceful empires."

"Peaceful empire," said Manolo, acerbically. "Empire, peace—the two words contradict each other."

"Isn't Tartessus where the bullfight originated?" asked Eva. "Isn't the modern Andalusian bull descended from there?"

"Exactly," said Manolo. "We have peacefully violent toros fighting in our arenas."

Angel stood up. "Bien, you'll have to excuse me now, I have to get going." He took Eva's hand. "Next time you go visit the Alhambra, come and find me, I will give you a private tour . . . perhaps I can even throw in a hidden passageway or two. Tell me, are you as interested in buried treasures as your husband was?"

"I'm interested in all your stories," she answered, flustered. But she had wanted to get back to the topic of Tony, and now Angel was leaving. Obviously she had left it too long, again.

"Then we must continue our conversation another time. But first, permit me to get you a drink."

He took her empty glass and returned with the refill, said his good-byes, and left.

"Are you?" Manolo asked.

"Am I what?"

"Interested in buried treasures."

She took a sip of sherry.

"You said earlier that you were on the lookout for us. What did you mean?" she said.

"Exactly that. My mother said you were coming, so I was watching, keeping my eyes peeled for your arrival."

"What do you mean, your mother said we were coming? How did she know?"

He shrugged. "My mother knows such things. Listen, Eva, the longer you boil an egg the harder it gets. In other words, you must not force things too much or work so hard at trying to make logical sense of everything."

"You mean, watch but don't think?"

"I mean, keep your eyes open and as sharp as the unsheathed

sword. But it will do you little good to think too much about what it is that you see, just as it will do you no good to plan ahead too much. Everything happens at its own pace. Nothing you do will change it."

"I really don't understand."

"¡Ojo alerta! That's what I'm saying." He pulled the skin below his eye, as Angel had done. "Learn to listen with your eyes, not your ears; think with your heart, not your head. Remember, words are nothing but clues. Observe instead the movements of hands, of fingers—the hand pressed to the heart in gratitude, the finger scratching the side of the nose, the averted eye. And pay special attention to those eyes that turn away from your own—look to where they look . . . There are many bad people about, people who are not as they would first appear."

"Maybe I should just avoid all Granadinos," she said.

She was getting tired of all this oblique advice. Her brain needed a rest. It had been a long, incredible day—more like three days in one.

"The trouble is," said Manolo, "it's not only us you have to be careful of."

She was about to ask if he was referring to anyone in particular when the taped music stopped abruptly, there was a small commotion, and everyone began to sing "Cumpleaños feliz." A cake with burning candles was carried out from the house.

At least that's just like home, thought Eva.

"My mother must be back," said Manolo.

Puri blew out the candles to general clapping and shouts of approval. Now me! Now me! a boy cried out, and the candles were relit and everyone sang Happy Birthday again and the boy blew out the candles. Me, my turn, my turn! cried another child, and the adults laughed and for the third time everyone sang and the child blew out the candles. Resa! Now Resa! shouted Puri, and the procedure was repeated, over and over, until it seemed that the Happy Birthday song had been sung at least fifteen times.

The flamenco music from the ghetto blaster resumed.

"Is that your mother?" Eva asked, indicating a plump woman in black with a surprisingly young face who was being greeted enthusiastically amidst the renewed dancing.

"Come, I'll introduce you."

As he spoke, the plump woman smiled to Eva from across the patio. Manolo picked his way through the dancing women and children, Eva following close behind.

"Mamá, this is Eva, Tonio's wife."

Mercedes immediately embraced Eva and bussed her on each cheek. "As young and beautiful as I had pictured you."

And you, not at all how I had imagined, thought Eva. "I'm so happy to meet you," she said. "I've been hearing so much about you."

"Let's talk, hija," said Mercedes. "Over there."

She took Eva's hand and led her to a stone bench under a tree near the far wall.

"Aquí, estamos tranquilas. We can see the others, but we are not so obvious to them that they will readily join us."

The two women sat quietly for a while. From under the tree, everyone on the patio appeared to be moving at a deliberate and rehearsed pace, the sky above a high black ceiling pierced with holes of light. Eva relaxed and forgot her fatigue.

Dance for us, Puri! called a woman, her voice sharp in the still night air. ¡Qué baile Puri! joined in the voice of Juán Pepe the baker. Manolito, get your guitar! and soon there was no question but that Puri should dance and Manolo should play.

Manolo tuned his guitar while the guests settled into chairs and Puri stood collecting herself. When he was ready, he nodded to her. She raised an arm and waited for quiet. When she began to dance, he began to play.

She plucked invisible apples from invisible trees, took nips from the apples, and scornfully tossed the leftovers to the appreciative audience, her mood intensifying until her hands and feet were lost in a fierce purple swirl.

It was all too much for Resa, who began to stomp her feet and leap about in earnest imitation of her new friend.

"Muy gitanaza, your daughter, a vivacious child, not cold and closed like most foreign children," said Mercedes.

Should I be flattered? wondered Eva. "Must be her ancient Granada blood," she said.

Mercedes smiled. "Yes, she will have no trouble fitting in."

"If we stay."

"No sense in making such a decision so soon."

"No, I guess not."

"It's good you came."

"Manolo said you were expecting us."

"Yes."

"Why?"

"Why because of your Tonio, of course. What is it you wish to know?"

There was something no-nonsense but comfortable about Mercedes. Eva decided to plunge right in.

"Well, for one thing, I would like to know why he came to Granada in the first place. He was in the middle of an important project in Italy, and yet he dropped everything to come here."

"He came because Manolo called him."

"Manolo called him?"

"Yes, about the book."

"The book?"

"Yes, the one that was found in the street." Mercedes pulled a folded piece of newspaper from her pocket and handed it to Eva. "I thought you might be interested in this one day, so I kept it."

Eva unfolded the clipping and read the article.

Early one morning, a very old-looking book had been found on the Carrera del Darro by an honest Japanese tourist, who had shown it to the well-known guitar maker, Manuel Carmona Heredia. Nothing more was heard of the book until the tourist returned to Tokyo and mentioned his find to a reporter there. When the Japanese press called the Granada police for more details, the police obtained the book from Sr. Carmona and brought it to the Institute of Arabic Studies to have it examined by scholars. Don Miguel Angel Sanlúcar from the institute had determined that the book was a tenth- or eleventh-century copy of *De Materia Medica* by Pedarius Dioscorides that had once belonged to a fourteenth-century Abencerraje official named Jacobo Abenabó, and three centuries before that, to one Yusuf Ibn Ezra. Its present-day value was incalculable.

So, had Tony come to claim a book that had belonged to one of his ancestors? And Yusuf Ibn Ezra: wasn't he the man Angel had just mentioned, the one who had been murdered and his library destroyed? This couldn't all be coincidence, could it? Eva felt lightheaded. "Imagine such a book surviving," she said, "outside of museums, I mean. It must have been well-hidden over the years."

"What's hard to imagine is anyone being so brave, or so foolish, over such a thing as a book."

Eva was about to ask Mercedes what she meant when the music abruptly stopped. Enough! shouted Manolo, putting down his guitar. Puri and Resa were standing looking at each other, giggling into their hands. Tell me, hijas, said Manolo, why should I play for you if you aren't going to take it seriously? The adults sitting near him echoed the sentiments. No sean feas, niñas. Show some self-respect, act beautiful.

Puri composed herself and recommenced. Rafael's wife Encarna began to sing and others to clap palmas secas, sharp syncopated spanks of the palm. Manolo picked up his guitar.

When Puri's dance ended the party ended, suddenly and without discussion, as if a silent consensus had been reached that the time had come to say goodnight.

Eva stood up to go.

Resa came running up and wrapped her arms around her mother's legs. "I'm tired, Mommy."

"Ven aquí, preciosa," said Mercedes, smiling and holding out her arms to Resa, who surprised her mother by releasing the grip on her legs and scrambling up into the lap of Mercedes.

"Mmmm, yes. You are very like your father, aren't you? The eyes, the hair, even something of his manner. You will have no trouble getting along here, none at all."

Although Resa could not understand the words, she allowed herself to be cuddled, responding to the warmth of the voice.

"You come and stay with me here in my house whenever you like," continued Mercedes. "I'll take good care of you." She looked up at Eva. "Really, I mean it. She will have Puri to play with, and children need other children. As for yourself, if you want anything, whatever it may be, you must also come here. Our home is your home . . . Oh, but Risita, you're so thin, I can feel your ribs."

Mercedes reached and took a sandwich from the small wooden table which was nearby.

"Here. Eat," said Mercedes, shoving the sandwich into Resa's face.

Resa clamped her lips together and shook her head.

"She's not hungry," said Eva.

"But she's too skinny, she has to eat. Hijita, here, a little pastel."

Resa shook her head again and slid to the ground.

"Really, she's not hungry. We ate earlier."

"Of course, but children need to eat more often than we do."

"Leave her alone, mamá," said Manolo. "Can't you see they don't eat as much as we do, one pastel after another. That's why they're so slim. That's why the little girl has the body of an artista."

Mercedes said nothing, but she did not looked convinced.

After a moment she said to Eva, "You, when you're sitting still, you could be one of us, too. Where did you get that dark skin and hair?"

"My father. He was Mexican."

"Let's go, Mommy," said Resa.

"Hija, come back here with me, come on." Even more to Eva's surprise, Resa crawled back up into Mercedes' lap and closed her eyes.

"Don't go, not yet," said Mercedes to Eva. "Come on, sit down. Stay a bit more. You wanted to talk, didn't you?"

Eva obediently sat down.

"I felt very bound to your Tonio, you know, and not just because he saved the life of our little Puri. Like my grandmother, your husband Tonio was born on a Good Friday and died on a Good Friday." Mercedes crossed herself. "And like my own dear mother, he was found dead in the shadow of San Pedro, except that she died of natural causes."

Eva felt the blood rush to her head.

"Those who are born on that day, on Good Friday, are gifted with the power to see into the earth and to discover hidden treasures. ¡Ay de mi! What a dangerous power to have!"

Eva waited.

"Oh but what a beautiful daughter you have! ¡Qué simpática! And how tired she must be, to have fallen asleep so quickly. Poor little thing–I don't think you give her enough to eat. She seems to have no stamina. I can feel her ribs. It's not normal."

"You met Tony's mother when she came for the burial?"

"She stayed here with us."

Of course, thought Eva, something else no one bothered to tell me.

"Teresa was beside herself with grief, as any mother would be. But what was hardest on her was the guilt she suffered."

"Guilt?"

"The guilt of the mother whose son does not fulfil his destiny. You have heard the story of King Boabdil? I often think of him, the poor young king in his long robes being admonished by his mother for not acting like a man. But some say his mother was right, that Boabdil abandoned his people, leaving others to do the fighting."

What did this have to do with Tony?

Mercedes sighed. "We all of us have our destinies to fulfil. Perhaps Tonio's destiny was to die on the day he was born . . . I suppose you will want to go to the Silencio next week."

"Is that one of the processions?"

"The same procession during which Tonio died."

Eva's breath caught at the top of her throat.

"The Silencio leaves from the church of San Pedro at midnight. All the lights of the city are turned out, and the procession passes through the streets in blackness and in silence. People come from all over, including many unsavoury types. Whatever you do, do not go alone."

Eva listened.

"If you wish, Manolo can accompany you. I myself don't go any more, so Risita can stay here with me. I would love to take care of her."

Maybe Mercedes was right—Eva should go to the Silencio. But did she really know this woman well enough to leave Resa with her?

"But perhaps you need to go alone. After all, to recognize the beast, it is necessary to see him."

Recognize the *beast?* I must have misunderstood, thought Eva.

"I saw Tonio just after they found him," said Mercedes. "Perhaps Teresa told you."

"No, she didn't."

"I happened to be walking by when his body was being pulled from the river. I examined him very carefully."

Eva glanced to make sure that Resa really was asleep.

"Hija, listen to me, Tonio may have drowned, but I am sure it was not in that river."

Mrs. Benabo had mentioned bruises, a broken arm, a broken jaw, a contusion on the back of the head. But she had said nothing about his dying away from the river.

"Some people say that he was killed by magical ways. The police of course would like his death to be accidental—it makes everything so much easier for them."

"And you?"

"I am more cynical. Let me tell you a story.

"Many years ago, at the time when many of the old donkey stables were being converted into car garages, I was urgently called to a house below, in the capital. A young man—a descendant of the Marqués de Villena—had fallen in love with a gitana from our quarter. When his family found out that his emotions were involved to the point that he actually wanted to marry the unfortunate girl, he was forbidden to see her any more. One thing led to another, until one morning the young couple was found dead—dead in one another's arms in the back seat of the father's car. It was said that they had snuck into the garage the night before, gone into the car, and started the engine. They died together, asphyxiated by the fumes. I could do nothing for them, of course, but I have never forgotten their smooth young faces, which were the colour of young cherries."

"Are you saying Tony was asphyxiated?"

"Let me see your hand."

Eva mechanically held out her right hand. "Do you mean he was choked? Gassed? What?"

"No, the other one."

"Choked?"

"The other hand. I notice it's the one you use the most."

Eva gave her left hand to Mercedes, who held it palm up in her own. "Your hands are graceful, the hands of an artista–your feet too, I imagine . . . And this ring, where did you get it?"

"Tony's mother gave it to me before she died. I had it on the other hand, but I switched it because Manolo said that on Good Friday I would be able to see enchanted soldiers." She felt foolish as soon as she said it.

"What would you want with soldiers?"

"I don't know, but Mrs. Benabo said the ring is supposed to bring luck."

"Is that all she said?"

"She said it was passed down in her family from a Granada poet named Ruth Shulam Delcampo. Was she also one of your forebears?"

"Yes, of course, but that's not what I meant. I was referring to this six-pointed star. It is the Seal of Solomon. You see the two superimposed triangles? This one, with the apex pointing upwards, signifies fire. The inverted triangle signifies water. Together they represent a dynamic consciousness. The double triangle of Solomon is a symbol of the human soul."

Mercedes turned Eva's hand over, examining it at different angles in the light. "Inside you is a buried passion that has never been properly awakened, a passion that is struggling to escape its bounds. Be careful of it, because once it surfaces, you will find it difficult to control. You are close to danger, sabes. The beast is near."

Maybe Eva hadn't misunderstood after all. "What beast? What sort of danger?"

"I'm not sure, but it may have something to do with a small metal object. A key perhaps?"

Eva could feel the key pressing through her pocket into her thigh.

Mercedes stared more closely at the hand, then released it. "Hija, if you care about yourself and your daughter, you must be more careful with whom you make friends."

Again, the warning.

"Let us go back to the story of our young lovers. Naturally no one believed the authorities when they said the deaths were accidental. News got out that the garage door had been sealed to confine the fumes, so everyone was saying that the deaths had been suicide."

Eva's mind was going in circles. What did any of this have to do with Tony? He had killed himself, is that what Mercedes meant? The harder she listened, the less she understood.

"Your Tonio was not the sort to kill himself," said Mercedes, as if reading Eva's mind. "As for our star-crossed lovers, it was the family of the young gitana who wanted me to have a look, not the family of the boy. The fact is, the police insisted the deaths were an accident, general gossip said they were a double suicide, but I knew that the two young people had been murdered."

"Murdered? By whom?"

"By the boy's father, of course. I knew it as soon as I arrived at the house and saw the face of Don Francisco de Villena."

"Why would he have killed them?"

"Because his son's death meant that the family would be saved from disgrace."

"Does this have something to do with Tony?"

"The death of those young lovers was not a usual killing. Perhaps not so odd for cristianos viejos, but our people do not kill with the exhaust fumes of a car. And certainly not with water."

What was this woman talking about?

"Often things are not as they first appear."

"Listen, my mother saw Tonio when he was pulled dead from the Darro," said Manolo.

She had not noticed him come up beside her.

"He looked like a beaten, drowned man. But the water in that river is filthy, and the inside of his mouth was clean."

Eva waited for him to continue.

"But that's not all."

What more could there be?

"The day he died, he was going to show me a tunnel he had discovered."

A tunnel?

"He didn't have time to tell me anything more than that, just that he had found it. He was very excited about it."

This was too much.

"I'm sorry," said Eva, "I'm having trouble absorbing all this. I think we'd better get back to the hotel." She really had to rest her mind.

"Of course," said Mercedes. "Manolo will drive you back. But listen: your Tonio risked his own life for that of my little Purificación, and we will do what we can for you, but we can do nothing against what you yourself have a will to do. Just keep the little one out of it. Leave her here with me as often as you must."

Manolo gently picked up Resa and carried her out the door.

"Look at that. My son," laughed Mercedes. "See that thick red beard? You know why he wears it? It's not to crow about the priest in his background. It's for protection. It's so he has something to hide behind, so you can't tell when he's up to no good."

†

That night, after the party, Eva had a troubled sleep.

Once again she was lying in the butterfly meadow, with Tony floating about her. But this time he did not come to her.

Come here, tell me everything will be all right, she cried. His arms flailed in the butterfly air, and he opened his mouth but no words came out.

Never mind, she said, just kiss me.

She grasped his hair, pulling him to her, but his mouth was filled with mud and weeds, not kisses.

The white butterflies withered and blackened.

Listen to me! she shouted, but the black butterflies fell into his ears and stopped them up.

And his fingers closed like cold iron bands around her throat.

Then and Now

NEXT MORNING WAS PALM SUNDAY. IT WAS hot and clear: a perfect day.

As they left the hotel, Resa stuck close to her mother. She checked out the sky and the plaza. No processions, but the bad man was behind the fountain.

"I don't like him, Mommy," she said.

"Who?"

"That man." But he was gone.

They arrived at the Gate of Elvira and watched the gradual thickening of the crowd under the ancient archway, the buildup of excitement, the craning necks, the ears straining to catch the first drum roll.

The people on the balconies were the first to hear–They're coming! they're coming! they called down to the others. Children darted out to the centre of the street, adults stepped out to pluck them back. Resa was almost swept away from her mother, who grabbed her and pulled her up the hill, wondering how the procession would ever manage to pass through the gate without crushing people.

But somehow the crowd rearranged itself and the huge paso of Jesus advanced through the archway–Jesus crowned with silver palm leaves, on a bed of carnations, riding his donkey; Jesus entering Jerusalem on the waves of a calm red sea, blessing the multitude. Beneath, a heavy velvet skirt hid the costaleros from the onlookers.

Accompanying Jesus was a military band and men in white capes and Murillo-blue cowls, and behind them, the Mother of God borne by a second corps of unseen litter bearers. Trailing in the distance was a group of women all in black.

"What a wonderful procession!" said Eva.

"*That's* the procession?" said Resa.

"Yes, love."

No flying dinosaurs, no dragons–just a parade!

"Balloons," said a voice. "That's what's missing."

The American from the cathedral.

Resa jerked her hand from her mother's and moved to her opposite side.

Eva turned to see her own distorted reflection in his sunglasses.

"I don't know, seeing them dressed like that in those pointy hoods with the slitty eye holes, it's kind of scary," she said.

"Klansmen protecting the purity of white womanhood. Hooded brothers guarding the Virgin. Should make you feel secure."

"But didn't all that originate in the Inquisition?"

"Only the costumes. The procession itself is pre-Roman."

"The costumes were the penitential dress of the flagellants, weren't they?"

"Later worn by attendants of the victims of the Black Death. So. Symbols of good deeds."

"Still, it's disconcerting. Maybe it's the masks as much as anything." Like your sunglasses, she thought. "It's eerie not being able to see people's faces." Or their eyes.

He smiled and folded his arms. She wondered if he wanted to perturb her. But why would he? she thought, and quickly put the idea out of her mind.

"The revenge of the Jesuits."

"Pardon me?"

"Moors and Jews weren't the only ones expelled from Spain. So were the Jesuits. In the eighteenth century. But they returned in the twentieth. Quietly but wealthy and active as ever."

The Mother of God was directly below them now, being greeted by shouts of enthusiasm.

"They're all the same. Tanit. Astarte. Isis."

"She does look Pagan, doesn't she, as if she's above it all, a goddess ruling over love and peace."

"Or war and death."

"I read somewhere that medieval painters always used blue to depict the Virgin because it was such an expensive pigment, almost as expensive as gold. The blue came from crushed lapis lazuli, if I'm not mistaken. Do you know?"

He either ignored her comment or didn't hear it.

"Goddess cults were death cults. Sacrificed animals. Humans too."

A man who had pushed out into the middle of the street spread his arms wide and began to sing—"Reina de los cantao-o-o . . . "—but the band did not stop playing and the Virgin did not stop to listen, and to avoid being trampled he was obliged to retreat into the crowd, where he finished his song.

"I thought the procession stopped for saetas."

"Sometimes."

"What's the logic? Who does it stop for? And shouldn't the band at least quit playing?"

"The band should be scrapped. Everything should pass in silence. Much more impressive. Nothing to distract from the theme of death. Like the Silencio on Good Friday."

"The Silencio," she repeated, as if saying the name out loud would give her some grip on it. "I've been told that the lights of the city are extinguished for it, for the Silencio."

"Except those of the Alhambra."

"If it's dark, how can you see what's going on?"

"Moonlight. And candlelight. The penitentes carry large candles."

"Do all the spectators actually stop talking and keep quiet?" From what Eva had seen of Spanish crowds, she had trouble imagining such an occurrence.

"Completely quiet."

"Is there any music?"

"Just the beat of a single drum. Boom. Boom. Boom. And chink chink."

"Chink chink?"

"The barefoot penitentes. Chains drag from their ankles."

"It sounds horrible, but I guess it can't be any worse than those poor women down there walking in spikes. For how long do they have to last, anyway?"

"Six, eight, nine hours."

Through streets that were undoubtedly conceived before the invention of high heels. "It must be sheer torture."

He turned his head to her. "Of course. That's the point."

She thought his eyes were probing hers, and she wanted to examine his in return, but all she could see was herself, one of her in each of the black mirrors covering his eyes.

"The Spanish Madonna is no sewn-up virgin. Forget the Joyful Mysteries. The Glorious Mysteries. The Resurrection. Spanish Catholicism is the hand of man plunged into the wound of God. The Spaniard loves Christ *because* he is crucified. And Mary *because* she holds her murdered son in her arms."

"Kazantzakis." Eva had read *Spain.*

"Passion and nonentity. Desire and death. That's what these processions are about. Death as stimulant."

Why was he always going on about death?

"I read that the brotherhoods were started by Queen Isabella," she said, "and that each has its own colours, like football teams."

"The poorer the brotherhood, the richer the colours."

"Wasn't each one connected to a medieval guild? To the candlers or the bakers or the shipwrights or whatever?"

"Others were to expiate an Act of God. A plague. Locusts. Or to commemorate a miracle. The unearthing of a statue buried during the Moorish invasion. Moors liked to decapitate the enemy leader. After killing him of course. They would bury the body. Parade the head through the streets. Much like what we're watching. Except the Christ down there isn't decapitated. Just dead."

She felt a couple of drops of moisture and gazed up at the sky, but there were no clouds. Maybe water or wine from a balcony, she thought.

"I understand that sometimes in the fall, the North African winds bring sand from the desert, and it rains red mud in Granada," she said. "Do you know if that's true?"

"You staying that long?"

"I don't know."

"Winter's cold."

"From what I've read, it sounds sort of warm and cozy, everyone snuggled around the table, sharing a blanket, the brasero under the table toasting your toes."

"Forced intimacy. You can get central heating. In the new part of town."

"I think if we do decide to stay, we'll stay in the old part, up there in the Albayzín."

"Most of those houses are small. Uncomfortable. Not made to receive guests. But don't worry. Spaniards don't ask foreigners into their homes."

"Manolo invited us to *his* house, right Mommy?" said Resa. She didn't like this man and she didn't like the way her mother seemed to have forgotten all about her. "Puri's birthday party was so much fun. We danced and danced and danced."

"You were lucky," said the man, ignoring Resa and addressing Eva. "Or unlucky."

"What do you mean?"

"You believe in omens? A door falling off a church. A log standing up and catching fire. A mute stranger sleeping in a doorway. A fake fortuneteller."

Eva looked curiously at the man. It seemed she couldn't talk to anyone without getting a warning.

"Could you be more specific?"

"Take the mute stranger. Take any of them. Your friend Manolo. What do you know about him? Could be a thief. A smuggler. Worse. He's a Gypsy after all."

The man was standing very close to her and she could smell his maleness, an assertive saltiness.

"You know, here we are standing talking to each other, and we haven't even introduced ourselves." She was trying not to sound flustered. "My name is Eva, Eva Bonilla. And this is my daughter, Resa."

"I know who you are."

"You do?"

She gazed up at him, looking for some clue. His moustache, his eyebrows, his hair, were so blond. She wondered if his eyes were blue.

"You're Tony Benabo's widow."

He said it matter-of-factly, not as a question.

†

The desk clerk had been right.

During the week, more than twenty processions would pass beneath the balcony of the Hotel de los Tilos, multiple Christs and Virgins carried on the shoulders of the men of the competing brotherhoods. Afternoon and night, procession after procession of unwieldy wooden Christs bowed under the heavy crosses of our sins, borne in turn by dozens of bent-over men. And one richly mantled Virgin after another, a Miss Universe pageant of crowned queens of heaven escorted by bloodied Christs with crowns of thorns, painted angels with golden wings, and hundreds of penitentes in colourful flowing robes and pointed hoods keeping funereal pace to the rolls of drums. Women and girls in sexy black mourning would shield, with scarlet-nailed hands, white candles that struggled to extinguish themselves. Crowds would line the streets. People would lean over parapets, shout, mumble the occasional prayer. Now and then a saeta would lift above the din and pierce Eva's lone but fervent heart like an arrow.

†

He hadn't told her his name. You're Tony Benabo's widow, he had said, and disappeared into the crowd.

Fire and Ice

BELLA WAS SEATED AT HER USUAL TABLE outside the Mesón de los Milagros hoping that her current lover, el Gallo, would show up. It was a couple of days now since she'd seen him.

Instead, it was Eva and her child who approached. Oh well, thought Bella, she seems pleasant enough.

"Well, how are you this morning?" she said. "Have a chair."

"Hi, we're fine thanks," said Eva, who looked genuinely pleased to see her. "Resa and I just had a lovely walk up."

"Not too hot?"

"Either we're getting used to the heat, or it feels different now that we know the way. How are you?"

"Suffering from what one might call a penitential hangover."

Eva smiled. "The bar isn't as full as it was two days ago."

"Weekdays are always less busy."

Bella shook a cigarette from the open pack of Fortunas on the table and passed the rest to Eva.

"No thanks."

"I forgot. You're one of those clean abiders destined to live a long life without having lived it."

"Well, not such a clean abider that I won't have a drink."

Eva put up her arm, tentatively, to signal a man who was serving a table five metres away.

"No, that's not our waiter, that's Paco, the owner of the other bar.

Contrary to appearances, this sidewalk holds two separate establishments. At certain hours of the day, lunch time for instance, extra tables are opened out as more customers arrive, until eventually the two bars run into each other and this side of the plaza looks like one giant outdoor restaurant. Every morning Moncho arrives early and places this table on the boundary between the two bars. It's a territorial thing. Now, if it gets really busy, he will be conceded the right to extend his tables into the alleyway."

"What about Paco? Doesn't he try and beat him to it?"

"Paco can't be bothered."

"Do you ever go to his bar?"

"Only if I'm desperate. Paco has the coffee machine, and better food, but I never eat there, not even on Tuesdays when Moncho closes."

"Why not, if the food's better?"

"To tell you the truth, I can't remember why exactly. I think I went there one night and Paco was rather rude. Moncho on the other hand has always been very kind and courteous, even after hours, so I like coming here."

She took a swallow of rum.

"Anyway, this is the best seat in the house. You have the breeze from the alley, shade from the tree, and a perfect view of all the comings and goings."

Moncho had made his way to the table.

"¡Orí! niña," he said loudly to Resa, pinching her cheek. "¿Y? ¿Qué?" he said to Eva, and stared at her expectantly.

Eva stared back at him, looking perplexed.

"One vino de verano, por favor," she said finally. "With ice. And Resa will have a coke."

"Another cuba libre for me, Moncho," said Bella.

"Muy bien." To Eva he said, "My cousin Manolo was here a while ago."

"Oh, we stopped by his guitar shop on the way up, but it was closed."

"Another time, then."

"Do you know when it's open?"

"Whenever he's there, it's open."

Moncho left the table and Bella said to Eva, "You have to make a point of saying it first."

"Saying what first?"

"'¿Qué?' If someone says it to you, it's the signal to open up, to tell them what's going on in your world. But if *you* say it first, the onus is on the other person to talk. Asking certain questions is bad manners—you may have noticed that no one has asked you directly what you do for a living or to otherwise justify your presence here, but unless you volunteer information about yourself, you will be judged to be cold and aloof, cerrada. And if *you* want to find out something, try and talk a bit about yourself first. It gives people a chance to look you over. But for polite chitchat? Those moments when your mind is exhausted from Spanish? Getting your ¿Qué? in first is essential. *¿Qué?* the moment you see someone. You may have trouble thinking of something to say, but Spaniards can talk without thinking. *¿Qué?* It saves so much agony . . . Speaking of agony, have you seen any of the processions?"

"Yesterday—we went to Elvira, and later we watched several others from the hotel balcony."

"What did you think?"

"It was incredible . . . but we've been told that the one not to miss is the Silencio on Good Friday. Have you seen it?"

"Yes, but I prefer the one that leaves our own little church of el Cristo—a celebration of life rather than death. As a matter of fact, you might enjoy coming here early on Thursday afternoon to watch the preparations. The procession itself leaves the church late afternoon and returns sometime before midnight. It's well worth the effort to see the Virgin's reaction when her Son finally makes it up the hill."

"Mary and Jesus are actors?"

"More like performing statues. I'll say no more, just come and see for yourself. And afterwards, if you do decide to catch the Silencio, you'll have plenty of time to get back down the hill."

Moncho brought tapas—a dish of salty shrimp—and the drinks: a coke with a slice of lemon for Resa, another rum and coke for Bella, and for Eva, something pink and fizzy with a hunk of jagged ice in it.

"How can you drink that plonk?" asked Bella. "You know what's in there, don't you? Bad wine cut with pop. Guaranteed to cause a headache, especially on a hot day, and too much of that ice will give you a sore throat. This lovely pale rum from Murcia, now that's good for you."

Just holding the glass gave comfort.

"Mommy! There's Puri! Can I go play with her?"

Manolo's daughter was indeed at the other side of the plaza, skipping rope with three other girls.

Eva said yes, and her daughter gulped down her coke and ran off.

"They're devoted to their children here," said Bella. "If your little girl makes friends, it will make you less of a stranger to them. I'm not interested in children, so the women keep me at a distance. In Granada children are adulated and women old enough to be grandmothers do not sit alone getting drunk."

Bella took a long swallow. Still no sign of el Gallo. But no need to watch out for him, really. She would know as soon as he came within a block of the plaza. People–women and men both–routinely applauded and called out as he strutted down the street. ¡Coño! how handsome and virile he is! What a man!

"Gypsy men are so childish," she said, rubbing her neck. "They need to leave their mark on you. If it's not a knife cut or a bite mark it's hickeys. Hickeys . . . I haven't had one since high school . . . "

Eva looked like she was trying to think of what to say.

"I expect you've read Gerald Brenan," said Bella. "A bit of a pompous ass, but he did say a few smart things. One was that in Spain the bald are balder, the thin are thinner, and the one-legged more limbless than in other countries. He could have added that if you live here long enough you get like that too: if you're old and ridiculous you get older and even more ridiculous."

"Why did you come here?"

"At my age, you mean? Because in a way, I feel perfectly at home here. The people are out in the street. They eat, they smoke, they drink, they fight, they sing, they dance all night. They fuck whenever they get the chance. And the fact that I don't know what they're talking about half the time keeps me on my toes. Anyway, people always sound more interesting if you can't understand what they're saying, don't you think?"

"I never thought about it."

"I mean, in Canada I spoke the language, but I always felt like an outsider. Especially when I returned."

"How long were you there?"

"One year. I was hired to be writer-in-residence at a university in Toronto. I thought it would be amusing."

"But?"

"The university was full of joggers and business students. No smoking allowed, no public drinking, no overeating. So much energy put into prolonging such humourless lives . . . Where are you from again?"

"Edmonton."

"Edmonton. I spent a few days there giving readings. It was my impression that at nine o'clock on a Friday night the entire population disappeared like puffs of smoke up a chimney. Tell me, is it true that Edmontonians get up on Sunday morning to go to church?"

"Some do, I guess."

"Just *in case* God exists."

Bella took another long swallow.

"Here, people sleep in. They don't make appointments, but if they do, they break them, because chances are they've run into another friend along the way."

"Why did you choose Spain to live in?"

"Why not?"

"I mean, why not Africa? or England? or Portugal?"

"Africa is so raw and rootsy. As for England, it was Théophile Gautier, I think, who wrote: 'L'infini dans le clair est bien autrement sublime et prodigieux que l'infini dans l'obscur.' In other words, who gives a shit about an infinite vista if you can't see it?"

"And Portugal?"

"I only went there once, to the Algarve for Christmas."

She and Zendi had spent two nights on the beach.

"The people had the loveliest soft whispering voices—I remember a mother remonstrating with her child—all those shshsh sounds at the ends of syllables, the woman couldn't quite manage to sound angry. But after Spain, Portugal seemed restrained, the people reserved and sombre. No edge to the voices or the music . . . even the buildings with their chipped layers of different colours seemed dilapidated and scruffy after the bright, brash Andalusian villages. And the Portuguese women, all in black, wearing kerchiefs—I thought, no Andaluza would be caught dead with her head covered. And it's true, you know, Moncho's wife gets headaches from the sun but she would sooner complain all summer than wear a hat."

"Now that's interesting. Do you suppose the reason for that could go back to the outlawing of Moorish dress?"

Bella brushed her wispy blond hair out of her eyes and examined Eva, trying to fathom what she must be thinking. "Why do you wish to hide yourself?" she said.

Eva looked away.

"This morning I was glad to see I'm finally getting grey hair," said Bella. She held out a few strands. "See, here above my forehead. It's a relief to get old. You don't have time any more to care what other people think of you. Beauty and intelligence are a curse. When you're young and beautiful, you never get the chance to find out what people are really like, the men are so busy sucking in their bellies and flashing everything they have at you."

"And the women?"

"They're busy worrying that you're after their paunchy men. And if you also happen to be a writer, other women regard you as men do sports heroes—they want you to live *for* them, as if it's your flesh and blood you're offering and not just a few words on paper. They project their desires onto you, and become angry when you don't say and do the things they secretly want to say and do. Being readily noticed is definitely not an asset for a writer. It's much more useful when eyes flicker away in automatic dismissal—you at least have a chance to get your bearings."

Her glass was almost empty. She drained it and lit another cigarette. "So, tell me, how are you getting along here?"

"Okay, I guess, but it's relaxing when I get the chance to speak English. In Spanish I have to think so hard, and I get mixed up between 'tu' and 'usted.' I'll be using 'tu' and inadvertently throw in an 'usted' and the other person looks a little hurt. I guess it confuses them."

"Things like that don't matter . . . ¡Moncho!" Bella called, holding up two fingers. "¡Dos más! ¡Un verano y un cuba libre! . . . There, you see. I may not know much Spanish, but I do have a grasp of the essentials."

"It's very kind of you, but thank you, I haven't even finished this one. And I don't think I'll want more, not so early in the day."

"Nonsense. Not only does drink render one gratefully insensible, it also unlooses the tongue."

In a few minutes Moncho arrived with two fresh drinks. He smiled and Bella heard him say quietly to Eva, "Don't worry. Yours has only the smallest drop of wine in it."

"Are the winters long here?" asked Eva. "Yesterday we were told that they are."

"Winter comes quickly. One day it's hot and sunny, the next all the cats have moved out from under the bushes to the open where it's not so dark and damp. Everyone says, You think this is bad, wait until

January, and then you don't see them until Spring. I remember my first winter here . . . "

No, not winter—it had been mid-September.

"What was it like?"

"I guess it was early fall. Zendi and I were in the habit of sitting here, not at this bar, which didn't exist yet, but at the other one, which was owned at that time by Paco's father . . . See that little window in the spire of the church? Every evening at about eight o'clock, a woman would appear there. She would lean forward with her forearms on the sill and her long black hair hanging straight down. She would stay like that for ages without moving, a Latin Rapunzel gazing forlornly into the darkness. Every night Zendi wrote a different poem about her.

"Then one morning—I was sitting by myself having a coffee—Zendi, damn the bastard, had gone off the night before with a Gypsy boy."

Even today, it angered her. She took a deep drag on the cigarette.

"Anyway, I had drunk ron pálido to the point where I was sober again. I was in that haze in which you're aware that you've lived through the night while the rest of the world has slept through it and missed it. You know, you've passed through to the other side, and it's as if you've survived something and beaten it, as if for once your time hasn't been wasted.

"It was raining, drizzling, an unusual occurrence so early in the year. One moment the streets were empty, and the next they were filled with people, all of them seemingly headed to the same destination. There were no cars in those days, no vehicles of any sort, just a flow of umbrellas all moving together, as if going to a village fair. I joined the flow.

"In front of me was the baker's wife holding an umbrella over her two daughters' heads, and beside me, with her grandson, the woman who tried to sell me a dancing doll every time I walked through Plaza San Nicolás. We passed the church, and a pack of children was pushed out the side door by—guess who—Rapunzel, screeching at the five children who tumbled out one after the other and scurried off, chasing each other like church mice. I realized this was no fair—it was the first day of school, and the mysterious nymph of Zendi's poems was just another harried mother who had to get her children off to school like everyone else.

"I looked around and saw all the women in a new context—the

dancers in the caves, the fruit sellers in the market, the hairdresser: on this morning, they were simply and complexly mothers and grandmothers.

"When we arrived at the school the gates were locked. The children and mothers on the outside of the gate and the teachers on the inside called to each other, but neither group had a key. A few of the biggest boys climbed the fence and jumped over. Eventually the principal arrived with his large iron key to save the day, and when he opened the gate, all the mothers and children tried to squeeze through at once.

"I went back to the bar and began to write a poem. And I stopped."

She finished her cigarette and stepped on it.

"I don't understand."

"Just that. I stopped. I haven't written a word since."

"Why not?"

"Because I realized that what I had just witnessed was in itself a poem, a perfect poem which did not require my name on it. Until that moment, nothing had seemed real to me unless I could translate it into my words. Now I found myself surprised to discover that what I had experienced required neither my presence nor my interpretation. Nor did it require the distancing that writing immediately bestows on an event. It did not need me to write about it. I did not wish to write about it.

"I returned to the apartment and looked through my notebooks—ten or twelve stories, some poems, the third draft of a novel. I burned them."

"You burned everything?"

Eva looked horrified.

Bella lost her train of thought.

She stared at Eva, waiting for her to say something, but Eva just stared back. She wants something, thought Bella.

"When you're young you're punished for being beautiful," she said. "When you get old . . . well, you're just old." There you go, an insight. She lit another cigarette.

"Did you mean that we have to choose to live life or to watch it? That we can't do both?" asked Eva.

"You know what they'll say after I'm dead? Not much, but those who know me least will have the most to say."

Eva still looked like a student expecting an answer.

Bella took a long swallow of rum, but it didn't help. The fog in her head thickened.

"Rubbish," she said. "It's all rubbish."

"Are you all right?" asked Eva.

"What do you want from me?" Bella could hear her voice inside her head, a little girl's voice, slurring the words. "*What* is it that you want from me?" she repeated, lowering her voice, shifting the emphasis. It still didn't sound right. "What do *you* want? *What* was it *he* wanted?"

"Zendi, you mean?" asked Eva.

Bella had a flashback of him with the Gypsy boy—in *her* bed. "He was a boorish ass, one of those men who feels the need to humiliate intelligent women who also happen to be beautiful."

"But why would anyone . . . "

" . . . stay with him, you mean?" Why *had* she stayed with him? Her mind was clearing. She waved her hand to dissipate the rest of the fog.

"Poor baby, you must be younger than you look. Zendi was an ass but he was an ass with style. He was my Spain. Someone has written that in most places, the day is broken up by so many little fences and obstacles, it is passed in struggle and effort, and by the time night comes, it's as if you haven't had a day at all; but in Spain, you get an enlarged sense of the passage of time, every day giving the sensation of a week. Who wrote that now?"

"I think it was Gerald Brenan."

"Brenan. Then that was the second intelligent thing he said. And it's true, you know, you go for a walk here and you stop to chat and you get invited to a party, you have a few drinks and run into another friend and end up at another party, you have a few more drinks . . . "

And drink was so good for the soul. Even Eva seemed to be enjoying this idle sitting around, watching the to-and-fro in the plaza, the boys booting a ball, the girls skipping Double Dutch.

Her daughter was with the skippers. At the moment she was trying to jump into the middle, but her feet kept tripping up the rope and yanking it out of the hands of the turners. The other girls were laughing and calling out instructions, content to restart again and again.

"Who is that woman?" asked Eva.

"What woman?"

"The Muslim woman walking in front of the crucifix."

The woman, wearing a chador, was striding straight ahead like a blinkered horse.

"'Lámparas de cristal/y espejos verdes,'" said Bella.

"Lorca," said Eva.

"A woman without a tongue . . . "

"What?"

"It's what the people say, that her tongue was cut out."

"Why?"

"They don't say. Her name is Zayda, but they call her Achinados, because of her Asian eyes, I suppose. I ran into her one night. We were the only two people on the street–it was very late, even by Spanish standards, and she seemed rather frightened, so I invited her home with me."

"Did she go?"

"She did."

"And what happened?"

"Nothing. I fell asleep. In the morning, or maybe it was afternoon, she was gone."

"Do you really think she's got no tongue?"

"What's the difference? If you don't use it you might as well not have it . . . You seem to know your Lorca. You must know this: 'Granada the persecuted, which, instead of protesting, turns into a dance' . . . "

Eva looked perplexed.

"What about this, then–'Sevilla para herir/Córdoba para morir' . . . And the next line, which he never wrote: Granada para vivir. Well look around you, dear Eva. You are in the land of poetry, of sudden bursts of colour–of shocking greens, yellows, reds against naked white buildings. As you sit, others pass, and as you pass, bits of song splash over the tops of walls to astonish you."

"It reminds me of something Claude Simon said, that he writes without commas because life is like that."

"It's not like that at all. Is your life like that? Mine is full of pauses: commas, semicolons, ellipses, parentheses, periods, new sentences, new paragraphs. Look, if you want a bit of advice from an old woman, it's this: pause at the commas. Leave yourself open to the unexpected. And those parentheses–sometimes there are very interesting things going on in parentheses."

Bella finished her drink and looked at Eva. What was this girl searching for?

"If you want truth, this is it: every single thing I've said is a load of old rubbish."

Eva looked flustered.

"What do you want?" said Bella.

"I'm not sure I want anything."

"Is it about Tony?"

"If anything, I suppose it is."

"Listen then—why don't you meet me tomorrow in Plaza Nueva. We'll have lunch, and afterwards, I'll take you up to the cemetery."

"Thank you, that's very kind."

"Not at all. I find that visiting once in a while with the dead encourages one to continue living."

"Just how well did you know Tony?"

"As well as all we foreigners know each other—we're a little leery of each other, especially at first—after all, most of us have come to get away from the rest of us . . . I met him through an American woman who had married a lawyer from Madrid—they lived over by San Nicolás—one of the best views in the Albayzín. She had planted a lawn in this tiny plot, a space where her husband would have preferred a couple of fruit trees, no doubt. I couldn't look at that pathetic patch of suburban U.S.A. without wondering what kind of foreign insects might be crawling around in the burnt yellow grass . . . Becky Smith, that was her name. I think she went mad."

"I knew Becky Smith," said a male voice.

"'Ah! when the ghost begins to quicken,'" said Bella. She heard Eva catch her breath. "I do wish you wouldn't creep up like that, Carl."

Eva's face reddened.

"I suppose you know each other," said Bella.

"We haven't been formally introduced," said Eva, "although we have met a couple of times—once in the cathedral and yesterday at the first procession."

"Carl Alonso, meet Eva Bonilla. Eva, meet Carl."

He sat down in the empty chair next to Eva and gave a dry laugh. From his neck hung an expensive-looking camera and concomitant paraphernalia. He set them carefully on the table.

"You're right, Bella," he said. "Becky did go mad. Overnight. She was terrified of water. Always had been, since she was a child. Her husband told me. One day I saw her drinking coffee in the plaza. Next day she was running around the market in skimpy shorts and Nikes.

Bumping into people. Her husband said she was getting up in the night to water the lawn. Every hour on the hour. By hand with a watering can. Wouldn't use the hose. Filled that can up over and over. And she talked to her grass. Told it secrets."

"Couldn't anyone do anything?" said Eva.

"Her husband took her to Salobreña. For a rest. One night she got out of bed and ran into the ocean. Nothing on but tennis shoes. Dead Becky, naked in her Nikes."

"Didn't she have any North American friends who could have helped her?"

"No sense diving in after someone who doesn't want to be rescued," said Bella. "You're more than likely to get pulled under while the supposed victim paddles off with her head above water. The most we can do for others is to say in passing—'Hello! Take care!' That, and share a bed now and again." If I go to the caves, she thought, I might run into Gallo.

"It's interesting about the coast," said Eva. "I read that in Muslim days, being sent to the coast meant you had been banished from the good life, because Almería and Salobreña were considered unhealthy places."

"Right. No fresh water. Polluted wells. Incoming ships bringing disease. The beach was for lepers and undesirables. The emirs sent their enemies there . . . Speaking of incoming ships, here comes la Muda."

Ruth Kostyk was striding towards them from the far side of the plaza. Today she was wearing a bright yellow hat and matching yellow dress.

"La Muda?" said Eva.

"Her nickname. The Mute One."

"You know that in Sacromonte, at night, you can hear a party from blocks and blocks away," said Bella. "The sound travels underground, from cave to cave, and it's as if the music is not just in the room with you, but under your skin, travelling in your veins, pumping through your heart."

†

The other night with Gallo . . . he had taken her from Sacromonte to Cartuja and back again, from bar to bar, cave to cave, inner sanctum to inner sanctum, and she had drunk vodka to the other side of drunkenness, until she had been peeled of all her layers of self-protection and had stood in his cave shivering like an unveiled virgin on her wedding night. The candlelight had burned his face an even deeper copper, and she had caught a glimpse in the mirror of her own white paper face with its staring eyes which were too bright and too blue. She had covered her face and peered at the mirror through splayed fingers. The skin on the back of her hands was like finely wrinkled parchment.

She had shut her eyes and he had pushed her up against the wall and kissed her hard, the stipple digging into her naked buttocks and shoulders. Her wrists were thin bones in his fingers.

"People still live in Sacromonte?" said Eva. "I thought that everyone had moved out after the mud slides. I read that people were buried alive, and that the survivors were too scared to return. Although it makes sense, I suppose, that over the years they would trickle back."

"It's changed since Bella lived there," said Carl. "Action's more spread out now. In the Cartuja. In the Albayzín."

"When were the slides, anyway—in the fifties, wasn't it?"

"I need another drink," said Bella, then heard in the distance: ¡Qué majo! ¡Anda! ¡Anda!

No drink, time to go.

El Gallo's red head appeared at the top of the hill.

"Excuse me," said Bella, standing up, "I have to leave."

Up and Down

EVA WAS MARVELLING AT BELLA'S RELATIONship with alcohol. One moment she was incoherent, head lolling sloppily on her shoulders, the next she had snapped her head to attention and was speaking both lucidly and expansively.

Bella plunked some money on the table and wobbled off towards the church, where there was a small commotion–people clapping, calling out, ¡Guapo! ¡Majo!

I hope she doesn't forget about tomorrow, thought Eva.

"El Gallo de las Crusadas," said Carl.

"Pardon me?"

"The Cock of the Crusades."

"Is that for real?"

"Refers to his conduct. And his red hair. Doubtless a legacy from an overzealous Crusader."

Ruth reached the table and sat down heavily in Bella's just-vacated chair.

"Hmmph. Thinks she's pretty smart, getting away from me again, prancing off down the street with some Gypsy young enough to be her son, young enough to be her grandson from the looks of it, mind you, she'd follow anything willing to drop his pants. But like my mother used to say: when you reach a certain age, coy is not cute."

"Still tracking the elusive Católica, are we?" said Carl.

The bright red head of el Gallo disappeared around the corner of the church, along with Bella and the rest of his entourage.

"Honestly, someone ought to tell her, but then the poor woman isn't interested in what other people have to say, I mean that would also explain why she only ever wrote that one book, wouldn't it? After all, how many books can you write if your only subject matter is yourself?"

"¡Cojones! Can you believe that car?" said Moncho, coming to take orders. "Parked right in front of the restaurant. Look at the licence plate—a Catalán, of course. And where is he? No one knows. ¡Maleducado! We could have placed two more tables in that space. But that's a Catalán for you—¡Soy yo!" Moncho stabbed his chest. "Now, señoras, señor, what will you have?"

"Nothing—I don't want anything," said Ruth, putting her hand to her forehead, " . . . unless, well, maybe a little of what Eva's having."

"The usual for me," said Carl. He turned to Eva. "Have you eaten?"

She shook her head no, and was secretly pleased when he ordered food for the three of them, although back in Canada she would have thought the gesture arrogant.

Moncho left, still muttering and shaking his head about Catalans.

"Just mention Barcelona. Worse than bragging about New York in Dubuque," said Carl.

"Or Toronto in Edmonton," said Eva.

"Well I happen to *like* Barcelona," said Ruth. "It's much more civilized than it is here, for one thing. Honestly, I don't know how much more I can take of this place, I tell you, the sun, the heat, the yappy mangy dogs—but I *have* figured out one thing about the dogs—do you know why people have them? I'll tell you why. It's not out of a love of pets, no sir, it's because they want *watchdogs,* I mean those poor animals are kept chained up on the terraces—they get almost *no* affection and *no* exercise—so tell me, is it any wonder that they spend all their time barking? You must have noticed how one will start and another will join in and pretty soon you'll have this whole chorus of yowling disenchantment, and it's always at night, but"—she took a deep breath, her mouth still open, precluding any interruption—"it really is so irritating when they bark all at once like that, even if I do know it's out of loneliness and misery, and if that's not enough, you have to put up with those horrible buzzing motorbikes all night long. Night after night it's yap yap yap and bzzz bzzz bzzz. I'm telling you, if it wasn't that I absolutely *have* to do this article on Bella—"

"—Unusual woman," said Carl.

Ruth harrumphed. "I'll give you that much. And I don't suppose *you're* so taken in by her any more," she said, turning to Eva.

"I like her," said Eva boldly. "She seems friendly."

A sound escaped from the side of Ruth's mouth. "Friendly, that's *one* way of putting it."

Eva gestured awkwardly to Carl's equipment, trying to change the topic. "Are you by any chance a professional photographer?"

"Carl does a lot of freelance work," answered Ruth. "He specializes in travel articles, especially places off the beaten track, little-known archaeological sites; he's a regular citizen of the world, aren't you, Carl? But why don't *you* tell her about it?"

"What could I possibly add?" he said dryly.

"Is the Albayzín out-of-the-way?" Eva asked.

"Nowhere is out-of-the-way any more."

"I guess not, if you judge a place by the number of Canadians who've discovered it. And there do seem to be quite a few of us here: Bella, Ruth, Resa and me."

"Probably all you're likely to meet," said Carl. "In this bar at least."

"Bella's over seventy you know," said Ruth, "as a matter of fact, I happen to know she's almost eighty, now I suppose that sort of thing might wash back home, and it certainly doesn't bother me personally, but one has to respect local customs, I mean imagine what the people here must think of her, and it reflects on us, you know, as Canadians, so if I were you Eva I'd keep my distance—the thing is, I have to do an article on her and then I'm gone, but you're in a different situation, so it's important to you how the locals view you and your daughter." Ruth lowered her voice. "I don't like to repeat gossip, but then it's not as if this isn't common knowledge in the writing community anyway—when Bella was writer-in-residence in Toronto she, well, ran off with a student, a Mohawk I think he was, and then she showed up two weeks later and said she had gone fishing and acted as if it were the most normal thing in the world. I mean think about it."

†

Eva was thinking again how pleasant the walk up had been today. Even the noises from the cathouse had been less perturbing, and she had taken the time to notice her surroundings—windows bordered with arabesques, and in one street a doorjamb covered in azulejos, the blue and golden geometric tiles of the caliphs. Some of the houses had their doors open, and she and Resa had peeked in at shady patios, and once at a white marble floor polished glossy like a mirror. They had stopped to talk to a woman who was emptying a pail of soapy water into the gutter. She had smiled and talked to Resa, who said it was the woman who had done her hair at the party.

"Eva, now tell me honestly. Don't you think it's sad?"

"Pardon me?"

"Don't you think it's sad to be carrying on like Bella does?"

Eva avoided the question by gazing determinedly towards the other bar. "I'm sorry," she said, "I was just wondering. Has either of you ever tried the other bar?"

"You mean Paco's bar," said Carl. "Best food in the Albayzín. But most people prefer Moncho's."

"Why?"

"Paco supported the Fascists during the Civil War."

"So you don't go there?"

"I go there a lot."

"I don't imagine that's why Bella doesn't go there," said Ruth, "I don't suppose she gives two hoots about the horrors of fascism."

"Paco won't have her," said Carl.

"Doesn't surprise me, not one bit."

"Actually, she did mention something about the owner having been rude to her," said Eva. "She said that *she's* the one who chooses not to go there."

"I can just imagine what happened," said Ruth. "She'd slurp up the Atlantic Ocean if it was whiskey."

Ruth had placed her elbows on the table and it jiggled every time she spoke. Moncho set the new round of drinks down and picked up a discarded matchbook cover from the ground, folded it, and placed it under one of the table legs.

Ruth gulped half her drink straightaway. "I'm so thirsty," she said, "it must be this heat. So Carl, exactly what *did* happen between Bella and the other bar?"

"She showed up after closing. Banged on the door. Demanded Paco sell her a bottle of rum. Paco refused. She insulted his mother."

"See, what did I tell you? I knew it was something like that, I mean honestly, it really is too bad, and with all the chances she had early in life." Ruth took another gulp. "Dear me, I'm going to have to be careful. I'm not used to drinking, you know, I can feel it already, it's going right to my head." She took a deep breath. "Now what were we talking about?"

Eva waited for Carl to speak, but he was looking across the plaza.

"Oh look, Carl," said Ruth, "isn't that your maid?"

Returning across the plaza, with a string bag full of oranges, was the reputedly tongueless woman named Zayda.

Carl threw some bills on the table and quickly excused himself, snatching up his equipment and half running in Zayda's direction.

There's just too much going on, thought Eva.

The food came, and Eva picked at it while Ruth continued talking.

After a while, the girls with the skipping rope left and Resa came running back to the table and sat down. She grabbed the edge of the table and pushed back until her chair was balancing precariously on its two back legs.

"Stop it!" snapped Eva.

†

Ruth could hear her own voice, droning on and on inside her head. She didn't know how much longer she could keep this up. She was tired of talking, but someone had to do it. Honestly, this Eva was so subdued, she seemed to have nothing to say. Well Ruth had plenty to say, but it was exhausting. You'd think others could do their share, hold up their end of the conversation.

Eva stood up and instructed her child to say good-bye.

Ruth watched their retreating backs and said to herself, Now what did you do wrong this time?

But it had always been like this.

†

First there had been her childhood, the other kids. Ever since she could remember, she had been conscious of her size—already at nine years old, taller than both her parents—and she had grown up alternating between feelings of awkwardness and overimportance. The other girls laughed at her behind her back, she knew it, but she despised their dolls and cutouts, and she defended herself by becoming the bossy girl who decides what game everyone's going to play. But her insides boiled when they snuck off in pairs, snickering. She tried to join the boys, but they laughed at her too and called her Stupid Bohunk. She hit them and ran home, wanting to shout at her parents to quit talking with their stupid accents.

I'll show them all, she had decided. It would not do to take over her parents' store, and certainly not to become a school teacher like the rest of the girls who finished school. Marriage—that was for those cliquey groups of unimaginative girls who walked hand in hand at recess. Ha! one day those imitation little Shirley Temples would be bragging in their kitchens that they had known her. She, Ruth Kostyk, would have the last word. She would be a writer.

But even that had not turned out.

†

It's not your fault, she said to herself, you can't help it if people don't speak up. Like the other day, she had come up to the plaza looking for Bella and she had seen Carl sitting with a group of people. He had introduced her to them—a dancer, the dancer's husband, who was a musician, and his or her parents, she wasn't sure. Then Carl had left and she had been alone with the Spaniards. They had drunk to her health and she had become suffused with a warm happy glow, and so overcome with good will that she had wanted to do something special for these lovely people, something big, something generous, and she had gone into the bar and paid for all the drinks. When the men got up to pay, she had eagerly awaited their delighted responses, but they had returned to the table with stricken looks on their faces, averting their eyes and speaking quickly to one another in low voices. The husband had taken the arm of the dancer and the group had left, no one looking at her or saying so much as thank you.

What faux pas had she committed?

Life and Death

On the way to Plaza Nueva next day, Eva decided to try the shop on Elvira once more. This time the door was open and Manolo inside.

"¡Hola! amigas, enter, come in."

Resa went straight to a guitar that she had seen on the wall the first time they had looked through the window.

"Where's your assistant?" asked Eva.

"Yukio? He's out on an errand."

Manolo noticed Resa staring at the guitar. "Ah, my little lynx, you have spotted the worthiest instrument in the entire shop."

He hoisted her onto a heavily carved wooden chair, lowered the instrument from the wall and placed it in her lap, gently arranging her arms and hands around its neck and body.

"This is a very special guitar," he said. "It was made in Cádiz long ago in the days of the Moors. Later it travelled with my family to Sevilla, and then here, to Granada."

He turned to Eva. "The first instrument of this type–the laúd–had four strings coloured yellow, red, white, and black to represent the humours of the body."

Resa plucked the fifth string.

"That one was added to enrich the others. In its day it would have been painted blood red."

"A laúd. How beautiful," said Eva. She thought it had the shape of a woman's breast.

"If played properly, it will throb with the pulsations of the human heart."

Resa began to strum hard on the strings.

Manolo laughed but took it from her hands and carefully returned it to the wall.

"This guitar is very delicate," he said to Resa. "But if you like, I will make you a special one of your own. ¿Qué dices?"

"Sí," said Resa.

"Muy bien, hija. When Yukio comes back we will choose the wood. Hoy mismo. It will be an excellent first project for him. Let's see now, we can use this piece of cypress—we want cypress, for the metallic tone—and I'll tell you what: for your guitar, we will use Canadian maple." To Eva's questioning look he added, "See that pile of wood? It's been drying now for ten years. It's my little corner of Canada."

"I didn't know you used maple."

"Not very often. I get most of my hardwood from Africa, but when I can afford it, I like to buy maple . . . I would love to visit Canada—mountains covered in trees, and the houses made entirely of wood. I've seen pictures."

"I guess it's like that in some parts."

"It's hard to imagine, a country with so many trees that you can build your house with wood."

"Can we watch you make the guitar?" asked Resa.

"What a good idea," said Manolo. "But I'll tell you what, let's go across the street first and have a drink."

Eva looked at her watch. "Actually, Resa and I have to get going—we're meeting someone for lunch." As long as Bella remembers, she thought.

"Can't we stay, Mommy?"

"You need to eat, sweetheart."

"Why not let Risita stay with me?" He turned to Resa. "Would you like to stay with me?"

"Yes," she said, nodding enthusiastically.

"Good. When Yukio gets back we'll choose the wood and then I'll take you home for lunch. Perhaps we can begin work on the guitar this very afternoon." He turned back to Eva. "My mother will be so happy for the chance to stuff some food into her. And after lunch, she can come back to the shop with me or stay home and play with Puri."

"Well, I don't know . . . "

"Please, Mommy, please."

"Well, I suppose it would be all right." It would certainly simplify things, she thought, especially if Bella does take me to the cemetery. "When should I come for her?"

"Whenever you like. Later."

"How late? Two o'clock? . . . Five?"

"Whenever."

"Where? Here or at the house?"

"Wherever."

†

Bella was seated smoking in the Plaza Nueva. She was in the same clothes as the day before and looking rather rumpled. Her hair hung down in thin strands and her eyes were puffy. Her red nail polish was chipped.

The two women exchanged greetings and for a while neither of them spoke, Eva content to take in the scene.

"I love the slow pace here," she said after a while.

"Don't let it fool you—their minds are quick as lightning."

Incongruous in the heat and traffic, a red-faced jogger ran by along the Carrera del Darro.

Had Tony jogged along there? At home he always ran in the early morning, before the air was polluted. "I saw on the map that at this point, the river runs underneath the Carrera del Darro," said Eva.

Bella waved her cigarette. "In the words of Angel Ganivet: 'Imagine covering a river! Whoever had the idea must have had it in the obscurity of night.'" She said it dramatically.

"Supposedly, the Moors fell head over heels in love with the rivers here," said Eva. "After the desert and the sea, fresh water was like a miracle."

Bella fixed Eva with her liquid blue eyes, which gave the impression of having seen all there was to see and of having endured all there was to endure. "'Water, cold and fresh as new snow! Delicious, clean water, a delicacy without odour or colour, a treat to smack one's lips over! Water which did not make men sick. Water which did not make widows of their women.'" She said the words as a Shakespearean actor might, then her eyes clouded and she lifted her glass to her lips.

I hope she'll be in shape to take me to the cemetery, thought Eva.

She gazed around the plaza and saw three women ambling across the other side.

"Do you know those women?" she said. "They look familiar."

Bella didn't bother to look. "After a few days everyone begins to look familiar."

"I think a couple of them were at Manolo's the other night."

Bella continued to puff on her cigarette.

"How do they manage to keep their hair so black, I wonder? Do you think it's diet? Olive oil or something?"

"I suspect it's *something* you get out of a bottle."

"Hair colouring you mean. Now why didn't I think of that?"

"Perhaps because you are not given to deliberate camouflage."

Was Bella being sarcastic? Eva blushed.

The waiter arrived at the table.

"What are you drinking, Bella?" Eva asked.

"My usual. Ron pálido–with decaffeinated coke. I want to catch a few winks this afternoon."

Eva asked for a limonada with crushed ice.

"I haven't eaten since yesterday," said Bella. "I'll have the estofado, por favor."

"Make that two," said Eva, and the waiter smiled and left.

"Where's your daughter, anyway?" asked Bella.

"With Manolo."

"How nice."

Eva saw a flash of yellow go by in a taxi.

"You don't seem to be overly fond of Ruth," she said.

Bella shrugged.

"Why not?"

"She's one of those women who wakes up one morning and realizes it's too late to have children."

"You dislike her because she's never had children?" The idea seemed preposterous to Eva, especially coming from Bella.

"Of course not. I mean she's killed her natural instincts, and in so doing has also killed all those little signals of desire and potentiality that most bodies send out to other bodies."

"Maybe it was necessary in order to have her career." Eva wondered if Bella had children.

"She's a blanket of talk, a quilt, an eiderdown of twaddle smothering a half-century of repressed urges."

"What's her writing like?"

"Never read it. But she probably saves her grocery lists for posterity and gives three-hour workshops to all those poor slobs who fantasize about becoming writers."

Eva blushed again. She had once taken a workshop called The Joy of Plotting, and enjoyed it.

"You think workshops are a waste of time?"

"They make people think writing is a communal activity, a sort of love-in where you get together with a bunch of other people and share all your good little bits. It's not like that at all. It's more like masturbation: the deed is best done alone."

She ground out her cigarette and lit another.

"Don't you save your notes and letters?" asked Eva. "To sell to a library or something?"

"I told you yesterday, I don't write any more, not even grocery lists." She raised her glass. "Yesterday is rubbish. Tomorrow is rubbish. Let's drink to today."

Eva clinked an imaginary glass to Bella's. "One thing I don't understand," she said, "why don't you just give Ruth her interview and get it over with?"

"She's not interested in my work, she wants to have pieces of me, like Saint Teresa's body. But at least with Saint Teresa, they waited until she was dead."

"You think Ruth is malicious?"

"She wants an interview. Interviewers are all the same. I had my share of them in Canada. The radio and TV ones were the worst. They would grill you as if you were a lying politician or a crucial witness at a trial. Or their voices would assume concerned tones, creating an illusion of intimacy. One of them, I remember, even had a little catch in the voice–he would ask a totally inappropriate question and then pause, expecting me to rush in and fill the awkward silence with something revealing about myself, I suppose."

"You don't think it would be different with Ruth, her being a writer too?"

"Ha! Canada's most underrated author interviewing Canada's most overrated one. I suspect that's how she sees it, at any rate. Canadian writers, academics . . . most of them haven't even bothered to read my book, but when I went back that once, they wined and dined me to try and find out if the latest gossip in *Maclean's* was true. Imagine professors of English literature ignoring my work, but checking me out as they might a prospective marriage partner for their eldest son."

"You're serious?"

"I'm bored. And chattering away about one's own work is always a mistake."

"You don't think there are insights to be gained from studying a writer's life?" Eva loved biographies of famous people.

"An arrogant notion. How can anyone presume to know what's gone on in someone else's head? There is more truth in fiction."

"In a way it seems as if you and Ruth are playing a game of hide and seek."

"Exactly. A silly game, and I don't want to play any more. Anyway, she sits too close. She pushes her face right into yours and her breath smells like stale doughnuts. Gurdjieff once told me that if two people sit too close to each other, their auras become entangled."

Eva smiled. "Still, I can't help feeling sorry for her. She seems so unaware or something."

"'Pity is not love; pity destroys love.' Who said that now . . . I can't remember."

Bella downed her drink. Her eyes clouded over again and Eva thought she had lost her, until the waiter appeared with the stew and a tall glass of pale yellow crushed ice. Bella immediately dug into the stew.

"What's in it?" asked Eva.

"Mostly pork and a few vegetables," Bella said, her mouth full of food. "Cabbage, carrots, onions, garbanzos. As in all such dishes the world over, what happens to be in the kitchen gets thrown into the pot."

"Resa and I tried those red sausages yesterday."

"Chorizos."

"Yes. Why do you suppose they eat so much pig here? Do you think it dates back to when the eating of pork was a test of orthodoxy?"

Oh oh, thought Eva, catching herself, that's the sort of comment that will make Bella's head loll.

She swallowed a forkful of food and said quickly, "That's one thing Tony probably didn't like here—the food. He never ate pork if he could help it, and nothing deep-fried."

"He may not have liked the food, but he himself was well-liked. It seemed to me he was easily accepted. He made a lot of friends."

What about enemies? Eva wondered.

"We'll take a taxi up to the graveyard as soon as we're done eating," said Bella.

†

The taxi took them up through the mottled shade of the streets of the Alhambra Hill and into the treeless cemetery where Tony was buried. The driver agreed to return in one hour.

Mrs. Benabo had sketched a map showing the location of Tony's grave, but Eva didn't need it. Bella knew the way.

She led Eva past impressive mausoleums sheltering the important families of Granada, past a patio dedicated to the dead of the Civil War, and other smaller gardens and chapels, to a hillock overlooking the city and the valley of the Genil.

Bella pointed to a simple stone marker—ANTONIO BENABO DELCAMPO (1942–1979) HIJO PRECIOSO—and discreetly walked away.

Over the last six years, Eva had imagined this moment many times. She had anticipated some sort of reconciliation: a release of sorrow strong enough to wash away the petty concerns of the past, a proper good-bye, or, at the very least, a simple verification of Tony's death.

What struck her instead was the foreignness of the marker in the stark light, the words: hijo precioso; and the name: Antonio Benabo Delcampo. Not her lover in the grave, but another woman's son—a stranger, not a Canadian called Tony Benabo. She wondered why she should be surprised to find him buried amidst other Granadinos, and not in some foreigners' suburb of the cemetery.

If you were going to die, why on earth did you come here to do it? she asked silently, and found herself desperately wanting to hear his answer, to hear his voice.

Oh Tony, I'm so alone here, I need you.

But he was dead.

Who was she to trust now?

She wished for guidance, some sign that might point the way. Her hand caressed the key in her pocket, but the hard metal gave no solace.

And then it seemed to her that there was nothing between the top of her head and the sun, between the dead and the sky, and she breathed in the heat and the dust and looked out at the city below and at the valley beyond and realized that here from her lover's grave lay the grandest view she was ever likely to see.

"Paradise. You want it? You can have it."

He seemed to be always coming up behind her. It was the wrong time for him to be here. He was intruding.

Bella was smoking a cigarette in the shade of the nearest mausoleum, her back to them.

"Other Spaniards don't think of Granada as heaven. Too ingrown. Isolated. Enclosed by its mountains."

But that was exactly how Tony had imagined heaven, with the commandments and prohibitions of the churches being walls erected to block access to it, to reserve it as a place for the few.

"Do you believe in God?" she asked.

Carl didn't answer.

Tony had said that belief in life after death was a lazy, cowardly response, one that rendered anything acceptable—as long as there was a god in this world, there was possibility of reprieve. For believers, it was easier to close one's eyes and pray, because nothing that happened on earth would ever be as important as what was to come after—redeem yourself now, save your real living for later. Anyway, had man ever worshipped anyone other than himself? What could be more ridiculous than worshipping a god made in our own image?

"I once read that heaven is modelled on fascistic principles," she said. "The higher the walls go, the smaller heaven gets, until it's just a little blue eye watching you."

"The priest would not have appreciated such sentiments."

There had been a priest? Why would there have been a priest? The closer she got to Tony, the more distant he seemed.

"Who was here?" she asked. "At the burial service."

"All of us. Mercedes. Manolo. Moncho. Pepa. Paco. The neighbourhood. Your mother-in-law."

"Did you see him?"

"The coffin was nailed shut."

"What was it like?"

"Hot. The priest talked. The priest left. Manolo played the guitar. Moncho sang."

"That was it?"

"Pepa danced. Pure unholy fire, that Luz. Satanic loins. A man trap."

Spanish women are traps, and inside the traps are cradles—Kazantzakis again. But what was it Angel Ganivet had written? In Finland he had been amazed to see the women walking unescorted in the streets, just like the men. The northern cities had seemed healthy to him compared to Granada, where the men still locked up the women.

"I wonder how much things have changed since Ganivet's day?" she said.

"Not much. Cut open a Spanish woman. Inside, vanity and indolence."

"And how many women have you cut open to find this out?" Bella had returned without Eva noticing.

Carl shot a glance at Bella. Eva was startled by his anger, which she sensed rather than saw.

"No point trying to stare me down like that," said Bella. "I'm too old to be frightened by a pair of dark glasses."

He turned to Eva. "Why did you come here?"

She had moved away from him and was looking at the white carmens of the opposite hill. Tony had written: One day I'll take you to Granada. We'll rent a carmen . . .

Carl took a step towards her.

"Why don't you leave her alone," said Bella. "Haven't you got more than enough?"

His face was red and his jugular vein throbbing, but he smiled.

"You surprise me, Bella," he said. "Grasp what you can now. Isn't that your credo?"

He put a rigid hand on Eva's arm and said, "Tell me why you're here."

"I'm not sure why . . . except that after Tony died . . . and then his mother . . . my own parents were already dead and there was only me and Resa . . . I bought two tickets for Spain . . . I packed three suitcases . . . "

"I could use a drink," sighed Bella. "I hope our taxi comes soon."

"Forget the taxi. I'll drop you off. My car's over there."

"But . . . " said Eva.

"I was driving by when you arrived. I told the driver not to bother coming back."

Carl drove down the hill to the Plaza Nueva.

"This where you want to be let off, Bella?"

"A little farther along, if you don't mind."

"Sacromonte, you mean."

He turned and drove along the Carrera del Darro, which narrowed and curved dramatically. On the right, the river was still above ground, the Alhambra high above.

"It's as if the river is running to hide," said Eva.

"My carmen on the left," he said.

Eva leaned to look out the driver side, but couldn't tell which building he meant.

"Where does that word come from?" she asked.

"From Arabic. Karm. Implies duality. In this case, of house and garden."

"How is a carmen different from a regular villa?"

"It isn't."

"Isn't it like a miniature Arab palace inside?" asked Eva.

"*Palaces* are inhabited by *demons,*" said Bella from the back seat, in her Shakespearean actor voice. "Palaces are *habitations* for demons."

"So you're looking for an apartment," he said to Eva.

"News certainly travels fast. We don't know—we haven't even unpacked our suitcases yet—but if we do decide to stay for more than a few weeks, Manolo says he knows of a furnished one that we could move into right now."

"Cagey guitar maker."

"You think he's unreliable?"

"He's a Gypsy. Never trust a Gypsy. Be satisfied with the gesture. You're wasting time if you wait for fulfilment. Right, Bella?"

"Here will be fine," said Bella.

He let her off and turned the car around.

Eva waved but Bella had already walked away.

"Funny," said Carl. "I didn't have her pegged as a meddler . . . But tell you what. I'll show you my carmen. Great view from the balcony."

†

The carmen was two stories high. Double doors opened onto the Carrera del Darro, over which hung a wrought iron balcony. The view from the balcony was as promised: the river trickling below, the palace of the Alhambra rising up out of the trees on the other side. But from here the palace looked disembodied from the rest of the city, more separate than it had from Manolo's house.

Inside, latticework arches led into rooms with plush ottomans, intricately carved benches, and murals dominated by turbaned warriors. One room, its corners piled deep in satin pillows, had walls covered in gold brocade and silk. In another room a marble floor reflected stalactites dripping down from a high ceiling, giving the illusion of a stalagmite floor.

"I've retrieved the Moorish echoes," said Carl. "Except for the size of the house. That's Italian. And I put in central heating."

He told her that the carmen dated back to the second half of the eleventh century, to the Zirite dynasty of King Badis. Originally it had been five small houses divided into many tiny rooms.

He took her up to the roof and showed her a bronze equestrian—visible from higher up the hill, but not from street level. The equestrian moved like a blown sail, his lance pointing in the direction of the wind. Carl told her that the statue had come from the ruins of a palace near Plaza del Cristo. He deciphered the Arabic script on the shield: "King Badis said this is the way Andalusia must show itself."

He led her downstairs and outside into the garden. She sat under a grapevine surrounded by several olive trees, an orange tree, a fruit tree she didn't recognize, and two languid cypresses. Vines crept up an ancient wall, and in front of it, rose bushes. A tiered fountain in the centre of the garden shot up a single jet of water that cascaded down into a small pool, which then overflowed into a larger one.

He returned with a pitcher of sangría and two chilled glasses.

"That wall seems very old."

"Called piedra viva. Living stone. Used to climb to the top of the hill."

He poured the sangría and they clinked glasses. "So. Like it?"

"It's a veritable garden of enchantment . . . What kind of tree is that?"

He went to it and picked a fruit. "Prickly pear. Try it. Prickly on the outside. Lush on the inside."

She bit into the pear. Its sweet juice dribbled down her chin. She caught the juice with her finger and licked it. She could feel him watching from behind his sunglasses, and she wanted to ask about Bella—about the animosity at the cemetery—but she was afraid of vexing him. Instead she asked, "What do you think of Ruth?"

"No comment. She comments enough for all of us."

He sat beside her and they were silent, listening to the fountain.

"All through *The Arabian Nights* people are having perfumed baths," she said after a while, "before they eat, after they eat, before they go to bed—all sorts of rituals involving water . . . "

"Rituals not to be ignored. Remember the newly-wed steward? Went to his naked bride. First time. So excited he forgot to wash. She smelled garlic on his fingers. Cried out. Whipped him. Sent him to the governor. Cut off his thumbs, said the governor. And the big toes for good measure."

He topped up their glasses.

"People here don't bathe much. They take quick showers."

"Like the women not covering their heads?"

"Yeah."

"How long have you lived here?" she asked.

"Six years. Seven."

She closed her eyes and said, "Then you must have come about the same time Tony did."

"Yeah."

"Did you know him well?"

"Not well."

She opened her eyes. Carl was standing over her.

"Come with me," he said.

He took her hands and she allowed him to pull her up out of the chair. He led her back inside the house, to a large wooden door with a half-moon at the top.

"The original front door. Complete with lock."

"How amazing, it looks perfectly intact."

"But not virginal."

"What's on the other side?"

"Two rooms. The back room once opened out onto the courtyard. But the opening is walled over now."

He was standing very close to her, so close his breath was disturbing her hair.

"The key is missing. I'd love to have that key."

"To unlock the door, you mean."

"No. To lock it."

He pushed it open and cupped her shoulders in his hands, the pressure of his fingers enough to guide her through.

All around, hanging on the walls and suspended from the ceiling, were weapons of every size and shape: bows and arrows, javelins, spears, lances, shields, crossbows, arquebuses, spurs, and other unidentifiable pieces of metal. In one corner was a glass-doored cabinet filled with knives, and near it, a small door that was closed, and another larger doorway that was covered by beaded curtains.

"My treasure-trove."

"It looks like a museum," she said.

"I'm partial to antique weapons, especially those in use before the Fall of Granada. Modern artillery was used there for the first time—by the Christians—thereby rendering walls and towers forever obsolete."

"This must be an expensive hobby." And chilling.

He considered her for a moment, then said, "I'm a good photographer."

"Pardon me?"

"I'm a good photographer. That's how I finance this."

"Where do you keep them? Your photographs, I mean?" It occurred to her that she hadn't seen any in the house.

"I don't collect them. I sell them. It's how I make money."

He pointed to a crossbow that hung directly above her.

"Now there's an efficient weapon, accurate over eighty yards. It fires metal bolts feathered with wood or leather."

Something in the lower ranges of his voice made her giggle nervously. "It looks ghastly."

"It is ghastly. It produces such deep penetration and such huge wounds that its use was forbidden against other Christians. Not that anyone paid attention, of course."

He walked over to a quiver and pulled out an arrow.

"This arrow was made to carry poison. Poisoning is an art that lost popularity after the invention of the arquebus. The Moors used realgar, which the Greeks and Romans called aconite, or lycotonos because it was good for killing wolves. It's also known as arsenic disulfide. You can still find the plants in the Sierra Nevada–they're black in colour and pungent. You pick them and cook them until they come apart in shreds and the juice runs out, and then you cure them in the sun until they curdle and become strong."

It was odd. Since they had entered this room, his voice was no longer the staccato of a machine gun, but more like a resonating bass fiddle.

"You either shoot the poison into your enemy or you trick him into eating it. It takes very quickly, directly from the wound into the blood stream. First the victim becomes cold and lethargic, then he vomits and foams at the mouth. He weakens, falls, and dies."

"Is there a remedy?"

"Not once it reaches the heart. Before that, you can try and suck the poison out."

"Isn't that dangerous?"

"Very."

"I've read that there used to be men whose job was sucking out poison."

He walked over to the cabinet and opened one of the glass doors.

"On this shelf are daggers, and this . . . " he picked up an Islamic-style knife, testing the weight in his hand " . . . is a navaja–the favourite arm of the people. Some of these are small as a ring and some as long as a sword. This one was made in Santa Cruz. It's extremely sharp and perfectly balanced. The handle is copper, carved and inlaid with niello and blue enamel. Notice the three parallel incisions. They're meant to brighten the blade and are painted red, to intimidate."

The blade itself was in the form of a fish.

"Is that something written on it?"

"Cuando esta víbora pica, no hay remedio en la botica."

"When this viper stings, there's no cure in the pharmacy."

"Exactly."

He grabbed a cape from the wall and wrapped it around his left arm.

"Fighting with a navaja had its own etiquette, like fencing."

He began to circle her, waving the navaja in the air.

"Each artist had his own bag of tricks, his favourite blows. It used to be that at the sight of a wound, everyone could tell who had inflicted it."

He leapt and slashed the air. She stepped back.

"No need to be nervous," he said, unwinding the cape from his arm and placing it over her shoulders.

He brushed her breasts with the navaja as he went to replace it in the cabinet.

Her nipples tingled.

"What's behind the beaded curtains?" she asked.

"My baths."

"Your *baths?*"

"I'll show you next time. Tell you what. Meet me up at del Cristo on Thursday. I'm photographing the Aurora for a travel piece. Then I'm doing the Silencio. I'll show you my baths afterwards."

When Eva finally got to the Carmonas to pick up Resa, Manolo said, "Tomorrow night there's a full moon, the perfect time to see the Alhambra. If you like, I will come to your hotel just before dark, before everything is blocked off for the processions. We can drive up to the top of the Alhambra Hill and watch the sunset, and then we can visit the palace in the moonlight."

†

That night Resa said to her mother, "Mommy, I love Mercedes. She's always smiling, and she's all soft and she gives me cuddles that make me feel cozy like a kitten. She makes me feel like putting my head on her and purring and purring."

Sun and Moon

RUTH WAS MAKING PROGRESS AND SHE needed to tell someone. Maybe it was a little early yet to go knocking on people's doors, but Eva seemed to like her well enough, she would understand.

Ruth knocked, and a disarranged Eva opened her hotel room door.

"Oh, Ruth, hi. We're not really up yet, but it's nice to see you."

Ruth marched in and didn't wait to sit down. "I'm sure you remember those books I was talking about the other day, the ones that disappeared from the library at the university. Well, remember how I said the theft was discovered when a professor went to look for a particular manuscript? Now I haven't exactly met that professor but I have met a friend of his, an incredibly interesting man–I'll have to introduce you–he's a historian or an archaeologist or an architect or something–anyway, he told me that it's not just the university that has books missing, it's the Alhambra as well."

Resa sat up in bed. "Mommy?"

"We got in quite late last night," said Eva. She sat on the bed and started trying to soothe Resa back to sleep.

Ruth moved a chair close to the bed and sat down. She took a huge breath. "Now just listen to this: the wonderful and charming señor, his name is Miguel Angel Sanlúcar, by the way–isn't that a perfectly wonderful name? Señor Miguel Angel Sanlúcar, I just love how it rolls along the tongue, I'll have to use it in one of my stories—and he's a proper gentleman, too, so distinguished-looking, with a thick head of white hair, and he speaks impeccable English—he owns a house in Madrid, and another one in Italy I think he said, but I don't know if he's got a wife or not, he didn't mention one at any rate—Miguel Angel Sanlúcar, the name is so grand, don't you think? Anyway, what was I saying? Oh yes, I started talking to him, and he told me all about these restorations he's involved in at the Alhambra, supervising them I think, but for the moment he's set aside his work to check out their book collection, because of the thefts at the university you see, honestly, you should see the room he has, right inside the Alhambra, and he's allowed free access to all the books, as well as those at the university, and he's set up a cot in his room so he can spend the night there if he feels like it—now how's *that* for professional dedication? Imagine a man like that spending a night on a little cot. I really will have to introduce you."

"I think we've met him."

"You've met him?" sniffed Ruth. "Exactly when did you meet him?"

"On the bus from Málaga, when we arrived, and we saw him a few days ago at Manolo's. We might see him again tonight, actually. Manolo's taking us up to the Alhambra."

"You met him before I did, then . . . Even so, he and I hit it off right away, and when he found out I was a writer he showed me his room, but you can't imagine, his desk is an absolute heap of books, descriptions in Arabic of the Alhambra, with all these lovely old engravings, some scientific treatises, although he does have lighter reading, too, of course, for when he's tired, especially late at night, he has trouble sleeping, you know, and don't I know what *that's* like—anyway, I asked Miguel Angel if he was familiar with any of the books that have gone missing from the university, and he told me *no one* seems to know how many or even which ones are gone, because until now, no one had bothered to catalogue them. I mean it's an amazing story, let me tell you. He said there's no way to know for certain *when* the books were taken, let alone *what* was taken, although he did tell me the names of a couple of them: one is *The World of Maimonides,* which dated back to the twelfth century, and another was a book of poems by someone called Ishaq Aben something-or-other—"

"—Ishaq Aben Abu?"

"Oh. You've heard of him. Yes, well anyway, Miguel Angel thinks he remembers that there was even a book by one of the women poets of the day, although he hasn't ever read it, because he's not that interested in poetry, and neither am I, actually, although of course I'm interested in women writers in general. Now what was I saying? Oh yes, when Señor Sanlúcar–Miguel Angel–found out that I'm a writer–now there's a good angle for a story: vanished books and vanished women writers–how many of those vanished books were by women, and how is it that most of them vanished? I bet there's a whole book there waiting to be written–anyway, as I was saying, Miguel Angel sat down and wrote me out a list of women writers of the day–now look at this . . . "

Ruth pulled the list out of her purse and slapped it down on the bed.

Resa slid out of bed and went to the bathroom.

Eva examined the list: Ruth Shulam Delcampo was not on it.

"Now I ask you, what happened to this tradition of great women writers in Granada? Why did their work disappear? I know what you think, you think that most writers' works disappear anyway, but it's not true, you know, not everybody's work disappears, but the work of the women on this list has disappeared, utterly and completely. I guess we should feel lucky we have their names, but–and this is ironic–the only reason we know their names at all is that they're mentioned in contemporary accounts by men, accounts which *have* survived, I might add. Now listen to this–"

She snatched the sheet of paper back from Eva and began to read aloud from it.

"–Hamda bent Ziyad, celebrated poet, and she may have had a sister, Zainab, who was also a poet. Alcalaiyya, Leila, la Racunia, Mocha ben Abi Abderrazác–all poets, all women born in Granada, and nothing remains of their work, nothing. And yet you can still read all kinds of worthless male poems–even anti-Jewish ones, says Miguel Angel."

Like the one by Ishaq Aben Abu that touched off that pogrom, thought Eva.

"You would think Bella, at least, would be more interested."

"Why Bella?" Eva asked.

"Why because she's Jewish of course."

Resa came out of the bathroom. "Mommy, can we go get churros?"

"Yes, well you'll have to excuse me, I have to get going," said Ruth. "I've got a zillion things to do, and it's so hard to get around, what with all these processions and everything, but Miguel Angel told me

I should make sure and see the one up at the Plaza del Cristo tomorrow. If it wasn't for him recommending it I probably wouldn't bother, but if Miguel Angel says it's worth seeing it must be worth seeing. By the way, if you see him tonight tell him I said hello."

And she left as brusquely as she had arrived.

†

That night, true to his word, Manolo showed up just before dark. Eva had been expecting him to be late.

"Sorry, we're not quite ready. Resa's having a nap—she was up very early this morning."

"Don't wake her, I'll go down and have a coffee. No rush."

But as soon as Manolo was out the door, Eva woke up Resa and they hurried down to find him in the plaza.

His car was parked in the same place as before. He drove up past the Alhambra and stopped a short distance above the Generalife.

"This is la Silla del Moro, the Moor's Chair. I wanted you to see this first."

The view made Eva think of the one from the cemetery.

"It's easy to imagine Jesus in the desert surveying all the dominions, and almost giving in to the temptation of the devil," she said.

"Many years ago, when I was a young man, this was a place to bring one's novia and it was indeed a place of temptation, especially on such a night as this."

"Where's the moose chair?" asked Resa, a perplexed look on her face.

"There isn't an actual chair," said Manolo, smiling. "It's called the Moor's Chair because King Boabdil used to come up here to observe his soldiers in the vega, or just to think, or to do whatever else it is that a king does when he is by himself. In earlier times, before King Boabdil, this hill was known as the Hill of the Sun."

"Because the top is close to the sun," said Resa.

"Exactly. And do you know, thc first Moors to arrive found a palace with walls so old that the Roman ones looked new."

The sun began to fade and the three of them witnessed in shared silence that brief moment when day and night are one, and the vega was a flood of purple and gold. Then it blackened and the lights of Sacromonte and the Albayzín shone like nearby stars.

Manolo drove down to the Alhambra and parked near the Gate of Justice. They climbed out of the car.

"Risita hija, look up there," said Manolo, getting down on one knee and pointing up so as to guide her line of vision. "See that huge hand over the gate? It used to be that if you looked at it and said the right words, any bad luck that might be headed your way would be turned aside. Sadly, no one knows them any more. The words have been lost."

"But I know what to do for mal de ojo."

"Resa, how do you know about stuff like that?"

"Puri showed me."

"Well don't be frightened, sweetheart, it's all just superstition."

"I'm not frightened, Mommy, because I know what to do if someone does it to you." She stuck the forefinger and little finger of each hand up in the air. "If you do this, nothing bad will happen. You won't go cross-eyed or anything."

Manolo ruffled her hair.

"Actually, I thought that each of the fingers over the gate represented one of the five paths to God," said Eva.

"You could also be right," said Manolo.

"Puri told me to watch out at night, because mal de ojos can see in the dark, and at night los tíos van en busca de las niñas."

Manolo laughed. "Qué bien ¡hija! Already you're learning Spanish! Tell me, what else did my Purificación tell you?"

"She said los tíos have cara mala, and that's why children can't go out alone at night, because in the dark you can't tell if a face is a tío's face or not, but tíos can see *you* because they've got cats' eyes. Mommy, I think that man from the church is a tío. He's got a bad face, and he hides his eyes."

"Well, sweetheart, people aren't always as they seem, you know."

"Unfortunately, some people are exactly as they seem," said Manolo, "and if your daughter is referring to that American, she's right, you should be careful of him."

Funny, thought Eva, he says the same thing about you.

"And what about you, Manolo . . . are you exactly as you seem?"

Manolo bowed half-mockingly and spread his arms, indicating that the conversation was over and that they should enter the gate.

Last week, in the daylight, the unpaned miradores had directed one's sight outward to the flowers and trees, the fountains, the blue sky, and the snowy mountain peaks. Now, at night, the Alhambra was a marvel of weightless marble pillars, of hedged-in patios and floodlit pools of water, a house of artifice that embraced the sounds of screaming swifts and the occasional plopping of a frog off a waterlily leaf. What had looked brash and disconnected in the sunlight seemed now in the moonlight to be imbued with deep sense and soft uncertainty.

In the Court of Lions, the fountain glowed like silver filigree. Manolo pointed to one of the stone lions and said to Resa, "When the water is not flowing, you can place your mouth into his and whisper your secret wishes, and if someone you love places his right ear against the mouth of another lion, your wishes will be heard."

"Just like in the room with the talking wall!"

"Ah, so you have been in the room of the ten thousand secrets. Do you know, since forever, people have been whispering their deepest secrets into those curved walls. You can imagine how heavy they get, to the point that they become in danger of tumbling down, so every hundred years, on the anniversary of the unhappy night when King Boabdil forever left this palace, the walls release their secrets, all at once."

"Can you listen?"

"Oh yes, but it's very dangerous. You see, because they come out all at once, the words are in such a jumble and make such a racket that you can't make anything out. As a matter of fact, if you don't stick your fingers in your ears, the words can kill you."

"Maybe you could go and hide in a tunnel."

"You could."

"Puri showed me one."

"Are there any tunnels here?" asked Eva. The other night, Angel had mentioned secret passageways.

"They used to run all through here, but most were blocked up or forgotten long ago."

"What were they for?" asked Eva.

"In the days of rivalry between the Albayzín and the Alhambra, high walls were built to keep out the other side. And people being as they are . . . "

"You mean, spies used them . . . "

"And thieves, and lovers . . . no one likes to be kept out of heaven."

"And children!" shouted Resa. "I bet children played in them too."

"Oh yes, I am sure children played in them."

"Can you show us one, Manolo? Can you show us a secret tunnel?"

"Actually, I do know of one that used to lead to what were once the gardens of los Alixares, behind the Alhambra overlooking the Genil. From there you could climb to la Silla del Moro, where we were a while ago. Come to think of it, there was another over by the royal baths. It was said to go under the Darro and come out again near the church of San Pedro. When I was a boy we used to dare each other to go in, from the Albayzín end of the tunnel. It was very scary inside—pitch black with a smell of dead chickens. It twisted and turned and you had to feel your way in the dark. At the third turn was a slimy spot where you always talked with your friend until you were through it so you did not have to think about what you might be crawling in. Further on you didn't talk because there was a fork in the tunnel that you didn't want to miss. If you took the right fork you were supposed to end up here, in the Alhambra; if you went to the left you came to a secret door that opened onto the gardens of the Generalife; but if you went down the middle you fell into a pit. In the blackness, because of the way the tunnel twisted, it was easy to confuse the three forks, and we were always too frightened to go any further."

"I bet there was a secret treasure at the end," said Resa.

"It's possible."

"Let's go see it, show us the tunnel."

"All right, but it might not be there any more. Señora, señorita . . . this way . . . " He turned into a sombre hallway.

"Do you think there are tíos in the Alhambra?" asked Resa, grabbing her mother's hand.

Manolo put his finger to his lips. "¡Chist! . . . On moonlit nights such as this," he whispered, "the thirteen butchered Abencerrajes wander along these galleries with their heads tucked under their arms. Listen carefully . . . Sometimes you can hear their moans and the sound of their patting feet."

" . . . I think I hear them."

"Don't be silly, sweetheart. That's just the sound of the fountains."

Manolo halted and cupped a hand over an ear. "You're right, hijita, I think I hear something, too," he whispered.

Why is he trying to scare her? wondered Eva. I wish he would stop.

"But we aren't worried, hija. The Abencerrajes don't like to be seen, and are especially shy of children. So if we get too close to them, they are sure to run and hide."

"Just like bears," said Resa. "Do Amen-say-aves have babies? Maybe we should make lots of noise so they know we're here. We can sing loud."

Manolo laughed and began to sing: "Los dos ríos de Grana'aoo . . . uno llantoo-o . . . "

Resa skipped on a few paces ahead. She looked around the next corner and froze in her tracks.

"I saw one!" she said, racing back. "I saw one of those Amen-say-aves carrying his head!"

"It's all right, honey, don't worry," said Eva.

"Let's go and investigate," Manolo said, taking Resa by the hand.

"He was over there!"

"¡Chist!"

They tiptoed down another poorly lit hallway.

Of course there was no one at the end of the hallway, nothing but a closed door. Eva didn't know how to politely ask Manolo to stop this game. She didn't want Resa having nightmares.

"In these shadows it's not surprising you thought you saw something, sweetheart," she said.

"But I saw him! He had a cape and his head was under his arm, just like Manolo said, and he saw me and he ran away!" Resa pointed to the door. "I bet he went in there."

"Do you know?" said Manolo. "This is exactly the place I was going to show you."

He tried the door.

"It's locked, but behind it are the stairs leading down to the passageway I was talking about."

"Those stairs haven't been in use for years and years," said a raspy voice from behind them.

"¡Don Angel! ¡Hola! ¿Qué?" The two men clapped each other on the back and Angel exchanged greetings with Eva.

"Now Risita," said Manolo, "you see who is your mysterious Abencerraje?"

"No! It wasn't Don Angel."

Angel laughed. "And you, my little angel, tell me, how are you enjoying our palace in the moonlight?"

"It's kind of scary, but Manolo said he'd show us a secret tunnel."

"Sadly, there is nothing to show," said Angel. "This door is kept locked, for safety reasons–after all, it would not be good to have tourists breaking their necks on decayed steps–and the tunnel itself is all bricked up now. In any case, I doubt that anyone knows where the key is any more."

"Well, Risita," said Manolo, "I will have to find you another tunnel. For now, let us take advantage of our expert guide, who has so opportunely appeared before us."

"Where are you installed?" asked Eva. "Is it where Richard Ford stayed?"

"You mean the Partal? No, señora, I am in the Palace of Charles V."

"By choice?"

"Yes, by choice."

"I agree," said Manolo to Eva, "the Palace of Charles is a heavy grey cloud that shuts out the sun."

"You may call it heavy," replied Angel. "I prefer the word, 'substantial.' And you must agree that the Palace of Charles V is an appropriate residence for a Christian interloper. Poor old Charles, he wasn't so bad—misguided, perhaps, but a fair man who wished to extend the peace. And it is ironic that the palace which he built to proclaim the victory of Christianity over Islam was never completed."

"This man will also tell you that the Inquisition has been exaggerated," said Manolo.

"It's true. Did you know, señora, that in Spain, the Inquisition lasted three-and-a-half centuries, over which period 25,000 people were killed? In Germany, on the other hand, the witchhunt lasted half that time, yet 100,000 were burned. As you say in America, do we have a poor public relations department or what?"

"What about the burning of books?" asked Eva. "Last week I was reading that the first order of Archbishop Xímenez was that the mosques be consecrated, and his second that all books written in Arabic be burned."

"That is no exaggeration. Books were considered more dangerous than the sharpest sword. In all, 5,000 were burned, many of them covered with gold and silver and filled with priceless illuminations."

"How many would have survived to our day?"

"Impossible to tell, of course . . . By the way, yesterday I met a compatriot of yours who is also interested in books, a señora Kostyk. Do you know her?"

"Ruth. Yes, we saw her this morning. She said to say hello."

"An intriguing señora . . . "

"¡Hija mía! what are you doing on the floor?" said Manolo. "You think you will find books under there?"

Resa was on her knees trying to see through the crack under the door. She just knew the Amen-say-ave was in there somewhere.

She bet he was listening to them right now.

"We have neglected this beautiful child enough," said Manolo, stooping down. "Perhaps it's time to continue our tour. Don Angel, would you honour us by accompanying us?"

Angel bowed. "A pleasure."

"Despite his biases, my friend knows everything there is to know about the Alhambra."

"Not true. Despite forty years of study, not a week goes by that I do not discover something new . . . Now tell me, señora, señorita, is there anything in particular that interests you? Other than secret passageways?" Angel patted Resa on the head.

He must have been teasing the other night when he offered to show them to us, thought Eva.

"I know what to do for the mal de ojo," said Resa, pushing her fingers in the air and punching them at Angel. She looked cross.

"Careful with that," said Manolo, taking her hand.

"I'm interested in the inscriptions on the walls," said Eva as they began walking back toward the Court of Lions.

"They are not mere decoration; they are meant to be read. You may have noticed that the majority are at eye-level."

"Are you able to read them?"

"Many of them . . . On first sight the words look like flowers in an exotic garden, but on closer examination you notice that the garden is overgrown with weeds. Most are poems of official piety written to cull favour from the monarch of the day, or fawning prayers to God—'O calyx of the flower, shell of the pearl,' 'All power belongs to God'—that sort of thing."

In the Room of the Two Sisters, Angel indicated a poem by Ibn Zamrak. "His chief claim to fame is that he plotted the assassination of his mentor, Al-Khatib, and replaced him as official court panegyrist. This particular poem is in praise of Mohamed V—'Love is but a glance which arouses passion and occasions something which not even the healing physician is able to cure.' Slipslop, is that not what you say in English? Ibn Zamrak was himself assassinated by Mohamed's men."

"For writing bad poetry?"

Angel smiled.

"No murderer can be a true poet," said Manolo.

"Hijo, one must not confuse life with art."

"What has murder to do with life?"

"More than you would care to admit. Like this little girl, I too believe in ghosts."

Eva wondered at the tension between the two men.

"I can almost imagine living here," she said, "wandering through these halls, from room to room . . . " She pointed to some tiles on the wall. "Those colours seem so vivid, as if they were painted yesterday."

"That's because they probably *were* painted yesterday, and very crudely at that," said Angel. "What ugly blues and reds. Those garish colours are not the original hues."

She felt rebuked.

"Why not go look at the baths now?" said Manolo, putting his hand on her shoulder.

†

In the daytime, the ceiling in the baths had been stabbed and pierced by sunlight, and Eva had had no trouble picturing herself stretched out in the great marble basin, gazing up at the pieces of sky. Now, at night, moonlight covered the floor with soft star patterns.

"The women of the harem would enter the room naked," said Angel. "The king could watch them from a window in the adjoining room without himself being seen, and whenever he desired a woman, he opened the wooden shutters and threw an orange to the one who pleased him best. She who caught the orange was the one who would lie with him that night."

He showed Eva the niche where the queen had placed her slippers.

"While the queen bathed," he said, "blind musicians played in front of her. If the favoured musicians were not already blind, their eyes were removed, for they were forbidden to see her."

†

On the way back to the hotel, Resa looked out the car window and said, "That must happen when you get old, your voice wears away."

"What do you mean, sweetheart?"

"Like Don Angel's voice."

Manolo and Eva smiled at each other.

"Tomorrow night, at sunset," said Manolo, "the Virgin of the Alhambra will leave the church of Santa María. She will be carried through the Gate of Justice, down through these lighted woods to the Plaza Bibarrambla. To see her, it is best to walk up to the start of the procession, or you can watch her go by the hotel later. Come to think of it, our own Aurora will also be passing your hotel tomorrow night.

Why don't you come to the plaza and watch her leave our little church? I will come and get you. And you, Risita, you can watch for as long as you like, and go with my mother when you get tired. My mother never goes to the processions."

"I won't get tired," said Resa, rubbing her eyes.

"Thank you, but I think we'll walk up," said Eva.

"But it's no trouble at all to come for you. I would like it very much."

"Actually, we're meeting Carl at the plaza. He suggested we go early enough to watch the preparations."

Manolo's lips tightened.

"Muy bien, Eva . . . It is your choice. In any case, Risita, you must spend the night with us, especially if your mother goes to the Silencio, which goes on very late . . . And Risita," he said with a forced laugh, "have no fear—there are no ghosts living in our house."

Resa didn't answer. She was not happy. No one believed her. As if she couldn't recognize Don Angel. It was not Don Angel she had seen, it was an Amen-say-ave.

†

They rode the rest of the way in silence.

Light and Dark

RUTH ARRIVED AT THE PLAZA DEL CRISTO IN a taxi.

Bella, Carl, Eva, and Resa were seated not at Bella's usual table but closer to the church, at Paco's bar. Resa was busy colouring in a book of Walt Disney characters with Spanish captions.

"Honestly, people are so rude here," said Ruth, claiming the empty chair between Carl and Bella. "Do you know what just happened to me? I was walking through the plaza down there, you know, the one by the cathedral, just walking along minding my own business and this Gypsy tried to sell me a flower, and when I said no she started chasing me, pushing this fake rose in my face, and I kept shaking my head back and forth, emphatically I might add, saying no no, and you know what she did? She called me a pig. Porky porky porky she shouted, running after me—porky porky porky—can you believe it?"

"Maybe she was saying ¿Por qué?" said Eva. "I had the same thing happen to me last week, and I think she was saying '¿Por qué?' as in 'Why not buy it?'"

"Well, the point is, the woman was ill-mannered and wouldn't accept 'no' for an answer."

"Why doesn't Porky Pig have genitals?" said Bella, sucking on her cigarette. "Look—nothing below that shortie jacket."

Everyone but Ruth automatically looked at the figure Resa was colouring.

"What are you doing at this bar?" said Ruth, deliberately, to Eva. "I thought you always went to Moncho's."

"Carl said we can watch the preparations better from here, and as soon as the women have finished dressing the statue of Christ, we can go into the church and see it."

"Not Christ. The Virgin," said Carl. "There's a saying–'Aquí Cristo no sirve pa na.'"

"Which means?" said Eva.

"As far as miracles go, Christ just won't do," said Bella.

"He isn't popular?"

"In the north, he's Adonis," said Carl. "But this is the Tierra de María Santísima. Our Lady of the Sorrows is god. Virginity and fertility wrapped in one."

"What a vulgar notion," said Bella. She took a drink.

"An honourable idea from the Old Testament, I would have thought," said Ruth.

"Actually the notion of virginity is Pagan," said Bella, "not Jewish."

Ruth pursed her lips.

"Wasn't it the Phoenicians who brought the virgin priestesses to Spain?" said Eva.

Bella began to yoo-hoo and wave ostentatiously in the direction of the Mesón de los Milagros. "You'll have to excuse me," she said, "but there's a friend over there I want to see." She gulped down the rest of her drink and fumbled in her pocket.

"Don't bother, Bella," said Carl. "I'm buying today."

She dropped the money on the table. "I'll pay for myself," she said, and left.

"Not following her, Ruth?" he asked.

"Oh, the hell with her. Enough's enough. As far as the famous Isabella Flowers is concerned, I've pretty much had it up to here, I can tell you. I might just go ahead and write my article without her cooperation, I mean it's not as if I'm going to get anything new out of her, is it? Anyway, I may be on to bigger and better things–I was telling Eva about it yesterday–about those books missing from the university, and it looks like the Alhambra might be missing some too. Tell me Eva, did you go up there last night?"

"Yes."

"Alone?" said Carl.

"No . . . Manolo took us."

"Did you see Miguel Angel?" asked Ruth. "Did he mention me?"

"Yes, we did run into him, and he did mention you, very favourably. He graciously showed us around."

"Did he show you his room or talk to you about the missing books?"

"No."

Ruth looked pleased.

"Missing books," grunted Carl. "Another buried-treasure tale."

"What do you mean?" asked Eva.

"All rumour, no proof. Easy to claim something's missing if no one's seen it. Books probably weren't in the library in the first place. You should be more suspicious."

"Of everything?"

"This isn't Toronto."

"I'm not from Toronto, I'm from Edmonton."

"Well I'm from Toronto and I believe Miguel Angel," said Ruth, "I mean he's such a knowledgeable man, such an interesting interesting man."

"Hombre de mucho bigote," said Carl.

"But he hasn't got a moustache," protested Resa, looking up from a picture of Minnie Mouse, whose dress she was altering with purple flamenco flounces and green polka dots.

"Resa!" said her mother with delight. "You really are learning Spanish. It must be all that time you're spending with Puri."

"What was that you said, Carl, about Miguel Angel? You called him a bigot or something. Tell me what you called him," ordered Ruth.

"A man of many whiskers. Just an expression."

"Well, say what you like, but if you ask me he's a real Christian gentleman. Just because he says there are a lot of romantic myths about the Moors doesn't mean he's a bigot, it means he's an unbiased scholar. He says if you were a writer under the Moors and they didn't like what you wrote, you weren't any better off than you would have been during the Inquisition, that it was a matter of choosing the method of execution. Now isn't that an interesting way of putting it? Miguel Angel says that crucifixion was very popular with the Moors, and poisoning even more so–he's going to lend me some books about it. He says that under the Moors, many writers died violent deaths."

"Palace life was risky. Writers were no different from anyone else."

"From what I've read, wasn't Muslim Spain more enlightened than other parts of Europe?" said Eva. "I mean, I thought the Muslims were quite sophisticated, and familiar with the Greeks."

"Miguel Angel says that's all been exaggerated, he says they completely misunderstood the Greeks, that they–"

"–maybe misunderstood them," said Carl. "But recognized their value."

"Miguel Angel says the Muslims wiped out all the groups who were already here, and that the Christians didn't do anything different than the Muslims had done earlier."

"Except spread dullness."

"What about the Iberians?" said Eva to Carl. "Do you know much about them?"

"None of their scripts has been deciphered. In the Levant and Catalonia the scripts go left to right. In the south they go right to left."

"Another way the south and north see the world differently, I suppose," said Eva.

"But the oldest written languages aren't native. They're Egyptian. And Semitic. Brought by the Phoenicians. Classical writers refer to the rich *oral* tradition of southern Spain."

"This is all too academic for me," said Ruth, rubbing her temple. "I see you've brought your equipment," she said to Carl. "I suppose you're doing a piece on Holy Week."

"On the procession. Start to finish."

"I'm surprised you're not taking pictures of the dressing of the statues," said Eva. "Now *that* would make an interesting introduction."

He laughed, a rumble from his lower chest. "I tried. The women were horrified. A man watching them dress Aurora! No one, not even other women, are permitted to see the Virgin with her clothes off. Thought they were going to stick sewing needles in my eyes. Blind me."

"Like Tiresias when he surprised the bathing Athena," said Eva.

Ruth lifted her chin. "If you ask me it all sounds quite ghoulish, I mean really, treating a statue as if it were alive. Honestly."

"Like Saint Teresa's corpse," said Carl. "But it was bent like an old woman. To dress it, the corpse had to be stood upright. One person propped it up with a hand between the shoulders. Like this." He demonstrated on Eva. "The others dressed her. All unnecessary once the limbs were chopped off, of course."

Resa belched loudly and swung her leg, kicking her mother, who grabbed the swinging foot and smiled at the others unconvincingly.

"I feel another migraine coming on," said Ruth. "That's why I took a taxi up. I don't usually get them so close together—I had one just last night." She rummaged around in her huge leather purse and pulled out a bottle of pills. "Anyway, I suppose only a fool would walk in this heat."

"Me and Mommy walked!" said Resa.

"Actually, it seemed like nothing at all today," said Eva. "We're catching on to the Spanish way, you know, of crossing the street back and forth, following the pockets of shade. And I guess it helps now that we know where we're going."

"If it wasn't that Bella is impossible to find at night, I wouldn't come out in the middle of the day at all, especially not up here," said Ruth. "Mind you, as I told you, I came up to see this procession on Miguel Angel's advice, and I expect he'll be around in a while, but I can't sit like this for hours and hours, I really can't, not with the sun and the noise. Give me a good Canadian winter anytime, nice short days and long quiet nights."

The plaza was filling up with people. Half a dozen men were hammering a wooden ramp into place over the stone steps of the church, with another five or six commenting and dispensing free advice. Neighbourhood women in plastic hair curlers and slippers stood in small groups trading information and discussing their own preparations. ¡Coño! your little Susana can wear the dress my Nuria wore last year—it will fit her perfectly!

Eva saw Rafael and his wife Encarna from the party, both in a small gesticulating circle of people that also included Don Elías the schoolteacher. La Abuela, the woman with the drunken husbands, sat in the shade, a shawl wrapped around her shoulders, her cane leaning against a doorjamb. Juán Pepe the baker was by himself in the middle of the plaza, his thin mouth stretched across his gums in an idiotic grin. Eva would have said novenas for him not to notice her, but she was saved when a thin woman holding her side with one hand came limping up behind and poked him in the back with a stick she had been waving around with her free hand. Juán Pepe turned and meekly walked away with her.

Chairs appeared on balconies and more people streamed into the centre of the plaza. Men in white robes jammed into Paco's bar and were joined by stylish women in black dresses and lacy mantillas over their sculpted hairdos. The dresses were long-sleeved with Pius XII necklines, but formfitting and hemmed to a length that touches the floor when kneeling. From each female waist dangled a shiny black rosary. The men barely glanced at the women, but slid along the bar to make room for them. Clusters of children ran in and out. Eva noticed Rafael's grandson Juanito-the-scratch pressing a conical hood under one arm and raising a beer with the other.

"Mommy, look! Puri and Manolo!"

Puri and Manolo were indeed approaching the bar, and with them, the princess and the harlequin. Today, the princess was dressed in black like the women, and the harlequin like a naughty-looking altar boy. Resa darted out to greet them, upsetting her teetering chair in the excitement.

"That Manolo," said Ruth, "now there's what I call a nice man, don't you think so, Carl? He's really just too nice."

"Nice?" said Carl. "Nice means stupid. Blind."

Ruth stiffened.

Elaborate and extensive Spanish greetings were exchanged all around before Manolo consented to sit down. The children ran off to play.

For some time, old women in black had been entering and exiting the church–importantly, quickly in and out. The word spread: Aurora's toilette is finished; any time now she will be ready to receive visitors. Soon the doors of the church would be open.

"I can't wait to see her," said Eva.

"Count me out," said Ruth, massaging her forehead with her fingertips, "I'm going to have to go back to my hotel–I think I'll phone now for a taxi–hopefully they can still get up here, but who knows, with the crowds and all. I probably shouldn't have come, despite Miguel Angel's insistence. I wonder if he's up here, has anyone noticed? Anyway, this is all a bit too realistic for me, and then–who knows?–if I leave now maybe I can get some work done this afternoon, after all, it's a writer's job to write, not dash around here and there watching parades–writing is hard work you know, it's not what people think."

She went into the bar to phone.

"That woman. Hasn't learned that the most interesting moments arise from silence," said Carl.

"Actually, I don't mind her at all," said Eva.

"Your friend la Muda has that type of illness which takes over a child when a new baby is born in the family," said Manolo.

"You mean jealousy?"

"My mother calls it——" Eva thought he said "protruding anus."

"On that note," said Carl, "let's check out this Virgin. I need pictures."

Eva stood up. "You're not coming, Manolo?"

"I've seen her many times. I'll sit here and watch the children."

Inside the church, María Santísima de la Aurora was being greeted by nods and murmurs of approval. She gazed out from under a sumptuous silver canopy surrounded by gladioli. Her veil of fine white lace was held in place by a gold crown, and her brocade mantle, also white, was intricately embroidered with golden thread.

I saw the Virgin of the Alhambra last year, said a woman, and she was terribly overdressed. I know, I saw her too, said another, and I saw the Virgin of Peace–now it's true, the work on her mantle was quite good, but not nearly as elegant as that of our Aurora. Yes, said a third, this is the best handiwork in all of Granada, and Aurora is the most beautiful of the Virgin Marys, everyone says so.

Off to one side, Aurora's wooden son, Nuestro Padre Jesus del Perdón, stood awkwardly tied to his pillar, his unblinking eyes directed to a faraway heaven in an invisible horizon. Painted blood poured out of his wounds into a bed of red carnations.

Back outside the church, the men were banging the last few nails into the ramp and the harlequin was kicking a soccer ball around with four other small boys in altar boy outfits. Carl snapped a few more pictures and he and Eva went back to the table.

Drums pounded close by.

The band! someone shouted. The band is coming!

"The return of the Falange," spat Manolo, who did not deign to raise his eyes when the corps of humourless young men in army boots and berets marched into the square.

The young men arranged themselves in front of the ramp and both bars emptied of their penitentes, acolytes, and coy women and girls veiled in black–all of whom were swallowed up into the church along with two or three dozen young men in white T-shirts and blue jeans who had been restlessly milling about.

"The costaleros," said Carl. "A relief squad takes over in Bibarrambla. The halfway point."

"How long from now will that be?" asked Eva.

"Three, four hours . . . They'll be coming out of the church any minute. I'll get the bill."

"No. Pago yo," insisted Manolo, jumping up and rushing inside the bar.

"Hasta luego to you too, Manolo. Never take Spanish pride lightly." He patted his camera equipment. "Listen, Eva. I want to get in close. Catch up to me later."

As Eva watched him make his way to the ramp near the church, the two girls came running up.

"Mommy, Mommy! Can I go play at Puri's house?"

"Don't you want to watch the procession, sweetheart?"

"I want to play with Puri. Please Mommy please?"

"Bien, Risita, you come back to the house with me–my mother will be thrilled to see you," said Manolo, returning to the table. "It's good for Risita to be with other children," he said to Eva. "How else will she learn to speak? She can spend the night at our house–one procession will be enough for her, anyway, and they go one after the other, all night long, and the later it gets, the more dangerous it gets. I see you left your purse behind–good. La Semana Santa attracts ladrones from all over Andalucía–purse-snatchers, thieves, professional outsiders of all descriptions. Especially the Silencio. When the lights of the city are turned out, the Albayzín is not a good place for a woman to be wandering about alone."

"It's all right, I won't be alone–I'll be with Carl."

"Even more reason to be careful."

Not again! Eva felt herself flush.

"I'm serious. Remember, you have a beautiful little girl to think about, a little girl who has already lost one parent."

Now that's really overstepping the mark, she thought.

"Can I stay at Puri's, Mommy?"

"Just a minute, let me think . . . " It did seem like an imposition, and she wasn't sure if she wanted to feel obligated to Manolo. She looked over at Carl taking pictures near the ramp. Who am I kidding? she thought. Six years is a long time.

Eva relented, eliciting squeals of delight from the girls. Not without mixed feelings, she kissed Resa good-bye and snaked her way through the crowd to the ramp.

Ruth shoved in beside Eva. "I don't know what I'm going to do, it's impossible to get a taxi, they won't send one up here, not for hours at least, so it looks like I'll have to walk back. Can you tell me the quickest way down? I've really got to get out of this sunlight."

But the crowd suddenly mashed in, everyone attentive and facing the front of the church.

At the top of the ramp was a cross bearer holding a splendid gold crucifix, flanked on either side by a penitente with a sanctuary lamp. Behind was a cluster of steepled cowls with the skulls' eye holes of the Ku Klux Klan. Under the menacing hoods, was it possible? Don Elías the teacher and Juanito the disc jockey, and presumably other innocent faces Eva had just seen in the bar.

The penitentes, three abreast, began the slow walk down the ramp, and the crowd pressed forward. Ruth groaned.

Eva looked at her with concern. "Are you all right?"

Ruth's face was drawn, her eyes sunken and lusterless. Eva mistook the migrainous signs as a reflection of her own discomfort with the dramatic scene before them. "I'll show you the way down as soon as the crowd clears," she said, feeling a surge of warmth towards Ruth.

The banner of the brotherhood was next through the church doors, followed by what was to be the first true test of the ready-made ramp—the unwieldy gold and red paso of Jesus del Perdón.

The band struck up a march. Two dapper men in black suits rushed up to the front of the paso and lifted the hem of its velvet skirt, checking that all was in order below. Then, shuffling backwards, buttocks in air, the two men successfully guided the paso to the bottom of the ramp. The men dropped the hem and smoothed down the skirt, and the rolled-up pants of twenty-four pairs of legs were again hidden from view.

Behind Jesus—girls in black, hands lightly pressed together in prayerful aspect, followed by the women who only hours before had been gossiping in their slippers and hair curlers. The procession paused, and the girls and women in black stood motionless, soaking in but not acknowledging the stares of the men in the crowd.

The crowd pressed even closer.

She's coming, Aurora is next, whispered a woman behind Eva.

And finally she, Aurora, looking decades younger than her hunched-over son, appeared at the doors of the church and floated languorously down the rampway above her own blind crew of costaleros.

Most of the people followed, moving towards the hill.

"I'm going to have to sit down," said Ruth.

Eva put an arm around her and Ruth allowed herself to be guided through the thick crowd. Eva spotted Carl in the wake of the procession, busily snapping pictures. Damn, she thought.

But she couldn't abandon Ruth. She would have to arrange a later rendezvous. She led Ruth to a chair outside Paco's now-deserted bar.

"Do you mind waiting here a minute?" she said, but when she turned Carl had disappeared with the others down the hill.

The crowd thinned more quickly than it had collected, and Ruth declared herself ready to go back to her hotel. Eva led her the quick way down to the Plaza Nueva, but the taxi stand was temporarily hemmed in by a second procession. The road up to Ruth's hotel was also blocked.

"It's okay, I'm feeling better, I'm sure I'll be all right," Ruth insisted.

But she didn't look better–if anything, she seemed to be sweating more profusely. Eva persuaded her to go back with her to Los Tilos.

"It's no bother, really. Resa's at Manolo's, and anyway, I want to watch the Aurora pass through Bibarrambla." Maybe she would see Carl pass by as well.

†

Night fell quickly. Ruth lay down on Eva's bed, and Eva went out on the balcony.

†

She watched the competing cofradías filing by with their heavenly burdens of wounded Christs and weeping dolorosas, the black trains of women with hands cupped to protect flickering candles from the breeze. Now and then a procession stopped for a saeta, and two or three penitentes nipped into the nearest bar for a quick drink.

†

Ruth came out on the balcony just as the Aurora procession was approaching.

"I can't sleep here, there's just too much stimulation, I'll have to get back to my own hotel."

"Do you want me to go with you?"

"I'm sure I can manage, but I'd also like a bite to eat while I'm at it. I know, I've got an idea, you come with me."

Eva's heart sank slightly, feeling intimations of times when, as a child, she had nursed her mother through certain drunken episodes.

"Miguel Angel told me about this fish restaurant that's supposed to be pretty good," said Ruth, "it's just on the other side of the plaza."

Maybe I can catch the end of the Aurora procession after dinner, thought Eva. Bella said that was the best part anyway.

The two women took the elevator down and picked their way through the crowd in the Plaza de Bibarrambla to the restaurant.

Eva wondered if she would see Carl again tonight. Nothing to do about it now, she thought, and ordered a carafe of white wine.

†

An hour later the wined pair of women made their way back out into the street.

Ruth, full of bonhomie and exuberance, had changed her mind. "I'm going back up with you," she announced to a disappointed Eva.

†

In the Plaza del Cristo, the two women stood pressed against one another in the crush of people anticipating the appearance of Jesus on the Pillar. Those near the church were the first to hear the roll of drums—¡Ya viene! ¡Ya viene! they called, tossing the news up and back until it had reached the people at the farthest edges of the plaza. ¡Llega ya!—He's coming! He's almost here! and then ¡Ya está!—He's here! Jesus is here! and the band struck up a tune just as Jesus was carried into the plaza, the costaleros under the heavy velvet skirt no doubt as exhausted as He Himself must have been after lugging the cross up Golgotha. A man on the balcony above the bakery spread his arms and began a saeta—O Cristo divino . . . No! Stop! Indignation from the group under the balcony: A paid singer!/el Zurdo says the brotherhood hired him/I know him, he's Conchita's nephew, from Córdoba/what have things come to, as if our Jesus needs a hired singer, one from Córdoba yet! The nephew finished his saeta to scattered applause. More indignation: Listen to that! What ignorance! As if one applauds prayers! Granada's getting as bad as Sevilla! The bearers of Jesus set down the litter and collapsed underneath in a communal groan. Above, with the patience of God, their carved Master awaited the arrival of his mother.

The wait wasn't long. The word spread—She's coming! The Virgin is coming! and then there she was, the band striking up once again, a rumba this time. The candlelit procession moved dramatically towards the resting Jesus. ¡Aurora! shouted a woman—¡Aurora! ¡Aurora! Another answered—¡Guapa! ¡Guapa! ¡Guapa! The cry was taken up by another, and another, until hundreds of sanguine voices were crying out their unabashed approval. ¡Aurora! ¡Aurora! ¡Guapa! ¡Guapa! ¡Guapa! Bodies pushed and fingers groped to touch the Virgin's paso. Aurora, weightless above the sea of people, resplendent in the light of a thousand candles; Aurora, gracious mother of God, dispenser of graces, deign to smile upon our desires and undertakings.

The men who had been resting under the haunches of Jesus stood and hoisted him anew onto their shoulders, and he began to sway and dip in time to the music, an impatient bridegroom at the altar watching his chaste bride move up the aisle. Aurora responded, and mother and son danced towards each other across the plaza. The people cheered. Those closest to Aurora snatched white flowers from her paso and threw the extras to those behind. Someone caught two at once and handed one to Eva. She stuffed the carnation into her pocket.

A voice said into her ear, "Isis. Keening for the dead Osiris."

Carl.

The band paused and above the crowd lifted the first strains of another saeta which carried traces of the solemn voices that had once called from the towers of the mezquitas. This time the crowd listened. Eva made an effort to understand the petition: You, Aurora, white as snow; Hear this Gypsy, all in black . . .

At the end of the woman's saeta, Conchita's nephew on the balcony took advantage of the silence and began to sing again, but the crowd would have none of it and with his first note began to mumble and cluck its disapproval. No professional singers for our Aurora! protested a woman, and the crowd worked itself up again—one song from you, fine; but two? no, it's too much, it's unacceptable—until soon there were so many hisses and boos that the nephew was forced to retreat inside the house midway through his song. The crowd applauded. When, a few minutes later he poked his head out (to see the pageant this time) he was shouted at so terribly that he was again forced to retreat, and after several other attempts finally gave up and stayed inside.

The band struck up a pasodoble, and Aurora and Jesus fell in with a swaying intensity, Jesus dipping and sliding before his swooning young mother. ¡Aurora! ¡Aurora! shouted a man, overcome. ¡Guapa! ¡Guapa! ¡Guapa! answered the crowd, moving as one, reaching towards her. ¡Eres la más guapa! Aurora, Aurora, queen of all else that is beautiful, glorious mother exalted above the choirs of angels, clothed in the light of the moon, source of power over darkness. ¡Guapa guapa guapa! the crowd in a frenzy of abundance.

Fireworks exploded high above, pounding the sky. Eva slumped back, relaxing the length of her body against Carl's, oblivious to the other bodies that pressed and pushed.

But does he ever take off those dark glasses?

†

The crush of people, the raucous voices, and now firecrackers—it was all too much. As her wine-induced exuberance wore off, Ruth became convinced that something sinister was afoot.

Once again she had fooled herself, pretending that if she ignored it, it would go away. Yet there it was, lurking behind the eyes, biding its time.

Three more firecrackers burst, boomed, shattered the sky into a shower of sparks, and immediately thousands of tiny white stars swarmed and flitted across her field of vision. She squinted her eyes shut, but behind her eyelids a kaleidoscope of disintegrating Virgin Marys whirled and tumbled like snowflakes, and she felt herself stumbling, being pushed from behind, and then she was losing her balance, falling through space. She opened her eyes and saw that she was being supported by the people in front of her. It was intolerable that they should be propping her up, she had to get out of here, right now.

Aurora shimmered, rippled, undulated through air which was like watered silk.

Ruth couldn't see Eva anywhere.

She felt abandoned. She said to herself, all right, if you can just get back down this hill, even if you don't make it up the other one to the hotel you might at least find somewhere quiet where you can sit and gather your forces.

But she was at the wrong end of the plaza. She would never be able to get through that huge crowd.

She was disoriented, but she had to get out of here, she would take a chance, try an alternate route. She chose the street from which the procession had entered the plaza, and commanded her unenthusiastic legs to pull her through, against the flow.

Silence

Oye, hijo mío, el silencio.
Es un silencio ondulado,
un silencio,
donde resbalan valles y ecos
y que inclina las frentes
hacia el suelo.

The huge crucifix of the Silencio was passing above the crowd. From the shared stillness and darkness Eva listened to the boom boom of the drum and the clanging of the chains of the barefooted penitentes as they escorted the Saviour along the cobblestone streets. The main sources of light were candles and the moon, but here and there a face in the crowd was briefly lit by the glow of an inhaled cigarette. Eva thought she caught a glimpse of Bella, fingers in a characteristic O around a cigarette.

Carl was explaining the procession. "The message of the Crucifixion–same as the Black Death. The strongest of men can be felled in a day."

A few people in the crowd began to object. ¡Chist! ¡Silencio!

Carl continued to talk, not lowering his voice. "The candles. Torches. All to exorcise the spirits of death. In the old days the penitentes whipped themselves raw."

¡Chist! ¡Chist!

Eva felt the muscles of his arm tighten.

"Sheep! Rule-bound fools!" he muttered between his teeth.

She thought she felt him harden against her, but when she turned he wasn't there.

He had warned her that it was likely to happen. After all, he was working, and sometimes he would have to move quickly to get a picture. In the dark, in the spill of the crowd, it was more likely than not that they would be separated. If so, he would meet her later in the Plaza Nueva.

She waited for a break in the procession and worked her way across the street to the spot where she thought she had seen Bella, but Bella wasn't there. Probably it hadn't been her in the first place. Eva, disappointed, made her way back to the river side of the street.

As the end of the procession neared, the crowd swelled and shifted to follow, then suddenly came to a dead stop. Eva breathed in the smell of burning wax and listened to the trickling of the Darro behind and below.

†

Lorca the moon poet was killed on a moonless night.

I'm a poet, he said, and no one kills poets. He was turning down a chance to escape to New York.

He was killed in the Sierra de Alfácar, near a fountain known in Nasrid times as the Fountain of Tears, and near the palace where the poet Al-Khatib had himself been murdered centuries before. Today Alfácar is famous for the sweet bread made from its waters.

After the first round of shots, Lorca realized that he was not dead. He got to his knees and cried, I'm alive! I'm still alive!

The coup de grâce was given by one Juán Luís Tres Castro, who boasted later that morning in Granada that, for good measure, he had fired two more bullets into the ass of the poet because the creep was, after all, a queer.

†

Everything had stopped.

Bella looked into the eyes of the hooded figure who was facing her, not quite touching her.

He was part of the crowd but he might as well have been invisible, a nonperson under a hood and robe. Only his eyes moved.

"I know those eyes," she said. "'The glittering eyes in a death's head.'"

She caught a glint of steel as his gloved hand drew something from inside his cloak.

"So that's it, you've come for me," she said.

Ahead, in the distance, a woman was singing.

En esa cruz enclava-o
te miro . . .

†

The hooded figure peered intently through the two slits of his hood at the woman who lay still at his feet. Satisfied, he took a couple of steps back.

One by one the people nearest the prone woman became aware of her. A man knelt and turned her face up. My god, he said, crossing himself, Es muerte. Others bent over her—Muerte, they repeated, the woman is dead.

The cloaked figure slipped away into the night.

A woman in black, also invisible in the darkness, finished her lament to the nailed Jesus giving up his soul to his father in heaven:

Cristo divi-i-no-o.
Eres un lirio troncha-o-o-o.

†

Eva was aware of some sort of commotion across the street, but slowly the mass of people began to move again, stopping and starting several more times. She stayed with it as far as the Plaza Nueva.

†

The alarm spread immediately up the Albayzín hill and down the other side into the rest of the city. A woman is dead, stabbed. A foreigner.

†

Ruth was lost in the midst of another loathsome procession. Above her the thorned head of the crucified Jesus seemed to stretch and rise up like a giant puppet head wobbling on an elongated el Greco neck. The distention in her own head threatened to expand into a crippling attack, and she squeezed her eyes shut.

The eyelids were no protection. Everything inside was blurring into a disgusting intimate otherworldliness, and she found herself wishing for a tragedy, some terrible occurrence which would correspond to and justify her misery.

She reopened her eyes. Jesus was gazing down at her meaningfully: He wanted something. No, she said, I have nothing to give, and his eyes rolled inward until only the whites showed. Blood ran down the face until the head was a maw circled in hair and thorns. The eyes rolled forward.

She turned and ran, bumping through the crowd. She could feel the head twisting towards her, the unblinking eyes following the back of her head.

She fled, but the next street and the next seemed overrun with Saviours and Virgins, and before she knew it, she was back on the Carrera del Darro facing the beseeching eyes.

Suffer the little children unto me, the red maw said, and Ruth realized that it was her uncle, her uncle with his scratchy face and veined nose and stained teeth. He turned slowly until he was facing her in three-quarter profile, like a painting, staring at her with the intensity of a self-portrait.

Come on, he said, you knew what you were doing, you knew exactly what I wanted. Remember? I hardly had to beg at all. Some girls are born knowing, I guess—no no, don't pretend to *me* you didn't know what was going on, don't try and tell *me* you didn't like it. You always were older and wiser than the others, old enough to know better, even your mother said so. Come on now, you liked it, admit it.

He smiled down on her with that special smile of his, the one he saved only for her. She could smell his yellow teeth.

Yeah, big for your age, you were, with a big wet mouth to match, but I sure shut it up fast enough.

But her mouth was small, dry, cold; she couldn't have spit if she wanted to.

The body seemed to have bloated out to gigantic proportions, shutting out the sky.

I know what you are, the maw spat out.

Ruth stuck a finger in each ear, but the voice was inside her head—Fruit of the womb, fruit of thy womb Jesus . . . Nothing happened! said another, familiar voice that could have been her own, but wasn't, for her tongue was too thick to speak, and her lips too numb . . . Fruit of the womb, fruit of thy womb Jesus . . .

Her head felt as if it were ripping from the inside. Surely this time the sutures of her skull must split.

Señora, what's wrong? ¿Señora? What's she doing? What's she saying? The woman is mad, possessed! Let her through! Several people crossed themselves and one old man raised his fingers against the evil eye.

She stumbled through the dark until she didn't have the strength to fight any more. Her legs gave out and she fell on the ground, in the weeds. Let me suffer in peace, she thought. Please.

†

How long had it been before she had noticed her swelling breasts? First had come the nausea, then weeks and weeks of overwhelming fatigue, the constant ache in her uterus, all those horrid baths in scalding water. Who had made her drink the turpentine?

There had been a strange house, a pale skinny man opening a side door, a woman nudging her through the doorway. The woman looked like her mother, but it wouldn't have been her mother.

The man had led them into a kitchen. In the middle of the kitchen was a table covered with a yellow blanket. Get up, said the man. Do what he says, said the woman who looked like her mother. Then the woman held her down while the man stuck something in her.

Why did you wait so long? he said. It's very big.

Her legs were shaking, the whole kitchen table was shaking. Keep her legs spread, he shouted, knees up, knees up! The woman who looked like her mother pressed her legs open hard. It hurt. The skinny man took a sausage fork and scraped around inside. Then he stuck his hand in and tore something out.

A small animal whimpered.

She hadn't seen any pets.

She sat up and slid off the table.

Jesus Christ! what's she doing, you're supposed to be holding her down! She's bleeding like a sow, bring her back, she's going to get it on my new carpet. The skinny man grabbed a towel and stuffed it between her legs.

But not before she had seen it hanging down, swinging from the cord.

†

No, no, moaned Ruth, it didn't cry, it couldn't have cried because it wasn't there. It couldn't have been there because nothing happened.

†

The yellow blanket was soaked in blood. Someone screamed. Shut her up, the man said, I've got neighbours you know. The woman who looked like her mother slapped her face and said shut up, haven't you caused enough trouble.

The man poked his head out the side door. The coast is clear, he said, don't let her wash for two weeks, not even her hair.

†

Ruth knew that she could not trust herself to stand, so she stayed down in the weeds. She felt horribly, completely out of control.

She drifted in and out of sleep. Once she thought she was awake, but then she knew she wasn't because the world was without colour. Another time she was sure she had woken herself up, but the sky was a ceiling of Arabic script: inscriptions, poems—all indecipherable—and she felt trapped inside a nightmare Alhambra. She tried to will her eyes open, but the ceiling began to chant: God knows all knows all knows all, is everywhere everywhere, there is no escape no escape no escape. The ceiling of chants moved lower. Tails and curlicues split off and dropped until she was smothering under a pile of mumbling broken words.

Her eyes were open. She was awake, really awake this time. But what did it matter? She pressed her throbbing temple into the ground. The moist earth smelled like her own blood—but no, it was more, much more than that—it was the intensely disagreeable odour of life.

After a while her heavy breathing subsided and her mouth filled up with sour vomit. She crawled to her knees and retched, again, and one last time, a dry hopeless heaving that brought no relief.

Never had she felt so weak, cared less about anything, about anyone, about herself. She entered a state of unmasked ugliness and of such deep self-loathing that she wished only to die.

It's no use, she said to herself, there's no one to help you, there will never be anyone to help you; you're alone, you will always be alone, you might as well accept it as the condition of your life.

And as she gave in to her despair, as she sank into a moment of stillness and timelessness in which she herself did not seem to be present, she began to feel relief. The thundering in her head began to subside and she could hear the trickling of water.

She opened one eye, to test. Yes, that was better. She opened the other.

The Alhambra was lit up, high above her.

She heard another sound, not water, more like falling pebbles.

She saw a shadow. A glitter.

She watched the shadow disappear into the ground not thirty metres away. She closed her eyes, and tumbled into a long, deep sleep.

†

Resa too was asleep, dreaming.

She was at the ocean. There was a bridge, a man with no face hiding under it, on the other side.

Her mommy was going to cross the bridge. But it was made of toothpicks, bent over the ocean like a bow aiming an arrow at the sky.

Then she saw sharks. They were trying to knock the bridge down. But her mommy was going to cross it anyway.

Resa tried to call, Mommy! Mommy! but the words stayed inside her head. She tried to run to her mommy but her legs didn't move. The sharks were getting closer and closer. The toothpick bridge was jiggling. Resa wanted to tell her mommy to come under the blanket where she would be safe.

But her mommy didn't seem to want to come under the blanket with her.

†

Ruth opened her eyes to a lightened sky and stumbled up the bank to the Carrera del Darro. Thank goodness, the streets were almost deserted. She walked to the taxi stand and took a cab up to the Washington Irving, hurrying through the front doors and up the back stairs to her room.

No one must see her in such a state.

†

Eva's immediate reaction was anger.

How was it possible? A woman killed, and yet the procession had continued, formally and deliberately as if nothing had happened, as if this grandiose piece of theatre still mattered.

Who were these people anyway? Strangers, indifferent unfathomable strangers. First they had killed Tony, and now someone else was dead, another foreigner, and not twenty metres away from where she had been standing. She was sick of them and their hot climate. They could keep their flaming blood and their superior pathos-steeped souls.

Yet she had kept moving along with the rest of them.

And then she remembered Resa and was frightened. What had she been thinking, abandoning her precious child to strangers? Manolo, Mercedes–what did she really know about them? She had to get up to the house right away.

She forced her way through the clamour and chaos to the nearest back street, but it was so dark and empty she lost heart. Perhaps if she went back to the Plaza Nueva, she could wait there for the lights of the city to be switched on. And if she was lucky, Carl would be there by now. She needed someone from close to home, someone with a common vocabulary, someone who could help her sort things out.

But what if he didn't show up?

And suddenly, unexpectedly, there he was, Carl taking hold of her elbows, talking sense, saying it's okay, I'm here, everything will be all right, there's no reason to panic, his voice telling her to come, come with me darling, consoling her, calming her down.

He's right, she thought, by now Resa will have been asleep for hours. What's the point of going up there at such an ungodly time of night, waking everybody up, upsetting Resa for nothing.

Carl walked her back to her hotel.

Darling, he had called her darling.

She wanted him to come up to the room with her. But once there, she found that she couldn't.

Not here, not in this hotel. Not in this room, not in this bed so permeated with dreams of Tony.

Oh I don't know what I want, she cried, but she knew that she didn't want to be alone.

Come on, said Carl, I'll take you out somewhere.

†

In the plaza again, looking up at him under the hotel balcony, she asked, Do you sleep with your dark glasses on?

You'll see, he said, and kissed her below the ear.

And it was not the singing of the Andalusian nightingale she heard, but the ringing of the hammer.

All or Nothing

EVA AWOKE IN A SMALL WINDOWLESS ROOM. Daylight entered through a grating high up near the ceiling.

She was alone in the bed, naked. Her throat was dry and sore, as if she had slept with her mouth open. Her anus was throbbing slightly. She had been dreaming.

Of what?

Of swan maidens, speaking apes, forbidden rooms guarded by ghostly Tartars and Berbers. In one room had reigned the Queen of Serpents with her attendant monkey. The queen had twisted her snake body and shaken her human head of hair and said, Come see the shifting sands of Bagdad. We'll visit the pope's cave, the baboon's prison. The monkey had peered at Eva with one yellow eye and waved a banana at her, but she had not been able to make out its face. That's not really a banana and he's not really a monkey, the queen had said, it's the mounted Saracen in disguise. He used to ride for Hippias. He possesses the sword of Sodom, the spear of Alexander of Macedon, the steel of Caesar, the blade of Bonaparte, the lance of Louis, the foil of Frederick, the pike of Peter the Great, the sword of Boabdil. Long live Carlo Gesualdo! the monkey had shouted, winking his yellow eye. Then he had transmogrified into Tony, who had floated up to the ceiling and grinned down at her. My Flower of Samos, my Aversa Venus, he said, but it wasn't Tony, it was something about to sink its fangs into her neck, and she woke up.

Eva looked down and examined herself. There were teeth marks on her left shoulder, more above the right nipple.

What had happened last night?

†

Only the beginning was clear—a noisy smoke-filled cave in Sacromonte, Carl leading her to a long table along the back wall, where it had seemed impossible that there could be room for one more person, let alone two, but the people on the bench cheerfully squeezing them in and offering sherry. In the middle of the cave, a young woman bounding up and down with great emotion, hair and skirts flying, hardly anyone paying attention.

So, how do you like Granada? the man on Eva's left had asked. I love it, she replied, eyes riveted on the dancer, I love flamenco. That furious hopping about is not dancing, he said, it is an epileptic fit, a nervous disorder which might impress the Japanese, or maybe even the Germans. He made no attempt to lower his voice. Even in Barcelona they didn't take her seriously, said someone else. Yes, it's muy muy fea, said another, and there was a general murmuring and shaking of heads. She may dance like a horse, said the first man, but she thinks she's the reincarnation of la Macarrona, except that those aren't zapateos, they're zapafeos. The others laughed and Carl said into Eva's ear, They don't like it when someone goes abroad and becomes famous. He ordered a bottle of vodka, with glasses all around.

After the epileptic stomper a couple came out onto the floor, a man and a woman. The male stalked, the female stalled dramatically, and still the audience continued to talk and laugh as if the dance was of little interest. Friends were greeted, seats exchanged, cigarettes passed from table to table. Another bottle of vodka appeared. Eva had no idea how much she was drinking, but her glass was never empty.

The dancing couple exited to slight scattered applause and a dapper man in dark slacks and an open-necked white shirt—Moncho!—came out and snapped open two metal chairs. Even more unpredictably, Manolo came out with his guitar, sat down, and began to play. But he said he only plays a little, thought Eva, enough to tune his guitars. Moncho came out again and sat in the other chair, knees apart. He patted his slicked hair, closed his eyes, and took a series of deep breaths. Listen to this, Carl said.

Moncho leaned forward, back straight, elbows on knees, glanced at Manolo, and began to sing—a series of variations on ¡Ay! ¡Ay! ¡Ay!—as if he were testing the dimensions of both his voice and the song. ¡Aaaaay!

Eyes half-closed, Manolo joined in, his guitar shadowing the song, prompting the singer, throwing in the odd comment of its own.

At first the audience continued to talk (though more quietly than before) as Moncho, voice harsh and metallic, slowly developed his theme, raising then easing the tension, building anticipation until the moment when the audience, sensing the punch line, was dead silent. In that moment of silence, he shot to his feet and ended the verse abruptly in an unexpected key, punctuating the last line with his hand. He was rewarded with an appreciative burst of applause and laughter. Several like songs followed, the crowd reacting to each as do children to the outrageous but inevitable last line of a puppet show. ¡Bien hecho! shouted the man on Eva's left.

She hoped to catch Manolo's eye but he disappeared. More drinks, more passing of cigarettes, and a gradual hush spread throughout the cave.

In the centre of the room stood a woman, gathering in the expectant silence with the stillness of an Alonso Cano statue. A family affair, said Carl. Moncho's wife, la Luz: no wonder she looked familiar. When the silence was complete and it seemed as if her tightly coiled body had absorbed all the energy in the room, la Luz began to snap the fingers of her left hand, slowly, not moving her feet or any other part of her body. Snap. Snap. First one, then two fingers. Then three. Snap. Snap. Snap snap snap. She curved one smooth arm above her head, and the fingers of the right hand joined in, then a heel, click click click on the wooden floor. The other heel clicked down, and she was gliding across the floor, fingers and heels snapping and clicking contrapuntally, feet gaining speed, the ruffles above the ankles swishing, sweeping the floor. A man stepped out from the shadows to accompany her with sharp rhythmic claps, palmadas—¡Anda! ¡Anda! ¡Venga gitana!—and then a guitarist, picking out the rhythm, drumming on the sound box, responding to her dry hard heels which were like the sharp cracks of whips. She swirled, round and round and round, her dress and feet whirlpools of sight and sound. The guitar joined in to the full—¡Tocaor!—and soon guitar and dancer were tossing the song back and forth, one taking the lead then the other coming back until the final extravagant release. ¡Hija del fuego! ¡Viva tu madre! ¡Faraona!

That one long moment of the dance took over the rest of the night, and Eva went back with Carl to his carmen.

†

You give me weak knees—had she really said that? Her cheeks burned in recollection: a scene more likely to have featured Bella.

Decidedly she had had too much to drink. There had been a discussion, no, more a manic monologue in which she had blathered on about passion and deep empty spaces.

But there was something else, something of tremendous importance. Something that had happened at the carmen? She tried to recall the sequence of events.

†

He had driven her back to his place. He had led her through the weapons gallery and swooped aside the heavy beaded curtains: My baths.

The room—she was still sober enough to realize—was almost twin to the Royal Room of Beds in the Alhambra. It was divided by columns and arches into alcoves, and included a balcony from which a king might spy on his harem. Lamps burned in small recesses and reflected lambent from burnished copper basins hanging on the walls. The walls themselves were partly covered with glazed blue tiles entwined with green foliage and golden arabesques. In one alcove was a sunken bath filled with steaming water, and beside it a long tiled bench with fresh-cut flowers on one end and thick red towels piled on the other. In the centre of the room was a raised, larger bath, also filled with water and surrounded by circular tiled steps, at the top of which was a lustreware vase about a metre high, cerulean blue and smoky gold, with wing handles. A high dome above the bath was cut so that half-moon and star shapes of light shimmered softly on the marble floor. It was a sultan's room, of a time when women spent the day bathing, scenting and resting themselves, preparing to be part of the evening feast.

It's as if he knew I was coming, thought Eva.

He led her to a low couch and she sank into the silk cushions. Beside her were jugs of wine, and food, baskets of it: bread, cheese, figs, dates, quinces, grapes. And silver goblets, embroidered napkins, a marble ablution vessel with carved animal designs. Lute music played softly in the background, and she thought again of the Alhambra, and Angel's story of the blind musicians.

Carl poured wine into a goblet and they both drank from it. He spread paste on a piece of bread and handed it to her, and she thought that never in her life had she tasted anything more sublime. I didn't realize how hungry I was, she said, and accepted a second one.

If what you're looking for is vanilla pudding sex, he said, better leave now . . .

He removed his dark glasses, and finally she looked into his eyes—one green, emerald green, and the other one, the left, a speckled yellow—cat's eyes.

. . . leave now leave now . . .

Too late.

The Arabic music stretched and intensified until it seemed to be coming from a thousand hidden speakers.

Time stopped.

No, time expanded into one of those moments which carries within it both the ambiguity and the clarity of the dream, and everything comes to pass as within the eternity of the dream. Carl clapped his hands (was it twice? six times?) and a slender woman with bare feet chinked through the curtains. She wore baggy silk trousers and a tunic of gold and red woven silk. A short veil covered the lower part of her face.

This is Zayda, he said, and left the room.

Zayda. The tongueless woman.

And the night became a voluptuous haze the colour of the peaks of the Sierra Nevada at sunset, and Eva was adrift in a world of pink aromas, pods of musk in willow-flower water, eagle-wood, mouths melting with pearls and heated liqueurs—a world without words and with no use for words. Waves swelled.

†

Eva's clothes were piled neatly on a chair beside the bed. Her watch was under the clothes: noon, already. She rolled out of bed and dressed with the distaste of putting on yesterday's clothes, reaching mechanically into the pocket of her jeans to check for the key.

The crushed carnation was there, but the key was gone. Not on the floor or under the bed or anywhere else that she could see.

She tried to remember—when she had put the flower in, had the key been in her pocket? Maybe it had fallen out then.

The way she had let herself go, it wasn't surprising she had lost it.

But there was something else.

She looked at her hand–no ring. But that wasn't it–yesterday she had removed it for her shower and forgotten to put it back on.

It was something else, something painful.

She cautiously opened the small door and peered out–the trophy room, the beaded curtains of the baths.

At least she was still here, at Carl's place. She crept out, into the room of spears and knives, and listened for a sound. Nothing–this part of the house seemed to be empty.

Then she remembered: last night, during the Silencio, a woman had been killed.

Resa. Of what had she been thinking? A murder, and she had forgotten all about Resa! She had to get up there right now, take a taxi.

No, arriving in a panic wouldn't help. First a walk, a walk to the hotel to clear the cobwebs, then a shower, clean clothes.

Outside in the street the sunlight hurt her eyes.

†

"Eva."

Manolo greeted her curtly, not returning her gaze, and ushered her in.

"So. You enjoyed yourself at the cave?"

Eva blushed. "You *did* see me then."

"Of course."

If he had seen her, why hadn't he shown it? Waved hello or something? "I looked for you afterwards but couldn't find you."

"I had to get home."

"I see. Well, thank you so much for looking after Resa."

"Thank my mother."

"Is she here?"

"Out running errands."

"And Resa?"

"Out playing. Sit down and wait if you like. I'll make some coffee."

He called from the kitchen, "Did you also see the Silencio?" She wondered if he knew about the dead woman.

"Yes."

"And?"

"It was very interesting."

From the kitchen came a series of short angry bursts from the coffee grinder.

"Interesting?" He came to the doorway. "In that case, I suppose you had a better time than your friend la Católica."

"What do you mean?"

"Just that." He went back into the kitchen.

He was confusing her. "When do you think Resa will be back?" she said.

"No te preocupa, she's with Puri."

"Do you know where?"

"Outside, somewhere, you know children. Don't worry, they'll be back as soon as they're hungry."

"It really is very kind of you and your mother to take so much trouble over her."

"No trouble. On the contrary, Risita brings us much pleasure . . . But you should take more care."

"What do you mean? Has something happened to her?"

"No no, that's not what I mean. I mean that I am very worried about *you*. As I said, I saw you last night with el señor Alonso, and you need to understand that he is a man capable of anything. Anything, do you understand?"

"Why do you say that?"

He stuck his head around the corner again.

"Because it's true."

"Can you give me an example? Something specific?"

"You know that servant he has? La Achinados?"

"You mean Zayda." As soon as she had said the name Eva felt a stab of pleasure in her abdomen. Now where was that coming from?

"Zayda . . . ¡Chisss! Zayda indeed! That is not her name."

"It isn't?"

"And she is no Arab. He tells people he brought her back with him from Fez, but I happen to know that he found her in a brothel in New York."

"How do you know?"

"I know."

"What *is* her name?"

"No one knows. She has no tongue. She can't talk ¿entiendes? The women say she shops by pointing at things."

"Well, if she is from New York, as you say, maybe she points because she doesn't speak Spanish."

"She can't speak Spanish, she can't speak anything, because her tongue was cut out—by el señor Alonso. Everyone knows."

"Zayda has a tongue," Eva said, surprising herself.

And then she remembered why she knew.

†

Zayda was emptying the contents of the lustreware vase into the large bath. Eva's nostrils filled with scents of ambergris and musk, and Zayda led her to another alcove, where Eva allowed herself to be undressed, massaged with oils, washed in the small bath and taken to the larger one. Then Zayda lifted her veil and stepped out of her silk trousers into the gently swirling water.

What else? Zayda with her black black hair and smooth body gliding over her, breasts and thighs slipping and sliding along her back and buttocks, arms encircling her from behind, from the side, from in front. And kisses–teasing nips of the lower lip, short little kisses on the mouth that begged permission for longer tender kisses. Oh, oh, oh.

Then a man–Carl–standing tall in boots, loose trousers tied with a golden cord, a scabbard and sword, a black shirt.

The water games stopped.

Zayda climbed out of the bath and went to him, water running between her thighs. He dropped the scabbard and Zayda untied the golden cord and knelt before him, nuzzling her head up under the long black shirt front.

And the music of the invisible lute players seemed to be inside Eva, emanating from within, as if created out of her own desires, each note bright and eternal, and then Zayda and Carl were both in the water with her, Carl claiming for himself the crest of the night.

But if that first long moment with Zayda had rendered words superfluous, the next was a confusing swirl of babble. Lips moved out of synch, ahead of the received words, and bells clanged, once . . . twice . . . bongngng . . . bongngng . . . bonging from the opposite side of another world . . . threeeee . . . foooour . . . and Carl looking down at her with one green eye and one yellow, feral eyes staring at her mouth, her breasts . . . fiiive . . . siiix . . . Carl turning her over . . . seeeveen . . . a voice counting the clangs . . . telling her something . . . eiight . . . they clang for the murdered Abencerrajes . . . nine . . . ten . . . listen . . . once for each murder . . . eleven . . . twelve . . . count . . . but she lost track and the bells were tintinnabulations burbling through space, as if the air were water, and then Zayda was facing her, Eva wrapping her legs around a neck, whose neck? and Zayda kissing her on the lips again, but no, it wasn't Zayda, it was Carl, no, Carl was behind, thrusting, his arms around both women who were front to front, and it was Tony, Tony who was kissing her, Tony with his black hair and smooth mouth, Tony giving thirsty sucking kisses, sweet aching long kisses which promised an eternity of kisses without end, and Eva vowed that if just tonight she could have this one undying kiss, she would never ask for anything else, ever again.

When finally the drug glow began to fade, the end of the night was like the beginning of the night, and her heart folded around it like a fist.

†

Manolo came back into the living room with a tray of pasteles and coffee.

"What's that you said? La Achinados *has* a tongue? Tell me, have you ever heard her speak?"

Eva reddened and reached for a cake.

"No." It was true, she had not heard a single word from Zayda's mouth.

"Well, then." Case closed.

"You said something about Bella not having a good time last night," said Eva. "What did you mean?"

"You mean you really don't know?"

"Don't know what."

"La Católica is dead."

"Bella is dead?"

"Killed. Murdered. On la Carrera del Darro, during the passing of the Silencio."

Eva put down what remained of the piece of cake she was eating. She felt the blood drain from her face. Bella . . . it was Bella who had lain dead in the street . . .

"Oh, I'm sorry, I see now that you truly did not know. Forgive my crudeness."

"Do you know what happened?"

"The police say she was robbed, stabbed once in the heart."

"You mean she resisted?"

Manolo shook his head.

"But you just said . . . "

"No, I said the *police* said it was ladrones. I for one don't believe it for a minute. Tell me: did you ever see her with a purse, or wearing jewellery?"

"But who would want to kill her? Maybe she was with someone and they both had too much to drink, something like that."

But if that *had* been Bella in the glow of the cigarette, she had looked perfectly calm.

"Eva, es algo muy feo, a woman drinking so much, but to kill an old woman for that . . . it's not gitanazo . . . Wait, I hear the girls coming . . . "

"*Darro tiene prometido*
El casarse con Genil . . . "

Puri and Resa came skipping into the house, singing.

"Ah, my little monkeys, so now you are arranging marriages between rivers."

"Only if Risita's mamá is the Genil and you Papi are the Darro."

Manolo laughed.

"Resa! There you are!" exclaimed Eva, "I was worried sick about you . . . Resa? Look at me."

Resa wouldn't look at her mother. "I had a bad dream. You went away. You didn't want to come back."

"Oh, sweetheart." But I know, thought Eva, I haven't been paying enough attention to you.

"I was scared."

"No need, love, no need, I'm here now." Eva gathered up Resa and hugged her hard. "Now tell me, what have the two of you been up to?"

Resa squirmed free and slid to the floor. "Playing school. Puri's the profesora and she's showing me how to write. We were going to play el segundo grade but we played the primero instead because in segundo if you're bad you get spanked but in primero you only have to stand in the corner." Resa said to Puri, with much hand motion, "Tell my mommy about primero . . . "

"Pues, two boys were acting badly, so the teacher sent them to the corner, and then two others started acting badly, so they were sent to the corner too, and soon all the boys were in the corner, so some of us girls started misbehaving, so we would get to go in the corner too, and at the end of class there were only three girls in their desks, and the rest of us were in the corner."

Eva smiled. "So sweetheart, what have you learned to write in this school of Puri's?"

"Risita bebe de una bota. I thought it meant I drink from a boot, and I told Puri it's not true, we don't drink from boots in Canada, but then Manolo showed me a bota and now I know how to drink from it too. I'll show you."

Resa ran to the kitchen and returned with a wineskin. "Here's what you do, you tip your head back and you tip the bota like this . . . " A sluice of water shot into her mouth. "Now you try, Mommy."

"No, it's okay."

"Come on, Mommy, try it."

"Another time."

"Come on, Risita, I'll teach you to write some more," said Puri, pointing to herself and making writing motions in the air.

"Ahora no. Let's go to our cuevita secreta instead."

Manolo laughed and pinched Resa's cheeks. "A secret cave, eh? Now what kind of a dismal world would this be without children and their fantasies. But I hope you know, cariña, that in the caves of Granada, it is impossible to hide from your friends and neighbours."

"You mean you know about our treasure?"

"Ah, you've found a treasure, have you? Muy bien, as long as you haven't touched it."

"Why not?" asked Resa.

"Because enchanted treasure turns to coal dust when it is touched by human hands . . . even such lovely little hands as these."

"Well, we touched some and nothing happened."

She took three coins out of her pocket and handed them to him. "See?"

"¡Hija mía! Where did you get these?"

"We found them yesterday in our secret cave. We're going to buy tortas with them," said Puri.

"I don't think these coins will get you tortas . . . Here, I'll trade you these for duros, what do you think." He fished in his pocket and gave each girl a handful of change. "Go buy your tortas, and then I think you had better show us this mysterious cave of yours."

"I guess our treasure's not enchanted," said Resa.

"No, but it might be Moorish." He bit one of the coins. "Maybe even Moorish gold."

†

Ruth had spent the morning under the covers, but had awoken with the sensation of having been given a reprieve, and with a corresponding feeling of reanimation, a determination to get things done. Her scalp was tender, but she felt refreshed.

She got up and finished writing the article on Bella. This afternoon, she would phone it in and that would be the end of it. Then she would go to the university and check out the library, find out more about this business of missing books. She would be aggressive—after all, you had to know how to deal with these people: you had to assert yourself, insist on getting the information you needed. Yes, that was the way—not take no for an answer.

She was on her second pot of coffee when Miguel Angel joined her in the hotel dining room.

He told her right away. "The police say she died instantly."

"You don't really mean it, you don't mean that she's dead, I mean she can't actually be dead."

"I'm afraid it is so."

Damn! she said to herself, now you'll have to rewrite that whole article, and immediately felt guilty. But why should you, why should you be made to feel culpable? Bella may have acted like you were pursuing her, but in reality it was the other way around, it's always been the other way around—Bella haunting you, tormenting you. And just when you thought you were finished with her, there she is again, intruding, offending all sense of order. Oh, why can't she leave me alone?

"It's a terrible thing to say, I know, but I'm not really surprised," she said, "I mean, all that drinking and carrying on, it was bound to catch up with her one of these days."

"She was murdered, stabbed to death."

Murdered! Ruth felt the inside of her head stretching in an unpleasant way.

Even in death Bella had to be dramatic, special: she couldn't have the decency to die of natural causes like everybody else, oh no. Cancer, heart attacks—they weren't good enough for Bella.

"I don't mean to trivialize her death or anything like that," she said, "I mean honestly, it's perfectly horrible, much too horrible as a matter of fact, but I'll bet you anything it was one of those Gypsy lovers of hers. I mean you can't go on forever flaunting the rules, can you? Sooner or later you're going to get your comeuppance. Play with fire, you'll get burned."

Yes, that must have been it, one of her Gypsy boyfriends, or maybe it was one of their women, a jealous wife or fiancée. Ruth was sure she had seen one of them up at the plaza the other day, a dark face with hot black eyes burning holes in Bella's back.

Bella's problem was she just didn't care about anyone else, she thought life was one long diversion invented for her own pleasure, she thought you could go about doing whatever took your fancy, with no concern for the consequences or the feelings of others.

It wasn't fair. It just wasn't.

Ruth poured herself another cup of coffee. If she could just drink enough coffee and stay calm, maybe she would be able to avoid having to lie down.

"Señora, is anything wrong?"

"You'll have to excuse me, Miguel Angel, I'm feeling a bit unsettled."

"Of course, I understand how distressing this news must be for you. Perhaps we can meet later, when you're feeling better. I've come across some more books which might interest you—I would have great pleasure in showing them to you, but when you're feeling better, of course."

"Yes, I think I'll have to forget about the books for now," she said in a little voice. "Bella—she's news in Canada, you see, and the newspaper will want me to get the scoop, I mean they'll be so thrilled to have a reporter right here on the spot." She gulped down the rest of the coffee. "I suppose I'll have to write some sort of eulogy." Ruth's teeth throbbed unpleasantly, the pain shooting down as far as the bottom of the neck and radiating into the tip of the shoulders. Another day ruined. Damn! Damn! Damn! Damn!

"Señora . . . " Miguel Angel was looking at her in an odd way, and she realized that she had just missed something he'd said.

"I'm sorry, I'll be all right. I shouldn't be drinking so much coffee. I'll be fine if I take a couple of pills."

"I'll get you some water."

As she watched his back recede, she thought to herself: you like him, you really like him.

But what difference did it make? Now that Bella was gone, Ruth's reason for being in Granada had ceased to exist. Even in death, Bella was running her life.

Miguel Angel returned to the table with a pitcher of water. He looked at Ruth with true concern, and she was touched by his sympathy.

I know you think it isn't possible, but I think he likes you too, she said to herself.

And in that moment of acknowledging and accepting his sympathy, Ruth experienced one of those seemingly inexplicable about-faces that sometimes occur in a life: she decided then and there that she had had enough of being despondent, she was sick and tired of it.

Why punish yourself alone in your room again? There's no reason, no reason at all, why you shouldn't go now with Miguel Angel.

"I've changed my mind," she said, "I'll come with you and look at those books of yours."

When was the last time she had wanted to be with someone, really wanted to be with him? It was time to stop denying herself.

But the dull pain around her eyes continued to press outwards as pieces of an image began to form against her will. Damn damn damn, she didn't want to think about that right now, it was too distressing. Oh, what was the use, she couldn't go out feeling like this, she might as well shut herself in her room again.

No Ruth, she said to herself, take control, come on, you can do it, look at it, let it surface, and she allowed the image to form in her mind.

There now, that wasn't so bad, was it? It was humiliating to think of herself spending the night alone on the ground, flat on her back, but it wasn't *that* bad, it was bearable.

"I wonder," she said, "could we go by the Carrera del Darro? There's somewhere I'd like to stop for a few minutes."

As soon as she had said it, she felt better.

Things were going to change, she knew it.

†

Puri and Resa scrambled down to where the river bank jutted out behind the church of San Pedro.

"This way! Down here!"

And indeed, not far from a pile of rocks and hidden in the partly trampled grass in the midst of broken bottles and other debris, was a horizontal opening into the bank.

"I can't believe it! It's right by the tunnel I was telling you about, the one we used to play in when I was a boy," said Manolo. "I wonder if they connect? I'm sure the other one was closed up long ago."

"This one might as well be," said Eva. "It looks too narrow." Back home, even the open-ended highway tunnels through the mountains made her claustrophobic.

Manolo stuck his arm in.

"No problem, it widens immediately. But we should have brought a flashlight."

"We don't need one," said Puri. "There's a light inside."

"Let us go first," said Resa, "we know the way."

The two girls crawled in, followed by a nervous Eva and a reassuring Manolo.

He was right: the tunnel was large enough to allow the crouched passage of a good-sized man. It snaked like a squared-off S, about twenty metres in all.

Eva became disoriented. She wished she had remained outside. "It's so dark in here. Where's that light?"

"There's a door, then some steps, then a room with the light," said Puri.

"Here's the door, Mommy. Feel."

Eva reached out in the pitch black and Resa guided her hand.

"Resa! Careful, you could get slivers from that."

Then their two hands settled on what felt like a simple garden latch.

"Let me, Mommy, let me. I want to open it."

"Chist . . . ," whispered Manolo, "we wouldn't want to wake up any ghosts."

Resa lifted the latch, and together she and Puri pushed open the door.

"Papi, Eva–wait here," said Puri. "We'll go turn on the light."

"Okay, but be very quiet, hijas."

The two adults waited in the darkness, the light went on, and they descended the five or six steps to a wider space. Around a corner was a small chamber in which they could stand upright.

The girls were standing proudly under a bare light bulb that hung from wires in the ceiling.

"It's amazing!" said Eva.

Manolo put his finger to his lips. "Sound travels well through these underground passages."

"Sorry," Eva whispered. "But I'm surprised there would be electricity in a place like this."

"Splicing into the city system is very common," he whispered back. "People do it all the time."

"Even lit, it feels kind of eerie."

"Entonces, niñas," said Manolo, "that must be your jug of coins on that old rug over there."

"Sí, Papi."

There was nothing else in the room but what looked to be a small pile of dark clothing in the near corner.

Manolo walked over to the rug and stomped on it. "Mmm . . . let's see if this is not covering up something more than dirt." He peered in the jug before moving it and pulled the rug aside to reveal a wooden trapdoor. He hunkered down and lifted. "At least the lid opens easily enough."

The group peered into a wood-lined pit about two metres square piled with five or six cardboard boxes.

"More treasure!" said Resa.

"Chissst hija–not so loud. And I don't want to repeat it." Manolo lifted out the top box, opened it, and removed an object folded in raw silk, which he passed to Eva.

"Unwrap it."

It was a carving–two alabaster sphinxes flanking a seated woman with a basin in her lap.

"She's beautiful," said Eva, turning the carving in her hand. "I've never seen anything like it. What's this hole in her head, I wonder?"

"For receiving wine or water . . . Yes . . . see . . . if you were to pour sherry into her head, sherry would spout from her breasts into the basin."

Next out of the box was a necklace of gold seals with delicate cloisonné patterns, the whole held together by a complicated chain. More unwrappings, and a second box filled with bronze razors, gold collars and bracelets, strings and strings of green and pink glass beads, and an egg painted in red and purple crescents and lotus flowers, which, except for the motifs, reminded Eva of a giant Ukrainian Easter egg.

"An ostrich egg," said Manolo, "very well-preserved, too."

The last boxes included some bowls decorated with geometric patterns and embossed dots, and a couple of incense burners and a silver flagon. Inside the flagon were five small iron rings, carefully wrapped.

The two girls were sitting near the pile of clothing, whispering. They had quickly become bored with a treasure they were not allowed to touch.

Eva, meanwhile, was becoming increasingly nervous. "Don't you think we should put everything back and leave?" she said.

"You're right," said Manolo. "Time to go."

"Good, I feel creepy, as if we don't belong here." She felt like a grave robber.

"We certainly belong here as much as whoever hid all of this," said Manolo, "otherwise it wouldn't be hidden. It's been hidden quite recently, too—I doubt that the Moors had such things as cardboard boxes. And you know what? I have a feeling that this is the tunnel Tonio was going to show me."

That idea disturbed her even more.

"Don't worry, we'll put everything back as we found it. After all, we can't carry this stuff down the street in broad daylight."

Eva watched him stuff one of the gold bracelets in his pants pocket.

"Just one thing. It won't be missed," he said.

"Can I take the pretty egg?" Resa asked her mother.

"It's not ours to take, sweetheart."

Manolo looked at Eva—reproachfully, she thought. "You think all this belongs to whatever ladrón hid it here? Tell me: who but a thief would hide valuables in a place like this?"

"You're right—I guess we'd better go to the police."

"The police! ¡Cojones! You want to donate our find to the police! Just as well to throw it all in the river! The police! They're likely to say, Thank you little fools! and throw *us* in the river. No no, for now we'll put everything away and go and think."

As they were speaking, Eva handed him items and he replaced them in the boxes.

"¡Coño! I should have been more careful. I should have paid more attention to the exact order in which I removed the items."

"Shouldn't we at least call in some expert, someone who can tell us what it is we've found and what we can do with it?"

"Money is like oil; a little will stick to the fingers of each who touches it."

"But wouldn't someone like Angel be able to help us?"

"Don Angel is a scientist. He will want to take our find to a museum in Madrid, or a big-shot one in New York."

"Papi," said Puri, "Abuelita told me that when you find a treasure and someone else finds out about it, you're supposed to give that person half of it. Does that mean that Risita gets half and I get half and you get half and Risita's mamá gets half? And Abuelita, will she get half?"

"Oh now wait, my little Purificación! We'll have to see about that. But you're right about one thing: the more people involved, the less for each. Now tell me, hijas: have you mentioned this cave to anyone else?"

"No," said Puri. "Just to you."

"Well be very sure you don't say a word to anyone. For now, it's our secret."

"But we'll tell Abuelita."

"Of course we will discuss it with your grandmother. But no one else. ¿Entiendes?"

"Sí, Papi. Entiendo."

"You know," said Manolo after he had carefully dropped the trapdoor shut, "I can't help thinking there must be another entrance somewhere. I have trouble believing in a tunnel with only one entry." He pulled the rug back over the trapdoor and replaced the jug.

"Resa! Don't touch that," said Eva. "It looks filthy."

Resa had picked up the clothes in the corner. At her mother's words, she dropped them and something clanked on the floor.

Manolo went over to look. "The garb of a penitente," he said, examining the tunic. Eva saw a flash of something shiny.

"Hijas, was this here yesterday?"

"No, Papi."

"Then someone's been here since then."

"I think we should leave right this minute," said Eva.

"Papi, I hear someone."

"The light, quick."

He appeared to tuck the shiny object in the back of his pants, under his shirt.

Puri turned the lightbulb and the small group stood huddled together, listening in the darkness. They heard nothing.

"Bien. Let's get out of here. We'll go very very slowly and quietly, me first, then you Puri, then Risita, and you last, Eva. Keep a hand on the person in front of you."

†

Manolo's head popped out to the sight of two pairs of feet planted at the entrance to the tunnel. He looked up. The feet belonged to Ruth Kostyk and Miguel Angel Sanlúcar.

"¡Hijo! ¡Buenos días! What a pleasant surprise! La señora Ruth and I were just passing by—such a lovely day for a walk."

The others crawled out one by one, and were each greeted in kind.

"¡Qué raro! What an enticing place for merienda."

"Yes, you must join us," said Manolo, "but not here, we've run out of coffee. But please, come with us to my house, I insist."

After three rounds of offers and protestations, Angel accepted the invitation.

†

The two men kept up a pleasant chatter all the way up to the house. The decision on whether or not to include Angel and, to a lesser degree, Ruth, had been made the moment Manolo's head poked out of the tunnel.

"That tunnel must go under the river as far as the Alhambra," Manolo was saying.

"I thought you said it ended in that treasure chamber."

"It appeared to, but didn't there used to be a castle right above?"

"Yes, of Phoenician construction. Why?"

"Well, everyone knows that in the old days most of the castles had secret tunnels, especially after that alchemist king walled off the entire Albayzín."

"Haxix, you mean."

"Eso."

"I think we should be a little more sceptical about our little tunnel. It's probably just an old Moorish well."

"Impossible. It doesn't go vertically into the ground, it goes horizontally, and the walls and ceiling are fortified with wood."

"Just the same, it's best not to jump to conclusions. All these hundreds of tunnels supposedly zigzagging under our feet—exaggerations."

"As are the hidden-treasure stories, yet we have found a treasure-trove."

At the house, Mercedes was waiting with iced water and fresh-made coffee, seven cups set out as if she had known the group was on its way.

She embraced Resa but not her mother, greeting the rebuffed Eva with a grunt and a curt nod. Reminded to keep quiet about the tunnel and instructed to keep-away-until-I-say-so! the two girls had a drink of water and ran off to play. The five adults sat down in the cramped Carmona living room.

Eva was exhausted and more confused than ever. In two days—in a single half day—she had experienced more intense and contradictory feelings than she had in the entire previous year: first, waking up hung over and naked in a strange room, filled with muddled emotions and unreliable memories of the night before; then, losing the key, and the shock, the unreality of Bella's death; and now, incredulity at the existence of the tunnel and its contents, and hurt, incomprehensibility, at the frostiness of Mercedes. What was going on? Too much too quickly.

Angel was listening intently to Manolo's description of the objects in the pit.

"And did you take anything out with you?"

Manolo smiled and passed Angel the coins.

"The girls found these. What do you think?"

"If they are genuine, they appear to be gold coins from the reign of Mohamed I."

"The founder of the Alhambra?" said Eva.

"The same . . . Did you take anything else?"

Manolo hesitated.

"Oh for heaven's sake!" said Eva, surprising herself. "Why don't you show him?"

Manolo frowned at her, but he took the bracelet from his pocket and passed it to Angel.

"The same sort of old jewellery that provokes thieves into severing hands," said Mercedes.

"In this case, probably Phoenician hands," said Angel.

"Like that castle that used to be above the tunnel," said Manolo.

"I don't know, it's possible the bracelet was made in Cádiz—Gadir in those days," said Angel, "but I would have to do a bit of research to be certain."

"What's the difference?" said Mercedes. "What's the difference where it comes from if it causes blood to spill?" She passed a plate of pasteles around.

"You know," said Eva, "while we were in that tunnel I had a strong feeling that we had no business being there, that we were not welcome. I almost expected the ghost of the owner to appear."

"I told you, there is no legitimate owner," said Manolo. "At least no more legitimate than us, the last people to touch the trove." He jabbed at his throat. "Don't constrict your gullet while pecking at the food."

"Manolo has a point," said Angel, "in the sense that our find surely has more than one provenance. Some of what you describe could be Moorish, but that libation basin is more likely seventh century, and much of the rest is typical of what might be found in a Punic grave of the fifth to third century B.C.–which would also predate the Moors."

"It doesn't make sense," said Eva. "I mean, that it should be all together in one place–the Moorish coins, the Phoenician jewellery–"

"What! What doesn't make sense?" said Manolo. "It's a treasure-trove, that's all."

"You found no books?" asked Angel.

"Why do you ask?" answered Manolo.

"Curiosity. You seem to have found a bit of this and that."

"But no books."

"I don't know what any of this is about," said Mercedes, "but I guarantee it has something to do with that foreign jackal who is too cowardly to show his eyes." She looked pointedly at Eva.

Eva said nothing.

"Let me tell you about your Carl Alonso," said Manolo. "He is a descendant of Martín Alonso Pinzón."

Pinzón. The name was familiar.

"You look puzzled, Señora Eva," said Angel. "El Capitán Martín Alonso Pinzón was the right-hand man of Cristóbal Colón."

Ah yes, now she remembered, Carl had mentioned him, that first day in the cathedral.

"At least three brothers went on the first expedition to America," continued Angel. "They were among the greatest of Spanish sailors who have ever lived. Martín Alonso was captain of the Pinta, his brother its pilot, and the third brother was captain of the Niña. Without them, the discovery of the New World would not have occurred. Now Colón was a proud man–he needed the brothers, but he resented the gratitude he owed them, so he made their lives as miserable as he dared."

Eva still looked puzzled.

"It is possible that those brothers, and their descendants, have felt that history has not properly appreciated or rewarded them. And, Señora Eva, those brothers were ruthless men who, once they got to America, did much worse than dispense sham beads of transparent glass."

So? thought Eva. As if we all of us don't have black sheep in our families. Anyway, wasn't Angel the one always going on about "the times"?

"A parent's actions affect his children, and his children's children, and so on and so on," said Manolo. "Revenge is a dish to be served cold."

"Yesterday I saw Don Pedro Alonso," said Mercedes. "Don Pedro is a genuine descendant of Martín Alonso Pinzón, and he says this jackal has nothing in common with the family, nothing at all."

"A fraud, I knew it," said Manolo.

Mercedes and the two men looked at Eva.

But what do they expect me to say? she wondered. She found herself idiotically wishing that Ruth would divert the attention to herself like she usually did. What was wrong with Ruth, anyway? She was being uncharacteristically silent. Maybe she thought her Spanish wasn't good enough. But that hadn't deterred her before, and these conversations always jumped back and forth from language to language.

"Let me tell you a story," said Mercedes, still looking at Eva. "Once, many years ago, many centuries ago, lived a young woman from a faraway country whose husband was murdered and his wealth stolen. She was left to cope with a small child. She became so lonely and desperate that finally, against the cries of her child and the advice of the people who loved her, against all the signs, the young widow took up with a good-for-nothing rich man. Months passed, one day following the next, until one morning the widow woke up to the realization that her keeper was the same good-for-nothing who had murdered her husband, and it was her husband's money, her own money, that the canalla was spending."

"¡Mamá!" interjected Manolo. "I think this is something that is better left between men."

"Ah sí, cosas de hombre—tonterías from which we simple women are to avert our eyes."

Manolo said something rapidly and in an admonishing undertone to his mother, then turned to Eva: "Please understand that my mother knows many things, but she occasionally forgets that some of them cannot be dealt with using the words and potions of old women, no matter how wise the words or efficacious the potions. Some things must be dealt with man to man. After all, the man who loses face is lost."

"Sí señor," said Angel, "it goes without saying. To lose face, to be afraid–"

"–is to be lost in the desert," finished Mercedes. "But even the man who is lost may stumble onto an oasis. And too, he must accept that he is lost before he can start looking."

Ruth turned suddenly to Eva. "Why do *you* think Bella was murdered?"

Eva started. "They're talking about something else, I think." But she had no idea what the Spaniards were talking about.

"Are we?" said Manolo.

"You know, I'm *sure* I saw someone there last night," said Ruth, mostly to herself.

"Where?" said Eva.

"At that tunnel, where you came out. I was near there last night, and the more I think about it, the more positive I am."

The others were carrying on with their own conversation.

" . . . perfectly horrible," Angel was saying, "killing a defenceless old woman." He turned to Manolo. "When do you think we should return to the tunnel?"

"The sooner the better, as far as I'm concerned. I think we should go back tonight after dark, take some sacks with us and get away with what we can."

"Hijo, don't be overanxious," said Mercedes. "Bear in mind how treasure turns to dust."

"This doesn't look like dust to me," he said, taking the bracelet from Angel's hand. "Are you suggesting, Mamá, that we leave the whole matter to the duendes?"

"Not a bad idea."

"If we don't hurry, our treasure might well vanish. It's unlikely our little visit will go undetected for long."

"Listen to me," said Mercedes. "On Thursday night I knelt before the cross, and last night I read the cards. I am certain that tonight is no good for such endeavours. Your bracelet did not turn to dust, but it is possible, hijo, that you yourself will return to dust sooner than would please your mother."

"All right," said Manolo. "But tomorrow night we'll go for sure."

†

As arranged, the next night a reluctant Eva went with Ruth and the two men to the tunnel. It had been decided that while the men went in to get what they could, Eva and Ruth would act as lookouts.

The group arrived at the tunnel to find the mouth completely plugged with rocks and concrete.

"The pile of rocks that was over there is gone," said Manolo. "It looks like they were used to block the tunnel."

"If only it were just rocks . . . we'll never get through all that concrete without making a lot of noise and attracting attention," said Angel. "We might as well forget it."

"We could wait for a noisy night," suggested Manolo, "a fiesta. The fiesta de toros—Día de la Cruz."

"But that's more than a month from now. And think about it—if the tunnel is blocked, the cave was probably emptied as well. Whoever it is will have found a new hiding place."

"Unless there is another entrance, and the tunnel was blocked from the inside. In that case, we can try to get in on Día de la Cruz, or earlier if an opportunity presents itself. What do you say, Don Angel, we just lay low for a while, stay alert and be ready to move at a moment's notice? It's worth a try."

"Bueno," agreed Angel, hesitantly.

Eva was bewildered to realize how weary she was getting of this whole business. If Manolo was right in supposing that the tunnel had something to do with Tony, perhaps with his death, then why wasn't she more concerned? And why didn't she feel more remorse about losing the key?

Water and Dust

"SEÑORA EVA, I SAW YOU AT THE CORRIDA THIS afternoon, in the sun seats. You must have been very hot."

"Carl said it would be more authentic to watch from there. He's quite knowledgeable."

Angel grunted. "Perhaps, but of course it would be quite impossible for him as a foreigner to grasp all of the subtleties of the corrida." Angel accented the word "corrida" with his chin.

It was late evening, Día de la Cruz, and he and Eva were with Mercedes in the Carmona patio, waiting for Manolo and Ruth to arrive.

"Where were you sitting?" Eva asked Angel. She hadn't noticed him at the bullfight.

"Below the president's box, with Ruth." He leaned towards Eva and said quietly, "I thought Día de la Cruz would be a diversion for her, especially the corrida. She still seems very upset by the death of la Católica."

And pensive, thought Eva. And yet Ruth had been the one to look after the details of Bella's death—the tracking down of relatives, the arrangements to have the body shipped back to Canada.

"Despite the fact that we were sitting in the shade, Ruth became ill, so she only saw the first toro. Unfortunately, it was a dewlapped cow with the legs of a chicken and more folds in its neck than the curtains in the throne room of the Royal Palace in Madrid."

"In a way, I'm surprised Ruth is still here. She seemed so anxious to get back to Canada."

"Perhaps Don Angel has something to do with that."

"Señora Mercedes, I would be honoured if that were so. I admire Ruth very much. She is outspoken. And you know, I have always liked tall women." He turned to Eva. "All the women in my family are over 1.6 metres."

"Some people use words as a means of letting others in," Mercedes said. "Others use them to keep people out."

"It's true, I think Ruth sometimes talks to hide things from herself, but it is only because, at heart, she is honest. Once she sees something is wrong she feels compelled to correct it–unlike we Spaniards, who look straight at reality but do nothing to change it."

"Pues, one must accept the inevitable."

"Sí señora, but we proceed as if life is a series of dreams in which we are the participants but not the dreamers."

Mercedes smiled. "You know, I could help your Dulcinea with her headaches if she would only let me get close enough. It is as if she is surrounded by an invisible shield and seeks to enlarge the space around her–like the toro charging into the middle of a crowded ring."

"The toro is certainly accorded ample space."

"Sí, Don Angel, but it is a space in which to die."

"In any case, she has been having fewer migraines lately."

Never mind Ruth, Eva was thinking. Why am *I* still here? Since Bella's death, Eva had lost heart in her original quest. And two nights ago, Carl had frightened her. But she had not tried to leave.

†

They had been in the bath.

Why don't you ever kiss me on the mouth? she had asked, and he had grabbed her and flipped her so he was on top, his face pushing down until her entire head was under water, kissing her so hard his teeth broke the skin on her lips. He had pulled her up by the hair. I know what you want, he had said from between clenched teeth. How, how do you know what I want? she had wondered, coughing up water, I don't know myself.

And yet today she had gone with him to the bullfight.

She was from a huge invisible country that for the rest of the world existed under a layer of colourless snow, a country blanketed in unnoticeability and insubstantiability.

†

"And you, Señora Eva, what did you think of it?"

"Pardon?"

"What did you think of the corrida?"

"Oh, it was all very interesting, I mean, you can't come to Spain and not go to a bullfight."

"Why not?" interjected Mercedes.

"Well, because it's something a person should see at least once if given the opportunity."

"Why?"

"Well, it's one thing to read about it, but to actually go and see one . . . " Her words trailed off—she could hear the insincerity in her own voice. But how could she say out loud what she had really thought of the bullfight?

"I never go to the fiesta de toros," said Mercedes, bluntly. "The whole spectacle is a disgusting display of imbecility and vulgarity."

"You, señora, would like to have the corrida outlawed, I suppose, as did Queen Isabel, but think—even a powerful monarch as she could do nothing in face of the appetite of the people."

"Didn't several popes try to ban it as well?" said Eva.

"Outlawing the corrida has never worked," said Angel, "because tauromachia, not religion, is the opiate of the Spanish people."

"Those popes probably didn't like the competition," said Mercedes.

"I grant you, there is something to that," said Angel. "If we consider the corrida as liturgy, what then is the matador but a sort of priest? Take the way he dresses—carefully, solemnly, each item of clothing in the correct order—just like the priest preparing to say Mass. And the tradition of not eating or drinking until the bulls have been killed—again like the priest who must fast until he has eaten and drunk of the body and blood of Christ. Yes, the vocation of matador is a holy one."

"Either that or the priest saying Mass is a butcher in a spattered apron," said Mercedes.

Angel laughed. "Nonetheless, the people demand the corrida, just as in the past they demanded the live sacrifice on the altar and the immolation at the stake. But you surprise me, señora. I would have thought you would be one to accept death more readily."

"Death? Sí, Don Angel, I accept death. I respect it. But its glorification? Its mystification? Its celebration? No. You men approach the corrida as you approach war—as a gathering of enemies at a feast of killing, of death by lot, a sentimental male rite that requires the presence of women to justify it. A moment ago you called a weak toro a cow, but tell me, Don Angel: why is it the dull-witted toro which is fought in the ring, and not the intelligent cow? I'll tell you why: it's because the stupidest cow knows to go for the man and not the cape."

†

Angel was right: it had been too hot in the sun seats. And when the matadores and their retinue had strutted in to the pasodoble, Eva had thought they looked goofy in their monteras pushed down to the eyebrows and tight pants pulled up to the armpits, and she had had to stifle the same urge to giggle that she had felt her first time at the opera.

The torture and death of the initial bull had jarred her back to reality: unlike the hero in the opera, the bull was not going to get up and take a bow. And there was something particularly numbing about the coup de grâce.

Don't judge it by that slow messy killing, Carl had said. If we're lucky it'll be done right at least once today. True alegría isn't the song and dance of the tablao. It's the dance and death of the toro. You'll see. The piques, the banderillas, the pases, the death of the toro: they'll all make sense. When it's done right, the corrida is true art.

The strict choreography of the toreros had reminded Eva of the flamenco dancers in the cave. But if art is imaginative, she had wondered, what was imaginative about the torture and killing of the bull? Its suffering, its death, were all too real.

I read something that Hemingway wrote, she said, and Carl interrupted her: Hemingway was a groupie who went to Ronda to fondle the relics of famous bullfighters. Spent one short summer with Dominguín and Ordóñez. Who humoured him. Poor old Papa. A voyeur trying hard to be one of the boys.

But the bullfighters must have gotten something out of it, too, she had thought to herself. Perhaps bullfighters were like Hollywood movie stars craving adulation. In exchange for international fame, immortality, Dominguín and Ordóñez gave Hemingway his story—a symbiotic relationship dependent on the magnetism of death.

She had asked about something else she had read, about the corrida being so important it was one of the few things in Spain that begins on time. True, said Carl. En España se empieza tarde y se acaba nunca. Except for the corrida. Always begins at precisely 5:00 P.M. And its ending is precise. A moment in the here and now when death asserts its power over the future. The corrida is heroic. The worthy warrior beneath the worthy hooves of his own horse.

Was Carl saying that the matador was an accessory to the whims of nature? But the matador seemed to be in full control, the fight itself an artificial construction in which the bull seemed not so much brave as frightened and violently stupid in its response.

The crowd's reaction to the sixth bull had been different than to the previous ones: ¡Música, maestro! ¡Música! the people had shouted at the first rhythmical passes of the matador. You're in for a treat, Carl said. He's going to kill the bull in the receiving position. Carl's face was red, intense, solemn. The bull died swiftly. It charged the matador, then fell to its front knees the instant the blade entered its neck, as if its legs had been severed.

But how could the killing be acceptable just because it was done skilfully and classically? And what could be forgivable about that first clumsy, undignified performance?

†

Mercedes was talking, and Eva realized that she was being addressed, if indirectly.

" . . . and while her mamá was relishing the death of the toro, the beautiful Risita was competing in the sevillana contest in the plaza."

"But Resa doesn't know how to dance flamenco."

"Oh? She won a prize."

"A prize?"

"She won a shawl," said Mercedes to Angel, ignoring Eva. "She's muy lista, that little girl, very quick to learn. We promised to take her with us tonight to visit the crosses. If her mamá were to leave the men to chase their Holy Grail, she could come with me and see for herself how her daughter dances the sevillana. But perhaps she doesn't want to do either. Perhaps she would rather go to the jackal's lair."

"You should go with la señora Mercedes," said Angel to Eva. "Día de la Cruz is unique to the Albayzín—the neighbours of each barrio erect a cross and decorate their placeta. The best ones win prizes. Tonight everyone will be going from cross to cross, comparing and admiring."

"But don't you need Ruth and me at the tunnel?"

"We can get along without one of you."

"Then again, perhaps she doesn't know that the jackal steals eggs from the lizard's nest," said Mercedes.

This is getting really annoying, thought Eva. So what if I *were* planning to see Carl? "Thank you, Mercedes, for offering to take Resa with you tonight," she said. "I'm very grateful."

"Grateful?" Mercedes pressed her hand over her heart. "This woman is thanking me, can you believe it? It is I who thank her. That little girl gives so much joy, she has so much gracia. Risita–listen, the laugh is in her name. Why just this morning, I spilled some milk on the floor, and Risita said, Oh look Mercedes, Moorish coins, and she bent as if to pick up one of the spots of milk."

Mercedes and Angel laughed.

Eva felt left out. But I suppose I deserve it, she thought. For the past month, Resa has been practically living with the Carmonas. On the other hand, it's not as if Mercedes isn't always encouraging me to leave Resa here.

But Eva knew that the cold treatment had to do with the time she was spending with Carl.

Okay, so maybe he isn't what's best for me, she thought. But what business is it of hers?

Oh, what was happening to her? How did she get into these situations? It wasn't the first time. The first time had probably been that phone call when she was twelve.

†

Eva had answered the phone. On the other end, a man's voice–friendly, chatty. It had asked her questions, innocuous ones which she had eagerly answered: her favourite colour, her favourite teacher. Imperceptibly the questions had changed, until she had answered, No, she had never kissed a guy, and then the voice had asked, the smile still in it, Have you ever been fucked? And it had stopped asking and started telling, and she had stayed on the line, listening, feeling too compromised to hang up.

†

But I'm not twelve any more, she thought, I'm thirty-one. Am I self-destructing, like my mother?

Ruth had arrived.

"Sorry I'm late," she said.

"It's all right," said Eva. "Manolo's not here yet."

"Do you think he remembers that this is the night?" asked Ruth.

"He knows," said Mercedes.

"And we're in no rush," said Angel.

"Do you really need me?" asked Ruth. "I have no desire to go crawling around inside dirty old tunnels."

"We wouldn't ask you to go inside," said Angel, "just to keep watch."

"If there's something else you would rather do, go ahead," said Eva. "I can keep watch. They don't need both of us."

"Thanks, I appreciate it. There *is* something I think I need to do."

Angel looked disappointed, but Ruth left, looking decidedly abstracted.

She seemed so indecisive these days. One day she would declare she was going back to Canada, the next she was still here.

"You know," said Mercedes, breaking into Eva's thoughts, "you are not so different from la Muda as you may like to imagine."

"What do you mean?"

"In the old days, if you were sick you would be laid on the street outside your door, in the hope that some passerby might be familiar with both the disease and the remedy. What each passing beggar or idiot said was taken as seriously as what the professional healer had to say."

Mercedes paused for a moment.

What was her point?

"What do you think about that–giving equal weight to the advice of each person who passes through your life? Both you and la Muda choose to place your destinies in the hands of others. The difference is, while you hear everyone, she hears no one, just echoes of her own self. She resists, you accept, but the end result is the same: inertia."

"Señora Eva, you look tired," said Angel.

"A weight on the conscience makes sleep difficult," said Mercedes.

"I suppose that the terrible death of your compatriot has been difficult for you, Señora Eva. And it is incredible to think that both she and el señor Tonio died almost in the same spot, and on the very same night–Good Friday, like Nuestro Señor."

"And both deaths were no more unassisted than was the death of Jesús," said Mercedes, crossing herself.

"You really don't look well," said Angel. "Have you been sleeping all right?"

"Not really," said Eva. "I've been waking up a lot in the night."

Mercedes looked at her for the first time. "Dreams?" she asked.

"Yes."

"What are they about?"

"Bella is in most of them. I can't remember much more than that, but this morning poison was involved, and a goblet."

"How interesting," said Angel. "This very morning I was reading an account of a feast that took place almost one thousand years ago. Badis the Zirid and a group of Berber chiefs were sitting around much as we are now, drinking sherry and discussing a Hamudid ruler named Al-Mahdi whom they all hated. They decided to get rid of him. A certain Kutami Berber was entrusted to carry a poisoned cup to Al-Mahdi and say: Badis received this cup as a gift but regards it to be worthy only of a caliph. Al-Mahdi was flattered by the gesture, which he accepted as an act of submission. He had the cup filled with his best wine, but as he lifted the cup to his mouth he suddenly sensed its poisonous content, and ordered the Kutami to drink the wine. The apparently innocent envoy drank from it and fell over dead. But you know, the poison was so powerful that Al-Mahdi, who had done no more than smell the wine, himself became ill and died three days later . . . Señora Mercedes, I understand that el señor Tonio showed signs of having been poisoned."

"Not poison, Don Angel. As you know, I saw his body, and the signs were of asphyxiation, or drowning."

"You said before that you didn't think Tony had drowned," said Eva.

"No. I said I didn't think he drowned *in the river.*"

"Oh. I see." But she didn't.

"A man in search of a treasure is like the lark who tries in vain to cover the eggs of the wild goose. On returning to its own nest, the lark finds her own eggs have spoiled."

Another enigmatic statement, for which Eva had no chance to elicit clarification. The door opened and in walked Manolo.

Greetings were exchanged all around.

"¡Hijo!" said Mercedes. "You're so dirty!"

Indeed, Manolo's face and shirt were covered in dirt.

Mercedes rushed to her son and started brushing off his beard and clothes.

"It doesn't matter," said Angel, standing up. "He's bound to get even dirtier once we start unplugging our tunnel." Angel rubbed his hands together. "¡Vámonos!"

"There's no point," said Manolo. "The cave is empty."

"Empty? What do you mean?"

"It's empty. I know because I was just there. Don Angel, I'm sure this will surprise you as much as it did me, but you know the door near the royal baths in the Alhambra, the one behind which is that old passageway? You know, where we ran into you that night. Well, it's the strangest thing, but not only does a key exist for that door, but the tunnel on the other side is not at all bricked up—it is open—and not only is the tunnel open and in good condition, but it leads under the river to the very cave in which we found the treasure."

Mercedes finished straightening her son's collar and sat down again.

Manolo turned to Eva. "If you enter the tunnel as we did, from the Darro side, you come to a hidden door—just before the one to the girls' cave. That door is covered in mud and dirt, so that at first touch it feels like part of the wall. But if you push hard enough, it opens onto an extension of the tunnel that goes under the river and exits at the bottom of those supposedly rotten stairs."

"But hijo, how did you find this out?" said Angel.

"I have a friend who works in the palace as a maintenance man, he's been there for thirty years now. The other day I mentioned to him—by chance, of course—how interesting it would be to have a peek on the other side of that door. No problem, he said, and—can you believe it?—he knew exactly where the key was, and this is the part that will really surprise you, Don Angel—the key was in your study the whole time, hanging on the wall."

"Really? How extraordinary."

"Anyway, I crawled through the tunnel to the cave, and there is nothing left, nothing."

"That settles it then," said Mercedes, slapping her hands down on her thighs. "Come, Eva. We'll visit the crosses. You will see your daughter dance with the other children."

"I don't think so," said Eva, not sure why.

"Once a woman decides to be seduced," said Mercedes, "she will allow herself to be charmed by the most commonplace of ruses, to be swept off her feet by the most inelegant of phrases . . . Tell me, hija, do you believe in another world?"

"You mean an afterlife? I've never thought about it very much. Why?"

In fact, Eva had spent much time thinking about it, but she wasn't really sure what she believed.

"Because," said Mercedes, "if you believe that you cease to exist at death, then for you, there will be no second chance. You must make the best of this life. There will be no belated reward or punishment."

Why should she try and make me feel guilty? wondered Eva. She's not my mother. "I'm sorry I've left Resa so often with you," she said.

"¡Chist! That's not the problem. I told you, we love her as if she were one of us. She's not at all like a foreign child."

There it was again: not like a foreigner.

What does that comment mean, anyway? wondered Eva. Did anyone ever declare to an Italian, You certainly don't seem Italian, or to an Englishman, Nah, go on, you're not really English, you can't be. What was a Canadian? A shell waiting to have some acceptable identity poured into it? Back home, you were a French-Canadian, an Irish-Canadian, a Chinese-Canadian, as if it were easier to be someone other than oneself.

" . . . if something should happen to you," Mercedes was saying.

Enough of this oblique meddling. "I'm sorry," said Eva, standing up. "I really do have to get going." But she had no idea where she was going.

"It's not right that you put yourself in danger unnecessarily. I told you, he claims to be an Alonso, but the Alonsos know nothing about him."

So what? He was Carl, an American. What did his background matter? At least he accepted her as she was (whatever that might be). Anyway, wasn't Granada pitos, taconeos, the hard heel on a wooden floor? Wasn't its musical soul the martinete, the fatalistic song of the persecuted blacksmith? Le-le-le-le.

†

Ruth took a roundabout route down from the Carmona house. Something was bothering her, something she couldn't quite put her finger on—something Miguel Angel had said? Maybe a walk would help.

She had not enjoyed the bullfight either, not even a little bit—squeezed on a hard bench between Miguel Angel and a stranger, a fleshy American with his legs spread so wide apart she was obliged to sit with her own legs pressed together and turned to one side, and in front of her, a greasy-haired man who smelled of damp fur. When the first bull had been killed, her mouth had filled with wet animal taste and she had known she had to leave—immediately. Miguel Angel had taken her back to his room in the Alhambra and made tea.

Ruth reached the Carrera del Darro.

The Albayzín was crowded and noisy. She didn't know if she could take three whole days of this Día de la Cruz—since when did one día make three días, anyway? The tree-lined avenues of Toronto seemed a lifetime away—optimistic Toronto, with its trusting visible houses set back from the road, houses with large windows and inviting shovelled walks.

She crossed to the river side of the street to avoid a group of revellers, and a familiar stride crossing in the opposite direction triggered an inexplicably disturbing vision of a man in a hood approaching a pile of rocks.

Turn and look, she told herself.

She did so and caught a glimpse of the strider's face as he moved under a street lamp: Carl Alonso, carrying a package. Another recollection tried to surface, something about that horrible night on the river bank. She felt a pinch in her forehead.

Stop, don't stuff it back in, you're not doing that any more, she said to herself, and with great force of will pulled the image back out where she could examine it.

Immediately her head lightened and the scene reconstituted itself in her mind, so clearly that she decided that the shadow she had seen disappearing into the ground that night had not been a hallucination, but a hooded man. The hooded man was Carl.

But what could it possibly mean? And why was it so terrifying to remember?

†

From the Carmona house, Eva went straight to Carl's, the quick way, almost running down the steep stone steps leading to the Carrera del Darro. She wanted something, some sort of reassurance.

As she rounded the corner at the bottom of the hill, she saw him, package in arms, unlocking the front door of his carmen. Carl! she called, Carl!

He went in, appearing not to see or hear her.

†

Ruth watched Eva rush in after him.

†

Before she knew it, Eva had followed him into the trophy room, and he was staring back at her.

"I called out to you, I guess you didn't hear."

He continued to stare at her.

"I saw you coming in, and . . . "

He didn't seem at all pleased to see her.

He set his package down on a table and bent to a small cabinet, his back to her. It sounded as if he were mixing drinks.

"Let's drink a toast," he said, standing up and facing her again. He had removed his dark glasses.

She was still out of breath, and she didn't really want a drink, but she accepted the proffered wine. "Are we celebrating something?"

"How about, a deepening relationship." He clinked his goblet to hers.

She drank. He tilted his own goblet back, his cat eyes watching her at the same time.

"So. Thought you'd trip me up? Catch me out?"

What?

His voice was hard, coming from between the teeth as if his real self were somewhere inside, being held back.

"Think this is a game? A simulated bullfight? You the mock bull? Me some punk novillero practising up for the alternativa?"

What was he talking about?

"I've seen through you all along. Acting dumb. Putting me on."

He took a step forward.

"Thought you were smart. But coming here with that key in your pocket. That was too much."

The key . . . She set her goblet down and took a step back.

"Time to cut the crap. What were you planning to do? Blackmail me?"

With the key?

"Where is it? Who's got the knife—Manolo?"

He picked up her half-empty goblet and held it out to her.

"Go ahead. Finish it. Too late for anything else."

She shook her head and looked towards the door.

"Hoping for a saviour? If you're too stupid to look out for yourself, no one will."

She knew she should turn and run, but she felt caught in the grip of some deep-centred force over which she had no control, like the bull which had stood mesmerized in the centre of the ring.

He set the goblet down. "Okay. Forget the knife. Tell me where the rest of the treasure is."

What?

He slapped her face.

"Stop playing cutesy. I already know it's not in the garden."

What was he talking about?

"Look at me."

She couldn't look at him. She looked down at the floor.

"I said look at me." He hit her again, hard enough to knock her down.

"Sit up."

This time she did as she was told, then tried getting to her feet.

"I said sit not stand."

He knocked her down again. She groaned.

"Look at me."

At last she looked up.

"You're not getting anything you didn't ask for. In fact, you showed the way."

The tiled floor was cold and hard, but she was only vaguely aware of it. A taste like dry castor oil was spreading from the back of her mouth and through her tongue; she felt a tremendous thirst.

He clamped one hand over her mouth and pulled her up. Her thighs, her extremities, were numb.

"Ignorant bitch. Thought you could make a fool of me."

His grip was hard over her mouth. Her tongue felt thick, her throat tight, her stomach on the edge of nausea.

"But I'm not like the others."

His hand shifted to cover her nose as well as her mouth.

"I'm not afraid to kill. Not afraid to die."

He released his grip and she slid to all fours, gasping and coughing for air. She felt an almost unbearable cramp in her abdomen. Never had she felt so cold.

"Tony was stupid like you. Naive."

No, please no.

"Know how I did it? With my bare hands. Know where?"

No, not there.

"In the bath. But you, you're in for a special treat."

He reached around behind the knife cabinet and extracted a sword.

"I was going to let the poison do it. But you deserve better. For you, the sword of Boabdil. How do you want it? Volapié or recibiendo?"

But she couldn't move.

†

Ruth realized what she had been trying to put her finger on, and it had nothing to do with Miguel Angel, nothing at all—if she had indeed seen Carl going into the tunnel the night of the Silencio, then the stash in the tunnel was probably his. If the stash was his, then he was a thief, a dangerous man. That meant Eva was in danger.

†

"Stay away from her."

Eva wasn't sure if she could trust her ears and eyes. Standing not five metres away was Zayda, Zayda whom she hadn't seen since the first night in the bath. Zayda in jeans?

"Get away from her," repeated Zayda.

Carl laughed. "What luck. Two at once. One recibiendo, one a volapié."

Zayda stepped slowly around until she was behind him. His body turned, following hers.

"Another fiesta, girls."

And Eva knew that she had to do something. The room was spinning, but somehow she had to overcome her terror, her nausea, her immobility.

"No!" she shouted, a loud roaring No! from the deepest part of her. Everything hurt, but she pulled herself up and threw herself at him.

She was aware of a struggle, a thud on the floor, a hideous gurgling, a gush of something warm and sticky, and then she sank into a profound blackness.

†

Ruth rang the bell of Carl's house. She didn't know what she was going to say when he came to the door, but she would think of something. No one answered. But she knew they were in there.

She rang again, pushing insistently, as if pushing harder on the buzzer would make it ring louder inside.

The door was ajar.

She entered cautiously and tiptoed down the hall, and froze in her tracks.

Carl's servant, her face and clothes covered in blood, was bent over Eva, shaking her, telling her to Open your eyes, open your eyes, stay awake.

But it was the scene behind the two women that shocked her. Blood, and a man—a dead man—splayed face down in the most grotesque position, ass in air, the tip of a sword sticking out the back of his neck—exiting from the sweet spot, she thought, absurdly. The sword had entered the man's stomach, and the whole body seemed to have collapsed onto the haft.

Ruth felt her mouth filling again with the same wet fur taste she had regurgitated at the bullring. She closed her eyes, and she saw a strange house, a kitchen, a sausage fork, blood on the floor. Something was whimpering. Someone, her mother, was shouting at her, shaking her.

But it wasn't her mother. It was Carl's servant.

"Stop, stop that noise! Get a hold of yourself!" she was shouting. "Go get help. Quick! Eva's been poisoned."

†

Eva was floating in the land of lost souls, a land of ebony horses hiding in the shadows and green-eyed devils hovering over lakes so deep the water was black. Then from far away she heard a violet voice chanting, about Maimón and Alamafi, about Solomon and the Seven Kings, and the voice came closer and she was a six-stringed guitar and the voice was plucking the strings, one by one, and it was so beautiful, so beautiful, but now the voice was tugging on all the strings at once, and oh, what pain, but the violet voice insisted it was time to leave the land of lost souls, but she couldn't leave, didn't want to leave, it hurt too much to leave, and for a long moment she was suspended between worlds.

Then Eva heard the voice of Mercedes bidding her to open her eyes.

She obeyed.

And she was back in the small windowless room of a month ago.

But nothing was the same.

Zayda was bending over her like a solicitous parent, and Mercedes looking concerned on the chair beside the bed, and Angel at the foot of the bed. And Yukio—Yukio?—was standing by the door.

"She'll be all right now," said Mercedes.

But Eva felt as if she had been eviscerated. Her throat was dry and sore.

"The girls will be getting up soon," said Mercedes. "Manolo is with them, but they'll want to eat."

"You go ahead, I'll stay with her," said Zayda, putting her palm on Eva's clammy forehead.

"Would you like some tea or something?" said Yukio.

"Tea won't help," said Zayda. "That's no viral infection she has."

"But I'm so thirsty." Eva's voice was a whisper.

"I'll go make you some chamomile," said Angel.

Hopes

"HOW ARE YOU DOING, EVA?" ASKED ZAYDA. Except that her name wasn't really Zayda, it was Mary—something else Eva would have to get used to.

"Stronger every day, but I'm still feeling rather weak."

"You're certainly looking better," said Ruth.

The three women were relaxing in the upper gardens of the Generalife. Despite the usual throng of visitors, they had found a shaded alcove that offered both privacy and a view of the lower gardens and the Alhambra and city beyond.

It was five days since the poisoning, and each day Eva discovered something new. First had come the revelation that not only did Zayda speak—with a fast-moving nasal voice—but that she was Canadian: Mary Lee from Vancouver. Her mother was Chinese from Vietnam, and her father "some American soldier named Johnny." Yukio was Mary's cousin Tom from New York.

"Isn't it absolutely splendid here?" said Ruth. "I'm really starting to take a liking to Granada, you know, especially during the day. All those caves and curves, it's such a feminine city, don't you think, next to Toronto, I mean, with all those grey skyscrapers full of money-grabbers in grey suits, and so pleased with themselves, too, like Peter Sellers in those Inspector Clouseau movies. But I'll tell you what, something's happened to me here, something profound. All right, why not say it? I'm in love. Isn't that something? Here I am, a woman on the verge of turning fifty-five, and I've fallen in love for the first time in my life."

"I'm so happy for you," said Eva.

"And guess what? I wrote a poem last night. I don't think I've ever written a poem before. I wrote it after Miguel Angel took me through the Alhambra. It really is the most incredible place, isn't it, a truly magical place."

"If you ask me, it's an overrated collection of rock chunks and embedded pebbles," said Mary. "And that sycophantic stuff on the walls is *so* tacky. And those ceilings, they remind me of the gooey witch's house in *Hansel and Gretel.*"

Eva looked at Mary and tried to reconcile the actuality of her with the fantasy of Zayda. Just thinking of the soft and languorous kisses in the bath still caused pangs of pleasure. But Mary was no longer Zayda.

"So Tom went home this morning?" she asked.

"Yeah, he had to get back. What about you? What are you going to do?"

"I don't know. I miss Canada—the big sky, the seasons . . . all that corny stuff." Eva remembered Resa running along the sidewalk, the fall leaves skipping after her. After a good rain on the Prairies, it was not just the sun that came out, it was the whole sky. "But then there's the fact that I grew up there, yet it never felt completely like home. I like the pace of life here, you know, the two days in one: you have a siesta, and when you get up, it's like a whole new day . . . Or as Tony said in one of his letters: Each moment carries within it the pleasure of the unexpected . . . "

†

. . . the beautiful in the face of filth and decay. You'll be walking up a little street and the smell of steaming urine hits you like a wall. You resume walking, but there's no shade, only the sun relentlessly following you, and you decide to book the next flight out. But then you turn a corner and there against a white wall is a spray of geraniums of a red so intense it takes your breath away, and from a window, a song—a flamenco air that pulls at your gut—and you decide to stay forever . . .

†

"I know what you mean," said Ruth. "Nothing seems to end up like you thought it would. I mean, just think about the three of us, for instance. You and I met because of Bella, but now she's dead and I feel closer to you than I ever did to her, and you and Mary met because of Carl, and he's dead, too . . . but what I really want to know is this–Mary, how did you take up with someone like that in the first place? I mean, did you know him in Vancouver, did you meet him here, or what?"

"In New York, actually. I was living in Vancouver, but my aunt phoned to say my mother was sick, so I went to New York right away–my mother had moved there to be with her sister. Anyways, when I got there I didn't know how long I was going to stay, so my uncle–who was high up in the tong–gave me a job in his garment factory. But that didn't work out too well. See, I was used to my own hours, lots of cash, stuff like that."

"So you met Carl at the factory?" said Ruth.

"Not really. I had seen him there a few times, talking with Uncle, and I knew he had noticed me, but I didn't talk to him until one day when I ran into him on Mott Street. We said hello and he bought me a cup of coffee, and that was pretty much it."

"You mean you went off with him, just like that?" said Ruth, looking shocked.

"Well no, not till a few weeks later when my picture was in the paper. See, I had made the mistake of talking to this reporter who was prowling around trying to dig up stuff about Chinatown gangs. I hadn't told her anything, but wouldn't you know it if my name and picture didn't show up on the front page of the *Times*. My uncle, who like I said was high up in the tong, was furious and humiliated, my mother too. And they were scared, because a few years earlier another woman who had talked to a reporter was found dead. Anyways, I ran into Carl again and he offered me a job I couldn't resist. I had sized him up anyways as the type who'll pay good money for a subservient Asian–'exotic' they call us."

"What kind of job did he offer you?" asked Ruth.

"As a fulfiller of fantasies, you might say. After some of the other things I'd done, it sounded kind of fun, and well-paid to boot. So, the next day I boarded the plane to Málaga with a new identity–different hairdo, fake I.D.–the whole bit."

I must have been part of the job, too, thought Eva. But then I guess that's how I wanted her–in disguise, jingling her ankle bracelets, Zayda the slave girl.

"Is it true you never spoke?" asked Ruth. "That's what Miguel Angel told me, that you couldn't talk."

"It was Carl's strictest command. I was supposed to act foreign, and he said it ruined the mood when I talked."

Like me, thought Eva, hearing your voice has ruined the mood for me, too. She felt ashamed.

"I can't imagine not being able to talk," said Ruth.

"Oh, I don't know, it's like anything else. You get used to it pretty quick."

"And what about your cousin? Did you get lonely and ask him to join you?" asked Ruth.

"No, the first time I saw Tom here I was surprised as anything. I didn't know whether to be ecstatic or terrified, whether he had come to Granada to visit me or to kidnap me. You see, I didn't know him all that well—he was a musician, a guitarist, actually, and he never came around the factory. Anyways, I saw him in the Plaza Nueva that day, and he acted like he didn't recognize me, so I was really mystified. Then a couple of days later I heard Manolo talking in the market about this new Japanese assistant of his called Yukio, and from the description I knew it was Tom. Well, I didn't know what to think, but I smiled to myself and thought—here I am posing as an Arabian slave girl, and there's my American-Chinese cousin passing himself off as Japanese."

"I don't understand why he wouldn't have approached you," said Ruth.

"Because he didn't want anyone to know who he was. See, when he finally did talk to me—he waited till no one could overhear us—he said that two days after I had left New York, Uncle had been found floating face down in the East River. You can imagine how I felt. At first I thought for sure it must've been revenge for my big mouth."

"And you found out otherwise?" said Eva.

"Not exactly, but Tom said he'd been going through the records at the garment factory and figured out that the import/export part of the business was also a fencing operation dealing in stolen antiques and stuff—the last batches had come in from Granada—so he wanted to try and find out who was involved, in case they had anything to do with Uncle's death. Tom had also come across Carl's name in the records."

"I should have known all along that he didn't get his money taking pictures," said Eva.

"Uncle had apparently let Carl know that he wasn't going to deal with him any more—because of some fobbed-off fakes that Uncle had unwittingly passed on to one of his best customers. Anyways, Tom had got to thinking that even if his father's death had nothing to do with the newspaper story, it might still be related to my disappearance. You see, in Chinatown, like here, everybody knows everything, and I had been seen with Carl—both times—and by now my mother, everyone, was really worried about me. So Tom decided to come to Granada."

"Do you think that Carl killed your uncle?" asked Ruth.

"Well, all the rumours in Chinatown said it was an outside killing. And Eva, you know as well as me that if you didn't do exactly what Carl wanted, he took it as a personal put-down."

Ruth whitened. "Mary, I don't understand how you could keep living with someone so dangerous," she said, "especially since there didn't seem to be love involved or anything like that. I mean, I could understand if you were in *love* . . . "

"Well, I was pretty sure I could handle most anything he'd care to throw at me. It's true, he did get kind of nasty sometimes—but you know about that too, Eva."

Eva reddened. "So how did Tom end up working with Manolo?" she asked.

"He found Manolo's name in my uncle's records, too."

"*Manolo's* name?" Eva was shocked. Surely Manolo hadn't been involved with *Carl.*

Mary shrugged. "I'm just telling you what Tom said. He said he looked up Manolo's shop and went in and started asking about guitars. I guess Manolo assumed he was just another Japanese tourist who had come to learn about flamenco, and he offered to teach him more. Tom jumped at the chance. It meant he could check out Manolo and hang around Granada more or less unobtrusively, and anyways, he really was interested in the guitars. When Manolo asked him what his name was, he said Yukio, because he had just finished a book by Yukio Mishima."

The three women sat in silence for a while.

"Doesn't it seem unreal, though, being alive in this glorious setting, surrounded by such beauty," said Ruth, "having survived so many dark things."

"Did you finish your eulogy on Bella?" asked Eva.

"Yes, and I have to admit, it was surprisingly effortless. I even found the process somewhat cathartic."

"You know, I spent the night at her place once," said Mary.

"Yes, she mentioned it to me," said Eva.

"Now Mary, why on earth would you have spent the night at Bella's?" asked Ruth. "I didn't even think you knew each other."

"Oh, one night when Carl sort of got carried away, I bolted from the house and ran into Bella. She was sauntering along, singing to herself. It was really late, and she invited me home, you know, one street person to another, no questions asked."

"And?"

"That was it. I left before she got up. Anyways, when I got back, Carl wanted to know where I'd been, but I wouldn't say–just in case I needed to go there again some time. He was furious, but he didn't do anything."

"I wonder if it was Carl who killed her. I mean he did try to kill you and Eva, and then there's your uncle . . . "

"Could've been Carl who killed her, I guess. Maybe he asked around and found out where I'd gone that night. Maybe he thought I knew more than I did about what he was up to, and that I had talked to Bella, but of course I wouldn't have."

"I wonder if Bella had seen anything, like I did that night she died."

"What exactly did you see that night?" asked Eva.

"For a time I wasn't sure, because I was very sick, and sometimes I do experience hallucinations with my migraines. Well, after you and I got separated at the Plaza del Cristo, I got lost and ended up by the river. I saw him going into the cave mouth. At first I thought he was a hallucination, but later I realized that I really had seen him, dressed in a tunic and hood."

"So, he might've put on that outfit so he'd look like one of the penitentes," said Mary, "then killed Bella, then . . . " Mary shot a glance at Eva, as if trying to read her face.

But the monstrous implication had not been lost on her: if Carl had indeed killed Bella, then it was mere hours later that Eva had made love with him.

Ruth shuddered. "Poor poor Bella . . . But what about you two? I mean, we know for a fact that he did try to kill you, although I'd sure like to know what was going on before I got there, if you feel comfortable talking about it, that is."

"We've already gone through it with the police," said Mary. "It still gives me the shivers, but I'm fine with it. Is it okay with you, Eva?"

"Go ahead."

"Okay, just interrupt whenever you want. Where to start? I was upstairs, above the trophy room where the sounds come up through the radiator. I heard him come in. I heard his voice, then Eva's. His was low and I couldn't understand what he was saying, but the tone wasn't nice. Then I heard moans and I thought he must be hurting her, so I went quietly down the stairs–I should've grabbed something first, but I didn't think of it. When I got there Eva was on the floor, her face all pale and everything, and Carl was standing over her with the sword in his hands. He said something to her about poison, and I said, Leave her alone. Then he came after me, but before I knew it Eva was flying through the air at him. It all happened so fast. Anyways, I managed to sidestep him at the same time as Eva threw herself at him, and we all sort of fell together in a heap, me half under him. I crawled out. And that's when you came in."

Mary looked at Eva. "I can't believe how lucky we were, the sword only getting him."

Eva did not reply. She considered Mary, Ruth, the magnolias, the green sculpted hedges below, the red towers of the palace, and thought: I won't waste it this time, I will not squander what I've been given.

"Ruth, how did you happen to show up when you did, anyways?" asked Mary.

†

Ruth had gone running up the stone steps and through the streets to the Carmona house. She had felt strong, as if for once she were running to something and not away from it, as if for once she possessed the required energy.

†

"You know," said Ruth, "it's the strangest thing, but I'm not sure why, either. At the time, I had it in my head that I needed to see Miguel Angel about the missing books. I thought I would find him at the tunnel–I didn't know at this point that the cave was empty, and that the unplugging project had been cancelled. Now I honestly can't remember why I needed to see him. Maybe deep down, it had nothing to do with the missing books, but with the missing me. In any case, I was on my way to the tunnel when I saw Eva follow Carl into the house. I don't know what made me decide to go in. I had a flash of him going into that tunnel and it scared me . . . I thought you were in trouble, Eva, but I didn't know exactly why. It was just a feeling, I guess, I don't know how else to explain it."

"Well, I suppose there's a lot that's unexplained," said Eva.

"Maybe Manolo and Angel can fill in the gaps," said Mary. "We can grill them on Sunday."

"I hope you're coming, Eva," said Ruth.

"I don't know—it seems to me it would feel too creepy going into that house again . . . How long are you planning to stay there, Mary?"

"Until someone notices, I guess. For one thing, I don't have anywhere else to go. I'm still afraid to go back to New York, and you've got to admit, Carl did fix up that carmen pretty nice."

"I still don't know how you do it."

"Oh come on, it's just a house, a roof and a bunch of walls keeping out the rain. Anyways, you should challenge what scares you."

"Sounds like you've caught some of that Spanish ¡Soy yo!" said Ruth, "but I agree. Take death, for instance: it can strengthen your fears, or it can open you up to life. Once you look death straight in the eye, it loses its ability to intimidate."

"Perhaps you're right," said Eva.

"So what's this fiesta on Sunday about?" asked Mary.

"Miguel Angel says it's the annual May eleventh sendoff for the pilgrims who are accompanying the Virgin of the Rocío to Huelva. He says they'll be gone about a week in all, drinking and dancing and carrying on around the camp fire."

"Sounds wicked," said Mary.

"Oh, I don't know," said Ruth, "I think I could use a bit more of that in my life."

Closed and Open

I'M GLAD YOU DECIDED TO COME, EVA," SAID Mary.

"Me too," said Ruth. "A new day, a new fiesta."

The three women were preparing a Canadian-style merienda in the kitchen of Carl's carmen—salad, sandwiches, fruit, a chocolate cake, but without frosting as they had not managed to find icing sugar in any of the stores. Resa and Puri were exploring the rest of the house. The other adults—Manolo, Mercedes, and Angel—were on the balcony awaiting the start of the Rocío.

"I still feel guilty being here," said Eva, "as if it's wrong to be enjoying anything in this house."

"Well, if you still feel bad next year, you can go to Huelva as penance," said Mary.

Eva smiled.

Mercedes came into the kitchen. "Do you need help?"

"Everything's ready," said Ruth.

They carried the trays of food and drink out to the balcony.

"Wonderful!" said Angel, reaching for the sherry. "What could be better on such a lovely afternoon than to be gathered with one's friends, eating and drinking . . . Los muertos en la huesa, y los vivos a la mesa."

Yes, thought Eva. The dead in their graves, the living to the table.

Avebury, not Stonehenge; Herculaneum, not Pompeii.

†

Below, graceful arabians mounted by horsemen in waist-high jackets and stiff-brimmed hats pranced up and down the Carrera del Darro. Perched in back of some of the riders were young women in flamenco attire, their skirts arranged over the rumps of the horses to give the illusion, from behind, of woman and horse as one—hind legs stepping and braided tails swinging out from under the flounces of the dresses.

Across, the Alhambra was spectacular above the church of San Pedro and the river that wound behind it.

"Just look at that view," said Ruth. "I don't think I could ever tire of it."

"I'm happy to see you're still here," said Manolo, "but I thought you missed the wide yawning spaces of Canada."

"Wide open spaces," said Ruth.

"What?"

"Never mind . . . Actually, I've decided to stay until next week and to come back in August. Miguel Angel says it's the best month."

Angel smiled at Ruth. "And who knows? I may decide to go to Canada with her." He turned to Eva. "And what about your plans, Señora Eva?"

"If it were up to Resa we would certainly stay," said Eva. "She loves it here—never being told to speak quietly, or to say please or thank you." Just Quiero, No quiero: so simple.

"And don't forget," said Manolo, munching a sandwich, "I haven't finished her guitar yet."

Mercedes reached across and picked a few crumbs out of her son's beard.

"Tell me," he said to Ruth, "did you finally get the story you were looking for?"

"Ruth's going to write a mystery story based on the stolen library books," said Angel. "I am personally helping her with the research."

"Actually, Miguel Angel, I've changed my mind. What I want to write about is not the books missing from the university, but the women writers missing from history—that is, the story of why so few of their books have even survived long enough to become objects of theft."

"Well, for the moment I'm interested in the missing details of *this* story," said Mary, "the one we've all been living through."

"I doubt that a single one of us is in possession of all the details," said Angel, "but you're right, with all of us here, it is a perfect opportunity for us all to fill in the lagoons of our knowledge."

Mercedes gave Angel a foggy look.

"Except for la señora Mercedes, who, of course, has understood everything from the beginning. I suppose the place to start would be with Boabdil's sword. At the very least, its existence brought out the worst in each of us."

Mercedes coughed conspicuously.

"That is, it brought out the worst in *most* of us. Let us begin in 1492, when Fernando accepted the surrender of Boabdil el Chico." Angel refilled his glass and leaned forward, elbows on knees. "Now, contrary to certain contemporary reports, Boabdil was in possession of his sword when he surrendered to King Fernando. On this one point, we—that is to say, Tonio, Manolo, and I—agreed. After that our family histories diverge."

Mercedes took two oranges from a bowl and stood up. "I'm going to make sure that those girls are nowhere near that room with the weapons." She went into the house.

Maybe I should go with her, thought Eva. For one thing, she wasn't sure she wanted to sit through another session about the history of the sword. But she stayed and listened while Angel explained at length why he believed that the sword had belonged to his ancestor, the Marqués de Cádiz, and while Manolo countered with his story of how Isabel had actually given the sword to Fray Juán. Eva declined an offer to repeat the Benabo version, and Angel did so on her behalf.

" . . . and before Alfonso Abenabó moved to Fez, he buried the sword in the garden of his home in the Albayzín . . . this very carmen, as it turns out."

"You mean this actually *is* the original Benabo house?" said Mary.

"Only the part containing the weapons collection," said Angel, "that, and the smaller, adjoining room."

"You mean the room Eva stayed in to recover from the poison," said Mary.

"Yes."

As well as being the one I woke up in after that night with you, thought Eva. She looked at Mary, but there was nothing in her demeanour to suggest that anything of importance had happened between them.

"I know how we could check for sure," said Manolo. "Tonio told me that he had left the key to the original door with his mother. Did she give it to you, Eva?"

"Yes, but I lost it . . . that is, Carl took it."

"I think I know where it is," said Mary.

She went into the house and returned with the key in one hand and a velvet pouch in the other.

The Benabo pouch? wondered Eva.

Mary held the key out to her. "You might as well have it back," she said. "I found it in the weapon's gallery."

"I'm not sure I want it," said Eva, not touching the key.

"For what it's worth, it does fit that old door," said Mary, tossing the key on a tray. "I tried it."

"Tonio mentioned a map as well," said Manolo.

"I found that too," said Mary, pulling it out of the velvet pouch.

It *was* the same pouch. "How did that get here?" said Eva. "I placed it at the bottom of one of our suitcases when we arrived, and I haven't touched it since."

"Was Carl ever in your hotel room?"

"Only a few times."

"Once would be enough," said Manolo, acerbically.

Eva flushed.

Manolo took the map carefully from Mary's hand. "According to Tonio, this should show us the spot where Alfonso Abenabó buried his treasure, and later the sword."

"Why was Carl so interested in that old sword, anyways?" asked Mary.

"Carl Alonso claimed to be descended from Martín Alonso Pinzón, the right-hand man of Cristóbal Colón," said Angel.

"My mother says it's not true, that Alonso was a fake," said Manolo.

"Let us assume for the moment that he was indeed a descendant of Martín Alonso, and that he also believed Queen Isabel had given the sword to Colón. If so, he could have been convinced that had the queen been aware of the role the Alonso Pinzón brothers would come to play in the expeditions, she would have given the sword to them rather than to Colón."

"That sounds familiar," said Eva. "Carl did say something to me about Columbus having usurped all the fame and glory for himself."

"Exactly. It is possible that he believed the sword morally belonged to him."

"That sure doesn't sound like Carl," said Mary. "He was just plain greedy. Anyways, the name on his passport wasn't Alonso, it was 'Smith.'"

"See?" said Manolo, "I told you he was a fake. And if he did find the sword in the garden, where the map says it was, then Eva–as Tonio's widow–and I are the true owners."

"Now why would that be, hijo?" said Angel.

"Because the first summer that Tonio came to Granada, I offered to help him find the Abenabó treasure, and he insisted that if we found anything, anything at all, we would share it. In any case, both our families have Delcampos in our background, so we are related."

"And you found nothing," said Angel.

"No, not that first summer, but we agreed to keep in touch. He didn't come back until a few years later–after I let him know about that book the tourist found in the street."

"The one I evaluated for the police," said Angel.

"I still don't see what was so important about that book," said Eva. "I understand about it belonging at one time to Yusuf Ibn Ezra, the rich man who was murdered because of a poem written by Ishaq Aben Abu–"

"–Aben Abu, which over the years became Abenabó. Now, the names of both Yusuf Ibn Ezra and Jacobo Abenabó were inscribed in the book. What if Ishaq did more than write a vitriolic poem? What if, after Yusuf's death, Ishaq also took books and other things of value from the palace? That would mean that if he was indeed Jacobo's ancestor–"

"–Jacobo could have inherited the stolen goods."

"Exactly."

"Which would mean that the supposed Benabo treasure was stolen property," said Mary, "I love it. So after Carl took the key from you, Eva, he probably figured out that this was the old Abenabó house."

"No, he already knew that," said Manolo.

"*How* did he know?" asked Eva.

"Because of the night Alonso found Tonio digging in the garden. You see, Eva, you're right to be sceptical–Tonio did not return here just because of that book. In the pages of *De Materia* was something even more interesting than Jacobo Abenabó's signature–a piece of paper which showed that this carmen was in the exact location of the ancient Abenabó house. When the police came for the book, I gave it to them but kept the map."

Why hadn't Manolo said so in the first place? wondered Eva.

"But I didn't see any map!" said Angel.

"It was slotted into the book, disguised to resemble the other illustrations."

"I can't believe I didn't notice it," said Angel. "Me the supposed expert."

"I've never heard about this book before," said Mary. "It was in the street?"

"Carl Alonso dropped it," said Angel. "He was carrying several packages and he was in a hurry."

"So if Carl had the book, doesn't that mean he had found the Benabo treasure?" said Mary.

"No," said Angel.

"How is it you know all this, Don Angel?" asked Manolo.

There was a moment's silence in which everyone looked at Angel and waited for him to continue.

Finally he sighed and said, "Very well. The book in question, *De Materia,* had come from the university library. I had been supplying Carl Alonso with books."

"What do you mean, 'supplying'?" asked Ruth, with a worried look on her face.

"Obviously he was stealing them," said Mary.

"Oh, Miguel Angel! *You* wouldn't steal *books!*"

He shrugged (not at all sheepishly, thought Eva). "I had open access to the library, and hardly anything was catalogued so it was really quite a trivial matter. Remember that night, Eva, when Manolo brought you to the Alhambra, and Risita insisted she had seen someone? Well, it wasn't her imagination. The mysterious Abencerraje was Carl in a hooded tunic, and he had disappeared behind the door."

"Then you *did* know all along about that passageway being open," said Manolo.

Angel shrugged again.

"So you took *De Materia* from the Alhambra library–"

"–no, that one came from the university–"

"–passed it on to Carl, who dropped it in the street, where it was found by the tourist, and so on."

"Exactly. After that, the university checked its collections and discovered other books were missing. The library was being watched, so we started removing items from the Alhambra—using that tunnel, which I had known about for a long time, of course. The books were easiest to steal—no one pays attention to books any more. Carl Alonso would collect them from me, at night of course, take them through the tunnel, and deposit them in the cave until he found a buyer."

"So Carl was stealing when Resa saw him," said Eva. "But why was he dressed like that?"

"To protect himself. The tunnel is dirty, and in places very narrow. He would put on the outfit at one end and remove it at the other, to emerge as clean as chorros de oro."

The outfit Ruth saw him wearing, thought Eva, the same outfit we saw later in the cave. She had a memory of Manolo examining the tunic, a flash as he inserted something shiny in the back of his pants. She had forgotten all about that flash.

"What about you, Angel?" said Mary. "What were you getting out of all this?"

"Carl Alonso was paying me for the items, naturally."

"Oh, Miguel Angel!" said Ruth.

"But I sold only the non-Christian ones. In that way I was able to enlarge my own collection of Christian memorabilia . . . I knew his morals were shaded, but a *murderer* . . . " Angel shuddered.

"When you met us coming out of the cave, you seemed surprised we had not found any books," said Manolo.

"Yes, because as I had recently supplied Carl Alonso with five more books—which he had not yet paid for—I wondered where they might be. The night he died, I found the package of books here in the carmen, exactly as I had wrapped it. I retrieved the package and hid it before the police arrived."

"What did it look like?" asked Ruth.

"About so big,"—he framed the imaginary package with his hands—"wrapped with brown paper and string."

"That must be the package I saw him enter the house with," said Ruth. "He did look like he was being careful with it."

"Perhaps he had gone looking for a buyer," said Angel. "And seeing as you found the cave empty, Manolo, perhaps he had managed to sell the objects that you saw in the cave—not a single one of which was anywhere in the house. I had a good look before the police arrived."

Amazing, thought Eva. There was Carl, dead, and Mary covered with blood, and me, dying of poison, and this man had the sang-froid to search the house.

"Where is that package of books now?" asked Manolo.

"Safely back in my room at the Alhambra."

"I just don't know what to say," said Ruth, "I'm so shocked by all of this."

Miguel Angel took her hand and looked into her eyes. "I didn't know he was a murderer."

"Well," said Ruth, "it will take some getting used to, but then I suppose I'm not lily white either."

"I'm sure the books have ended up in museums, or with private collectors who will care for them properly," said Angel. "And most of the artifacts Carl Alonso dealt in probably came from our poor little villages—statues and such which the people do not have the means to preserve."

"The dignity of the people does not belong in those houses of death you call museums," said Manolo.

"Do you really believe that, hijo?" said Angel. "Everything you found in that cave would have fallen to ruin if left with the villagers. And once they are dead, do you think their children will be interested in out-dated jewellery and sculptures of fat goddesses? They will want fast cars and trips to America. At least this way, the past is preserved for future generations, and a few of us are able to profit concretely at the same time."

Mercedes came back out on the balcony and leaned over the railing. "The pilgrims will be leaving soon," she said. "They're assembling near the church."

"Manolo," said Eva. "Mary says that your name, along with Carl's, was in her uncle's records in New York."

"Right," said Mary. "That's why Tom went to your guitar shop in the first place."

Mercedes sighed and sat down. "Aren't you done talking about that yet? . . . I never thought the day would come when I would be praying for the start of a procession."

"And I believed him when he said he had seen la Luz dance," said Manolo.

"It wasn't really a lie. He said you asked him if he had seen her dance, and he nodded yes. Actually, he *had* seen her dance—in New

York—but you assumed it was Tokyo because you assumed he was Japanese."

Manolo laughed and raked his beard. "In any case, Yukio was a fine assistant, and I'm sorry to have lost him."

"Were you involved in this fencing operation, too?" said Eva.

"No no," said Manolo, "but I think I know why my name was in the records. A year or so ago Carl Alonso gave me an order for a flamenco guitar—from a señor Lee in New York. That's all."

Eva felt relieved.

"You mean Uncle ordered a guitar from you?" said Mary.

"It sounds like it was him."

"But the guitar must have been for Tom. And all that time, Uncle acted like he had nothing but contempt for what Tom was doing. Did my uncle ever get the guitar?"

"No, it's one of the ones Yukio was helping me with. It's not quite finished."

"And he didn't even know. How ironic," said Mary.

"There's another little thing I've been wondering about," said Eva. "Why did that Japanese tourist bring the book to you in the first place?"

"I suppose he knew me a little and imagined I would know what to do. Actually, there were four of them, four friends travelling together—I had given them a tour of the Alhambra, and they had spent an afternoon in my shop, where I talked to them about bulerías and rumbas."

"So you got in touch with Tony, and he came here," said Eva. "Then what?"

"We watched the carmen for several nights, unobtrusively, which was not difficult as it was Semana Santa and there were so many people about. Tonio thought he remembered from his map approximately where the treasure was buried—a certain number of paces from the north corner of the wall. On the night of the Silencio, we came here with a small spade and waited, hoping for a chance to dig. Sure enough, soon after the street lights were extinguished, Alonso left the house. We crept around to the back and I tossed the spade over the wall. Tonio climbed over—he insisted on going himself into the garden—and I returned to the Carrera del Darro to keep an eye on the front door. The procession passed, and I waited and waited, the procession returned to the church, and still I waited. No Alonso, no Tonio. The sun came up and I didn't know what to do—I couldn't go to the police. I was sure Alonso had not returned, at least not through the front, but I rang the bell a couple of times, just in case. Zayda—María—answered and indicated that neither Alonso nor Tonio was here. You can imagine how worried I was."

"But *had* Carl come back?" asked Eva. An image formed in her mind of Tony digging in the garden, in the light of the moon, Carl coming up behind him . . . Oh love, poor love!

"I remember that night very clearly," said Mary. "Carl was only gone for an hour or so. He must've come back a different way and snuck in the side door. Maybe he had seen you, Manolo."

Manolo looked a little embarrassed, and said, rather aggressively, "On the other hand, you insisted that Alonso was not in the house, and yet he was there the whole time."

"Of course he was, but I wasn't very well going to say so. He was standing right behind me."

"So Alonso discovered Tonio digging in the garden," said Angel.

"He must've," said Mary. "After Manolo left, Carl told me to serve sangría in the garden. Tony was sitting on the bench under the grapevine."

Just like I did, thought Eva.

"They seemed to be playing some sort of cat and mouse game. Tony was apologizing, insisting he had thought no one lived in the carmen. He said that he had been drinking with some friends and he had scrambled over the wall on a dare. Carl was laughing, acting like it was all a pretty good joke. A little later, Carl rang for me to bring food and wine into the room with the baths—part of my role as slave girl. He often did this with his guests." Mary looked at Eva, an unfathomable look. "I served the drinks and went back to my room, where I was supposed to wait in case I was summoned again. I wasn't."

"So you don't know what happened after that?" said Manolo.

"I know," said Eva. "Carl killed Tony. He told me. He killed him in the bath."

"Then it was just as you said, Mamá: Tonio did not drown in the river."

Mercedes did not reply. She appeared not to be listening.

"María, do you know if Tonio found anything in the garden?" said Manolo.

"As far as I know Tony found nothing."

"But he must have found the sword."

"Not that night, I don't think. But I think Carl found it after Eva spent that first night here. As soon as she left, he went out to the garden."

So the house wasn't deserted after all, thought Eva. You were both here the whole time.

"He must have taken the map from our hotel room before we came here," she said. "He probably went through my suitcase when I was in the bathroom."

"So Alonso went to the garden . . . "

"Yeah, and after a while he came back in waving this stupid sword in my face—I remember, the handle was caked with dirt. He was making all these careful, deliberate strokes in the air, like he was performing a ritual or something. It was freaky."

"What about the rest of the treasure?"

"Like I said, I only saw the sword."

"And even that has been confiscated by the police," said Angel.

The police. Two peremptory men had visited Eva and suggested that it would be much simpler to no mover las aguas. She would have no further questions to answer, no more bother. And what would be the point of exhuming the body of la señora's husband, of trying to prove that he had been murdered, now that the presumed murderer was himself dead? Would it not be simpler to keep el señor Benabo's death officially recorded as an accident?

"Who gets the sword now?" asked Mary.

"Probably a museum, or a Japanese investor," said Angel. "The police can't profit from it for themselves—too many people know about it."

"So in the end, there was no treasure," said Eva. And yet four people were dead: Tony, Bella, Mr. Lee, and Carl.

There was a long moment of silence.

"You know, my mother knew all along that this fake Alonso had bad things in mind," said Manolo. "She had been doing things to him for quite some time."

"What do you mean," said Mary, "doing things?"

"Things," said Mercedes.

"Spell-like things," said Manolo.

"You mean like the evil eye?" said Mary.

Mercedes grunted, as if in scorn. Eva thought she heard her mutter, "cosas de principiantes"—beginner stuff.

"She performed manipulations that weakened him," said Manolo. "That's why you were able to overcome him so easily. Jondo ¿no? Impaling himself on the sword of Boabdil."

"Clean through," said Angel. "He had obviously sharpened it."

"Please don't talk like that," said Ruth. "It was too horrible."

Yes, thought Eva. His blood in my ears, my mouth.

"I still have a bruise on my thigh where the haft of the sword dug in," said Mary. "He was heavy, like a felled tree pinning me down. It took all my strength to crawl out. Then Ruth appeared, and I told her to run and get help."

"You were very brave to walk into the carmen the way you did," said Manolo. "Tienes cojones."

"Actually, I wasn't really thinking clearly, I was looking for Miguel Angel," said Ruth.

"Why did you want to see me?"

"I can't remember any more, but at the time it seemed important."

"I think it was important not that you see Don Angel, but that you walk by this carmen at that particular moment," said Mercedes. "It was a question of your presence on the scene, an act of fate."

"Why did you go get Mercedes?" asked Mary. "Why not a doctor?"

"A doctor? Why a doctor?" said Mercedes.

"I didn't think about it," said Ruth. "When Mary said Eva had been poisoned, I immediately thought of Mercedes, I don't know why, but I thought she would know what to do."

"You did the right thing," said Manolo. "Doctors work against nature."

"You must have moved quickly," said Angel.

"And it's good that she did," said Mercedes. "It was a close call. As long as Eva was conscious, the remedy would have been simple enough: the Jackal had given her realgar; I would have given her quince juice. But it turned out to be a little more complicated."

"What did you do?" asked Eva. "Did you suck the poison out?"

Mercedes waved her hand at Eva.

"Did Alonso want to kill la señora Eva because she knew things?" asked Angel.

"Alonso was evil," said Mercedes, as if that were reason enough.

"I think Carl had been keeping tabs on me because he thought I knew where the rest of the treasure was," said Eva, " . . . and then, before I passed out, he said something about a missing knife."

She looked at Manolo. "Do you know what he might have been talking about?"

Manolo half stood and pulled a knife from back inside his clothes. It had a fish-shaped blade.

"This navaja. I found it in the tunic in the cave."

"But why didn't you show it to me at the time?" asked Eva.

"I thought if I could discover the owner of the navaja, I would know for sure who had placed the objects in the cave. When I got home and was able to examine it, I noticed blood on the blade, and thought right away of la Católica. I suspected Alonso, but I wanted to be sure before I did anything."

"Before you did what?" Eva was incredulous. "If you had shown that navaja to me when you found it, I could have told you it was Carl's. He had taken great pains to show it off to me."

Manolo held out the navaja to her.

"It won't do any good showing it to me now. I can tell you what the inscription says: Cuando esta vívora pica, no hay remedio en la botica."

Eva picked up the key from the tray and threw it overhand as hard as she could. Everyone watched it spin through the air and disappear into the Darro.

The band in front of the church of San Pedro struck up and attention was redirected to the procession of pilgrims on foot, on horseback, and in horse-drawn carts that was beginning to move slowly along the Carrera del Darro. The first carts were being pulled by large white horses wearing blinkers festooned with orange flowers.

Resa and Puri came tearing out onto the balcony. "Are they coming? Are they coming?"

Resa climbed up on her mother's lap.

"Look," said Puri, "the Virgin."

A two-wheeled cart pulled by a pair of oxen was carrying the Queen of May, who was surrounded by yellow roses and protected by a beautifully carved canopy. As she passed beneath the decorated balconies, people opened their hands filled with white rose petals. The white petals floated down to blanket the cart and the street. Some floated to the river.

"Snow flowers," said Resa.

Outset

"SO. MY SON WANTS TO MARRY YOU."

"Yes," said Eva.

"He is a good man," said Mercedes.

"I know, but I hardly know him." And, like Tony, he had kept things from her. He hadn't even told her about the knife. The next time, I want someone who trusts me with what is important to him, she thought.

"You could get to know him, and he would take good care of you. It would be good for him, too, to have a wife. One day I will be too old to cook."

"What happened to his first wife?"

"She died after giving birth to little Puri."

Eva gazed out the Carmona window at the Alhambra which looked pink today.

"Well, I'm flattered, but I don't think I'm ready to get married again."

"You know, from the moment he saw you on the bus, he kept watch over you. Because of Tonio."

And it's because of Tony that he wants to marry me, too?

"For all that interest, I was certainly kept in the dark."

"Do not be too hard on him, he did the best he could. He is only a man, after all . . . Perhaps you should look more closely at what is being offered. Think of Risita–you would be giving her a father."

It's true, thought Eva. Resa would have an instant father, an instant sister, an instant grandmother—a proper family. Resa would be overjoyed if I married Manolo. And who was it, Thornton Wilder? who had written something about it being better to make mistakes through generosity than gains through caution.

"What is it?" said Mercedes. "What is holding you back?"

It's my loins, thought Eva, but why should I pay attention to them? It's not as if they haven't misled me before.

"I don't know. Maybe I just need more time to think."

"What's to think? Do you not have a gut?"

But no matter how hard Eva wished her gut to say, "Manolo," it did not.

"Think of this then—you are a healthy woman, alone. You are too young to be alone. Solitude can be like a death."

"I know." But did she want to live with a man whose mother still cooked for him? And the other night, Manolo had said: Woman is the right-hand castanet, the hembra trilling off the bac-sic of the macho castanet. Not me, Eva had thought. Not any more. ¡Toma!

"The poets say, the Mecca you seek is inside your own heart. You must not ignore what is in it."

"But Manolo is not in my heart."

"Well, why didn't you say so in the first place?" Mercedes patted Eva's hand. "I have done my best on my son's behalf. Now, hija, let me read your hand again."

Eva held out her left hand.

"The other one. We will do the past first . . . Yes, you see . . . you came here with a key, thinking you were coming for your husband, and you came with this ring, thinking you were coming for his mother. The key led you to the sword, and the ring allowed you to see inside the cave. The trouble is, you did not use your own eyes to find the way . . . *Now* the other hand."

Eva extended her left hand again.

"A trip."

"I'm going back to Canada?"

Eva had never gotten around to unpacking—she and Resa were still living out of the suitcases. It was time to decide what to do. Staying in the hotel, even by the week, was expensive. If they were going to stay, they should rent an apartment; if they were leaving, they should leave now.

"Not to Canada. Not to a cold country, across the ocean, but somewhere hot . . . ah yes, that's it, I see it now . . . your journey is not over . . . Your other hand told us that until now, you have been following a path that was made by others. This hand is telling you: Listen to the wisdom within . . . Now, hija, close your eyes and look inside."

Eva closed her eyes.

"Empty your head of all extraneous thoughts. Listen. That your heart and mind be one–that is what is important. Only then can you hear your soul speak."

Mexico.

"Mexico," Eva said.

And she knew. She and Resa were going to Mexico City.

"Your mother was from Mexico?"

"No, she was Canadian. My father was Mexican."

"Ah."

Mercedes let go of her hand.

"I have something for you."

Eva opened her eyes. It was a book, a small, leather book with elegant, curved script.

"Is this Arabic?"

"Yes. It is a book of poems written hundreds of years ago by Ruth Shulam Delcampo. The book is called *The Song of Lutes.* Don Angel gave it to me before he left for Canada with la Muda, but I would like you to have it."

"But this is the poet Mrs. Benabo mentioned. And if she was Mrs. Benabo's ancestor, she must be yours, too."

Mercedes shrugged. "I don't read. I never learned how. And I know that books have special meaning for you."

She handed Eva a folder. Inside were about fifty sheets of typewritten pages.

"When I told Don Angel that I wanted to give you the book, he did a Spanish translation for you. He apologized, but he did not feel able to do it in English."

"No, this is wonderful. But where did he find the book in the first place?"

Mercedes shrugged again. "Does it matter?"

"If you know, I would like to know."

"I think he reclaimed it from that last package of books he had given to the Jackal."

"Oh . . . Are you sure this is Arabic and not Hebrew?"

"That is what Don Angel said."

"But I wonder why Ruth Shulam Delcampo didn't write in Hebrew?"

Mercedes laughed and slapped her knee. "Don Angel told me that you would ask that question. He said to tell you that our Jewish poets usually wrote in Hebrew when they were writing to their god—they did not wish to praise him in the language of Islam. But to express worldly love, they wrote in Arabic. Most of these are love poems set at night in the gardens of the Alhambra and Generalife."

Eva examined the titles in the table of contents: Under the Apple Tree, All Green is Our Bed, From the Desert, Tree of Life, Daughters of Jerusalem, The House of My Mother, Sixty Queens and Eighty Concubines, Countless Maidens, The Nut Orchard, From the Heights of the Alhambra . . .

"And now, hija, you have your ring to protect you from harm, and this book of poems to remind you of our little corner of the world."

†

Eva finished the last poem and closed the folder.

The bells of the cathedral started to ring—four times, then six in a lower tone.

Six in the morning! No point going to bed now.

She wondered how long Resa would sleep—she had promised her one last breakfast in the Plaza de Bibarrambla before going to the airport.

†

Resa was dreaming.

It was night, and she and her mother were on their way to eat churros y chocolate.

They walked past white walls that threw back the light from the street lamps. The street shone wet from the night's rain, the cobblestones reflecting irregular patterns in cleansed shades of grey, black, and yellow.

A bored German shepherd dutifully tossed a few barks over the wall of one of the cármenes, and was heard by a mongrel chained to another lonely rooftop, who passed the warning to another dog guarding another carmen, and so on and so on, until the whole city was a chorus of barking, challenging guard dogs.

The church bells stopped ringing and the dogs were quiet.

†

Resa opened her eyes.